ON THE HOUSE

A MADAME PRESIDENT MYSTERY

Book 2 of the House Mystery Series

by

Denise Tucker

International Standard Book Number 13: 978-1-60452-139-9
International Standard Book Number 10: 1-60452-139-2
Library of Congress Control Number: 2018938036

BluewaterPress LLC
52 Tuscan Way Ste 202-309
Saint Augustine FL 32092

www.bluewaterpress.com

This book may be purchased online at -
www.bluewaterpress.com

Please note that address information is subject to change. At the time of printing, the address was correct, but may have changed since. Please check our website for the latest address information for BluewaterPress LLC.

Painting of Versailles Palace cover art by Richard Phillips

This book is dedicated in loving memory

Of my father

Robert Milton Tucker

And in loving memory of my publisher

Ardis Clark

Ardis, this one is for you.

Preface

In the Garden

Versailles Palace
July 1785

It was summer in a restless, brooding Paris. At the crowded court of Versailles, even the royal family and their well-dressed courtiers struggled to maintain their composure and the rigors of etiquette amidst the merciless heat of this hot summer day. With his morning worship and meetings concluded, the King quietly withdrew to his cool private cabinet. There he could sit at his father's gilded desk, attend to matters of state, and escape the heat and the endless crowds that streamed through the outer public rooms of his palace. The Queen and her ladies-in-waiting quickly departed for a day's rest at a shady lakeside hamlet, where they dressed in light muslin peasant dresses and straw hats and pretended to be shepherdesses. With the royal couple thus retired, the court relaxed, collectively free to mill about the palace and its expansive palatial gardens. Some would seek sustenance, others would seek shade. It was late afternoon when an energetic young nobleman arrived at court, dressed in the king's military uniform—a jacket of turquoise and red outlined with silver and gold braid. The young man was anxiously looking for a close friend.

He was told to look outside in the vast royal garden park. A crusty old gardener carrying a bucketful of weeds stopped, wheezed, and directed the young nobleman towards the bright blue pools of the Water Parterre, past the cooling mists of the Latona Fountains, out towards the green stretch of the Royal Avenue. The young man kindly thanked the old gardener and walked briskly onward, stopping twice to speak briefly to several noble acquaintances. He pressed forward, passing twelve large white statues that lined the wide grassy avenue until, following the gardener's directions, he reached the sparkling pool of another massive fountain. Here the great god Apollo, the original ancient Sun King, arose from the crystal waters and greeted him.

There was no sign of the young man's friend anywhere. Frustrated, the nobleman gazed at the gilded statues of Apollo and his mounted horses. He paused and then knelt to take hold of a shell-pink rose blooming beside the fountain. He held the fragrant flower close and inhaled its delicate aroma. Suddenly he heard it, the melodic sound of a violin floating high over the trees. The music made him smile broadly. He threw the rose into the fountain and dashed off towards its source deep inside a secluded grove to his left. There he found them, a middle-aged father with his teen-aged daughter on the steps of the garden's Colonnade—a pretty round peristyle graced with thirty-two white marble columns, delicately carved archways, and decorative urns. The young lady was radiant wearing a pale blue silk dress in the latest Paris fashion. She was sitting on the marble steps, resolutely holding a pad of paper in her lap while sketching a nearby pair of life-size statues of Pluto and Persephone. Standing behind her, a redheaded gentleman carefully supervised his child's drawing while he played a gentle melody upon a rather beaten-up old brown fiddle. The song was English. The man was American.

The French nobleman greeted them enthusiastically. "Bonjour, mes amis. Bonjour! Such crowds today! And so many pathways and gardens for you to avoid them! Thank the Bon Dieu for that old fiddle. Otherwise, I would have never found you! And how is Dr. Franklin's replacement this afternoon?"

The fiddle player looked over at the nobleman with a raised eyebrow.

"Hot. And no one can ever replace Dr. Franklin, sir. I am only his successor. Now come and sit down before you melt."

Laughing, the young man obediently plopped himself down on the white stone steps beside the young lady.

"Dr. Franklin echoes your sentiments, I am sure! And bonjour to you, too, Mademoiselle Patsy! You are hard at work at your drawing, n'est-ce pas? I hope the nuns at your school recognize your talent and are providing you with a good instructor. Paris has many great artists. You must see some of their work while you are here. Perhaps my wife and I can take you." He paused and peered over to look at her drawing. "Oh, that is good, very good!"

"Thank you kindly, General," the young artist said in her pleasant southern drawl. She held out her drawing for her own critical inspection. She frowned. "I didn't get her face quite right. The eyes are good, but her brow is not so wide there and there. Drawing people is ever so much harder to do, but I'm determined to try. I'm mighty tired of sketching flowers. You can only draw so many roses, Monsieur! Papa has brought me to Versailles several times to see the gardens." She paused to glance around and drew her breath. "Aren't they beautiful? I'm told the King has his greenhouse flowers freshly cut and placed outside in pots, even in winter! They say that the orange trees bloom all year, too."

"Oui. So I have heard," murmured the French nobleman with a slight frown at the royal extravagance. "It is a practice the King has learned from his great, great, great grandfather!"

The southern belle took no notice of the man's grimace and continued with her chattering. "Have you been to Marly? Papa and I have been invited to go! Father's been before. He's told me all about it, the chateau with twelve glorious pavilions surrounding it and the wonderful fountains."

"A good design," observed the father thoughtfully. "On a smaller scale, it would make an excellent academic village."*

The nobleman nodded with a knowing smile. "Ah, mon ami, always the architect. There are many structures for you to study at Versailles. The main palace belongs to the King's court, for the work of government. It is mostly a public place, very big, very formal. But Marly, that exists to entertain the King and Queen and their closest friends. It is a great honor you have been invited! You will be amazed at its wonders! Marley's fountains can shoot one hundred feet in the air!"

The nobleman paused and looked at his friend who tried his best to look unimpressed while he adjusted the fiddle strings. Smiling, the Frenchman continued.

"There is another palace, *mon enfant*, you must see. It is called Trianon. It is a private residence for the members of the royal family only." He suddenly sighed. "Too bad the petite porcelain palace was torn down. That was the original building, created to resemble blue and white china. The Sun King, King Louis XIV, had the roof covered with blue Delft tiles and the walls painted with blue and white fresco. In the garden, large Delft pots were kept full of jasmine and lilies all year long. The scent was *magnifique*."

The girl sighed dreamily with her eyes closed. "It does sound heavenly."

"I have not been to Marly," said the French nobleman honestly, "but I have been to the Menagerie. We must get you an invitation to visit there also. The Menagerie is to the far left of the Grand Canal. It is a circular palace with many walled gardens and aviaries. The Old Sun King kept his royal animal collection there. He even had elephants in one of its gardens!"

"How exciting!" exclaimed the girl. "Papa says there is going to be a grand fête when we go to Marly. I hope there will be ships floating in the Grand Canal and thousands of candles lining the waterway and fireworks like there was at the Queen's wedding. I can't wait to see the Queen in her evening gown and her jewels. I wanted to draw her today, but Papa wouldn't let me!"

The fiddler hit a dreadfully wrong note at that comment.

The nobleman turned and addressed his American friend. "I see you share the common people's sentiments, mon ami. You do not like the Austrian woman?"

The fiddler scowled. "In the presence of my young daughter, let me simply say the King continues to drink and the Queen continues to sin."

The Frenchman laughed. The father continued. "She is a hard-willed woman, she controls him, and she will not make it easy for you to teach the principles of democracy to your nation."

The young man gazed at his revered friend soberly, his eyes burning with fire at the mere mention of the word sacred to him.

"Democracy! This is the real reason you have been sent here! Who else can preach to the French people of the revolutionary principles of equality and freedom?"

The red-haired fiddler shook his head and sighed. The music stopped, and the father said nothing until he put his instrument and bow away in their battered case. "Preach? I am not a priest! Don't speak to me of priests! How often priests become hostile to liberty! True, I am a theologian, my dear General, but I am not a preacher. Preaching is not what your people need. They need to know themselves and their God-given rights of self-government. They need to know that every man possesses the right of self-government and displays such in the exercise of self-will. I have seen far too much of kings and judges and priests and how they can degrade and corrupt governments! Only the people themselves are the safe depositary of power and equality under the law. And I have sworn before the altar of my God eternal hostility against every form of tyranny over the mind of man! I have said and will continue to declare that rebellion to tyrants is obedience to God." **

"Rebellion!" The young general savored the bold word like sweet dark honey upon his parched lips, having fought not long ago across the ocean in the War of American Independence. He fervently grasped the sword that hung by his side.

The fiddler extended his strong hand and pulled the young man to his feet. "Don't be too anxious for rebellion yet, my friend. Be patient. These things take time. But do not worry. With a woman like Marie Antoinette, you may get your revolution sooner than you think! Now, enough of this talk! The day is drawing to a close, and I'm famished. Will you and Madame Lafayette be joining us for dinner tonight?"

The General, the Marquis de Lafayette, nodded his head in happy agreement. "Mais oui, she will dine with us at the Adamses' apartments this very evening. She would not miss a party given by Madame Abigail!"

"Nor would I," said the father readily as he looked down at his daughter. "Put away your pen, Patsy, and let us find refreshment."

The threesome walked from the quiet grove of trees into the wide expanse of the Royal Avenue. A gentle evening breeze blew across the treetops, signaling the end of the day. General Lafayette gazed thoughtfully towards the golden palace of Versailles and asked, "But do you think you can get us something to eat at this hour, Monsieur Jefferson?"

Thomas Jefferson, the author of the Declaration of Independence, smiled confidently at his friend.

"Marquis, have no fear. As you said, I am Dr. Franklin's successor. I am America's Minister to France. And anything I want around here is *On The House....*"

Chapter One

East Wing
November 9, 2001

"That's right. Twelve trees. We need them to be exactly the same height and shape — I believe you have the specifications we faxed over to you this morning? . . . Yes, that is correct. Now, the trees are to be delivered to the White House the week *before* Thanksgiving. . . Yes, I'm quite aware that's only two weeks away and ahead of schedule, but we suddenly find ourselves unexpectedly hosting the King and Queen of Spain that weekend for dinner. So the trees must be up and decorated in the Cross Hall earlier than we originally planned. We want to make a good impression...."

The caller on the other end of the phone cared not one whit for making good impressions on Spanish royalty and continued his heated protest. Delivering twelve trees was not a problem. They had a whole farm full of trees thank you very much. But to meet those exact height specifications (for twelve trees, mind you) and to have them delivered to Washington at short notice? Well, that was another matter entirely. Gary Craig, Social Secretary of the White House and husband to America's first female president, leaned back in his chair in his tiny East Wing office, pulled the receiver away from his ear, and sighed heavily.

How his life had changed! Just two years ago, Gary was divorced, depressed, and consoling himself by decorating his quaint backyard cottage in Greensboro, North Carolina for the upcoming winter holidays. Such was his fate. But Fate, having a hilarious sense of humor, promptly turned Gary's world completely upside down. Gary was now husband to the brilliant and beautiful blonde woman running the nation from her desk in the Oval Office, a stepfather to three very independent children, and co-owner of three equally independently-minded cats. The youngest of the felines, a rambunctious black creature named Sheba, was presently curled up on his desktop, draped comfortably over his daytime planner on the exact page he needed to see.

Cats!

Appealing for help, Gary looked up at his assistant, Ryan Adams, who was standing in front of Gary's desk with his trusty clipboard in hand. Adams was looking rather tense. Seeing his boss's predicament, he nervously pushed up his tortoise-shell glasses, quickly flipped through his papers, pulled out a single sheet, and promptly handed it over. One glance at the document did the trick. Gary cleared his throat and interrupted the unhapted caller.

"Of course, Mr. Gleason, I understand completely. Sorry to impose. If the deadline and specifications of our order cannot be met, then we can certainly withdraw the contract. My assistant has just given me the name and address of another tree farm, one I believe not far from your own, Winter Wishes Farms, owned I believe by...let's see... oh, yes, here it is, a Mr. Archibald Hamilton. I can give Mr. Hamilton a call this afternoon...."

The telephone's protestations abruptly ceased. Mr. Gleason, while not caring much for international politics or diplomacy, cared very much about beating out the neighborhood competition. He had a sudden change of heart and immediately acquiesced to all the White House's demands, willing by God to deliver his trees on schedule. The call concluded, Gary put down the receiver, picked up his napping cat, and got to his feet

"Well, that's that. Nice work, Ryan. What's left on the list?" Adams stared down at his clipboard.

"This afternoon, we're inspecting the ornaments submitted by different state organizations on this year's Christmas theme, *The Twelve Days of Christmas*. The states' ornaments will go on Mr. Gleason's trees in the staterooms on the main floor and the trees in the Diplomatic Reception Room on the ground floor. The White House florists called a little while ago to report we have plenty of partridges, but we're one box short of milkmaids."

"Yow!" said Sheba.

"Milkmaids, kitty girl, not milk," Gary clarified to his hungry pet. "Well, call FedEx and find our missing maidens. Ryan, are you okay?" Gary noticed that his assistant appeared uncomfortable and had glanced at his wristwatch more than once during the phone call.

"Yes, sir," replied Ryan. "It's just …it's just that our meeting ran over a bit and I promised to call my wife. She's working in Paris this week."

Gary nodded with understanding. "Not good to keep a wife waiting! Feel free to stay and use my phone if you like. I'm going to take Sheba upstairs and check on Abigail. You know how Abigail can get into trouble."

Adams winced. He certainly did know about that. Abigail, who had just turned six, had this week tried out a new set of watercolor paints on his white office door.

"Yes, sir. I do, sir. And thank you, sir. I think I will use your phone if you don't mind. I'd like a private line when speaking to my wife," he said meekly. He and Gary exchanged places in Gary's cramped East Wing office.

Gary watched as Adams sat down, said goodbye, and quickly left.

Ryan Adams waited several moments. Once assured Mr. Craig was out of earshot, he picked up the phone and asked the White House operator for a secure, outside line. Waiting for the connection, Adams took off his glasses and carefully laid them on his clipboard which he had placed on Gary's desk. He pulled out a small piece of paper from his pants pocket and rapidly punched in the overseas numbers once the connection was secured. The phone barely rang before the other line was quickly picked up.

"Olá!" answered the overseas voice.

"Hello, may I speak to Mr. De Silva?"

"That's me! What the hell took you so long?" demanded an impatient voice with a clear Spanish accent. "I've been waiting for your call almost half an hour. This is dangerous, calling you from this public pay phone. I do not like it."

Adams apologized. "Something came up, and I couldn't get away till now."

The man on the other end of the line made a frustrated noise. "I was beginning to think The Seven was no longer interested in our offer."

Adams patiently assured Mr. De Silva this was not the case. "On the contrary, The Seven is most interested in your proposal. I have been told to relay their acceptance. Tell me, for I am naturally curious, exactly what is your connection to the Columbian Drug Cartel?"

De Silva replied proudly. "I work for a man who is indebted to one of The Seven for actions better left unsaid. As a token of my employer's deep appreciation, he wishes to make a gift, a parcel of exquisite Columbian emeralds, which The Seven may use to finance future criminal operations."

"That is certainly a generous offer. Please extend to your employer our sincerest thanks. When and where will the jewels be delivered?"

The voice spoke in a hurried whisper. "The emeralds will arrive in Paris the same week as the G-8 summit, which, as you know, has been recently relocated to Versailles Palace. Your American President will be in attendance?"

"Of course," confirmed Adams. "She and her entire family will be flying overseas after the New Year."

Mr. De Silva continued. "During the summit, there is going to be a cake competition at Versailles. We understand that one of The Seven will be there, correct?"

There was a pause.

"Why do you ask?" said Adams coolly.

"I have been given an anonymous email address for this person's assistant," replied De Silva anxiously. "Once the gemstones are deposited, I am instructed to email the bank account information to this assistant while at the contest. I want to make sure this member of The Seven and his assistant will be at Versailles when I complete my assignment."

Ryan shook his head in annoyance. He hated dealing with people with no control over their nerves.

"You have nothing to worry about, Mr. De Silva. A member of The Seven will be at the conference. I can assure you of that."

"Good," said De Silva sounding relieved. "Then inform the Master about the emeralds and the plans for their delivery. I will tell my employer the offer has been accepted."

"Excellent," said Adams looking down at his sheet of paper with the phone number on it. "I will call you again at this same time and number in two weeks for confirmation of delivery and any additional details on the exchange."

Mr. De Silva balked. "But is that necessary? I have given you the instructions. Speaking again could be risky."

"It will be," said Adams ignoring De Silva's fears while making some notes on his small piece of paper. "The Master requires me to take care of details, and I want to make certain nothing goes wrong with this exchange. Please tell your bosses we can have an agent pick the emeralds up once the summit begins. Thank you again,

Mr. De Silva. The Master greatly appreciates your organization's contribution to the cause. I'll speak with you again in two weeks."

"Okay," said De Silva gloomily. He hung up.

Adams smiled to himself and reached over to put down the receiver. A giant hand interceded.

"I'll take that."

General Charles McKay, National Security Advisor, stepped forward and quickly removed the phone from Ryan Adams's outstretched hand. The assistant gasped as he looked up. The General was standing in front of him, with Gary standing behind in the doorway. Next to Gary were three Secret Service agents, Rick Pullman, Sam Lewis, and Dan Harkin, all with weapons drawn. Gary remained silent as the General held the receiver to his ear, pushed several buttons, and returned the phone to its cradle with the speakerphone on.

"McKay here. Did you get it?" he asked solemnly.

The speakerphone immediately replied. "We did, sir. The call was recorded and traced to a pay phone inside the Louvre museum, near the gift shop. French police are on the way, but given the normal tourist traffic this time of year, it might be impossible to intercept the man."

"That's fine. We really don't want to pick the fellow up right now. We just want a good look at him. Be sure our agents get hold of all the film from the museum's security cameras. Inform me when he is identified. But take no other action." McKay stared frostily at Adams. "We want Ryan Adams to call him back in two weeks, don't we, Mr. Adams?"

Ryan Adams said nothing. He slowly picked up his glasses from his clipboard and held them tightly in his steady hands.

"Get a copy of the phone recording over to the CIA and NSA today. See if they can identify the man using their voiceprint technology. That's all." McKay barked out his orders and briskly pushed another button to end the call. The General, a huge military man with broad shoulders and a resounding voice, gazed down at Adams with complete disdain. "Anything you want to say before we arrest you?"

Adams managed a calm smile. "If you arrest me, General, how will you be able to make that phone call in two weeks?"

"An excellent question, Mr. Adams. You told Mr. de Silva that you like to pay attention to details. We pay attention to details, too. We have a new agent assigned to Mr. Craig. Step forward and introduce yourself, Agent Harkin."

The tall blonde agent stepped forward, his handgun pointed straight at Adams's chest. The agent spoke.

"The Master greatly appreciates your organization's contribution to the cause."

Adams's eyes grew wide. Harkin had repeated his own words verbatim, mimicking his voice very well. The assistant looked up at the National Security Advisor silently, then shifted his gaze over to Gary.

"How long have you known?"

It was a simple question.

"Since the wedding in September," answered Gary flatly. Gary looked at his assistant with a mixture of anger and disappointment. He had depended on and trusted Adams so much during his first months in the White House. He had considered Ryan Adams a true friend. When he learned of Adams's position as an informant and double agent to The Seven, a deadly secret criminal organization that had tried to kill his wife a few months ago, he simply couldn't believe it. It had been excruciating to keep up the façade of friendship for several weeks now, watching and waiting, until today's bust.

Adams nodded. He fingered his eyeglasses carefully.

"I assume that you know about The Seven?" he asked in a steady voice, barely a whisper. The three agents slowly inched their way into Gary's office, their black guns drawing closer to their mark.

McKay answered in a tone that sounded more like a growl. "Oh, yes, we know about them, too, Mr. Adams. We know The Seven was responsible for killing President Taylor, his friend and Vice Presidential running mate, Eric Peters, and White House Counselor, Donald Hooper. We know they planned to kill President Johnson and put their own man, Senator Miller, into the White House as her replacement. And most importantly, we know The Seven is a secret criminal organization made up of the late Senator Miller, a French chef, a Vatican Priest, an English Lord, a world banker, a U.N. ambassador, and the leader of the group. What did you call him? The Master?"

The assistant's eyes widened even more in surprise. Apparently, they knew more than he anticipated.

"Yes, that's what I call him." Ryan looked up at Gary and nodded his head. His eyes looked sad. Then he leaned forward, rested his elbows firmly on the desk, put one end of the earpiece in his mouth, and bit down hard.

McKay crossed his arms and stared at the man for a few moments, giving Adams time to think things over. The General then addressed him slowly. "I think we've answered enough of your questions for now. We have many more questions of our own that will need answering. To begin with, we want to know how your organization got started, where do they meet, what are the members' individual responsibilities, and how they communicate with this Master of The Seven. What an interesting name, by the way. What does it mean? Who is he? Is he a military man? A businessman? Is he a foreign or domestic terrorist? What is his agenda? And how did he come to hire you? Trust me. We want to know a lot more about this Master of yours. And I'm happy to report that we've made special arrangements for a place for you to stay where we can have plenty of time to chat until the next phone call to Mr. De Silva."

Adams didn't appear to be listening. His head was bent over, eyes almost shut.

"Who is the Master of The Seven!" demanded the General hotly.

Adams did not answer. He could not. The glasses slipped through his fingers and fell to the floor. He suddenly stood up, jerking as he painfully clutched his sides with his arms, his breath coming in convulsive spasms. He looked at Gary apologetically.

"I remain. . . true to those . . . I serve. Both...of...them."

Ryan Adams crashed face down on the desk. McKay grabbed the body and flipped it over. Adam's eyes bulged out, staring blankly at the ceiling. There was no breathing. Adams was dying. McKay began administering CPR and yelled for medics. Agent Lewis hastily put away his gun and radioed the situation through his wrist microphone to the Secret Service command center. Agent Pullman grabbed the desk phone and started dialing. Gary heard people running up the steps, and soon sirens were racing down Pennsylvania Avenue towards the White House. Agent Harkin took over the CPR for General McKay.

In the midst of the pandemonium, Gary reached down and picked up the glasses that had fallen to the floor. The tip of the left earpiece was broken and hollow inside. There was still some dark fluid remaining at the edges. It must have held some sort of poisonous substance. He showed it to McKay.

"Hellfire and damnation!" exclaimed the General.

The medics arrived, but it was too late.

Ryan Adams, the loyal assistant to both the White House Social Secretary and the Master of The Seven, was dead.

Chapter Two

White House Family Dining Room

Saturday
November 17, 2001

"**P**arley Vous Fran-cey. Fran-cey, Fran-cey. Parley Vous Fran-cey. Très bien!"

Six-year-old Abigail Louise Johnson Craig, the youngest daughter of America's first woman president, proudly serenaded her family early Saturday morning. She enthusiastically sang her original song to the tune of "Here we go round the Mulberry Bush" while tapping her way around the breakfast table. This morning she was sporting a new pair of black patent leather tap shoes, and a pretend crystal tiara she got for her birthday.

Enjoying the early morning performance were Madame President Martha Dameron Johnson, her aunt and acting First Lady, Sophie Johnson McKay, Sophie's new husband and National Security Advisor, General Charles McKay (who was hiding behind his morning paper, quietly tapping his foot under the table keeping time with the music). Also present were Mildred Long (Abigail's nanny), dark-haired teenage sister, Eliza Johnson, U.S. United Nations Ambassador, Maurice Porter, and White House Press Secretary and family friend, Blaze Phillips. All adults and siblings praised Abigail's serenade, all adults except for one.

"Okay, who's been teaching Abigail how to speak French?" Gary asked critically while buttering his toasted sesame seed bagel. He looked around the table with displeasure.

"Well, don't look at me," said Blaze holding up his hands defensively. "I flunked French in high school."

"Not me!" said Eliza as she picked up her orange juice. "I'm taking Spanish."

General McKay remained silent behind his Wall Street Journal.

Finally, the guilty party, Nanny Mildred, slowly raised her hand. "It was me. I thought she should know a few lines before we went to Paris."

"Humph," said Gary crossly, taking a bite of his bagel and chewing it hard. "Mildred, you know we have to be careful about what is said *around* Abigail. It can get her and us into a world of trouble."

"Yes, we know," said the cynical voice behind the newspaper.

"World of trouble, world of trouble" sang Abigail, her blonde curls bouncing up and down as she struck a ballet pose and expertly pointed her toe.

Gary looked over at his wife for moral support, not sure if he should be the one to reveal their daughter's secret skills to present company. Madame President smiled with understanding and turned to Ambassador Porter.

"My husband is complaining because our youngest daughter has a photographic and eidetic-auditory memory. This means she remembers everything she sees and hears, talents which played a rather significant role in the events that took place here in September."

"Good Lord!" exclaimed Ambassador Porter, putting down his cup of coffee. The white-haired gentleman, tall and distinguished in appearance, was quite astonished, for he immediately understood Madame President's meaning. The events of September last had rocked the nation — the attempted assassination of Madame President by her now deceased chief of staff, Jim Myers, and the suicide of the Secretary of State, former New York Senator David Miller. Both deaths and the foiled murder attempt on Martha had made headlines around the world, as had Madame President's subsequent appointments of then-Treasury Secretary Kingsley, as the first African American Vice President and Gary's friend and UNC law professor, Dr. George Washington Campbell, as the new Secretary of State. Porter stared at the blonde-haired tyke apprehensively. Gary could see the Ambassador's mental wheels spinning, most likely reviewing everything he recently said in front of the precocious child.

Martha smiled at the Ambassador. "Abigail's talents are not public knowledge, Maurice, for obvious reasons. So please keep this information to yourself, for her protection and mine."

"Of course," said the Ambassador, still eying the child.

"The deaths of Myers and Miller and the attempt on my life are one of the reasons we invited you to breakfast this morning, Ambassador," continued Martha. "The General and I felt you should be fully apprised of the situation before we travel to Paris after Christmas. The press got some of the story, but some things we did not tell them."

"Did not tell. Did not tell," sang Abigail twirling.

Mildred immediately wiped her mouth with her napkin and stood up.

"Abigail, Eliza, time for us to go. Your mother has official business with the Ambassador. Let's go wake your brother. Joshua is making a bad habit of sleeping late these days. I won't have it."

"Do we have to? I know what happened,." complained Eliza.

"Don't argue," instructed Nanny Mildred firmly, "and set an example for Abigail. Come, Abby, let's drag Josh out of bed and go downstairs and see how the new Christmas trees in the East Room are coming along. They arrived yesterday morning. The florists said you could hang some ornaments today."

Abigail clapped her hands in excitement, went over to kiss her mom, and rushed off with Nanny Mildred and Eliza following in her wake. Ambassador Porter took a sip of coffee and looked at Madame President expectantly.

"What don't I know?" he asked.

"Well, an attempted kidnapping or worse, an attempted murder of my daughter, Abigail, for starters," replied Madame President sipping her coffee.

Porter's eyebrows raised in alarm.

"Who in heaven's name tried to do that?"

McKay finally lowered his newspaper. "The butler," he said in a displeased tone. "And he's dead now and certainly not in heaven, thanks to the quick thinking and deft shooting of our former nanny, Miss Jane Michaels — "

"Who is really a secret agent with the British MI6 and Charles's daughter," added Aunt Sophie with pride. She reached over and proudly patted her new husband on the arm.

"Good God!" exclaimed Porter. He shook his head as he tried to take it all in.

"The press wasn't told about Jane's role in the butler's demise either, so do me a favor, Maurice, and keep that information to yourself," requested the General.

Porter promptly nodded. He knew better than to cross General Charles McKay.

"And there's more," added Gary, sitting back in his chair. "It was Abigail who overheard the assassination plot that Myers and Miller had concocted, Abigail who saw Myers plant a poisoned lipstick in Martha's purse, and Abigail who overheard my former assistant, Ryan Adams, reporting to his boss, a man in charge of the assassination attempts known as the 'Master of The Seven.'"

"The Seven!" cried Porter, rising halfway out of his chair. Shocked, he quickly turned to Martha. "You believe *The Seven* did this?"

Martha immediately shook her head, put down her coffee, and reassured her ambassador to the United Nations. "Sit down, Maurice. It's alright. It's not the UVA Seven that we are concerned about. As a fellow UVA alumnus, I knew you would jump to that conclusion. It's another Seven completely, a very bad one, I'm afraid."

Gary slowly nodded his head in agreement. The good organization his wife referred to, was a band of University of Virginia alumni known as "The Secret Seven," a group that historically gave large donations of cash, always in amounts of seven, to various projects and causes associated with Mr. Jefferson's university.

"Are you sure?" asked Porter with a worried look on his face. He bit his lip. "I'm on the UVA Board of Trustees, as you know. I have many friends around the world who are noted UVA alumni. Many are now working in rather high places. Could it be any of them? Are you sure they aren't involved?"

"Oh, we are quite sure!" said Martha emphatically. "Abigail overhead Adams mention that The Seven is an organization comprised of a French Chef, a Vatican Priest, an English Lord, a world banker, a U.N. ambassador, and the leader of The Seven, the Master. Believe me, we've checked out the possibilities thoroughly, and there isn't any former UVA student currently working in Paris as a chef or working in the Vatican as a priest or one who has obtained the title of English Lord or who serves in a top leadership position in the World Bank."

Porter glanced over at McKay and Martha with an extremely uncomfortable gaze. "And the U.N.? An ambassador? This is rather awkward, but how do you know it's not me?"

"We wouldn't have invited you to breakfast if we thought that," replied the General flatly as he reached for his coffee. "The Seven's agent inside the White House (that would have been Myers) was supposed to nominate one of The Seven to become Vice President after Peters' death. You were already serving in the U.N. before President Taylor was put into office, and your name was not brought forward as a possible V.P. candidate after Peters died. Myers nominated Senator Miller. Thus, you are eliminated."

"Well, thank heavens for that!' murmured Porter, reaching up and loosening his collar. His shoulders relaxed as he let out an audible sigh and sat back down in his chair. He grabbed a glass of water and took several sips. Looking up, he asked, "Why are you telling me this?"

"Well, for one thing," replied the General, "you can keep your eyes and ears open for us at the U.N. We know someone there is involved. Tell us anything you see as unusual. That will do for starters."

"Of course," agreed Porter promptly.

"Next," said Martha, "we want you to attend the G-8 summit. Secretary Campbell will be there, obviously, but we would like you there as well."

"No problem," said Porter. "But what reason can we give the press?"

The General let out a groan and picked up his newspaper.

Gary smiled. "We'll get to that in a minute."

Martha leaned in closer. "But first, as our ambassador to the United Nations and as a member of the UVA Board of Trustees, you can help us by giving us access to some of those important friends of yours, people, how did you put it, in high places?" Martha paused briefly and then added solemnly. "You see, we are determined to go after The Seven, one by one, and unmask them and bring them to justice."

"Your friends," added McKay gravely, "might be able to provide various 'reasons' for our people being in certain places at certain times." His eyes narrowed as he spoke. "It's called 'cover' over at CIA headquarters."

Porter's eyes widened. "General. Say no more. I am willing to help in any way I can. When shall we start? Paris, I presume, with the French Chef?"

"Exactly," said Martha nodding her head. "Gary can tell you our ideas for setting a trap."

Gary took over the conversation. "Martha has contacted the French President Mansart and requested that both the G-8 summit and the cake competition be moved from Pau to Versailles. Given the attempt on her life in September, the French president felt, and we agreed, that Versailles would be a more secure location. President Mansart contacted the other summit leaders and their security advisors to get their agreement for the move. They concurred, and the venue was changed."

"I was wondering why that had happened," mused Porter softly. "It's a good location. The World War I treaty was signed there. The summit move makes sense just on the historical aspect alone. But why move the cake competition there? Wait! You don't mean you know the identity of the French chef? Is he part of the competition? You want him there at the conference?"

"Yes and no," replied Martha. "Yes, thanks from information we intercepted from Ryan Adams, we know that the French chef will be part of the competition, but unfortunately we don't know who it is. Not yet. So, the old adage, 'hold your friends close and your enemies closer,' makes a lot of sense in this situation. My Secret Service detail is screaming, but let them scream. I want to draw this man out into the open, so the cake competition comes with us to the summit."

"Okay. But I still don't see how I can help," said Porter frankly.

Gary quickly responded. "That's where I come in with one of my crazy ideas."

The General disappeared behind his newspaper again. "Mr. Craig's crazy ideas almost drove me to drink last time around. I don't know why I agreed to this new scheme."

"Because Gary's ideas are ingenious," assured Sophie soothingly. "Here dear, have some more coffee cake."

Porter politely coughed. "Well, speaking of cake, did you know my daughter, Marie, is a pastry chef in New York City? I know I'm biased, but she is rather good. Might I take her along with us? I'm sure she would love it!"

Gary nodded his head in agreement. "Perfect. Actually, this will add to our 'reason' for your presence in Paris, Ambassador Porter. We would like to invite you to help judge the cake competition, along with myself and Aunt Sophie. This cake competition will include the use of sugar construction. Understandably, your daughter would want to be present when her father judges such a prestigious event."

Porter looked completely astonished. "You want me to be a judge? But I'm no gourmet!"

"But you've eaten in the best restaurants in New York City, have you not?" asked Martha grinning. "Okay, it is a stretch I know, but given your position in the U.N. and the importance of this summit, I think the White House can spin it."

"We're very good at spinning," added Blaze with a smile.

"And we'll get our friend Jack Parish to promote the story. He's rather good at spinning, too!" added Gary.

"Okay, I'll do it," said Porter, "Spin away, Mr. Phillips. Do you need anything from my daughter before we go?"

"Yes," said Martha promptly. "We will need her full name and birthdate so Charles can run the necessary security clearances. But it should be no problem."

Gary continued. "This afternoon Blaze, our new White House Press Secretary, will hold a press conference and will announce that we will hold a Winter Arts Festival at Versailles Palace during the summit. We will celebrate the past glories of Versailles in food, fashion, and art! Of course, we won't announce what took place behind the scenes to get the countries attending the summit to agree to all this! But McKay has been working closely with the other security advisors, and they have given their consent and are supportive of the idea. So, in addition to the cake competition being moved to Versailles, we will also hold a fashion show. Maurice, could you possibly help us in that regard?"

Porter nodded. "Yes, I can. I am friends with fashion designer Roland Martin. He lives in Paris. I went to school with him at UVA. He can help you put on that fashion show."

"Wonderful," said Madame President. "Gary's new assistant, Nick Vasquez, will assist in the organization and planning of the fashion show. Nick will also be assisting me, Sophie, and the girls with our wardrobes for the trip, along with D.C. designer, Max Jones. You know Max?"

Porter chuckled. "The crazy wedding designer who created your wedding dresses? Who doesn't know Max!"

McKay's newspaper rattled loudly, expressing his sentiments towards Maximilian Jones.

"Oh, one more thing," said Gary. "Blaze will announce that we are sponsoring an art competition. We have selected four relatively unknown artists from different countries to draw and paint events during the summit. Since journalists will have limited access to the Palace during the meeting, the artists can more securely capture the events. We'd like the U.N. to help sponsor this event."

"Certainly," said Porter. His attention was briefly distracted by the approaching sound of Abigail's taps shoes. She popped into the family dining room again, lugging a little pink suitcase behind her. She sat on the floor, opened the case, took out a box of crayons and two coloring books, pulled off one of her black patent leather tap shoes, and put it in the suitcase.

"I'm packing," announced Abigail.

"She packs daily," observed the voice behind the newspaper.

Abigail, encouraged by an audience, pulled off the small tiara from her head and packed that too.

"Which brings us to the subject of the final event," said Gary solemnly. "We're going to hold a Masquerade Ball."

Porter gasped. "With an unidentified assassin loose? Martha, have you lost your senses? I agree with the General. It's sheer lunacy. You certainly don't mean a masquerade ball like they did before—"

Madame President interrupted. "Oh yes, Ambassador, just like they did during the reign of the Sun King, Louis XIV. It will be a splendid ball, held in the sparking Hall of Mirrors, with fine foods, wine, medieval music, dancing, and Rococo dresses to die for."

"That's not funny," complained McKay loudly from behind his newspaper.

Martha ignored her uncle-in-law. "Amid food and fashion, we will catch him, Maurice. Now, you must promise to tell no one of The Seven and our plans to capture them. We are limiting the number of people who have access to the full story. Not even my Vice President or my Cabinet, including Secretary of State George Campbell, knows about The Seven. Tell no one!"

Chapter Three

Lighting the Tree

Late Sunday afternoon
November 18, 2001

"So, who killed President Taylor?   A secret international cabal by chance?"

Stunned, Gary Craig gaped at Jack Parish, the flashy, white-haired CNN reporter, who was standing in the middle of the White House Blue Room with masses of silver Christmas tree tinsel draped liberally around his neck.

How on earth did Jack know? How did he always know?

Blaze, Sophie, and Martha all turned and stared at Gary.

"Well, don't look at me," said Gary. He was standing next to the tree holding a yellow and blue glass partridge ornament. "I didn't say a word."

The First Family and their friends were gathered in the Blue Room to decorate the most special Christmas tree in the entire White House. The giant spruce was full and fragrant and reached all the way to the ceiling. With this year's theme, *The Twelve Days of Christmas*, the Blue Room tree featured ornaments depicting all twelve days.   Twelve additional trees, each representing verses from the familiar Christmas carol, were scattered throughout the house. In the Green Room, Scottish piper ornaments adorned a tree filled with red and green balls and holly berries. In the Red room, little drum decorations from various countries around the world hung on a pine tree and around the fireplace mantel. Milkmaids, the leaping lords, and the ladies dancing filled the branches of the State Dining Room trees. Bird-theme trees (swans, calling birds, French hens, turtledoves, and partridges) were set up along the blazing red carpet of the main floor's Center Hall. And in the East Room, five thick pine trees from Mr. Gleason's tree farm were covered with various sized golden rings— decorative ornaments submitted from all fifty states in the union. The golden trees were covered with oodles of white twinkling lights, gold tinsel, and artificial snow.

Jack beamed at Gary. "I'll take that as a non-denial denial, which, in Watergate terms, confirms my suspicions, thank you so much." He paused and looked down at the family's black cat, Sheba, poised underfoot, ready to pounce. Jack pulled out a single piece of tinsel and held it out for the playful cat to attack.

Martha shook her head and crossed her arms with a sigh.

"Sorry," muttered Gary.

"Tut, tut, my children," said Jack reassuringly as he dangled the silver tinsel up and down in front of Sheba. "Nobody technically squealed. I deduced. It is what I do best. When Gary's former assistant keeled over dead last month and every agency that stands guard inside this house went bananas, I added two and two together and came up with conspiracy. I figured there must be more to Adams's death than meets the eye and another round of fun and games about to begin, especially with half the household traipsing over the Atlantic after New Year's Day. Rest assured, I won't blab to my producers…not yet, anyway. I'm a good boy, remember?"

Gary and Martha both threw Jack a skeptical look.

"Hey, you can trust me," said Jack looking offended. Sheba objected, batting the tinsel away with her front paw.

Martha gave Jack her most presidential severe look. "Well, alright. But let's get one thing straight, Jack Parish, we were going to brief you anyway. You were helpful to us the last go round, and the General and I believe your journalistic talents might prove beneficial on this next trip. You've demonstrated to us that you can keep your mouth shut when necessary, and your reporting skills do come in handy at times. You recently were given a moderate level of security clearance. That was done because we want to officially use you on this next mission."

Jack looked flattered. "I won't let you down, Madame President."

"See that you don't," said Martha.

"Okay, tell me everything," said Jack.

"Do I have to leave the room again?" whined Eliza with a distinct note of bitterness in her voice. She was still cross about having to leave the breakfast table early the day before.

"Yes," said Martha. "I'm sorry, sweetheart. We have to talk about national security. You know the rules."

Eliza frowned. Clearly, she knew and didn't like them.

"Well, what about everyone else? Do they have to leave, too?"

The definitive answer to her question came from below the tree, where a toy train set was noisily being assembled.

"Yes, everyone has to leave, including the plumber," barked General McKay, surrounded by a mass of cardboard boxes and tissue paper. Seated next to him on the floor were Madame President's son, Joshua, age eleven and a half, and Bert, the Greensboro plumber, who was now married to Gary's former landlady, Harriet. Joshua and Bert knew better than to argue about the rules with the General and promptly reached for more boxes. They would finish assembling the train in the adjacent Green Room. Eliza declared it all very unfair and begrudgingly took Abigail upstairs where Mildred and Harriet were visiting. Aunt Sophie went along with them to cheer up Eliza.

Once the room was cleared, Gary handed Jack some more tinsel and launched into the story. He told him the full details of Ryan Adams's death, what they knew about The Seven and how they knew it, and outlined their plans to seek out the remaining members of the organization and bring them to justice.

Jack looked dazed.

"Well, alright then. I guess that means I'll be spending New Year's Eve overseas. CNN's finance department will be thrilled." He paused and looked down at the dancing lady glass ornaments hanging on the Christmas tree. They were Abigail's favorite.

"Abigail really did all that? I mean — repeated everything Jim Myers and Ryan Adams said, word for word?"

"She did," replied Martha in a voice full of warning. "Jack, you are a reporter, but you are also a friend of this family now. And as a friend, I must insist that you don't make Abigail's talents public. Promise me that."

"Cross my heart, hope to die, or the General can stick a needle in my eye," replied Jack solemnly.

"Don't think I won't!" replied the General.

Martha quickly added, "It's a good idea to keep Abigail's talents in mind and not to underestimate her."

"She's a force to be reckoned with," advised Gary proudly, "like her mother."

Jack pondered the warning thoughtfully. "A kid like that could be kinda dangerous around here. She hasn't been in the Situation Room by chance?"

A strangled noise came from underneath the tree.

"Not yet," said Gary.

The impromptu security briefing and tree decorating were suddenly interrupted by the arrival of Maximilian Jones,

D.C.'s flamboyant wedding-dress designer. Max ran an exclusive boutique in Georgetown, where, as he liked to put it, "Our nation's best brides-to-be *flock for frocks*." Fortunately for Max, his ability to design clothing far surpassed his skills in alliteration. Today, the strawberry blonde fashion guru arrived carrying several big boxes of dress samples for Martha to try on. Having designed the President's wedding dress, he was now branching out into day and evening wear for the nation's first female leader. Max arrived wearing an obscene chartreuse silk shirt (loosely draped) and his trademark black leather pants (tightly tucked). He was accompanied by his two assistants, Michael and the punk, pink-haired Christina. They, too, were laden down with boxes.

"Greetings! Greetings!" exclaimed Max brightly as he strode into the Blue Room, ceremoniously dumping his brightly colored boxes on the floor. "Never fear. Max is here. God, the traffic around the Mall was simply awful! Next time, Madame P., I demand you send the family helicopter."

"I'll put the Marines on standby," said Martha grinning.

The family welcomed Max heartily. Eliza and Abigail reappeared to greet him, and White House Chief Usher Morgan popped in to announce the status of dinner, which would be served shortly. Abigail excitedly took Max by the hand and gave him a tour of the Christmas trees located within the three main staterooms. Joshua and Bert returned with the train assembled, and the General got it running on tracks underneath the Blue Room tree. Michael and Christina were invited to help hang ornaments and then joined the children in a pirate card game called Plunder. Later on that evening, the adults chatted about the lighting of the National Christmas Tree, holiday college football games, and the menu for tomorrow's private dinner with the Spanish royals.

Chief Usher Morgan returned to announce, announcing dinner was ready to be served in the family's private dining room on the main floor. The children hurriedly left with Blaze,

Sophie, Michael, and the General. Eliza dashed upstairs to get Mildred, their nanny, and Harriet. Martha stayed back and knelt down to look into one of the boxes. "So, what have you brought for me?"

Max quickly stepped up and pulled the box away.

"Ah-ah! Not yet! All will be revealed in good time, including your glorious gown for the ball." Max pointed to the biggest box on the floor, the one being closely guarded by Christina. "Magnificent! We've been sewing our fingers to the bone, even sending some work up to New York for detail finishing." He turned and flashed a satisfied smile at Gary. "And speaking of the Big Apple, the news on the street is your ex, the wicked witch of the South, is creating havoc up and down Fifth Avenue. My sources tell me she is raising holy hell in the entire fashion district, trying to find 'the right people' to create her wedding trousseau. Darling, trust me when I say Janet Marie Benson-Craig gives a whole new meaning to the word *tirade*!"

"I can only imagine," said Gary acerbically.

"We all can," countered Jack snidely. The reporter had previously met Gary's former wife, the wealthy textile business heiress from North Carolina, currently engaged to the junior senator from South Carolina, Evan Daniels. Jack's final judgment: he did not like the woman. He detested her. This was a rare decree coming from Jack Parish, for Jack loved women of all ages, shapes, and sizes.

Max continued airily. "But no worries. Uncle Max has worked equally hard to prevent Ms. Benson-Craig from finding a New York designer for her wedding trousseau. Thanks to me, no one in New York City will sew a buttonhole for that woman! Oh, by the by, I met your ambassador's daughter on my last trip. She's a pastry chef at a lovely new place in downtown Manhattan. The things that girl can do with chocolate! My waistline still hasn't recovered!"

"I'm glad you like her," said Martha approvingly. "We've invited her to join us in Paris."

"Oh, yummy!" declared Max enthusiastically. "Ask her to bring some samples for the flight over. Now, come along, kiddies, I'm famished. Feed me first, and then we'll have a little family fashion show afterward!"

Madame President took Max by the arm and led him out of the Blue Room, leaving Gary alone for a moment with his close friends, Blaze and Jack. Blaze had been Gary's friend for years. Jack, on the other hand, had entered Gary's life during the past twelve months. Given his position as White House Social Secretary and husband to the most powerful woman in the world, Gary appreciated having two male friends that he could informally hang out with and talk to. Despite all the cameras and the drama, Gary was learning the White House could be a very isolating place.

The three men raised their glasses and toasted friendship, Blaze and Jack with wine, Gary with his Diet Coke. Gary didn't drink alcohol due to a rather extensive history of alcoholism in his family. He had never been addicted to booze, and he was determined to keep it that way. He preferred to be addicted to Diet Coke instead.

"Where's your new Chief of Staff?" asked Jack, refilling his wine glass before dinner.

Gary answered. "Ned? Oh, he and his wife went down to Florida for the holiday weekend. He says he's practicing for retirement."

"Sounds nice," said Jack. "I totally get that 'Retire- And-Move-To-Miami' deal. The older I get, the further south I want to live! And where is your wife's new chief counsel? Why spend the holidays with a computer when there are so many wonderful, unattached young women t be thankful for?"

"Knock it off?" said Gary laughing. "Ken flew to California to visit family and friends. He wants a new laptop, so he's going to attend a high tech computer convention to pick one with the latest new gizmos."

"How nice—a cyber day-after-Thanksgiving sale. To each his own," said Jack dismissively, sipping his wine. "I wouldn't spend the holidays with a computer, not when there are so many wonderful, unattached young women to be thankful for."

Gary ignored Jack's bantering and noticed Blaze was staring forlornly at the train circling the tree. He looked positively glum. Jack noticed, too.

"What's with you?" asked the reporter, putting down his wineglass and picking up Sheba. The cat was circling Jack's feet, demanding attention.

"I don't know," said Blaze morosely as he watched the train move slowly around the tracks. "It's just the holidays. They can be pretty depressing. You know, all this family stuff can make a single guy feel kind of lonely inside. I'll spend the holidays like Ken on my computer, answering emails."

Jack held up his hand. "You're going to Paris, the city of love, son. You'll soon be surrounded by the most beautiful women in the world. Trust Uncle Jack. I'll make sure you are anything but lonesome. Now, here. Take the nice kitty into the kitchen. She hasn't eaten for at least twenty minutes. I want a word in private with Gary."

"Okay, sure," said Blaze, looking a bit happier. Obediently, he put down his glass, took the cat, and left. Gary turned and faced the reporter. Jack stared back at Gary, clearly waiting for him to say something.

"You have tinsel on your sweater," observed Gary.

Jack scowled and brushed it off. "I'm surprised it's not in my teeth. So, okay, talk. Give."

"Pardon?"

Jack leaned in and spoke in an urgent, precise whisper. "You know what I mean! What the hell is really *hap-pen-ing*?"

Gary grinned at his new friend. Even though they had given him an important security briefing, Jack sensed there was more. Which was true, and Jack wasn't going to be easily diverted. Gary cleared his throat and tried his hand at diversion anyway. "Well, we're about to have this wonderful turkey and rice dish. I got the recipe out of an old cookbook I found upstairs — not sure who left it there. Barbara Bush? I hear she was a wonderful cook. Anyway, it calls for a white sauce made with mushrooms...."

Jack groaned. "Not that, Fred. I mean, what's happening over there across the ocean in gay Paree? I mean — hello — that was some pretty serious stuff you dished out before Max made his big entrance. God, was Ryan Adams really part of this Seven gang?"

"Yes," said Gary somberly. "He was the liaison between Myers and the Master of The Seven. Some name, huh? There's no telling how long Ryan was in their employ and how much information he turned over. The damage could be enormous, and the General is pretty furious about the breach in security. The FBI and the CIA are not very happy about that prospect either. I admit I'm still pretty shaken. I trusted Ryan. His betrayal was deeply personal."

Gary paused for a moment to observe the lights flickering on the tree. The powerful scent of pine washed over him, a comforting fragrance to his still frazzled nerves. "Ryan's last words were a pledge of loyalty to the two persons he served, which would be me and the Master of The Seven. It was a rather chilling statement. I don't understand how he could compartmentalize like that. How could he be so devoted to the White House, to me, and at the same time be a traitor to the country and its president?"

Jack shook his head. "I don't know, Mack. Beats the hell out of me!"

Gary took a sip of his Diet Coke and continued. "I never suspected Ryan. He was hard-working, responsible, and competent. He was so quiet, too, never seeking the spotlight. He just blended into the White House life seamlessly, which I guess made him a perfect spy."

"And does his death ruin things?" asked Jack. "I mean, everyone in the press covered it, although we weren't given the entire story. Just the fact he collapsed on your desk and gave up the ghost. Does his demise hamper your effort to go after The Seven?"

Gary took another sip of his soft drink and answered, "Not necessarily."

Jack's eyes narrowed. "Uh-huh. Then it would be my humble journalist's guess that you, the General, and Madame P. have something clever up your collective sleeves?"

Gary paused to look up at the tall glorious Christmas tree, sparkling brightly in the darkening room.

"Yes, you could say that," he said quietly.

"And?" urged Jack breathlessly.

Gary stepped forward and carefully fingered one of the crystal dancing lady ornaments twirling amid the white flickering lights. A lady — how appropriate!

"Well," said Gary smiling. "Let's just say if things go well, one of their henchmen is about to have a run in with some of our best operatives, a group of well-trained secret agents. You might even say this meeting will be completely out of the *blue....*"

Chapter Four

The Louvre

Friday
November 23, 2001

C arlos De Silva looked at his watch, licked his lips nervously,
and swore silently to himself.
Damn! Damn!! Damn!!!
*He did not like being here again, waiting all day for a phone call
in such a public place!*

*A highly skilled and cautious crook, Carlos did not believe
in taking unnecessary risks, especially in broad daylight. Yet, as
ordered, here he was, standing in the center of Paris, in the middle
of the day, inside the Louvre Museum for God's sake, surrounded
by hundreds of camera-carrying tourists, waiting for a call beside
a public pay phone. A phone call, he thought cynically to himself,
which probably would not come. After all, the man who should
be calling him today was dead. The American newspapers had
reported this man's death, since this man worked at the American
White House. Worse yet, this man died on the same day he made
initial contact with Carlos.*

Carlos De Silva did not like this. He did not like it at all.

But Carlos shuddered, knowing that in working for the Columbian Drug Cartel, one is not paid to feel or to think, especially to think independently. His employers were not interested in his suspicions, his thoughts, his opinions, his pain, or his worry. On the contrary, they thought it was quite possible that the Master of The Seven received their offer and follow up instructions that Carlos had supplied Mr. Adams with before he died. Adams's position had apparently been compromised; and when threatened with exposure, he took his own life to protect his leader. That loss was not the concern of the Columbian Cartel. In fact, they rather admired Mr. Adams for his efficiency and sense of duty and expressed this opinion to Mr. De Silva. Carlos shuddered again. Point taken. So, given the fact that cell phones are too easily traced, it was now Carlos's job to stand beside this damn public pay phone and wait to see if the Master of The Seven had hired a new assistant.

The pay phone in question was situated on the main floor just outside the entryway to the Louvre Museum Gift Shop. There were lots of interesting people milling about, none of whom gave Carlos much cause for alarm. He prided himself on being able to detect the presence of any covert agent from either the American or French governments. Looking around, Carlos didn't see any cause for concern. There was a dark-haired boy, ten years old perhaps, a street urchin, not far from him, dressed in shabby clothes and playing an old, beat-up violin. His violin case lay open upon the ground, and people were dropping coins inside as they walked past. There was a young American couple with twins in strollers nearby, the father consulting the museum map while the mother handed out snacks and bottles of juice to the fussy children. There was a group of old ladies, too obviously American by their touristy attire, holding packages from the gift shop, taking pictures, and arguing about when and where to eat lunch. The oldest gal in the bunch complained the loudest and appeared to be winning the debate. A group of four Middle Eastern-looking men was standing at the entrance of the gift shop, talking rapidly in Arabic and pointing to some art prints on display in the window.

Terrorists?

Oh, how he wished they were.

Radical Islamists fascinated Carlos and, frankly, made him a bit jealous. They were free to recruit publicly in many countries abroad. They had well-funded training camps, televised announcements, and even websites! Whoever heard of a Columbian cartel website or training camp for prospective promising drug smugglers?

The phone rang.

Carlos practically jumped out of his skin and rapidly reached for the receiver.

"Olá," said Carlos in a hasty whisper.

"Mr. De Silva?" a man's voice queried.

"Yes," said Carlos tentatively, his fears rising again. It was a different voice addressing him of course, one unknown to him. "Who is this?"

"I am Mr. Adams's replacement."

Carlos swallowed hard. Damn!

His bosses had been right. The deal was still on.

"Your name?" insisted Carlos quickly. He may have been forced to work in open daylight, but he would not make foolish mistakes. He was a professional!

But the new caller ignored his request. "Immaterial. The Master has asked me to call. You heard of course of Mr. Adams's... unscheduled departure?"

"Yes, of course. It was in all the newspapers, on television everywhere. I have been most upset. No one has contacted me since his death."

"That was not what we arranged," the man said coolly. "You were told to wait two weeks."

"But I've been worried. Very worried! Did Mr. Adams get my message to you?"

"No," was the curt reply. "He left us most abruptly. But the Master wishes to confirm his interest in your employers' gift and to get the details about the offer."

Carlos grimaced, and for the second time, he hurriedly relayed the message about the emeralds, their scheduled delivery during the G-8 summit, and the planned transmission of the account number by their agent to the member of The Seven at the cake competition.

Carlos then added, "The emeralds will be delivered to the Banque Nationale de Paris. I anticipate their arrival into the country on the third day of the summit. That will be the first day of the cake competition. I will deliver the account number and access code to your representative at the Summit. You will see that the Master gets this information?"

"Yes."

"Will I need to call you again?"

"No. I assume you have the email address of the chef to whom you are to deliver the information?"

"Yes, of course," snapped Carlos. He felt insulted by the question. What kind of businessman did they think he was? Of course, he would have the information needed. What The Seven didn't know was that he even had the name and email address of the chef's assistant.

"Excellent," said the caller. "Then our business is concluded. Good day, Mr. De Silva. Please give our regards to the Columbian Drug Cartel with our deepest thanks."

With that, the line went dead. Carlos let out a sigh, replaced the receiver, turned to leave, and ran straight into one of the old ladies who had been arguing about restaurants. It was the short one, the old one, the loud one with the attitude. She was petite and looked like she couldn't have weighed more than 100 pounds. Their collision caused her to lose her balance, sending her, him, and all her packages tumbling to the ground.

"I am sorry," said Carlos apologetically while glancing around nervously. The last thing he needed was to have a museum security guard take notice of him. Carlos did not like security guards or policemen. He hurriedly offered his assistance to the old woman on the ground. "Let me help you."

The old lady sat up and then winked at him. "No need to apologize, sonny! I don't mind bumping into a good-looking man like you!"

Taken aback, Carlos managed a polite smile and helped the old woman to her feet. She leaned heavily on his arm as she stood up. Once she was stable, he rapidly gathered up her handbag and packages and handed them back to her. She leaned in very close and patted him on the shoulder.

"Let's do it again sometime!" she whispered with another wink.

The pay phone rang again.

Horrified at the woman's flirtation and frightened at the sound of the phone ringing again, Carlos did what any rational, red-blooded man would do in such a situation—he bolted straight into the museum shop. Once inside, he looked around, pretending to shop, all the while praying the awful old lady with the gray-blue hair would quickly disappear.

Maddie waited till the man left, picked up the phone, and spoke for a few minutes. Then she walked back to the group of women anxiously waiting for her return. All seemed pleased, except for one woman who stood slightly apart, looking critically at her friends with her hands on her hips.

"Don't you think that was a bit over the top?" asked Gertrude flatly.

"No. I enjoy taking a tumble now and again," replied Maddie breezily. "It keeps my knees in shape."

Gertrude looked down at the thin, knobby knees and rolled her eyes.

Standing next to Gerty, Eileen shook her head unconvinced. "There's nothing wrong with those knees."

The youngest member of the group, Olivia, asked impatiently, "Well, did you get it?"

A satisfied smile spread across Maddie's face as she produced the man's wallet. She promptly handed it over to Dotty, the newest member of the uncover team. "There! Search through that! It should get us a name and address. Oh, by the way, I'm afraid our bird got the real call from The Seven. The call I just answered was from Agent Harkin back at the White House. He was supposed to pose as the replacement. Looks like the Master has a new assistant, and they beat us to De Silva. But I overheard some of what was said. We should call Langley right away."

"Good heavens, girl, you are good!" said Dotty in her strong Texas accent. She quickly flipped through the wallet and found Carlos De Silva's Brazilian driver's license. She handed it over to Eileen, who began copying down the information. "Mildred wasn't kidding when she said you were a great pickpocket!"

Maddie blushed. "Well, I am the best."

A young male voice unexpectedly chimed in. "Mais, non, Madame. You are good, très bien, but I am the best pickpocket in all France."

Startled, the women abruptly turned to see the impudent boy who had been playing the violin standing right beside them, grinning appreciatively from ear to ear. Maddie was not taken in by the boy's smile or assertion.

"You bet I'm good, kid! I was picking pockets before you were born!" Clearly, Maddie's professional pride had been injured.

"Maddie!" hissed Eileen in a hoarse whisper. "Lower your voice!"

"Well, I was!" said Maddie with a sniff.

Dotty ignored her friends and stared at the boy intently. "What's your name, sugar?"

"Philippe," said the waif.

"Do you come here often, Philippe?"

"Oui, Madame. Every week! My violin, I play for the tourists."

"Yes, Philippe, you play very well. Now, Sugar, have you seen that man before?" Dotty asked. "The one Maddie—er—bumped into?"

"No, Madame. I have not seen him before. He is Spanish, no?"

"Brazilian," said Eileen, putting the man's license back in the wallet.

Dotty nodded and took the wallet back from her associate. "I see. Thank you, Eileen. Now, Philippe, you aren't going to tell the museum guards about Maddie taking that man's wallet, are you?"

The imp looked aghast. He shook his head violently and placed his hand melodramatically over his heart. "Mais non, Madame! I will tell no one. I only came to help!"

"Help?" asked Dotty in surprise.

The boy glanced over at Maddie and then pointed at the window of the Museum shop. "Oui, Mesdames. You took the wallet out, I will put it back. We must hurry, no? He is about to make the purchase."

The boy was right. Carlos De Silva was in line, holding a book and a magazine in his hands. He was almost at the register. Apparently, De Silva decided to do some real shopping as a cover.

Dotty shook her head. "No, Philippe, it's much too dangerous. I really don't think...."

Maddie instantly stepped forward, grabbed the wallet, and resolutely handed it back to the child.

"I do think. He says he's the best pickpocket in France. Well, then, let him prove it! Here, kid, show us what you got!"

Philippe took the wallet and beamed a kindred smile at Maddie. All five women peered into the large storefront window. They could not hear, but they watched intently as Philippe entered the store, walked briskly around a large wooden table stacked with over-sized books, bumped smack into De Silva, and said something to the Brazilian in rapid French with a lot of animated gestures.

Were there tears?

Carlos De Silva sympathetically reached into his jacket pocket… pulled out his wallet and handed the boy money!

"Well, I declare!" muttered Dotty in her southern drawl.

"Poor boy," said Gertrude sympathetically.

"Poor boy nothing!" declared Eileen. "Philippe is nothing but a petty thief."

"Yes," said Maddie approvingly. "Isn't he wonderful?" She reached into her oversized black handbag, pulled out a handful of Euros, and tossed them into the open violin case.

The old ladies waved goodbye to Philippe and hurriedly left the Louvre Museum. Once outside, they stopped in front of the glass pyramid in the museum's exterior courtyard. Dotty pulled out a cell phone and placed an overseas call to CIA headquarters in Langley, Virginia.

This group of five retired females was an ultra-top secret CIA team known as "The Blue Hairs." Their name came from the fact that these gray-haired ladies often used a blue hair rinse on their missions. Each woman was a widow of a US military officer and underwent extensive training in various intelligence-gathering procedures. Their call was received and quickly routed to the office of the Director of Central Intelligence, DCI Tim Robbins, who promptly put "The Blue Hairs" on speakerphone. Robbins greeted Dotty and announced he had a visitor in his office waiting to hear from them.

"McKay here," answered the National Security Advisor darkly. "I understand our fake call wasn't received by their agent. Not good. What do you have to report?"

"Good afternoon, General," said Dotty crisply. "The Blue Hairs were successful in making contact. The Columbian agent is a man named Carlos De Silva. Age thirty-six, born March 20th. He is from Sao Paulo, Brazil. From his passport, it appears he arrived in Paris six weeks ago. Eileen took pictures of him with her camera when he was talking on the phone.

She'll email those to you immediately. Unfortunately, as you know, De Silva received the real call from the Master's new assistant before Agent Harkin's call came through. Maddie can tell you more. She overheard some of what De Silva said. However, we don't know where he is staying...."

"Yes, we do," corrected Maddie. She pulled out a small electronic keycard from her handbag, the kind hotels give out to guests. "He's staying at the Abbatial Hotel Saint Germain on the Left Bank, room #206."

Dotty gasped. "Madeleine! You got this, too? Why didn't you say so back inside?"

"Well," replied Madeline kindly, "I didn't want to hurt Philippe's feelings."

Chapter Five

The Marble Courtyard

Saturday afternoon
January 5, 2002

T he winter holidays came and went at the White House with much happiness and splendor. The Thanksgiving meeting with the Spanish Royals went exceedingly well, and the royal couple joined Martha and her family for the lighting of the National Christmas Tree on the South Lawn. Gary's office, working closely with the Usher's office, completed the spectacular decorations of the President's house; and the First Family hosted numerous holiday luncheons and suppers throughout December, including a grand Congressional Ball in the East Room.

Christmas came, and Gary reveled in the magic of the season, it being his first officially as a father. He splurged on gifts for all the children, for Sophie and McKay, for his beloved new wife, and even for the three cats! Victoria, Martha's Ragdoll, got a white plush pet bed (suitable for the West Wing); Cleo, Sophie's fat tabby, got green pottery bowls (size extra-large!) from O'Quinn Pottery in Seagrove, North Carolina; and Sheba,

Abigail's rambunctious black kitty, got a rhinestone-covered, blue velvet collar with a silver bell. The bell had been Usher Morgan's contribution. He wanted a warning system for tracking the naughty feline throughout the historic house! For Martha, Gary bought a large watercolor painting of the Bodie Island Creek by Outerbanks artist E.M. Corsa.

On New Year's Day, the family celebrated on a much smaller scale. With friends, they enjoyed a holiday lunch and afternoon of watching football games on television upstairs in the family quarters. Martha was able to take the day off, after completing a very busy week. Items on her agenda included a major fire in Sydney, Australia (she made several calls to their Ambassador offering assistance); Argentina naming a new president (more calls involving Secretary of State Campbell and Ambassador Porter); Israel's Prime Minister Sharon demanding seven days of peace before coming to the conference table to discuss a truce (more work for Campbell, having been sent to Israel before the meeting in Paris); and naming a special envoy to go immediately to Afghanistan.

Gary invited Jack and Blaze to watch the college bowl games with him and his stepson, Joshua. Gary also asked his former landlady, Harriet, and her new husband, Bert, the plumber, to come up from Greensboro, North Carolina. Mildred, Harriet, and Aunt Sophie spent the afternoon in the kitchen, cooking and cackling. Bert and Charles watched football with the guys. Eliza talked and texted her friends on her cell phone. Abigail colored. Even Max made an appearance, with his two assistants, for free food and additional top secret fittings. Max wanted everything to be *"perfect,"* so there were some last minute minor alterations to Martha's wardrobe before *"the big trip."*

Finally, on Saturday, the president and her company boarded Air Force One for the overseas journey to Paris. It was Gary's first trip on the president's airplane, and it sure beat the heck out of flying commercial. Martha had an office onboard, and there was even a small bedroom for her and Gary in the front of the plane. There were private chefs for meals, and Gary discovered he could order anything he wanted. Blaze, the-always-starving, was in hog heaven. He ordered a lot. Abigail got out her tap shoes and tiara and danced up and down the aisles, much to the staff and accompanying press corps' delight. And Jack with his dry wit kept everyone in stitches as they flew across the Atlantic.

Upon arriving in Paris, the party separated. McKay and Sophie left for a brief tour in Normandy. They took Joshua with them, as he wanted his new uncle to show him around the World War II sites. Eliza stayed in central Paris to attend a workshop on modeling sponsored by Vogue magazine. They were planning a feature spread of Madame President's teenage daughter in the upcoming May issue. Mildred would stay with Eliza in Paris, acting as chaperone. Only Abigail would accompany Gary and Martha to Versailles for the summit. Also attending were Ambassador Maurice Porter and Secretary of State George Washington Campbell, who arrived early that morning from his travels abroad.

It was a relatively short journey by car to the home of the famous Sun King, Louis XIV. The approach to Versailles was through vast, winding, busy streets; and since the enormous royal park was situated behind the palace, the front of the castle was deceptively hidden in the outskirts of the city, appearing suddenly beside an ordinary looking city block. Gary marveled as their car pulled in, passing underneath the enormous gilded gates surmounted by the golden Royal Arms of France. During the summit, the palace and its gardens would be closed to the public and most of the press. Nevertheless, on this chilly January afternoon, scores of media vans with satellite dishes were parked up and down alongside the entrance. Dozens of reporters were standing at the palace gates. Cameras flashed and almost blinded them upon their arrival.

There were three courtyards situated in front of Versailles. The armored car drove first through the Great Courtyard, going directly up to a second more narrow cobbled area known as the Royal Courtyard. The car slowed and stopped beside this area's grandest feature, the equestrian statue of Louis XIV located in the center of the square. Secret Service agents immediately jumped out of their vehicles and came around to assist Gary, Martha, Abigail, and the others out of the car. Martha and Abigail were wearing matching dark navy wool coats trimmed with white faux fur around the neck and cuffs. Even at this distance, many feet away from the gilded gates, Gary could hear the frantic clicks of cameras and see the flashes of hundreds of light bulbs going off. Abigail, the un-shy child, turned and waved. More flashes of light. Soon, a second limousine pulled up carrying Blaze Phillips, Max and his two assistants, Jack Parish, and Jack's big cameraman, Al. Jack and his cameraman had been given security clearance and were assigned to officially document the trip for the White House with Al serving as photographer.

Waiting for the American president and her party inside the third courtyard, the Marble Courtyard known for its dazzling black and white tiles, were the President of France, Robert Mansart, several of his associates, the senior official of the palace, Gervaise Lavel, and Versailles's chief gardener, Jean Dumont. Once everyone was out of their cars, the American party turned to greet the French president, his associates, and the Versailles staff. Gary's French was basically nonexistent. Gratefully, President Mansart was fluent in English and had provided several interpreters for them as well as a British photographer who joined Jack and Al in taking pictures of the initial meeting.

Once the official welcome had taken place, with handshaking, greetings, and more photographs, President Mansart turned the First Family over to the competent care of Messieurs Lavel and Dumont, as the Americans were being given the great honor of actually staying at Versailles during the summit. They were going to stay in a smaller palace within the garden park known as the Grand Trianon. Foreign dignitaries had stayed at Trianon in the past; and given the recent attempt against Martha's life, Mansart insisted she and her family stay there. He bid them a hasty *adieu* and, with a satisfied smile and a final wave to the press corps lined up at the gates, the French President climbed into his limousine and sped off.

Monsieur Lavel, the man in charge of Versailles, was a tall, lean man with thin graying hair, narrow distinguished face, long classic nose, and lips firmly set. His look was serious, his manner refined. He stepped forward to address them in crisp, clear English.

"Would Madame President and her family wish to tour the Palace before going to their quarters?" he asked with great formality.

Martha paused, looking around at the magnificent palace. Gary gazed at the honey cream colored royal buildings that surrounded the marble courtyard on three sides. Massive columns, elaborate facades, black iron balconies trimmed in gold, tall sparkling paned glass windows, and stunning arches adorned the exterior of the palace. Numerous life-sized statues stood along the edges of the expansive roof. Everything shimmered in the golden sunlight, reflecting the glory of the former Sun King.

Martha turned and shook her head.

"No, thank you, Monsieur Lavel. I think my husband and I will tour the palace later. Right now, we would prefer a brief look at the gardens. Then we shall retire to our rooms. It's been a long flight, and I suddenly feel quite tired."

"Très bien, Madame President," said Lavel. "We will be honored to show you the gardens. Unfortunately, today's weather it has turned too cold for the fountains to be turned on. Perhaps if the weather warms up later this week, you will see our glorious fountains before you leave." Lavel turned to Gary. "I understand, Monsieur, you like to garden, n'est-ce pas?"

"Yes, very much," said Gary. "I grow roses."

"Oui. We grow them, too. Unfortunately, our roses, they are asleep. But there are still many things to see — the Grand Canal, the Apollo Fountain, the Colonnade, the Ballroom, the Orangery, the Fountain of Neptune. All are available to you during your stay. Monsieur Dumont will give you a guided tour anytime you wish."

"Thank you, gentlemen," said Gary. "I shall look forward to it."

The gardener now stepped closer. He was older, short with a thick rounded middle section, a kind face, snow white hair, and light blue eyes that reflected wisdom and humility. His hands were large, strong, and calloused, evidence of his life's work in the garden park.

"I am at your service," said Dumont. "Though it is winter, the gardens, they are still magnificent."

Gary readily agreed. "We must come back in summer when everything is in bloom, but I'm looking forward to seeing the gardens in wintertime. It will be quiet, and in winter the gardens will show their bones, their underlying structure."

Dumont clapped his hands together enthusiastically, appreciative of a kindred spirit. "Oui, monsieur, it is so!"

At this point, other Versailles staffers stepped forward to assist the Secret Service agents in unloading their guests' luggage. Several small electric-powered carts appeared, used by summer tourists to explore the expansive grounds. Luggage, agents, and staffers were loaded onto the carts and quickly left for the Grand Trianon, located on the northwest end of the massive royal park. Ambassador Porter and Secretary Campbell would be staying at the Petit Trianon. The two men announced their desire to retire early. They got into their cart and, with their security teams, immediately left for their quarters.

Once Porter and Campbell departed, Messieurs Lavel and Dumont led Martha, Gary, Abigail, and their secret service detail on a brief walking tour around the south side of the palace and back to the west porch overlooking the first set of twin pools and fountains known as the Water Parterre. Blaze, Jack, and Al accompanied them, with Al filming the event. From this vantage point, Gary and his wife got their first glimpse of the massive Versailles gardens. Thrilled, Gary looked down to the now quiet round Latona Fountain and the famed Royal Avenue. He felt his heart skip a beat with excitement as he looked across one of the most beautiful and historically important gardens in the world. Jack whistled at the sight, Blaze excitedly pointed at everything he saw, and cameraman Al filmed Martha as Dumont spoke to her about the gardens.

Gary suddenly became acutely aware that Abigail was unusually quiet. She hadn't said a word since getting out of the car. This was not a good sign with Abigail. It was like those dark purple clouds out on the horizon, hovering at the end of the Royal Avenue, threatening trouble over the waters of the Grand Canal.

Calm before the storm?

Gary looked down at his step-daughter. She was not facing west towards the gardens like the rest of the party but east towards the house. She was looking up and waving.

"Abigail, what are you doing?" asked Gary.

Abigail pointed up to the rooftop statues.

"Look at the pretty boy, Papa. I'm waving at him!"

Heads quickly looked up.

Secret Service men rapidly reached for their microphones and weapons.

Al turned his camera upwards.

There he was, a pretty young boy indeed, about ten years of age, standing three stories up on the roof, right on the ledge of the balustrade between two life-sized statues. He was very near the edge in fact. Gary drew in his breath, afraid the boy would fall.

Monsieur Lavel gasped, his face suddenly turning red, clearly mortified.

"Mon Dieu!" he declared incredulously in a lowered voice. "I cannot believe it! Not today! We specifically told him to stay inside!"

Dumont raised his voice and fist and yelled, "Philippe! You bad boy! Come down at once!"

Philippe ignored Dumont's instructions and solemnly addressed Martha.

"Bonjour, Madame President, welcome to my home." He then proudly spread his arms out wide and bowed.

Abigail giggled. "He looks like Peter Pan, Momma. Can he fly?"

Martha's eyes widened. She turned to question Monsieur Lavel. "His home? Does that boy live here?"

Lavel's face turned almost purple with embarrassment.

"Oui," said Dumont candidly and shook his fist again at Philippe.

"You know this boy?" asked Special Agent in Charge Pullman. "We were told nothing about him in our briefings." He didn't look pleased.

Lavel reluctantly nodded his head in confirmation.

"Oui, monsieur, the boy lives here and is no danger to any of you, only to myself, my nerves, and my reputation."

Agent Pullman turned to Martha who ordered her men to stand down. Jack looked like he was about to faint. Gary could see the mental wheels inside Parish's reporter's brain spinning furiously. Here was a great news story!

"Is he in danger of falling?" asked Gary with concern.

"Mais non," said Lavel miserably. "Philippe knows the castle inside and out. He is like the nimble mountain goat. He's played up on that roof since he was a little child."

"In the old days, the Sun King would walk upon that balustrade with his guests in the evenings to view the gardens," whispered Dumont softly, "to smell the lime trees and to watch the fountains play underneath the stars."

"Tell me about the boy," insisted Martha.

Lavel spoke with an awkward look on his face. "It's a long story, Madame President. It goes back for decades."

"Centuries," said Dumont.

"You see," Lavel explained," Philippe's family has been in Paris for over 200 years. Before the Revolution, his family relations were nobility. They were present in the royal court. After the Revolution, some of his family returned to Paris and began working here in the gardens, even though the house stood empty. His grandfather came to work here when the Palace was reopened and restored. Philippe's father and mother both were employed on the estate as well, but they were killed in a tragic car accident when Philippe was only three."

"Four," corrected Dumont.

"Philippe then lived with his grandfather, who worked here with Dumont in the gardens."

"He worked in the Orangery," said Dumont wistfully. "He was a good man. He loved this garden—especially the trees."

Martha smiled and looked down at her daughter.

"Abigail likes trees, too," she said.

Jack made a snorting sort of sound.

Lavel continued. "Then the grandfather died when Philippe was seven…"

"Eight," countered Dumont politely.

Lavel turned and glared at the gardener. "I am telling this story, monsieur. Where was I? The grandfather had a heart attack. He died instantly. He left Philippe some money, enough for meager food and clothing, but not enough for housing and education. So we, the staff, decided…"

"Voted unanimously," clarified Dumont smiling.

"…That we would take care of him, watch over him. We agreed that Philippe could stay here. He lives in the attic apartments of Madame du Barry. The rooms are upstairs, out of the way, old, mostly unfurnished, not open to the public. We put in a small bed for the boy, a table and chair, a small chest of drawers."

"Amazing," muttered Jack, his small notebook out, his pen flying.

"That information is private," snapped Lavel with disapproval, suddenly remembering a reporter was in the crowd. He glared narrowly at Jack and his alert cameraman.

"But, it would make a terrific side story," argued Jack earnestly. "The public will eat it up!"

"No," said Gary firmly. "Leave the boy alone."

"But—"

"Why are you and your cameraman here, Jack, and out there behind the gates with the rest of the banned reporters?"

Jack huffed. "Because I'm a family friend and I do what I'm told."

"Correct. Put your pen and your camera away."

"Killjoy." Jack and Al obeyed.

The boy called down again. "Madame President, today is a special day. For you, I will play a beautiful song!" He disappeared briefly behind the wall, only to reappear with an old brown fiddle and bow in hand. Secret service agents again drew to attention, but Martha quickly assured them she wasn't about to be assassinated by a fiddle-playing child.

Philippe's song began. A tender melody floated serenely over the walls and out into the gardens. The effect was hypnotic.

"Why, he is wonderful," Martha whispered, dazzled.

"That sounds like Mendelssohn," said Gary.

"It is," said Dumont proudly.

Martha closed her eyes to listen more intently to the heavenly music. "I wish I had brought one of my instruments. I would relish the chance to play with him."

Lavel raised his eyebrows with interest. "Madame President, you are a musician?"

"She is," said Gary jumping into the conversation. "Martha plays the violin, the piano, and the harp!"

"Magnifique! Recently, our historical department commissioned a reproduction of Marie Antoinette's harp. It is here now in the palace. You are welcome to play it anytime you like, Madame President."

"How kind you are, Monsieur Lavel. Well, perhaps I will get a chance to play a duet with Philippe while I'm here."

Seeing that Martha approved of Philippe, Lavel now added with some pride, "He will not disappoint, Madame President. The boy has to hear a song only once, and he can play it perfectly. In summer, we have music playing in the gardens—Lully, L'Aisne, Marais. Philippe knows them all by heart. Too bad the boy is too poor for any formal training."

"A child prodigy?" asked Gary.

"Yes, he is a boy with many talents."

"He has other talents?" asked Martha opening her eyes wide.

Lavel bit his lip. "I'd rather not say, Madame President."

Dumont said sighing, "I will tell you. Philippe, he is the pickpocket, 'the best in all France,' he claims. Keep your purse closed when you are around him, Madame President."

"Then Philippe will get along very well with my daughter," said Martha laughing. "Abigail is a bit of a thief herself. She's known for stealing my lipsticks."

Hearing her name again, the behavioral storm clouds finally broke, and Abigail's quiet obedience came to a screeching halt.

"I want to play with him!" she cried. She let go of Gary's hand, took off in a mad dash running up the stone steps, and disappeared straight inside the castle.

"Abigail, come back here!" yelled Gary.

Too late.

She was gone.

Looking up at the rooftop, Gary could see that Philippe had disappeared as well.

Gary turned to his Secret Service detail and ordered, "Well, don't just stand there! Go after her. Monsieur Dumont, lead the way!" Agents Pullman, Harkin, and Lewis promptly took off, with Monsieur Dumont running behind them.

Gary turned to his wife and observed, "There are far too many rooms and far too many trees here for Abigail to play her hide and no-seeking game."

"Hiding?" asked Lavel warily. "This child likes to hide? That is not good, Monsieur."

Gary made his wife an offer. "Let's trade. I'll go to the G-8 summit and deal with the Russians, and you can be in charge of watching Abigail."

"Sorry, darling," said Martha wisely. "This week I'd rather face the Russians."

Gary surveyed the vast expanse of grounds, buildings, and fountains stretching out before him and frowned. A strong wind blew from the west, carrying with it a chilled feeling of apprehension. A storm was indeed approaching.

"It's going to be a long and exciting week," said Gary.

The President of the United States put her arm lovingly around her husband's sagging shoulders.

"Yes, my love, it most certainly will be that."

Chapter Six

Family Drawing Room

Sunday morning
January 6, 2002

G ary awoke late the next day feeling a bit discombobulated. He never handled jet lag well. Today was no exception.

He slowly opened his eyes and blinked, bedazzled by the opulent surroundings. He and Martha were given the Grand Trianon's *Queen of Belgium* bedchamber. The Grand Trianon was a delightful structure in the midst of the lavish royal park. Yesterday, Monsieur Lavel explained that Louis XIV desired to expand the castle property and, therefore, purchased Trianon in 1668. At the time, Trianon was only a quaint town bordering the outskirts of Versailles. The Grand Trianon palace that the king created was made of white stone with pink marble pilasters and a courtyard flanked by two long wings. After the French Revolution, the small castle remained empty until Napoleon arrived and restored it to its past glory. History records that the new emperor often stayed in this lovely palace with his wife, Josephine, and other family members. After Napoleon's fall, the building again fell into neglect and ruin for almost one hundred years until President Charles de Gaulle rediscovered the forgotten palace and repaired it for use by visiting heads of state.

Gary and Martha's room was divine, decorated in a royal palate of vibrant reds and gold. Gary estimated the ceilings to be at least 15 feet high. The walls were painted stark white with wide, ornately carved crown moldings. Two tall French glass windows were adorned with lush red and gold tapestry draperies across the room from the bed. A bright red and gold rug stretched across the floor. The same fabric made up the bedspread and bed tapestries. Dazzling crystal chandeliers hung in front of both windows, casting tiny rainbows of light across the room. To Gary's left was a black marble fireplace. Someone had apparently been in that morning, for a warm fire was lit and burning.

Gary felt Martha stir beside him.

"Good morning," he said softly, holding her close.

"I don't think so," answered Martha weakly. "I think I'm going to throw up."

And she did. Martha jumped out of bed and went to the closest thing she could find to a basin - a black urn sitting on a nearby table. She stood over it and retched.

Gary got up and went over to her, putting his hand on her back as she continued to be sick. When she was done, he took her in his arms and carefully led her back to the bed. They both got in, and Martha snuggled up against him in a tight ball under the covers.

"Feel better?" asked Gary with concern.

Martha nodded. "Much. I've wanted to do that for two days now."

Gary was suddenly alarmed. Was Martha coming down with something? That would be catastrophic the day before the international summit began. He put his hand up to her forehead. It felt cool to the touch.

"Are you ill?"

"No, just my nerves I think," said Martha sleepily. "After all, this is my first face-to-face meeting with the world's most powerful leaders. My stomach has been bothering me for a few weeks now. I'm just anxious about all the things going on at home and about giving the opening address after President's Mansart's welcome. I don't really know why. I'm not usually this nervous about speaking in public."

Relieved, Gary smiled to himself and hugged his wife tightly. He gently brushed several blonde hairs from her face, kissed her cheek, and whispered encouragement.

"No worries. Just be yourself, work hard, and throw up all you want to afterward. I'll be waiting here with rare Chinese porcelain vases at your disposal."

They laughed and lingered in bed a few minutes longer until they heard the pitter-patter of little feet, or in this case, the tap-tap-tap of Abigail's tap shoes fast approaching. Abigail had been given the smaller, yellow and gold Emperor's bedchamber, the bedroom used by Napoleon himself. Gary was apprehensive about that arrangement, concerned that his forthright stepdaughter was sleeping in the bed of France's former forthright dictator. The spirit of Napoleon might rise up and unduly influence his already headstrong little girl.

While Nanny Mildred was with Eliza in downtown Paris, the Versailles staff had provided a young and all too innocent French maid named Gabrielle to keep up with and attend to the First Daughter's needs. Poor girl! From the sound of it, Gabrielle had fallen too many steps behind.

Gary got out of bed to assist Gabrielle in capturing a fleeing Abigail. Soon, the excited, wiggling child was washed, dressed, and ready for breakfast. She and Gary joined Martha and the others assembled in the Louis-Philippe Family Drawing Room. Waiting for them were Secretary Campbell, Ambassador Porter, fashion designer Roland Martin, Gary's assistant Nick (who had flown over during the night), and

Max Jones. Jack was not present, as he and cameraman, Al, were already at the main palace setting up their equipment in the Chateau's chapel for the opening session. Nor was Blaze at breakfast, as he was setting up for his first televised press conference of the week. As reporters had been banned from the palace, Jack's news feed would be shared with other US and international networks.

A plain set of dining room table and chairs, not part of the historic furnishings, had been placed in the drawing room for the family's use. This modern arrangement required a beautiful green malachite bowl stand to be moved over towards the gold-colored fireplace. Magically, servants appeared, carrying silver trays of hot croissants, eggs, bacon, fresh buttermilk, coffee, and cut fruit. Campbell sat near Martha talking state business. Gary sat by Abigail and assisted in buttering her croissant. Porter introduced his friend, Martin, to Gary, Max, and Nick; and naturally, a lively discussion about Paris fashion ensued.

Monsieur Lavel appeared just as breakfast ended, followed by Philippe who came bearing a long-haired, gray cat in his arms.

"Bonjour, Madame President, honored guests, ma petite fille," said Lavel looking down at Martha, Gary, and then at Abigail. "And how is everyone this magnificent day?"

"Wonderful," said Martha smiling.

"Excellent," agreed Ambassador Campbell nodding.

"Très bien," said Abigail while chomping on her croissant.

Gary nervously glanced over at his daughter. The little parrot hadn't been in Paris twenty-four hours, and already she was quickly picking up some French. He hoped it was only an echo without any real comprehension. He wasn't quite ready to handle a bilingual child, definitely not one with a preponderance for mischief and a photographic memory. Gary gazed at Philippe and his pet with curiosity.

"And who is this?" he asked.

Philippe brought his cat over to be admired and petted by Gary and Abigail. "This is my cat Sebastian," said Philippe proudly.

"I have a cat named Sheba," said Abigail while sipping her milk. "She's black and likes to climb trees."

"And ankles," added Max dryly.

Philippe grinned. "Sebastian, he is a good cat. Observe. He will not eat his *petit déjeuner* until his prayers are said."

"A religious cat!" exclaimed Max brightly. "Oh, how I do love the French! Even their pets have class!"

"This I've got to see," said Nick putting down his coffee.

Philippe put the cat on the floor and asked Gary for a piece of cheese. Gary handed a small piece to Philippe, who bent over and placed it on the floor in front of Sebastian. The gray cat leaned over and hungrily sniffed, paused, and looked up. Philippe bowed his head and recited a well-known child's prayer.

Merci pour le monde si doux
Merci pour le nourriture que nous mangeons
Merci pour les oiseaux qui chantent
Merci, Mon Dieu, pour toute

The prayer ended, Sebastian immediately pounced on the cheese and gobbled it up. The adults in the room and Abigail applauded. Porter shook his head in amazement.

"I've seen a lot of things in my world travels, but that takes the cake — or in this case, the cheese," he declared as he reached over and patted Philippe on the back.

"We must show this cat to Jack!" exclaimed Max enthusiastically. "Maybe Al can film the pious kitty saying grace before tonight's dinner and dessert!"

Martha laughed. "What an amazing cat you have, Philippe! Abigail, you've finished your breakfast. Why don't you and Philippe go out and play with Sebastian?"

"Come, Mademoiselle Abigail," said Philippe eagerly, "I have brought my violin for you. I will play a song, and you can dance!"

Abigail didn't need any more encouraging. She quickly jumped down from her chair, blew her mother and Gary a kiss, and followed Philippe and Sebastian out of the room. Once the children left, Monsieur Lavel straightened his back, raised his chin, and made a formal announcement.

"Madame President, Monsieur Craig, Ambassador Porter, Secretary Campbell, Monsieur Martin, and Monsieur Jones. The four artists that will be here during the conference have arrived. They are waiting outside to be introduced. *Pardon-moi* while I go supervise the children and Sebastian." Lavel bowed and left.

"Artists drawing at the Summit?." questioned Campbell with uncertainty. He put down his fork and turned to Porter. "I just don't know. Are you quite sure about this plan, Maurice?"

"Quite certain!" said Porter reaching for more coffee. "It's a wonderful idea. Roland, why don't go over the details for Secretary Campbell."

Roland Martin nodded. "Paris is known for its art. So, for the Winter Arts Festival, we will capture the highlights of the meeting through an artist's eyes. With President Mansart and Madame President's recommendations, four young artists were selected to sketch and paint during the summit. Once the meeting concludes, their works will be shown later this month at the Louvre."

Secretary Campbell tilted his head contemplatively. "Well, alright, but make sure they keep a respectable distance during sessions. I don't want our discussions interrupted."

Roland agreed, got up, and went out of the room. In a few moments, he returned with four individuals— three young men and a young woman. He paused to pull a piece of paper out of his coat pocket.

"I have the information on our artists here. I will read this as I make the introductions. First, from Britain, we have Mr. Tom Parker. Mr. Parker is known for his modern viewpoint, expressed in stark black and white drawings. He'll be sketching this week in charcoals. Welcome to Paris, Mr. Parker."

A tall young man with a fair complexion, black hair, and bright blue eyes stepped forward and bowed.

"Hello," said Tom brightly with a chipper English accent. "Pleasure to meet you all!"

"Welcome," said Martha. "Thank you for coming. I'd like for you to draw the opening session for me if you don't mind."

"Right," said Tom, "Opening session it is then. I'll do my best, I promise."

"Next," said Martin, "we have from Japan Mr. Kiyoshi Ito. Mr. Ito is known for his exceptional bold use of primary colors and will be painting this week with acrylics. Greetings, Mr. Ito"

Mr. Ito, a short and muscular fellow, said nothing and formally bowed to all in the room. Martin continued.

"Then from French-speaking Canada, we have Monsieur Jean Bardou. Monsieur Bardou is something of a traditionalist, taking his inspiration from Pre-Raphaelite art. He will be working in watercolors. Bonjour, Monsieur Bardou."

The handsome young Canadian, with sandy blond hair and big brown eyes, stepped forward briefly and smiled to all in the room. Gary thought this artist might be a nice distraction for Eliza later that week.

Martin acknowledged Mr. Bardou with a nod and then took a deep breath.

"And finally, we have from France, Mademoiselle Babette Moreau. Mademoiselle Moreau is a relatively new artist. Although not well known in the States, her work was recently well received in Paris. She follows the tradition of the French impressionists and will be working this week with pastels. Bonjour, Mademoiselle."

The young lady stepped forward. She was a lovely woman with a slim model's figure, bright makeup, short-cropped platinum blonde hair (obviously bleached), and high-end designer clothes. She wore a shockingly short cream cashmere mini dress paired with sheer cream leggings and knee-high cream boots. Over this ensemble, she wore a full-length coat made of light pink fur. Mademoiselle Moreau softly murmured her "Bonjour" and stepped back.

"My God, what's she wearing?" whispered Secretary Campbell staring at her clothes.

"Nina Ricci," replied Max wistfully finishing his coffee. "That outfit just came off the Paris runway. Isn't she grand?"

Mademoiselle Moreau cast Max an appreciative smile.

Martin put his list away and then gave the artists his final instructions. "Each of you has been given access to all summit locations. You may walk the grounds and palace hallways freely. I'll be giving you an outline of the events for the week. You are to draw, sketch, or paint scenes from all the events, especially scenes from the ball, this Tuesday night."

"Thank you," said Gary appreciatively to the artists. "If you need anything, please contact me, Mr. Martin, or General McKay who is in charge of security. General McKay will be working with the French police and American Secret Service. The grounds will be closed except to the members of the G-8 summit and their staff, so you should not have any interference from tourists or unwanted reporters. When Monsieur Lavel returns, he will show you to your quarters in the Petit Trianon."

"And don't forget the cake competition on Thursday and fashion show on Friday," added Max enthusiastically. "We'll want detailed drawings and paintings of all the cake creations and the models coming down the runway."

Secretary Campbell sighed with resignation. "Chefs, artists, and catwalks! The only thing missing is a chorus line! Well, I'll leave it to McKay to keep it all under control."

Gary smiled. He well remembered Dr. Campbell's dislike for surprises from his college days. Campbell had been Gary's professor in his first year of law school.

Campbell wiped his mouth with his napkin and stood up. "Martha, gentlemen, if you will excuse me, I want to send my Mrs. Campbell an email before our meeting with the French President at ten o'clock. Violet should be back from physical therapy by now."

"Has your wife been ill?" asked Martin with concern.

"Rheumatoid arthritis. Violet's recovering from her second hip replacement, or she'd be here with me. She takes an interest in my work and she loves Paris. She had the surgery in early November, and she's doing fine. She's a tough cookie, my Violet."

"Give her our best wishes for full recovery," said Martha sincerely.

"Will do," said Campbell. He promptly left to go to the Petit Trianon where he was staying.

Martin cleared his throat softly and finished his instructions to the artists. "You will begin tomorrow at the opening session inside the palace's chapel. That meeting begins at 10:00 A.M. sharp. As mentioned, I will see that you get a written handout of the week's events, including the times of the fashion show and cake competition. The chefs will be arriving tomorrow morning and will be setting up their stations inside the Hall of Battles tomorrow afternoon. Any questions?"

They had none.

Madame President stood up. "Excellent. We look forward to seeing your work during the week."

At that moment, music began to play. Strains of a violin concerto floated into the room. Then another sound was heard.

"What is zat strange noise?" asked Babette Moreau with a questioning frown.

Loud echoes of tap, tap, tap in time with the music resounded from a nearby hallway.

"That," explained Gary meekly, "would be our chorus line."

Chapter Seven

Garden Drawing Room and Chapel

Monday Morning
January 7, 2002

The first day at Versailles ended well. Martha returned late in the afternoon to the Grand Trianon with positive reports of her private meeting with the French President. Gary spent the day touring the Palace and walking the gardens with Monsieur Dumont and the children. There was much to see and learn. It was hard to take it all in. Gary loved the staterooms, particularly the Queen's bedroom and the Hall of Mirrors. Abigail liked the Meridian Cabinet because it was small, cozy, and filled with soft silk blue cushions and draperies.

During their outside tour, Philippe talked nonstop. The boy took pride in showing Abigail the Grotto and the Children's Island. Dumont took them to see all the fountains. Standing by the Grand Canal, he described in detail how the park had been lit up by the biggest fireworks display in Versailles history at the marriage of Louis XVI and Marie Antoinette. By mid-afternoon, Abigail was in dire need of a nap, although

Gary didn't think it would be possible to convince her to take one. Nevertheless, Gary and Abigail returned to the small palace for an afternoon rest. The First Family was joined that evening by Blaze, Jack, Ambassador Porter, Max, and Roland Martin for a quiet, Sunday night dinner. Secretary Campbell begged off, requesting a meal in his room. He wanted to call Violet again and then check and see if Senator Evan Daniels had arrived yet. Senator Daniels was from the Senate's Foreign Relations Committee and assigned to work with Campbell on this trip. He was also engaged to Gary's ex-wife.

Early on Monday, General McKay and Aunt Sophie arrived. The couple left Joshua in Paris with Mildred and Eliza, as Joshua wanted to visit the museums and see the sights with his sister. Charles and Sophie, technically on a postponed honeymoon, were given private accommodations in the secluded Queen's Hamlet, buildings once belonging to Queen Marie Antoinette. They arrived just before breakfast and were greeted by the first family before being whisked away by the ever attentive Lavel, who had arranged appropriate furnishings, linens, and a delightful breakfast for the newlywed couple.

Jack Parish and Blaze Phillips joined Gary for breakfast in the Garden Drawing Room. This room was built directly over the location of the former blue and white Porcelain Palace. It was bright and cheerful with morning light streaming in from the many floor-to-ceiling French door windows built into three of the four standing walls. These windows looked out upon formal garden plots that Gary could imagine were once filled daily with purple, white, and red flowers from the Sun King's greenhouses — even in the midst of winter.

A blue, white, and gold rug currently covered the floors of the Garden Dining Room. The furniture was white with gold trim. The cushions were a luscious dark blue-purple, and the walls were pure white. This morning's breakfast was served on two gold and glass tables.

"So this is how the other half lived," observed Jack as he helped himself to seconds of a brie-cheese omelet and crème brûlée oatmeal. "I think monarchy agrees with me. Where can I sign up?"

"Be careful what you wish for," cautioned Gary relishing his morning coffee. "There was more to it than just eating well and living in splendidly adorned palaces."

Jack looked unconvinced. "Oh, yeah? Like what?"

"Well," said Gary thoughtfully, "when Dumont gave us the tour yesterday of the house and gardens, he described the formality of the Sun King's day. It was all done by strict protocol from sunup to sundown. The King arose promptly at 8:30 in the morning…"

"Hold on, Fred. I thought Kings slept in late."

"Wrong. Louis XIV was awakened early each day by the First Valet de Chambre…"

"There was more than one valet?" asked Blaze.

"Many valets," replied Gary. "The ceremonial rising was called *the Levee*, and many courtiers, hundreds according to Dumont, came to watch and assist the King rise, wash, and dress in the morning. An estimated number of more than 160,000 noble persons once lived at Versailles."

"You're joking!" said Jack with astonishment. "The King dressed and bathed in public?"

Gary nodded his head. "Yes. In fact, there was a complex protocol, a complicated system called *Etiquette* that determined who held the King's shirt, his shoes, even his undergarments — every piece of clothing he wore. The more important your position in his court, the closer you were physically to his majesty's presence. That closeness was very much in play during the morning and evening rituals."

"Stop right there," said Jack. "No committee is going to give me a bath and manhandle my underwear!"

Gary laughed. "But I'm just getting started. After publicly dressing, the King went to mass, which was held at 10:00 each morning. They said the Sun King only missed one mass in his entire adult life."

"Church every day?" asked Blaze amazed.

"That was to make up for all the partying he did every night," said Jack sarcastically. "When do we get to the nightlife, his majesty's need for daily repentance?"

"I'll get there eventually," said Gary smiling. "First, however, the King met in Council at 11:00 with his courtiers and government officials. He was extremely disciplined in his work habits. He worked every morning, with lunch at 1:00."

"Finally, food!" exclaimed Blaze. Food was Blaze's favorite topic.

Gary smiled at Blaze and continued. "Lunch was usually private in the King's Cabinets. Afterward, starting approximately at 2:00, the afternoon was devoted to leisure activities. These varied by season and location, for the King and thousands of members of his court went on *journeys* — at Compiègne in the spring and Fontainebleau in the fall. Some days, the King, his family, and courtiers would *promenade* or formally walk the gardens. Most often, the King engaged in his favorite pastime of hunting."

"Not interested," said Jack firmly, "I may kill reputations, but I don't kill animals."

"Not to worry. You could enjoy the *soirèes* that took place in the evenings, beginning at 6:00. Supper was held at 10:00 each night. These were usually public events. Townspeople could come inside the palace, walk through the staterooms, and watch their King eat. You will notice most of the formal staterooms are designed in the outer ring inside the castle. That's where the public could walk. The inside ring of rooms was private for the royal family. Finally, at the King's bedroom, another formal public retiring would take place, called the *Couchee*, and again, valets, officers, family members, and the aristocracy would come and assist the King in disrobing and dressing for bed. The King retired at 11:30."

"You didn't mention the wigs," said Blaze. "Didn't they wear those big white fluffy things?"

"Yes. Dumont says there was an entire room called the Wig Cabinet that contained the King's many wigs. There were hundreds of those. Louis changed his wig several times a day."

"Enough! I'll stick to my own hair, peasantry, and reporting," declared Jack, downing the rest of his coffee. "I did hear a story from Lavel that caught my journalistic attention. You like mysteries, Gary, so you will like this one. When King Louis XIV lay dying in his bed, he did four things before shuffling off this mortal coil. First, he said goodbye to his second wife, Madame de Maintenon. Second, he said goodbye to his heir, his great-grandson Louis XV, who was just a child at the time. Then he met with his nephew, the duc d'Orléans, and officially made him the Regent of the realm, to rule over the kingdom until his great-grandson came of age."

"That's three," observed Blaze.

"Correct," said Jack. "Care to guess what the King's last act on earth was?"

"I have no idea," said Blaze. "Tell us!"

Jack leaned back in his chair with a smirk. "The King of all France, with his dying breath, whispered to his nephew, the Duke, the identity of the man in the iron mask!"

"You mean the man who was locked up in the Bastille?"

Gary nodded. "Right. That is a good mystery, Jack, but not one we'll ever solve, I'm afraid."

"There's more," Jack said. "The nephew told King Louis XV, and that king told King Louis XVI. But that king of France took the secret with him to his grave. Several theories are floating around as to the identity of the man in the iron mask. One theory says he was the King's twin brother or older illegitimate brother. Another theory claims the man in the iron mask was King Louis XIV's real father. Queen Anne of Austria and her husband Louis XIII hated each other and were childless for many years. Then suddenly, poof, she gets pregnant. This theory suggests that she slept with someone else, and this man returned later with plans to blackmail the king. He ended up in the Bastille instead."

"I've heard that story," said Gary. "According to one person who worked in the Bastille, the jailor assigned to the man in the iron mask addressed his prisoner as 'my prince.' "

"Sounds like a modern-day soap opera!" exclaimed Blaze. He then stared down at his piled-high plate. "I love this French food! I could just eat everything!"

"You do eat everything," replied Jack drily. "While we're here, son, let's see if we can slow down your rate of consumption and try educating that enthusiastic palate of yours."

"Educate my what?!"

"We'll start with gastric anatomy," said Jack.

"Okay, you clowns, try not to forget this is a working trip," warned Gary as he finished his green apple crêpes. "You need to be up and running when the big brass arrives at 10:00 for the opening session. Jack, where is Al?"

"I left him behind at the Petit Trianon. The poor guy is smitten with a little French maid there. Monsieur Lavel had a nice breakfast service set up for the artists, Porter, Campbell, and Martin. So, Al is breakfasting with them, hoping to get another glimpse at the cute young thing before her morning rounds."

"Yeah, she's a looker," agreed Blaze.

Gary's eyes widened as he took a sip of hot coffee. "Maybe you should check her out, Blaze. You were feeling rather lonesome at Christmas, you know."

"Nope, I'm waiting for Jack's models to arrive."

"Jack's what?"

The reporter paused with a spoon of steaming oatmeal close to his mouth. "They're Martin's models, actually," said

Jack, "although I intend to lend a helping hand when the little darlings arrive."

"You're pathetic."

"I know. Pass the crêpes."

"You're starting to eat like Blaze."

"With the prospect of love on the horizon, I must keep up my strength," replied Jack with his hand outstretched.

Gary laughed and handed the dish over to the reporter. He then looked down at the English newspaper resting on the table. Along with photos of his wife shaking hands with President Mansart (lead story, page 1), there were articles about European nations giving economic loans to Egypt. More unrest in the Middle East followed, a story about the celebration of Stephen Hawking's birthday, and the latest details on the probe into the Enron disaster. Reporters then covered the brouhaha stirring over actress Brigitte Bardot and her foundation launching an anti-cat-dog-eating campaign amidst the World Cup soccer event scheduled in South Korea in May, and a movie critic's take on the release of *Gosford's Park*. One final item caught Gary's eye. The weather report said a sudden, unusual front was headed for Europe, with dire predictions of heavy snow for Paris in the forecast. The news made Gary pause. Would this help or hinder their plans?

Gary put the paper down, got up, and went over to the window. He paused, opened the French door, and stepped outside. The morning sky was still clear, but dark gray clouds were gathering on the distant horizon. The air was cold, giving Gary a sharp uneasy feeling, a chilling sense of foreboding. He pulled on his wool jacket tightly and shivered.

The approaching storm made him question again his decision to bring the entire family to Paris. They had thought about it, discussed it, and argued over it at length at Christmas. Initially, Gary was against bringing the children, but General McKay convinced him otherwise. Charles explained that The Seven had successfully penetrated the White House twice before and had attempted to kidnap Abigail with relative ease. At least with the children in Paris, they could keep an eye on them themselves. Gary couldn't deny this was sound logic, especially where Abigail was concerned.

But were they headed for disaster? A terrorist would be waiting for them in the palace, and here he was with his wife and youngest child. Was it pure insanity to think that they could corner this chef, unveil and capture him before he could do them harm? He closed his eyes and silently prayed for their success. Gary felt a driving force pushing deep inside, a raw determination to find justice for those who had already died at the hands of The Seven. It was a determination shared by his wife and General McKay. If they left now, the opportunity to identify The Seven's "French chef" would slip away. Gary sighed and opened his eyes. Leaving wasn't an option. The Seven must be stopped before they grew more powerful and struck again.

At least Versailles would be enclosed with top security during the Summit. No one else would get in, and those trying to get out without good reason would be closely scrutinized. And, if the danger became too great, the Secret Service would simply evacuate Martha and their family. Comforted by that final thought, Gary looked around. Four secret service agents were standing sentinel nearby. He saw Abigail, wrapped up in her new winter coat and hat, out on the steps playing with Philippe and his cat, Sebastian. Philippe's coat looked very worn. He smiled at his daughter. Gary noted that the Japanese artist, Mr. Ito, not far away, was drawing the children playing outdoors, another set of eyes squarely focused upon his child. Gary nodded a greeting to the Japanese artist, shook off the chill, and went back inside.

"It's going to snow," announced Gary, turning back to shut the door closed.

"Snow?" Blaze looked up from his plate in surprise. "Here? Are you sure?"

"It's in the papers, and some nasty looking clouds are appearing outside."

"Wonderful," said Jack sarcastically. "Things are going downhill already." He lowered the sports section of the paper, wiped his mouth with his napkin, and stood up. "Come on, Mack," he said to Blaze. "Let's get going. Oh, morning, Madame P. Nice outfit. Morning, Max. Nice outfit."

Martha hurriedly entered the room with Max and his two assistants in tow. Gary felt a glow of pride as he beheld his beautiful wife. She was wearing a classic, navy-blue suit with matching blue pumps, a smart outfit designed by Max for the opening session of the summit. Her shoulder length blonde hair was pulled up and back into a lovely French Twist, the handy work of a local French hairdresser, Monique, whom Max had brought in from Paris.

Gary walked over and gave his wife a kiss.

"Morning, sweetheart. You look lovely."

Martha smiled weakly. "I wish I felt lovely. My stomach is in knots again. I should be wearing green to match!"

"Ah-ah. No throwing up on the navy suit!" cautioned Max.

"I'll do my best."

"Sit down. Eat something," suggested Gary.

"Oh, no, I couldn't eat a thing," said Martha. "That would be tempting fate."

"But you should try. The weather is going to get worse, and I don't want you getting sick. The paper says it's going to snow."

"SNOW!"

Max shouted the word in sheer panic and immediately dropped his head in his hands. "Oh, dear gussy, the humidity will ruin her hair! We need more hairspray. And we'll need the Monet water lilies print umbrella. We spent too long on that French twist to cover it up with a scarf or hat." He quickly turned and issued orders to his assistants to run and gather the necessary items.

"Toast?" asked Gary as he lifted a small plate towards his wife.

"I don't think so," said Martha warily.

"No, absolutely no toast," interrupted Max. "It will leave crumbs."

Stirred with concern for his wife and the continued feelings of foreboding, Gary's temper suddenly flared. "Max, SHUT UP! Martha shouldn't go on an empty stomach. She needs her strength, so chill out!"

"Sorry," said Max meekly, surprised at the sudden outburst. Gary rarely lost his temper with his friends. "I just want her to look her best."

"So do I!" said Gary testily. "But she can't ignore her health. Martha, sit down and drink some hot tea and try a little bread. It will settle your stomach. You'll see."

"Yes, dear, you're right. I should try." She sat down.

Gary took her hand and held it tightly. Then he pulled out a small card from his pocket. "Don't worry, my darling. You're a terrific speaker. You'll do fine! Remember that you've decided to give a brief speech, which is exactly what Mr. Jefferson always advised. I found this quote back home that I wanted to give you this morning before you go."

Martha took the card and read it aloud.

"*Speeches of sententious brevity, using not a word to spare, leave not a moment for inattention to the hearer. Amplification is the vice of modern oratory. It is an insult to an assembly of reasonable men, disgusting and revolting instead of persuading. Speeches measured by the hour, die with the hour.*" ~*Letter from Thomas Jefferson to David Harding, April 20, 1824.*

"In other words, stand up, speak up, and shut up," clarified Jack.

"Thank you, Jack," said Martha smiling.

"No problem."

"I think I like Jefferson's version better," said Blaze.

*   *   *

Two hours later, Gary stood with his assistant, Nick, and Monsieur Lavel on the second-story gallery of the Chapel. The first meeting of the G8 summit had begun, and seated at a long oval table placed in the first floor Nave of the Chapel were the heads of state. Gary scanned the table, noting the faces and names of the leaders sitting there. At the head sat France's President, Robert Mansart, whom they had met the day they arrived. To Mansart's left sat Britain's Prime Minister Alan Foster, a likeable man in his late forties. Martha sat next to him. To Martha's left sat Canada's Prime Minister Pierre Laurent. At the other end of the table sat Germany's Chancellor, Kurt Herrman. Gary smiled as he remembered the visit of the German Chancellor and Ambassador Schneider to the White House last summer. To the German Chancellor's left sat Russian President Alek Voronova. Beside him sat Japan's Prime Minister Kuto Yutaka. Finally, there was Italy's President of Council Vincetio Gallo. It was an impressive- looking bunch. No wonder Martha's stomach was in knots. Gary suddenly felt queasy himself, and he wasn't even speaking!

Martha made her opening remarks, and then the British Prime Minister spoke. Gary paused and looked around. The Chapel was magnificent. Everywhere there was sparkling white marble and bright gilding. Below there were white, ornately carved marble pillars. Before coming to Paris, Gary had read up on the history of the Chapel. Over 14 sculptors worked on carving the pillars, so each one was unique. At the High Altar, there was an incredible gilded bronze bas-relief called "Deposition from the Cross." Above, on the second story, there stood the grand organ, recently restored in 1995. The most beautiful sight of all, thought Gary looking upward, was the painted ceiling. Legions of angels floated amid bright turquoise blue skies and delicate white, rolling clouds surrounding the glorious form of God, the Heavenly Father. The power and glory and love emanating from the God of all mankind seemed absolutely real, close enough to touch. It was worth the entire trip just to see this painted masterpiece.

Gary then glanced across the gallery. There, sitting in a wooden chair with her board and paper in her lap, was the artist, Babette Moreau, silently working on a pastel sketch of the summit meeting below. She was wearing a lovely, navy-blue dress that laced up the front and a matching navy beret. Beside her, on the floor, sat his daughter, Abigail, quietly coloring. Philippe was sitting next to her, watching both the coloring and the meeting intently. Next to him, Sebastian lay perched with his head and paws hanging dangerously over the ledge, like a vulture, closely watching the proceedings below.

"Mademoiselle Moreau is lovely, is she not?" whispered Monsieur Lavel.

"She should be," commented Nick with the voice of authority. "That dress is another item just off the Paris runway. She's wearing Michael Kors."

Lavel and Nick sighed in unison.

There was a profound stillness in the air.

Again, Gary mused, quiet before the storm?

Something stirred in Gary. That strong terrible sense of foreboding returned as he noticed a flickering in the bright sunlight falling against the marble walls. He gazed upwards at the windows.

It was snowing.

Chapter Eight

The Hall of Battles

Monday Afternoon
January 7, 2002

I t snowed heavily all morning.

By the time Gary, Martha, and the children left the Chapel and were driven back to the Grand Trianon for lunch, a cloudy veil of pure white snow heavily dusted the gardens of Versailles. At the Fountain of Latona, mounds of freshly fallen snow covered the frozen blue waters of the fountain. Along the Royal Avenue, the marble statues and urns quietly arose from the pearly white ground. The Grand Canal looked like a gigantic cross of aqua-colored ice.

The unexpected wintry weather had everyone at the Grand Trianon palace in a major uproar by the time they arrived. Max was in full panic mode, frantically walking around in circles with his cell phone in one hand while his other hand shooed his assistants off into the city to buy umbrellas, boots, woolen mittens, scarves, and (for Abigail) more cotton tights. The Secret Service was regrouping, rethinking their plans, and calling out for necessary protective clothing and footwear.

Aunt Sophie and the General were present, ready for lunch and full of questions about Martha's speech. Jack, Blaze, and cameraman, Al, were huddled in conference, deciding how best to handle press coverage amidst the inclement weather. And last but not least, Gabrielle was all aflutter, lavishing her attention on two very wet and very cold children.

Lunch was served in the Garden Drawing Room, a wonderful fare of hot cream of zucchini soup with freshly ground parmesan cheese, crusty French baguettes with thick creamy butter, and cherry almond tarts. For the children, there was freshly made vanilla ice cream. For the cat Sebastian, Lavel sent over a plate of tuna tartare. Once fed, Martha returned to the Palace for more meetings. Gabrielle whisked the children away for a quiet afternoon of board games in the Games Room. The General left to make phone calls back to the states and to continue his oversight of Martha's security inside the Palace. The General's first call would be to Chief of Staff, Ned Baldwin, who was manning the West Wing with the Vice President in Martha's absence. Max's team returned with packages as lunch ended, Gary and Aunt Sophie, warmed by their delicious luncheon, bundled up in their coats and newly purchased scarves and mittens and left for the palace to meet the chefs for the upcoming competition.

It was 2:00 o'clock when Gary and Aunt Sophie entered the South Wing of the palace. As they climbed up a small staircase, Gary felt a twinge of excitement in his stomach. *The moment* had finally arrived, and he was not feeling afraid at all to face another member of The Seven. Filled with this unexpected courage, he spotted Secretary Campbell talking to a distinguished looking man on the landing. Campbell stood, his arms crossed, his face calm and serious. As Gary and Aunt Sophie approached, Campbell looked up and curtly nodded his welcome.

"Ah, there you are. Let me introduce you," he acknowledged as Gary and Sophie stepped up on the landing.

"Monsieur Dubois, this is Madame President's husband and White House Social Secretary, Gary Craig. And this is the President's aunt and our acting First Lady, Sophie Johnson McKay. Mrs. McKay is also the new bride of our Secretary of State, General Charles McKay. Gary, Sophie, this is Dean Paul Dubois, perhaps the finest chef in Paris."

"Bonjour," said Dean Dubois graciously, taking Sophie's hand and kissing it in the European fashion. "Congratulations are in order, no? You are the blushing bride. It is a pleasure to meet you. I look forward to you and Ambassador Porter joining me in judging the cake contest." Aunt Sophie smiled with embarrassment at the excessive praise.

"The pleasure is all mine," gushed Aunt Sophie. "Is Mr. Porter here?"

"Oui, Madame," said Dubois quickly. "He is waiting inside along with my assistant, Angelique du Pré. I will introduce you to her shortly. Monsieur Campbell, good to see you again. Please express my best wishes to your wife, Violet, for a speedy recovery. Violet Campbell is well known and loved by the best chefs in Paris for her exquisite taste. I hope to see her again very soon. And may all go well with your summit."

Secretary Campbell replied, "Thank you. Good luck with the competition. Now, if you all will excuse me, I believe Madame President is expecting me inside the Chapel. We have a few important matters to discuss. Good afternoon." He turned and left.

Gary felt a great deal of pride as he watched his old professor walk away. Who would have thought all those years ago that he, Gary Craig, a young and eager and somewhat idealistic law student at Chapel Hill, would someday be married to the President of the United States? That his famous, brilliant, and often daunting first-year law professor would become his mentor and his wife's Secretary of State. He let out a sentimental sigh. Life truly was stranger than fiction!

Gary turned his attention to the present and towards Paul Dubois. The noted chef was a polished-looking man of medium height, slender build, graying hair, and receding brow. His facial expression was earnest and strong, accented with a pale complexion, thin lips, and a resolute, square jaw. He wore a perfectly fitted dark suit and perfectly framed black square glasses. This was a man of refinement and precision.

Dubois wasted no time and got down to business.

"I am founder and Dean of *Par Excellence*, the most prestigious cooking school in Paris and the sponsor of this competition. All five contestants are French master chefs. Most have taught at my school, so I am well acquainted with their work. Each of these chefs has selected a newly graduated chef from my school to assist them. Each team will construct an original cake creation, which features some part of the palace or its grounds, in its past or present history. On the first day of the competition, they will be putting together the major pieces of the cake, made earlier this month at their cooking establishments, and subsequently, they will add decorative icing and spun sugar creations to those structures. The additions will be added the second day of the competition. Some of the sugar elements, such as handmade flowers or human figurines, were also made before the competition begins this week. Each team was allowed one month to create these spun sugar pieces. On day two of the competition, they must combine all these elements of their designs and then create one additional colored spun sugar element. All of these chefs are very good in sugar creations, as you will soon see. Now, if you will follow me please, we will meet the chefs? Monsieur Craig, you will please join us in making our first inspection?"

"Thank you," said Gary somewhat in awe. Dubois needed no real introduction. He had read about Dean Dubois in numerous newspapers and gourmet magazines.

Gary was genuinely looking forward to judging the competition with him.

Dean Dubois brightened and asked, "You are also a chef, a good cook, *n'êst-ce pas*? I have heard of your work in the American White House."

Now it was Gary's turn to feel embarrassed.

"Well, I've taken some gourmet cooking classes and experiment now and then in the White House kitchen."

Dubois's thin lips curled in appreciation. "Such modesty! I shall like you, Monsieur Craig. We are kindred spirits, no? You love food and the art of cooking. Come and see what we have done in the Hall of Battles!"

Dubois took Aunt Sophie by the arm, and Gary followed behind as they turned left and entered the Great Hall. As they rounded the corner, Gary let out an audible gasp. Aunt Sophie put her hand to her chest and whispered, "Oh, my goodness!"

"Ah, you experience what I discovered long ago as a boy," said Dean Dubois with a satisfied expression. There was national pride in his voice as he spoke. "You come to this palace and think you have seen all. Then you turn a corner, wander into a room, and suddenly, *Voilà*! Versailles has surprised you once again."

"What is this place?" asked Sophie mesmerized as she looked up at the transparent vaulted glass ceiling, where the mixed glare of winter sun and clouds of snow cast their brilliant light into the massive hall.

Dubois cleared his throat. "This is the largest room inside the palace. Originally, this was the South Wing, the Prince's wing. There were once five apartments on the first floor for the Sun King's brother, the Grand Dauphin, and other members of the Royal Family. There were also fourteen apartments in the attic level for members of the court. But, after the Revolution, King Louis-Philippe turned this wing into an art gallery. There are 35 paintings here that portray fourteen centuries of French history in battle."

While Dubois lectured on the paintings, Gary's attention turned to the architectural glory of the hall, with its massive gray columns topped with gold, the golden brown wooden inlaid floors, and the gilded carved tiles on the ceilings. Amid all this beauty, there were five industrial cooking stations made of metal and glass set up for the chefs to work. The teams were in place, and already there was a flurry of activity, unpacking, stacking, inventorying, arranging, and organizing. Here we go, thought Gary excitedly.

Ambassador Porter appeared and joined the group as they approached the first station where two men were carefully unloading a number of cardboard boxes. Dean Dubois introduced them to master chef, Pierre Rousseau. The handsome man was tall with a well-built, aristocratic face. He appeared to be in his early forties, with straight dark hair, prominent square jaw, and intense brown eyes. He greeted Dubois with a lofty air and a confident smile.

"Welcome, mon ami! Coming to inspect the winning team first?"

Dubois's silvery eyebrows rose ever so slightly. "Time will tell."

The handsome chef seemed unaffected by Dubois's reserve. Rousseau's manner was all ease and confidence.

"Only the time it takes for me to create my masterpiece," replied Pierre with a winning grin.

"It will be a wonderful masterpiece!" cried Pierre's assistant, who suddenly appeared from behind the counter carrying a huge cardboard box. "You will see, Dean Dubois! Magnifique!" He patted the box carefully. Gary guessed it contained a major portion of their Versailles cake.

"You are ever the loyal assistant," dismissed Dubois, waving his hand at the younger chef. He introduced the assistant as Chef Antoine Bernard. He looked to be in his thirties, with a clean-shaven head, dark eyes, and thick eyebrows. Antoine radiated the air of a true artistic personality — excitable, energetic, and flamboyant, as evidenced in his over-the-top attire. Underneath his white cooking coat, Antoine was wearing a loud printed shirt in lavender silk.

"Pierre is the finest pastry chef in all Paris!" bragged Antoine. "It is an honor to work with him." He glanced over at Pierre with immense admiration. "He will win the competition, you will see!"

"Hush, hush, Antoine!" ordered Pierre in a voice that was both soft and sharp. Clearly, he was the leader. He quickly glanced down the row to the final table. Blaze was standing there with Jack and a lovely brunette. "We must not tip our hand. There are wandering eyes about. Our design is most secret. Now, Dubois, I must speak to you about that beautiful assistant of yours!"

Dubois raised his finger and shook it with reproof at Pierre. "Do not bother her, mon ami. She knows about your reputation with women. I have warned her."

"Then I must go and live up to my infamous reputation, no? Antoine, finish unloading these boxes." And with that, Pierre bid them a hasty adieu and departed to the back of the hall.

Aunt Sophie, Porter, and Dubois moved on ahead, but Gary lingered for a moment to watch Antoine at his station. The message from De Silva specified that one of The Seven and his assistant would be here at the competition. So, apparently one of these five team leaders, these master chefs, was the man, or perhaps, the woman, they were looking for. Gary noticed how Antoine stared at Pierre with an injured look on his face, his singular devotion ignored. The younger chef suddenly looked moody and volatile, and yes, those were characteristics, thought Gary, that could play deadly into the hands of one of The Seven. Pierre, so calm and confident, indeed looked like a promising suspect. He was all too sure of himself. Gary mentally positioned Pierre high on his list of five suspects.

Gary quickly moved on to the second station and its two female chefs. He and his group were immediately greeted by a young black woman who was unpacking a stack of metal mixing bowls.

"Bonjour, Isabelle," said Dean Dubois crisply. "Let me introduce you to the judges, Monsieur Craig, Ambassador Porter, and Madame McKay. This is Isabelle Villeneau, the youngest of our competitors. She just finished her training at our school."

"Hello," said Isabelle cheerfully in a clear British accent. She enthusiastically extended her hand in greeting. "Pleasure to meet you! Do come and watch us while we work tomorrow. We have an absolutely lovely cake planned."

"You're English?" asked Gary mildly surprised. "But your name is French!"

Isabelle's flashed a proud look. "My Dad was from Paris, but I was born in London, actually. My parents divorced when I was young, and my mum raised me in England. Grew up in London, I did. But when I turned eighteen, I decided to come and live with Dad for a while. I always fancied cooking, and Dad thought I was pretty good at making desserts. So he sent me to Monsieur Dubois's school. I've worked hard and now, well, here I am! It's all a bit thrilling. I just hope I'm ready!"

Dubois gazed affectionately upon the young lady. "But of course, *mon enfant*! You have the gift, one of the best students I've ever taught."

Isabelle beamed.

Gary liked the young woman immediately. She was straightforward and down to earth. Like Antoine, she was quite young, mid-twenties at the most. It was early, but Gary seriously doubted Isabelle would knowingly be in cahoots with a killer. She appeared too intelligent for that. But could she be too young to know what was really happening, young and innocent enough to be deceived? Suddenly a sharp voice rang out with displeasure.

"Isabelle! *Qu'est-ce que je ferrai avec vous*? If you spend all afternoon talking, we will lose the competition before it begins!"

A tall and slender beauty marched towards the front of the station, her hands on her hips and her eyes flashing furiously. Her countenance caused Gary a moment's pause, an uneasy moment indeed, as this woman's ivory complexion, violet blue eyes, and shoulder length red hair was all too reminiscent of his ex-wife. Come to think of it, that stinging tone of voice matched that of the former Mrs. Craig to a tee!

Isabelle seemed unperturbed by her mentor's vexation. She bent her head over and whispered conspiratorially, "Better run then. Camille can be rather beastly when she's like this, under pressure and all. See you later."

Staring coldly, Camille watched her protégé rush away. She then sauntered forward and greeted the judges with an aloof smile. Dubois introduced the beautiful master chef as Mademoiselle Camille Aumont, owner of a fine restaurant located on the west bank of Paris.

"What is *she* doing here?" demanded Camille pointing to the last table where a man and a woman were in the midst of setting up their station. "Dubois, I cannot believe you invited *her* to participate! That woman, she is très horrible. She is an amateur. She cannot cook even a baguette by herself."

Dubois raised both his hands defensively.

"Ah, Camille, do not blame me. Monsieur Bonnet selected Mademoiselle LaClaire for his cooking assistant. I had nothing to do with it."

Camille sniffed indignantly. "Then George Bonnet is a fool. Josette La Claire is a she-devil. She is bad news, Monsieur. You wait and see. She will create havoc, and bad things will happen!" Her iris-blue eyes flashed defiantly at Dubois with clear warning.

Dubois shrugged his shoulders dubiously. "Do not fret, Mademoiselle. I am in charge. I will be keeping a close eye on everyone. But report to me immediately anything out of the ordinary."

"You will be the first to know," she said sharply.

Gary and his group left Camille to her preparations and proceeded to the third table where perhaps the most celebrated chefs were stationed. Dubois promptly introduced the famed Louis Girard and his assistant, Gerald Matisse. Of all the chefs in the competition, Gary was most familiar with the work of Louis Girard, an avant-garde artist known for his superb cakes and exotic chocolate creations. Gary had seen the Girard and Matisse team perform in several competitions broadcasted on cable television, which they usually won.

Girard lived up to his celebrity. He was an extremely attractive man, even more handsome in person. He was of medium height, with a sleek build and muscular arms. He pulled back his shoulder-length, dark-blonde hair into a ponytail during competitions. Today his mop of wavy dark blonde hair was worn down, perfectly framing his face and shining in the midday winter light. His face was roughly shaven with a hint of moustache just above his full lips. An expensive pair of dark, wire-rimmed glasses completed his look. Behind those glasses, Girard gazed at Gary and Dubois with moss-green, hazel eyes.

Dean Dubois introduced Girard, and the young chef greeted them with a gracious and easy manner.

"Bonjour, Mr. Craig. It's an honor to meet you. I watched your marriage to Madame President on television. It was amazing. And your wife, she is most ravishing."

"Thank you," said Gary heartily. "I agree! My wife is the most beautiful woman in the world!"

"You are the romantic! I look forward to meeting her, Monsieur," said Girard smiling. "And I understand you are a new bride as well?" Girard reached over and took Aunt

Sophie's hand and kissed it. "Since you are also a newlywed, you might particularly like my creation."

"Don't give them any more hints," cautioned his assistant, Gerald Matisse, as he approached, carrying a tray with rows of brightly colored bottles. "It will ruin the surprise." Matisse was a smaller man, dark and muscular. He put down his tray and shook hands with Gary, Porter, and Sophie. His accent was weaker than Girard's, evidence of the time Matisse had spent in New York and London during his career.

"What are those?" asked Sophie peering down at the miniature flask-shaped glass bottles filled with vivid, multi-colored liquids.

"Those are Louis's specialty," answered Dean Dubois with pride. "Louis is known for his masterful work in handmade food dyes and colored sugar."

"I am the world's best in sugar creations," said the chef simply. He said it without ego.. It was stated as humble fact.

Dubois added to the statement. "Notice the various shades of blues and purples and greens in those bottles. Look at the reds and the oranges. They are wonderful, no? Louis makes and mixes his own food colors. No other master chef has such an eye for color. His ability to shade is extraordinary!"

Girard's eyebrows arched in slight disagreement. "Not true, Monsieur. Any skill I have I learned from my teacher," he said appreciatively while bending his head towards Dubois. "No one in this hall can match your abilities in the kitchen."

Dubois blinked modestly.

"You are too kind."

"I am anxious to see your work in real life," admitted Gary honestly. "I watched the broadcast of last year's international cake competition honoring Chef Antonin Carême, the man who cooked for Napoleon, King George, and the Russian royal family, the Romanovs. Your recreation of Carême's Grecian temple centerpiece was unbelievable!"

"What are you talking about, Mr. Craig? Who was this Carême?" asked Porter.

Gary explained. "Carême was the world's first celebrity chef. He was born in Paris, lived through the French Revolution, studied architecture, and became perhaps the greatest pastry chef of all time. He used his knowledge of history and architecture to build amazing sugar creations — pyramids, castles, temples, and fountains. He traveled all over Europe and into Russia. He even made Napoleon's wedding cake!"

"The one recipe Carême failed to record. Ah! I remember now. Dubois told me that you are a chef, too. You like Carême?"

Gary nodded emphatically. "Oh, yes, I've read a lot about him, and I have to confess I have tried to make some of his recipes: the salmon with Genovese sauce, curried turtle soup, meringues stuffed with vanilla cream, raspberry mousse, and of course, his orange jelly."

Louis's hazel eyes narrowed. "I, too, have studied his recipes. I have all of his published works. How fortunate for us and the world that Carême kept detailed journals and published his own recipe books. As a belated wedding gift to you and Madame President and you, too, Madame McKay, allow me tonight to make for you the dessert that Carême made for the table that displayed his temple centerpiece here in Paris at the Château Rothschild in 1826. Tonight, Gerald and I will make for you Carême's *Nectarine Plombière*."

"Oh, how wonderful," cried Sophie clasping her hands together. "I can't wait to tell Charles!"

"Holy cow," said Ambassador Porter most impressed. "I can't wait for dinner!"

"*Magnifique*," murmured Dubois with a look of extreme ecstasy on his face. "I shall personally see to it the necessary ingredients are ordered and brought to the palace for you this very afternoon."

Gary was completely taken aback by Girard's generosity. For a brief moment, he forgot all about The Seven.

"Thank you so much," said Gary simply. "My wife will be touched."

Looking satisfied, Louis suddenly glanced down the hallway and shook his head with disapproval.

"Dubois, you must do something. Your poor assistant, Angelique, she is surrounded by three men, and one of them is Rousseau. You know what a cad he is. She is the innocent. She cannot handle such men. Do something—immediately!!!"

"Do not fret. Angelique can take care of herself," said Dubois nonchalantly. "Besides, she doesn't seem to be bothered by the attention."

Gary glanced down the hall where a group of men had gathered near Jack's new platform. Joining Jack and his faithful cameraman, Al, were five more CNN employees: Peter, a backup cameraman; Joe, lineman and computer technician; Russell, the lighting technician; Roger, the sound technician; and Bob, the producer. Dean Dubois's assistant's back was towards them so Gary couldn't see her face. But her profile was lovely. She was slender with dark brown hair falling carelessly about her shoulders. She wore a brown wool, babydoll dress, black tights, and black boots. Pierre Rousseau was standing beside her chatting away. Listening to the chef's rambling were Blaze and Jack. From their collective facial expressions, Mademoiselle du Pré clearly had the entire cast of male admirers mesmerized.

"Who are those two gentlemen?" asked Louis with his finger pointed.

"The tall skinny one is my best friend, Blaze Phillips," answered Gary quickly. "He works at the White House as our Press Secretary. I can assure you that Mademoiselle du Pré is in no danger whatsoever around him. Blaze is a true gentleman."

"And the other one?" asked Louis with his eyebrows arched skeptically.

Gary hesitated. "That's Jack Parish, a family friend and CNN reporter. He's a bit of a flirt. Once we finish with the introductions, I'll make sure Mr. Parish behaves himself."

Louis Girard nodded his head in appreciation. "*Merci beaucoup*. Keep an eye on her, Monsieur. Angelique, she is a very shy, quiet girl, and men of the world, like your Mr. Parish, are out of her league. I would not want to see her hurt in any way."

With that, the master chef bade everyone adieu and turned his attention back to his liquid dyes and sugar preparations. Gary, Porter, Dubois, and Aunt Sophie moved to station number four where Dubois introduced them to master chef, René Michel, and his assistant, Claude Breton. Unlike the other teams they had met so far, the master chef was actually younger than his assistant. Chef Michel couldn't have been more than thirty years old, and his appearance reminded Gary of a young James Spader. Michel was short with a slender build and dark blonde, close-cropped hair. His straight bangs fell across his forehead, and his eyes were pale gray-green. Unlike the previous three vociferous chefs, Chef Michel's demeanor was quiet and reserved. He greeted the party with a soft-spoken voice that exuded confidence, respect, and professionalism.

"Bonjour, Dean Dubois," said Michel affectionately to his former teacher. "You are well, I trust?"

"Très bien," assured Dubois with a nod. "And you?" Dubois glanced around Michel where his assistant was in the back of the station bringing in many stacked square white boxes. The assistant smiled nervously and waved. Gary studied the fourth chef's assistant, introduced as Claude Breton. Claude appeared to be in his late forties. Like Bernard, his head was clean-shaven. But his face was longer than the other chef and his build more lean. In fact, Claude Breton was a bit too thin, which might be the result, thought Gary, of a nervous disposition.

Michel shrugged his shoulders with uncertainty. "I am fine. Claude is a bit anxious for the competition to start, but then he is always on edge, you know. It's his way."

"Yes, I know," murmured Dean Dubois reflectively. "Claude was always a perfectionist."

"That's why I selected him as my teammate," replied Michel candidly. "Claude's worries translate into great attention to detail. And I always pay attention to detail, especially with the theme we have chosen. It must be perfect."

Dubois nodded his approval. "I would expect nothing less from the most precise student I ever taught."

Aunt Sophie noticed a small oval blue and white plate on the table in front of her and picked it up. It was a plate of Delft china.

"What's this?" she asked.

Chef Michel took the plate from Aunt Sophie with an impassive face.

"That is a *petite* hint, Madame," he said winking.

"We look forward to your creation with great expectation," stated Dubois as he bid his former student adieu.

They moved on to the last station that was occupied by the only male/female team in the competition, Chef George Bonnet and his assistant, Josette La Claire. They were greeted with an angry outburst.

"Josette! What are you doing?"

George Bonnet stood inside their station, hands on his hips, his round face reddening, and his eyes full of fury. Bonnet was a short, stocky man with graying hair and receding hairline. He was the oldest chef in the competition, in his early fifties. He glared at his assistant, a beautiful brunette who had put her tray of utensils down and was leaning over the counter, her head in her hands, staring dreamily at Pierre Rousseau.

"I am taking a break," she replied lazily.

"Idiot! You've already taken two," snapped Bonnet, now fingering his full chin with vexation.

"So, I am taking another," she said continuing to gaze in Pierre's direction.

Bonnet looked like he was about to explode at his assistant's insolence, but he held his tongue, nodded his head quickly in recognition of Dean Dubois and his guests, and turned his back to begin unpacking his boxes all by himself.

"I will introduce you to Monsieur Bonnet at another time," said Dubois judiciously. He pursed his narrow lips together as he glanced at Josette and shook his head with displeasure. After taking a deep breath, he turned and smiled and held up his hand. "As you can see, we have a group of extraordinary chefs for the competition. Now let me introduce you to my assistant, Mademoiselle Angelique du Pré. But I must warn you, she is a very reserved person. She is also an extremely efficient businesswoman and an excellent chef herself. I would be lost without her. She is as smart as she is pretty, but humble and shy, an interesting blend of traits for someone working in Paris, no? Oh, men flock to her, but she has little time for them. Like Louis, I sometimes worry about her. She is unaffected by the world and delicate in spirit. She is there, over at the television stand with your reporter friend."

Indeed she was, and Jack was utterly spellbound. So were Blaze and the rest of the all-male CNN crew. Pierre was standing next to her still chattering away when they arrived. Dubois instantly cut him off.

"Enough, Pierre! You will talk the poor girl's ears off. Now, go back to your station and get to work!"

Frowning, Pierre obeyed his former teacher and hastily bid the girl goodbye.

"Angelique," said Dubois kindly. "Please turn around and meet our guests. This is Mr. Gary Craig, Madame President's husband, and the other guest judges, Madame Sophie Mckay and Ambassador Porter."

Angelique Du Pré slowly turned around.

Gary did a double take. He couldn't believe his eyes!

"Why, how extraordinary!" said Aunt Sophie putting her hands to her face. "What a resemblance!"

"It's uncanny!" whispered Gary.

"What is wrong?" asked Angelique uneasy at their reactions to her appearance.

Porter looked confused. "What are you two talking about?"

"Don't you see it, Maurice?" asked Sophie. "Look at her face. Who does she remind you of?"

Angelique looked extremely uncomfortable as they stared at her.

Porter gazed at Angelique and then snapped his fingers.

"I know! She looks like that British actress, Rachel Weisz!" She's the one in that new Mummy movie!"

"Well, yes, she does look like her, too," agreed Aunt Sophie. "But she looks like someone else, someone *here* at Versailles."

Angelique glanced over at Aunt Sophie with a startled expression.

"I do?" she asked anxiously, looking quickly at Dubois.

"Yes, you do," said Gary, shaking his head in amazement. "You could be her twin."

"Who is this woman?" demanded Dubois.

"The French artist, Babette Moreau," answered Gary. "She is one of the artists working at the summit. Her hair is different from Miss du Pré. Babette's hair is blond and cut short, but the facial resemblance is striking."

Dean Dubois straightened and patted his assistant on the shoulder reassuringly. "Do not be alarmed. They say we all have a twin. Now, it seems, you will soon meet yours."

"We'll introduce you," offered Gary.

Angelique bowed her head meekly. "I would like very much to meet her." Her face, however, did not look so eager to meet her double. Gary couldn't blame her for that. He wasn't sure how he would feel if he ever came face to face with a man looking just like himself.

Suddenly Ambassador Porter turned.

"Oh, look! My daughter Marie has arrived. She flew in late this morning. With all the dire weather forecasts, I was afraid she wouldn't make it. Marie! Marie!!! Over here!"

A vivacious little redhead rushed over to hug her father. She was a tiny thing, couldn't be more than five foot two, thought Gary as he was introduced. Marie Porter, New York chef, had an oval face, translucent ivory skin, and dark blue eyes the color of sapphires. She greeted her father with a kiss and then took a moment to shake the snow out of her short curly hair.

"Dad! It's like a blizzard outside!" she exclaimed excitedly. "I had to practically bribe a cab driver with double fare to drive me out here. He didn't look too happy about it either when the Secret Service stopped him and asked to see his license. I never thought they would let us through the gates. I'm lucky to be here at all! They closed the airport right after we arrived, did you know?"

Her father shook his head emphatically. "The airport is closed? No, we didn't know that. Was it a bad landing, sweetheart?" His face suddenly looked concerned.

"Oh, no, Dad, it was fine," she said breezily, waving her hand in the air.

"Well, I should check in with my staff and tell General McKay about the news, if he doesn't know already. The airport closing might have a significant effect on security, especially if we can't get people out of Paris. Stay here and enjoy yourself, sweetheart, and I'll see you later for dinner. And guess what? Chef Louis Girard is making dessert for us tonight!"

Marie's mouth dropped open.

"Dad, you're joking!"

Porter smiled. "No, my dear. I'm quite serious. If you don't believe me, ask him yourself. He's right over there! Now I must be off."

"Will you excuse me, too?" asked Aunt Sophie politely. "I have a meeting with the other first ladies in half an hour, and I don't want to be late. Lily Mansart wants to meet with me before our official group tour of the palace begins. We're going to see the Revolution, the Empire, and the 19th century rooms. That means lots of Napoleon this afternoon! Dean Dubois, I look forward to the competition. I'm sure it will be wonderful. Gary, see you at dinner."

"Au revoir, Madame McKay. And I must go, Monsieur Craig, and check with the palace kitchen staff on how the weather is affecting the delivery of foodstuffs," Dubois added gravely. "If we should end up snowed inside the Palace, we must have sufficient stock for not only the competition. Who knows? My teams may end up cooking breakfast for the leaders of the free world! Angelique, I leave you here to introduce Mademoiselle Porter to our celebrity chefs. Remember Mademoiselle Porter, she is a chef, a kindred spirit. Show her around."

Porter kissed his daughter goodbye and then left the hall with Dubois and Aunt Sophie. Marie looked around, her short hair bouncing as her head turned back and forth.

"I'm just so excited," she said to Gary happily. "I can't wait to see the chefs in action! I've been to several cake competitions in the states, but this is my first international competition."

She paused a moment and looked past Gary at Blaze and Jack. An infectious darling smile spread across her face.

Jack immediately stepped forward. "No time like the present, Miss Porter. Would you like to meet them now? Please, allow me!"

But Marie's attention was focused elsewhere. She brushed right past Jack and extended her hand to a surprised Blaze Phillips.

"I know you! I've seen you on television! You're the guy that does the press conferences at the White House!"

Startled, Blaze nodded. "That's right. I'm the White House Press Secretary, Blaze Phillips."

"I'm on television, too," observed Jack softly.

"That's nice," said Marie staring steadily at Blaze. "Your job must be so interesting, Mr. Phillips, getting to work for the President and meeting so many important people!"

"Well, yes, I do meet lots of important people on my job," said Blaze modestly.

"I interview important people all the time," murmured Jack.

"That's nice," said Marie. "I'd love to hear more about your job, Mr. Phillips. Why don't you walk around with us while we meet the chefs. Will that be alright, Mademoiselle du Pré?"

Angelique hesitated, her eyes gazing intently at Blaze. Gary couldn't quite read her expression, but his gut told him Angelique didn't want to be a third wheel. Did she want Blaze, too?

"But of course," she said quietly. "Please follow me."

She led a bewildered Blaze and a bouncy Marie off towards Louis Girard's station.

"Did you see that?" exclaimed Jack. "She blew me — ME — off for Blaze Phillips!"

"I think your ego can handle it," said Gary with no sympathy whatsoever.

Jack sighed. "And Blaze was worried about meeting a woman on this trip! From the looks of it, he's already landed two!"

"So, you noticed how Mademoiselle Angelique was eying Blaze?"

"Hey, it's me! Of course, I noticed. But Blaze, the innocent wonder, didn't notice a thing! Mark my words, that poor boy is headed for trouble with a capital T. Enough talk about love! Let's talk treachery. Any first impressions after meeting the chefs?"

"A few," said Gary candidly. "George Bonnet has a vile temper, and his working arrangement with Mademoiselle LaClaire is certainly odd. Why would he choose someone so disrespectful and lazy? Chef Michel is a pretty cool customer, completely in control of himself and his work. Yet his assistant is a bunch of raw nerves. Makes you wonder why he is so anxious. So that is another odd pairing. Pierre appears to be extremely egotistical, a bit of a snob actually. Camille, she's full of herself, too. Louis is personable but proud. So, all of them, in their own way, are worthy of suspicion. It could be any of them."

Gary was interrupted when Agent Pullman swiftly approached. He seemed quite agitated.

'Mr. Craig! Someone is outside the hall and demands to speak to you *immediately*."

Gary suddenly felt alarmed.

Had something gone awry at the summit? He glanced at his watch. The afternoon session wasn't supposed to end for another hour.

"Is something wrong?" he asked as he walked out with Agent Pullman.

Pullman's lips tightened, and he refused to meet Gary's eye.

"You'll see," was all he said.

Now Gary's anxieties really intensified. Last fall, The Seven tried to kill Martha by putting poison in her lipstick. Had The Seven's chef already succeeded where the last member had failed? Martha had been slightly sick the last two days. But poisoning at this stage of the game wasn't possible! All of the chefs and their assistants were in plain view inside the Hall of Battles. Then another horrible thought entered Gary's mind. Marie Porter had reported the airport was closed. What about the roads? Eliza and Joshua were in downtown Paris! Had something happened to the children? Had there been an accident? What if Martha were sick and needed to get to the hospital? Could they get her out in time?

Gary's thoughts were racing madly as he and Pullman exited the hall and rushed down a narrow passageway in the south wing. They made a sharp left turn and passed through another small room. Pullman led the way into a bigger room, the Coronation Room. Gary followed, took one step into the doorway, and stopped dead in his tracks. A cold voice and an icy blue glare were waiting for him.

"Oh, there you are, my precious! It's about time you showed up. Where the hell have you been? I'm getting absolutely nowhere with this annoying little man. Please tell him who I am and that I am used to getting my way and whatever I want. And what I want is to stay in this palace in that cute little bedroom down the hallway, the one with the rosy pink bedspread! I think it will suit me quite nicely."

The annoying little man in question was Monsieur Lavel, whose face was turning purple with frustration and rage.

The cute little bedroom down the hall was the Queen's bedroom which once belonged to Marie Antoinette.

And the woman who was used to getting her own way was Gary's ex-wife, Janet Marie Benson Craig.

Chapter Nine

Venus and Diana Rooms

Monday Afternoon
January 7, 2002

"Janet, what in earth's name are you doing here?"

The former Mrs. Craig smiled triumphantly at her former husband. "I'm here with Evan, of course. We've just arrived."

Gary eyed his former wife narrowly. "I thought you were going to stay home on this trip."

"Yes, dear heart, I was. But thanks to you and that evil Mad Max, I changed my mind."

"Thanks to me?" Gary tried sounding surprised. It didn't work.

"Yes, for some strange reason, I couldn't get a soul in New York City to make my wedding dress. Don't think I don't know why. Really, you and Max should be ashamed of yourselves. But when I heard that the *fabulous* Roland Martin was here at Versailles and that he was going to put on a fashion show, I decided I had to come with Evan. Roland Martin is just the person to design my wedding gown. And you, my angel, will set it up for me."

Gary held his tongue. He knew from years of experience it was no use arguing with Janet when she used that tone of voice. It was best to humor her and quickly change the subject.

Gary managed a weak smile. "How did you get here? I heard the airport just closed due to inclement weather."

Janet peeled off her white leather gloves and handed them over to Lavel.

"How concerned you sound! Well, since you asked so nicely, I'll tell you. We flew in last night on my fiancé's private jet. Evan's family is filthy rich, you know."

"Yes," answered Gary dryly. "You've mentioned that before — several times in fact!"

Janet stretched out her bejeweled hands, one sporting a very large diamond ring, and sighed. "It's so nice to finally date someone with money, someone who can spoil me. I love being spoiled. Poverty simply didn't suit me!"

The implication was, of course, that Gary had been quite poor when he was married to her and was not able to so provide. But Gary listened patiently to his ex complain without reacting. He was accustomed to Janet's constant little insults.

Janet took off her long white fur coat and tossed it over to Lavel.

"Anyway, my sweet, Evan and I jumped into his cute little jet and flew straight here."

"Where is Senator Daniels?" asked Gary.

Janet flipped her hand around in the air. "Oh, he went to see Secretary Campbell. He's somewhere about. Now, our bags are downstairs, so if someone could retrieve them and bring them right up, I think I'll take a nap before dinner. Who's cooking dinner by the way? Do I get to pick which celebrity chef I want to make our supper? I hear that chef Louis Girard is very good and very good-looking, too!"

Finally, Monsieur Lavel had had enough. He unceremoniously dumped Janet's things on the floor and exploded.

"Madame! *C'est impossible!* You cannot stay here. And you cannot under any circumstance stay in *that* room! That is the Queen's bedroom! It belonged to Marie Antoinette! No one has slept in *that* room since 1793!"

Janet's eyes widened in horror!

"Oh, yes, I see. I understand completely! If no one has slept in that room since 1793, the sheets must be filthy!"

She reached a well-manicured hand down into her black LV handbag and pulled out a bulging wallet. She opened it, extracted several hundred dollar bills, and tossed them into the air in Lavel's direction.

"I shall need fresh sheets every day. I only sleep on Egyptian cotton. I never sleep on synthetics! That should cover the expense. See if you can get pink or red sheets to match the room décor. I like my linens to coordinate. Now run along."

Monsieur Lavel looked like he was about to have a stroke.

He turned and earnestly appealed to Gary for help.

"Do something, Monsieur! I beg you."

"May I be of any assistance?" asked a smooth voice from behind.

It was Jack.

Janet took one look at Parish as he approached and bristled. Those two had an understanding. He hated her, and she detested him.

"Well, well, well, the ice woman cometh," said Jack with a devilish smirk. He came and stood resolutely beside Gary with arms crossed. "That would explain the furious blizzard raging outside. All nature doth protest too much!"

Janet glared at Jack frostily. "Jack Parish, what a surprise seeing you here. I thought all low-life reporters were banned from the conference. Shouldn't you be outside freezing your buns off with the rest of your kind?"

Jack chuckled. "Sorry. I was invited, unlike you, who just tagged along. Now, why don't you be a good witch for a change and fly back home on your broomstick? There's plenty of wind outside to carry you straight across the Atlantic."

A mournful gale outside beat upon the windows and verified Jack's invitation.

Janet straightened her shoulders defiantly and jutted her chin.

"If anyone leaves this palace, it will be you, you half-witted hack! I am not going anywhere!"

Jack stepped forward and began rolling up his sleeves. "Oh, yeah? We'll see about that, missy. Just say the word, Gary, and I'll pick her perfumed carcass up and dump it outside into the deepest snow drift I can find!"

Lavel's face brightened at the prospect.

"Enough!" ordered Gary impatiently. "Janet, stop insulting him and be respectful to Monsieur Lavel or I will NOT introduce you to Roland Martin! I mean it! And Jack, stop egging her on! From the sound of it, we are going to be stuck here for quite some time, for days perhaps. So you two will just have to get along."

Janet sniffed haughtily, closed her eyes, and tossed her head back. "Very well, my precious. But Evan and I still need a place to stay. We certainly can't go back to downtown Paris in this weather, and the hotels nearby are full of scruffy-looking reporters! I checked."

"Fine," said Gary, "We'll find a place for you and Evan to stay. But you can't stay inside the main Palace. Is that understood?"

Janet's red mouth turned upside down into a childish pout as she nodded her head.

Gary turned to Lavel. "Isn't there one more room available in the Petit Trianon? Could she and Senator Daniels stay there, please? The senator serves on the Senate Foreign Relations

Council and works closely with Secretary Campbell. It would be good to put them together."

Lavel hesitated and then reluctantly agreed. "Oui. There is one more room, and as a favor to you and Madame President, we will accommodate them."

Gary knelt down and picked up some of the bills that had fallen to the floor.

"Thank you, Monsieur Lavel. Take this and see if one of your staff can find the sheets she requires. If there is any problem, come find me. Agent Pullman, has the Secret Service given any thought as to how we will be transported back and forth from the Trianon in this snow?"

Pullman immediately stepped forward.

"Yes, sir! We've located two snowmobiles and will soon have them on site should the snow get that deep. They will arrive before nightfall."

"And perhaps we — that is, the palace — can lend a hand," offered Monsieur Lavel meekly. "I have an idea that might assist you."

"Excellent! Agent Pullman, if you will see to it that Ms. Benson-Craig and Senator Daniels are taken to the Petit Trianon with their luggage, I will go and break the happy news to my wife that my ex and her fiancée will be joining us for dinner."

* * *

One thing Gary loved about his wife (the current one) was that Martha didn't have a jealous bone in her body. When Gary caught up with her as the early afternoon session concluded and told her about his former wife's untimely arrival, Martha did not get angry or upset. Instead, she threw back her pretty blonde head and laughed out loud. Then she patted her husband playfully on the shoulder, assuring him before she left for her second round of meetings that if he needed any help dealing with the former Mrs. Craig, she could call in the Marines.

Marines sounded good. Monsieur Lavel most certainly would concur.

His mid-afternoon duties complete, Gary bundled himself up against the elements and rode back to the Grand Trianon in a motorized cart. The Royal Avenue was now covered with several inches of snow but was still passable at this hour. Dumont and his staff were doing their best to keep the pathways plowed, but at this rate, their machinery could not possibly keep up with this storm.

Gary arrived at the Trianon to find the French maid, Gabrielle, all in a dither because Abigail and Philippe had gone missing for a few minutes, only to innocently pop up in another part of the small palace. It was not her fault, she protested. With tears, she questioned where had they gone?

Wonderful, thought Gary. Abigail was indulging in her favorite pastime of hide and seek, or in his daughter's case, hide and no-seek, something he had forgotten to warn Gabrielle about. Apologetically, Gary explained, consoled, and dismissed the maid for a much-deserved break while he went in search of the two disappearing children. He found the little Houdinis in the gold and green Malachite Drawing Room, eating popcorn and watching *The Little Mermaid* on a VCR the palace staff had set up for them that morning. Gary was shocked to discover Abigail sitting on the sofa with an oversized grey and black fur hat perched on top of her head.

The source of the new hat was soon evident. The artist, Babette Moreau, was nearby, sitting in the corner, drawing Abigail. Babette was dressed warmly in a structured black wool jacket and pants outfit, complimented with shiny black, lace-up boots. The hat naturally went with her outfit. Two other Secret Service agents were in the room, officially standing guard, unofficially watching the movie.

"Bonjour, Mademoiselle," said Gary greeting the artist first.

"Bonjour," replied Babette softly, her steady gaze focused on Abigail.

"Lovely weather we're having," said Gary chattily.

Babette grimaced. "Très horrible! Obviously, the weather, it forces me to work inside. The other artists are working inside the big castle, but I choose to work here, in petite palace, drawing the children. I like children."

"Make yourself comfortable then. Tell me, what is Abigail wearing?"

"Louis Vuitton," replied Babette nonchalantly. "The hat goes with my outfit. It is from his fall collection. Mademoiselle Abigail wanted to wear the hat. I have another one in lavender."

"Very nice. By the way, I met someone today in the Hall of Mirrors that looks just like you—just like you," said Gary informatively. "Her name is Angelique du Pré, and she is the assistant to Dean Dubois, the chef heading up the cooking contest. The resemblance is quite astonishing. She could be your twin. You don't happen to have a sister or distant cousin living in Paris, do you, Mademoiselle Moreau?"

The blond artist stopped drawing and looked up wide-eyed at Gary and shook her head. "Mais, non. I am the only girl in my family." She paused. "Perhaps I should go and meet this person. I can come back later and finish the drawing."

"Please join us for dinner," offered Gary.

"Merci! You are very kind."

Babette Moreau put down her paper and pen, retrieved her hat, gathered up her art supplies and coat, and bid the children and the two agents a hasty adieu. Gary went over to where the children were watching the movie. One of two gold print sofas in the room had been rearranged to sit in front of the black stone fireplace, where the small television sat placed on the mantelpiece. Sebastian was curled up in a ball in front of the fireplace snoozing. Gary sat down by Abigail on the sofa, kissed her, and then gently asked her an important question.

"Abigail, Gabrielle was quite upset when I arrived. She tells me you were missing today for a while. Is that true?"

"Uh-huh," confirmed Abigail.

"And why did that happen, dearest?"

"I'm teaching Philippe to hide and no-seek," said Abigail matter-of-factly while munching on a handful of popcorn. Then she stopped eating and complained. "Gabrielle wasn't supposed to look, Papa Gary. She's no fun to play with! She doesn't know how to play my game. But Mademoiselle Babette knows! She is very smart!"

Gary cleared his throat unsympathetically. "No, Gabrielle doesn't know how to play, which is why you shouldn't have disappeared. Now, Abigail, where did you and Philippe hide?"

No reply. Only the sound of chomping and the singing of "Under the Sea" by a hyperactive crab could be heard. The agents in the room grinned. Abigail was not forthcoming.

Gary tried again. "Abigail, I need to know where you and Philippe went. Remember we talked about this before we left home. There is a dangerous man here that Mommy and Papa Gary are trying to find. We need you to be a good girl and stay safe."

"I was safe," explained Abigail solemnly. "I was with Philippe."

Philippe put down his popcorn. "There is a dangerous person here inside my castle?" he asked.

Gary smiled. Philippe considered Versailles his castle!

"Yes, Philippe, there is, and he might try to harm Abigail."

Philippe sat up straight and spoke with fervor. "Then I will help guard Abigail, Monsieur. I will watch her day and night! Nobody knows the Palace like me! Nobody! I know every room, every corner, every secret passage!"

"Secret passages?" Gary felt his insides tighten into a hard knot. He glanced over at the Secret Service agents. They weren't smiling anymore. This was not something they had been briefed on.

"Philippe, are there any secret passages inside this building?"

'Oui, they are in all the buildings. I will show you!"

Abigail leaned over and whispered conspiratorially into Gary's ear.

"There are *secret* passages, Papa Gary. I promised not to tell."

Well, thought Gary with some resignation, as long as they remain secret and The Seven doesn't find out about them, the children should be safe. Certainly, there were plenty of people watching them! He smiled, grabbed a handful of popcorn, and settled down into the sofa to cuddle with his daughter and to enjoy the movie on this snowy afternoon.

"You can show me later, Philippe. Tomorrow perhaps. And remember, the secret passages must remain our secret." He paused and glanced back at the two agents standing sentinel. "And it can be their secret, too. They like secrets. And we'll tell Madame President. She will need to know."

"What about Babette, Papa Gary? Can she know, too? She likes us."

Gary smiled again with satisfaction. "Since she is spending much of her time drawing you, yes, you can show her, too. But tell no one else."

The remainder of the day proved quite enjoyable. Martha returned from her long afternoon of meetings, tired but pleased with their progress and her performance. The Russian Ambassador came around to her position on climate changes and global warming. She was encouraged by their discussion on setting targets with regards to the spread and treatment of infectious diseases, such as HIV/ AIDS, tuberculosis, and malaria.

Later that day, family and friends joined Madame President and Gary for an informal dinner at the Grand Trianon. Janet and Senator Evan Daniels showed up, much to Jack's dismay. But true to her promise, she pulled in her claws and left the reporter alone during the evening. Instead, she hung around Senator Daniels and Secretary Campbell throughout the night, praising the qualifications and accomplishments of her senator-fiancée at every opportunity.

This was the first time Gary had been around Senator Daniels. The star senator of the south was undoubtedly a very handsome young man. He reminded Gary of Ben Affleck. Senator Daniels had a striking face, dark hair, light brown eyes, and a winning smile. Although known for his exceptional command of the Senate floor with his extraordinary gifts of elocution, Daniels was surprisingly quiet and reserved in a social setting. Perhaps this was one reason Janet found him so attractive (besides the money and the power). She did all the talking in this relationship. Evan appeared modest in the wake of all of Janet's public praise of him. Janet, of course, never lost an opportunity to advance her own causes.

As promised, Chef Louis Girard arrived and presented several platters of Carême's *Nectarine Plombière*. The dessert was the hit of the evening. Louis remained for the rest of the night, proving to be an extraordinarily talkative and entertaining fellow. Gary never forgot that Louis was still a suspect, but a likable suspect all the same. Louis even got down on the floor and played with the kids. Sebastian carefully watched from a safe distance. The evening festivities came to a close near midnight as the storms continued in earnest. Those staying at the Petit Trianon and Queen's Hamlet hurried to get back to their lodgings while they still could.

* * *

Tuesday morning
January 8, 2002

The next morning, the wicked weather persisted. It continued snowing heavily throughout the night; and the morning news reported that a record three and a half feet of snow had accumulated on the ground during the past twenty-four hours, with another sixteen to twenty-four inches expected by noon today. With the constant winds, snow drifts of seven to ten feet were reported in some parts of town. The one bright spot in the forecast, however, was a predicted break in the precipitation from noon until several hours past midnight, literally a break in the storm. But another wave of heavy snow was on the way, another one to two feet of snow expected to arrive sometime early Thursday morning.

"It is as we feared," lamented Monsieur Lavel at lunchtime. He stood by the table that was set up in the Venus Drawing Room for Gary, Max, and Jack. The old man was looking extremely stressed. He mopped his glistening brow with a wrinkled white handkerchief and continued.

"The snow has made travel between the hotels, restaurants, and the Palace almost impossible! The newspapers are already making comparisons to the historic blizzard of 1789 when it snowed for two months. People froze to death trying to travel from Paris to Versailles. Your American president, Thomas Jefferson, likened it to visiting Siberia. So, given the circumstances, we have made the monumental decision to move all the foodstuffs for the conference luncheons and dinners and the cake competition inside the castle today. We've also moved all support staff into the castle and given them housing until the end of the summit!"

Gary nodded sympathetically at Lavel. Being Social Secretary and thus responsible for the official functions of the White House, he could relate to all the administrative pressures Lavel was experiencing.

"Versailles is coming to life again!" murmured Jack in awe of his surroundings.

"Oui, Monsieur, it is so," agreed Lavel as he stared at the life-size white marble statue of Louis XIV beside them in the alcove.

"Well, this arrangement for our lunch is wonderful," commented Gary with admiration, looking about the large room adorned with dark brown marble pillars and gilded ceiling.

"*C'ést pratique*," admitted Lavel with an exasperated sigh. "It was as in the old days. We set up the buffet tables and drink tables in the Drawing Room of Plenty, the closest room to the Chapel. This space, it is easy for the leaders to come and get their food. Then we set up tables and chairs in the Venus and Diana State Rooms, the Diana Room for the G-8 leaders and their translators, and the Venus room for the chefs, the artists, and other guests. In the days of the Sun King, this room was used to serve light suppers. Voilà, it is so again!"

"If I can be of any assistance, just let me know," offered Gary sincerely.

"Garçon! Some assistance, please! I need more coffee!"

Janet's piercing voice rose above the din of the crowded room. She waved her arm over her head, beckoning Lavel's attention to where she was sitting with designer Roland Martin. Martin looked absolutely miserable.

Lavel closed his eyes.

"Can you not make her disappear?" he pleaded.

"Sorry," laughed Gary. "I'm afraid I was never any good at doing that!"

Lavel sighed deeply, excused himself and dashed off towards Janet's table.

"Look at the bright side," Max suggested as he sipped his warm chicken white bean with bacon soup. "The sun is going to shine this afternoon, and the ball is going to take place tonight as planned. That is good! And the tent at the Apollo Fountain will indeed go up."

"Tent?" said Jack in disbelief. "OUTSIDE? In this weather? You're not serious!"

"Oh, but I am! It is a large tent made of clear, heavy-duty plastic. There will be electric warmers inside and lots of warm drinks — hot chocolate, hot cider…"

"Hot rum?" asked Jack hopefully.

Max laughed. "Yes, many hot liquors! I met with Monsieur Dumont early this morning, and his crews stand ready to start clearing the Royal Avenue and the other garden walkways as soon as the snowfall completely stops and the winds die down. They will clear away as much snow as possible so that the guests may walk the gardens tonight underneath a full moon."

"Whatever for?" asked Jack morosely, reaching for more crusted bread and butter. "I've been in Paris several days now and haven't found a single *la jeune fille to* shower my attention upon."

Gary tried to placate his reporter friend. "We are going to put out luminaries, all up and down the Royal Avenue, the other walkways, and around the Latona and Apollo Fountains. It's supposed to be reminiscent of the lavish parties of the past. Tonight, guests can bundle up in their winter coats and walk up and down the Royal Avenue at their leisure, with the Apollo tent as a stopping-off point to rest and get warm drinks. Actually, with all the snow and candles, it should be quite a display. You and your cameraman will document the event."

Jack sputtered.

"Me, spend the evening out there, in that snow? Sorry, Fred, I didn't bring my long johns."

"We can get you some," offered Max.

Jack huffed. "Thanks. Get me two, so I don't freeze. Good thing I brought my mittens."

Max laughed and stood up. "Courage, you silly man. Courage and faith. If you don't feel like walking, you can take a fabulous ride in a Cinderella coach."

"Coach?"

"Didn't Lavel, tell you? In throwing open the doors to Versailles, they've decided to open up the doors of the Grand Stables and the Coach Museum as well."

Jack's jaw dropped. "The palace's coaches?"

"Hmm, yes. They don't make them like they used to. Think about it, my darlings! These old coaches were built over 200 years ago to handle all kinds of weather. Truth is, the Secret Service couldn't find enough snowmobiles in the area, but they did find lots of horses. So they got together with Lavel and Dumont and came up with a new means of transportation. I hear there are at least ten coaches and six sleighs. Seven of the coaches were used for Napoleon's wedding. Lavel got the word out, and local people put on their boots and brought in their horses and hay. Amazing! Now, if you two will excuse me, I think I'll go over and rescue poor Roland. The poor man isn't looking particularly cheerful at the moment."

The designer left. Jack looked around the room quickly, leaned over, and whispered. "Well, how's the detective work going? Any leads in the case?"

Gary shook his head and glanced about, taking notice of where people were sitting. At the table next to them sat Dean Dubois, his assistant Angelique, and Louis. The two men were engaged in an animated conversation, ignoring the quiet brunette sitting between them. Angelique fiddled with her soup and stared morosely over at the next table where Blaze and Marie were having lunch with her father, Ambassador Porter. Marie was a bouncy little thing, full of pep, a real pistol. Her gay laugh, like a silver bell, rang happily amid the crowd. Blaze's face was singularly focused on the lively redhead, his countenance full of pleasure. Clearly, the situation brought no pleasure to the sullen Angelique.

Two tables were set up in the middle of the room. One was an all-male table, with Antoine, Pierre, and Gerald sitting together, drinking wine and talking cheerfully amongst themselves. Antoine appeared in better spirits today. His face was bright and held a happy expression. At the other center table, Claude, René, Isabelle, and Camille were enjoying their steaming soup and bread. Camille wore a lazy, bored expression as if she could not stand to be among such mere mortals. Isabelle was in control of the conversation, chattering away with René and Claude's complete attention. At the far end of the room, beside Janet's table and the artists' table, Josette and George sat together in a shadowed corner.

George appeared gloomy, attacking his soup and avoiding all conversation with his assistant. Josette had finished her lunch and was leaning back in her chair. She held her wine glass to her lips and threw seductive glances in Pierre's direction. Pierre ignored them.

Frowning, Josette finally put down her wine glass, got up, and left the room. Babette Moreau, who according to Max was wearing Valentino this morning (a knee-length plaid wool skirt with a short-waisted, gray woolen jacket) suddenly got up and followed the female chef out. Babette's departure got Angelique's attention, who gazed after the stylish artist with a disconcerted look. Gary felt empathy for the shy girl. It was hard enough to come face to face with one's twin. But to be outdone in looks and fashion at every turn, that must be a bitter pill to swallow.

Gary brought his attention back to Jack and his question.

"Nope. No leads yet. Just taking things in right now, getting to know the chefs and their assistants. The hunt will begin in earnest tomorrow. Tonight, we shall celebrate and enjoy the ball."

Jack sighed. "If only I had a date! Can you believe it? Blaze, the bottomless pit, has two beauties dangling on a string. And I, the fabulous international playboy reporter, don't have a single girl in sight. Well, there is the pretty maid at Trianon, but Al has dibs on her. I tried picking up your nanny, Gabrielle, but she's taken, too. Who am I going to share a romantic carriage ride with, in this blasted snow?"

Gary opened his mouth to reply but was interrupted by the sudden arrival of his assistant, Nick.

"The models have arrived, sir," Nick reported breathlessly. "We were able to get them down from Paris last night before the roads became impossible and got them all rooms inside the Palace with the rest of the staff. They were exhausted and slept in late, but now they are waiting outside in the Hercules Drawing room with the children. Philippe is saying grace and feeding his cat for their entertainment. The cat got a plate of Beef Wellington! It looked so good, I was ready to get down on my hands and knees and join him. I need to tell Martin they've arrived."

"Models?" Jack jumped right out of his chair. "No, don't bother Martin, Nick. He is busy aiding and abetting Max at the moment with the dragon-lady. Let me be the first to greet the poor maidens. You run along and tell Lavel he needs to set up a new table...for six."

"Seven. I'm coming with you," said Gary pleasantly, "as a chaperone."

"I don't need a chaperone," said Jack.

"But they might," countered Gary.

"You're right, "conceded Jack, grinning from ear to ear. "Let's go!"

Jack hurried out of the room and raced towards the Hercules Drawing-room at full speed. Gary had to dash to keep up with him. He was just able to hear Jack announce as he crossed the threshold, "Bonjour, Mademoiselles!"

To which he was greeted:

"Oh, look, it's Mr. Parish! We met him before at Madame President's wedding! He must be covering our fashion show!"

"Isn't he handsome, Gerty? I think he is the handsomest reporter on television!"

"Oh, I don't know about that. I'm kind of partial to that weatherman on CNN myself. Jack's hair is too white for his age. I don't think it's natural."

"Well, your hair color isn't natural, Eileen! It's straight out of a bottle!"

"Hi, Sugar! Is that any way to greet your old Auntie?"

"Sonny boy! How about a kissy-poo?"

"Madeleine!!!"

Jack froze dumbfounded. He gaped at the group of five, blue-haired old ladies standing in front of him and exclaimed, "Aunt Dotty? What in hell's name are you doing here?"

Chapter Ten

The Announcements

Tuesday Midday
January 8, 2002

It took two bowls of soup and a big glass of wine to calm Jack down. Once recovered, he leveled his question again directly at his relative.

"Okay, Aunt Dee, what gives? What are you doing here?"

Dotty (Aunt Dee to Jack) gazed affectionately at her nephew with a tranquil smile on her face.

"Didn't Mr. Craig tell you? It was his idea to have us come and be models in Mr. Martin's fashion show. It is such a groundbreaking concept to use a bunch of old gals like us, so much more like real life. I mean really, what normal woman is that skinny? I hope you don't mind, but then you might be partially to blame. You must have told him we were here in France touring."

Gary enjoyed his soup and listened in on the conversation in silence. Dotty was giving the cover story to Jack, and Gary hoped the savvy reporter bought it. The truth was that General McKay had sent his top-secret CIA team to Paris to monitor De Silva's movements and to come to the palace; and Martha had informed Gary, since the Blue Hairs were there, they would provide extra security for them and the children. Hopefully Dotty would be able to hide her new role as a U.S. undercover agent from her nephew's sharp reporter instincts.

Jack bit his lip. "Yeah, I guess I did. You sent me all those postcards from Normandy and Provence over Thanksgiving and Christmas. I wondered why you weren't home for the holidays."

Aunt Dee blithely continued. "Oh, I've been touring abroad with the girls for two months now. It's nice to get out of dreary old Texas for a change. Remember, Mr. Craig introduced me to my new friends at his wedding? They are all war widows like me, and they like to travel as much as I do. All of their husbands were in the service. Mildred's husband and my husband were in the Army."

"Navy," said Gertrude for her spouse.

"Air Force," said Eileen.

"Coast Guard," said Olivia.

"Marines," said Maddie winking at Jack.

Jack ignored Maddie's impertinence.

"Well," said Jack, "you still should have told me you were coming to Versailles! I would have met up with you in town and brought you to the palace myself."

Dotty reached over and patted Jack on the shoulder. "Don't be silly. It was supposed to be a surprise."

"Oh, it was that," replied Jack dryly. He downed another mouthful of wine and then cast a spiteful look at Gary. "Any other little surprises you have in store?"

"One never knows," said Gary vaguely.

So far, so good, thought Gary. Jack seemed to be buying it. The Blue Hairs had been trailing Carlos De Silva in France for several weeks. Now that they were here, their assignment was to keep an eye on the First Family and to interact with all the suspects. Certainly, the chefs would never suspect them as CIA agents!

Their meal finished, Gary stood up and announced, "Ladies, join us in the Hall of Battles to watch the competition officially begin. The chefs are going to reveal their cake themes, and tomorrow they will begin assembling their creations. Aunt Sophie and Ambassador Porter will be waiting for us there. Come on. Let's get going."

Hall of Battles

According to tourist literature, the Hall of Battles is 120 meters long (393 feet) and 13 meters wide (42 ½ feet), an ample space to host the pastry competition. When Gary and his party arrived, they found a packed hall waiting for the show to begin. If tensions were running high among the chefs, perhaps it was partly because their audience consisted of the leaders of the free world and their spouses. The afternoon session of the summit had ended early, and the G-8 leaders with their spouses were present, ready for an afternoon of fun and relaxation before the grand ball.

There were two rows of chairs set up in front of the five cooking stations. In the front row, the seating arrangement was as follows:

- The French President's wife, Madame Mansart
- French President Robert Mansart
- Philippe (with Sebastian in his lap)
- Abigail
- Gary
- Madame President Martha Dameron Johnson-Craig
- Aunt Sophie
- Ambassador Porter
- Marie Porter
- British Prime Minister Alan Foster

- Mrs. Foster
- Secretary Campbell
- Dean Paul Dubois

Behind, in the second row, the seating arrangement was:
- Madame Laurent
- Canadian Prime Minister Pierre Laurent
- Mrs. Voronova
- Russian President Alek Voronova
- Japan's Prime Minister Yutaka
- Mrs. Yutaka
- Mrs. Herrman
- German Chancellor Kurt Herrman
- Italian President Vincetio Gallo
- Mrs. Gallo
- Blaze
- Angelique du Pré

For the Blue Hairs, some chairs were quickly found and set up in the back, near the press stands. General McKay stood beside them.

As they took their seats, Gary looked up and down the hall. Dean Dubois had created the seating chart, and Gary couldn't help but notice that he placed Blaze right next to Angelique, not Marie Porter. Ambassador Porter's daughter was looking rather sour at the moment, her arms crossed, her mouth turned upside down in an unbecoming frown. Ambassador Porter smiled at his daughter and put a comforting arm around her sagging shoulders. Angelique sat close to Blaze, whispered quietly in his ear, and looked triumphant. Blaze was entranced by the lovely shy brunette, completely oblivious of the battle being waged over his attention. Gary was a bit worried about Blaze. He was inexperienced when it came to matters of the heart, and here he was playing with fire, bouncing back and forth between these two intelligent women. Before the week was out, Gary was afraid Blaze would more than likely be the one to get burned.

In front of Blaze, Secretary Campbell sat in his corner chair looking very uncomfortable and out of his element. Gary was pleased to see that Dean Dubois had the foresight and perhaps the intuition to place the crusty old professor beside him. Dubois was whispering, busily pointing things out and explaining procedures to a fidgety Secretary Campbell.

The press was set up behind the chairs. Jack and his crew were on a large middle platform in the center of the staging area. This afternoon, CNN was not the only press allowed inside the Palace. Two more camera crews had been given admittance, due to the wicked weather, the oversight of General McKay, and the kindheartedness of Monsieur Lavel, who could not stand any longer witnessing the freezing reporters huddled up against the icy palace gates. Today, a crew from England's BBC and a crew from Euro TV, which broadcasts to more than 150 European channels in nine languages, were allowed inside. The BBC crew, headed up by Jack's arch-rival, Derrick Brown, was to the right, and Euro TV was to the left. Gary quickly glanced back, and Jack gave him a thumbs-up sign. Jack was looking a bit glum, no doubt over Derrick Brown's sudden appearance. Gary knew he would hear all about it later.

But Gary couldn't worry about Jack's ego just now. He had his own problems to deal with which included: 1) finding out the identity of the next member of The Seven; 2) keeping an eye on his ex-wife, Janet and making sure she behaved herself; and 3) worrying about what Philippe was so excitedly saying to an amazed President Mansart. At least Janet and Senator Daniels were not present this afternoon. That was a good start.

"You look nervous," whispered Martha into Gary's ear as Gary sat down.

"That's because France's best pickpocket, the one who secretly lives inside France's royal palace, is having an unsupervised conversation with the President of France."

"You have a point there," concurred Martha smiling. "Oh, look, it's about to begin."

Dean Dubois stood in front of Louis's table with a microphone in his hand. The five teams of chefs were at attention beside their stations, each holding a white poster board. Dubois bowed his head quickly towards the chefs and formally began the competition.

"Mesdames and Messieurs, welcome to the *Par Excellence* Cake and Sugar Competition. Gathered here in the Hall of Battles are five of the most talented master chefs in all of France, and working with them are five of the most promising chefs ever to graduate from our cooking school. This afternoon, each team will announce the theme they have chosen to create this week. They are holding a watercolor painting of their chosen theme, painted by our guest artist, Jean Bardou, from Canada. We will begin with team Rousseau and Bernard. Gentlemen, if you please."

Pierre and Antoine looked at each other, and then Antoine melodramatically turned over his poster. "For this competition, we will bring to life the lost magical palace of Marly." There was a pause and then applause from the diplomatic audience. Pierre took over the narration.

"Our construction will involve building thirteen petite vanilla cake palaces, with the central royal palace here, surrounded by six smaller buildings on each side. We will use spun sugar to recreate the cascading fountains, terraces, arbors, pergolas, and flowers."

"Holy smoke," murmured Gary to his wife applauding again as Pierre and Antoine stepped back to their station. "That looks amazing."

"Marly reminds me so much of the U.V.A. Lawn," whispered Martha. "Of course, Jefferson was there — I mean, here—when Marly existed, and he was important enough to be invited there by the King and Queen. I wish it still existed. Too bad Napoleon had to go and pull it down."

"That's a dictator for you," replied Gary smiling. "Okay, here comes the next one."

George Bonnet took the microphone and announced his theme while Josette melodramatically revealed the watercolor painting. It showed a large grotto covered with greenery set by a small pond. Inside the grove was an ensemble of magnificent white sugar statues. Masses of roses surrounded the pools.

Monsieur Bonnet proceeded. "Mademoiselle LaClaire and I will present the Baths of Apollo. We will create the *Bosquet des Dômes* with cake, and the *Horses of the Sun* and *Apollo Served by Nymphs* statues is perfected with white spun sugar. We will also use spun sugar to create the surrounding grounds and flowers."

Again the audience applauded. Next, the ladies team made their announcement. Isabelle revealed a painting showing a lovely palace and gardens full of wild animals. Camille proudly announced they would be recreating the famed Menagerie. Spice cake would make the octagon-shaped palace, and the gardens and wild animals made of spun sugar. Abigail stood up in her chair and clapped her hands, much to the audience's delight, as specific animals were pointed out in the drawing. The Blue Hairs cheered, too. Gary turned back and noticed all three television crews were filming his daughter. It looks like Abigail would be headline news again on international T.V.!

Once the excitement died down, Chef Michel took the spotlight. Claude held up a small blue and white plate in one hand and then revealed a lovely painting of a small blue and white palace.

"What you see Chef Breton holding is a plate of blue Delft china. Long ago, the Sun King built the Porcelain Palace for a royal family retreat. For this competition, we will recreate the palace using lemon cake and white frosting. Then we will use spun sugar to recreate the blue and white Delft tiles that once adorned the palace's rooftop. We will also use sugar to create the petite gardens that surrounded the palace, gardens once filled with roses, lilies, and white jasmine."

Of all the creations shown thus far, Gary felt this theme and drawing was the most beautiful and perhaps the most technically difficult. If it turned out half as wonderful as the artist's depiction, then this one had an excellent chance of winning. Gary quickly glanced back and looked at Blaze who was leaning close to Angelique. He was whispering excitedly into the young woman's ear. She looked happy and satisfied. She pointed proudly to Louis Girard, who was the next to announce his creation.

Gary turned around to see Matisse holding a lovely watercolor of one of the most famous events ever to take place at Versailles. Gary took one look, and he knew that Louis and Gerald had chosen a real winner and would be giving Michel and Breton a run for their money.

Louis took the microphone. "Tomorrow, Chef Matisse and I will create for you the Wedding of Marie Antoinette! As you can see in the painting, this event took place in the gardens beside the Grand Canal. We will use cakes to recreate the Versailles palace and gardens and spun sugar to create the Grand Canal, fountains, flowers, statues, fireworks, and the flotilla that once sailed in the canal." Louis paused and reached down to pick up one of his precious vials of dyes. He held it up. "To bring the gardens to life, I will be using my own created color dyes. I have here a platter containing over one hundred shades of blues, greens, purples, and reds that will achieve a spun sugar creation the world has not seen since the days of Antonin Carême!"

There was thunderous applause from the diplomats and loud cheers from the press and Maddie. Louis bowed to the audience and then glanced over at his assistant with a satisfied look.

Dean Dubois took the microphone back and announced that the diplomats and their spouses were welcome to meet the chefs during a wine and cheese reception. Gary saw that a table filled with food and drink had been set up in the back of the hall near George and Josette's station. He quickly took advantage of the moment to round up Abigail and Philippe (who was still standing far too close to the French President's coat pockets for Gary's liking) and take them over for snacks and soda. Gary was relieved to see that the ever-watchful Lavel had included some refreshments suitable for a child's palate. Aunt Sophie and Charles showed up and told Gary they would watch the children for a while and for him to join Martha and the other delegates. Gratefully, he handed over Abigail and walked to Chef Michel's table where Martha and British Prime Minister Alan Foster and his wife were engaged in conversation. The Fosters and the Craigs made a good foursome. Together they walked up and down the hallway to view the paintings and to talk with the chefs. They were stopped at Pierre's station when suddenly there was an angry outburst.

"Put it back!" ordered an angry George Bonnet in a thunderous voice that rang through the hall. His assistant, Josette, was standing beside the middle cooking station, her one delicate hand hovering over Girard's tray of little vials. A green one was in her other hand.

"I cannot believe your insolence," continued George fiercely marching towards Louis's station. "You are an embarrassment to me and the entire competition! You should be at your post greeting the guests, not sticking your nose and your hands into other people's business. The judges will think we are cheating!"

Conversation in the hall abruptly died down. and all eyes turned to Girard's station. Josette merely looked annoyed at her employer's public reproof.

"I was just looking at them. They are very pretty, no? Louis doesn't mind, do you, Louis?" She cast a flirtatious smile in Louis's direction.

The handsome chef had been talking to Italian President Gallo, his back turned away from his station. Louis glanced around and studied the pouting brunette with a narrow gaze.

"She may have it," said Louis generously. "I have plenty more on another tray in the refrigerator. And besides, I've given some of this color to René for his sugar garden. So, no one can call it cheating. But only this one," he cautioned with a dark sound of warning in his voice. "Now, run along, cherie, before I change my mind."

Josette marched past George triumphantly, holding the little vial tightly in her hand. Chef George apologized profusely to Louis and Gerald and followed his truant partner back to their station. Gary noticed Dean Dubois leaning over and whispering to his assistant, Angelique, both of whom were staring hard at the young female chef. Dean Dubois frowned in disapproval.

"Ghastly," muttered Isabelle at the next station, within earshot of Gary and Martha. "How absolutely ghastly! Why on earth did Louis let her get away with it? Her behavior was indefensible, really."

"Because Louis is a fool," said Camille shaking her head. "I told you so, Isabelle. That girl, she will cause trouble. Much trouble. Mark my words. You will see."

Chapter Eleven

Hall of Mirrors

Tuesday night
January 8, 2002

A glorious full January moon cast its radiant blue light across the snowy gardens of Versailles. Beneath the bold Orion, the grounds sparkled with the splendor of majestic days gone by. A golden carriage drawn by a team of four black horses slowly processed through the cleared frozen pathways of The Royal Avenue now illuminated by hundreds of white luminary candles. The glistening carriage pulled up to the palace ablaze with lights burning at every window, the staterooms full of international guests awaiting the final guest's arrival in exalted expectation.

On the back terrace, staff and Secret Service agents waited for the gold carriage to come to a complete stop. Two men swiftly moved round to open the doors; and somewhere overhead, no doubt at the careful command of Monsieur Lavel, the music of Jean-Baptiste Lully, his *Prélude des Trompettes et autres Instruments pour Mars*, began to play into the winter night air. Gary first stepped out of the carriage, turned, and reached back to take hold of his true love's velvet-gloved hand. Dozens of frozen reporters, who had stood sentinel at Versailles's golden gates for the past few days, were allowed inside the grounds for this moment only. Their camera lights flashed brilliantly as Martha descended from the coach dressed in an exquisite navy blue Rococo silk gown, her head, and shoulders covered with the thick folds of a matching navy blue velvet cape and hood.

Around her neck shone a treasure known as *The French Blue*, a diamond that King Louis XIV himself wore on ceremonial occasions, a stone some say is cursed but, tonight with the rarest of blessings from the Smithsonian Institution, a stone worn again into the grand halls of French kings and queens. For this was the ultimate of Gary's wild ideas, one that literally caused Martha to gasp, Aunt Sophie to cheer, and General McKay to openly swear in front of the children. This moment was Gary and Martha's greatest surprise and greatest gift to the gathered diplomats of the free world and for their new friend, Monsieur Lavel, who openly wept when he saw the necklace hanging gently around Martha's lovely neck. Not even Max whispered to any the great secret. The designer stood proudly beside a bedazzled Ambassador Porter, an astonished Dean Paul Dubois, and a pleased Secretary Campbell as Martha gracefully ascended the white marble steps wearing the immortal Hope Diamond.

Waiting for them inside the Hall of Mirrors were General McKay and Aunt Sophie. The First Lady was dressed in an exquisite burgundy velvet gown, also created by Max. The General wore a traditional black and white tuxedo with a burgundy cummerbund. Upon arrival, Charles and Sophie greeted Gary and Martha, then immediately took charge of a wide-eyed Abigail, the first daughter wearing a matching blue velvet gown. Her blonde hair was done up in ringlets and navy blue ribbons. Philippe and Sebastian were waiting, too. Sophie quickly gathered up the children and cat and directed them towards the Apollo Drawing Room where they found games, refreshments, and drinks . Aunt Sophie's working motto was, "When in doubt, ply Abigail with food." Free of the children, Gary joined his wife in mingling with the G-8 summit leaders and their wives in the grand reception.

Gary spent the first hour visiting the guests, enjoying cocktails (his drink being Diet Coke with lime), and admiring the architecture and art inside the historic Hall of Mirrors. Gary and Martha greeted German Chancellor Herrman and his wife, Helga, a buxom woman dressed in a peach silk gown. They discussed European gardens, European money exchange, and free trade with the German couple. Next, they visited with French President Mansart and his wife, Lily. The French First Lady was an elegant person; and tonight, the brunette looked beautiful in her cream organza gown. Lily was a proud historian, and she shared with Martha and Gary some of the history of the Hall of Mirrors and its recent restoration. As she spoke, Gary could envision the tall silver throne that once stood in this hall. He could almost smell the King's potted orange trees.

Soon Jack and cameraman, Al, came begging for some pictures of Martha with President Mansart. While Martha posed, Gary went over to say hello to Blaze and Angelique. Blaze was completely smitten by the charming chef, dressed in a startling dark green Rococo gown. They talked about the pastry competition and the themes for the cakes. Martha and Jack soon returned, and Jack announced he was going to explore the other staterooms in search of wine, women, and song—not necessarily in that order. He left, and then Gary and Martha caught up with the talkative Adelaide Foster, the wife of England's Prime minister.

"Extraordinary!" exclaimed Adelaide admiring the blue diamond necklace up close. "Simply extraordinary! How on earth did you manage it?"

"The Smithsonian gave it to General McKay and he's been hiding it at the Queen's Hamlet," said Gary smiling.

"Quite right," said Adelaide laughing. "No criminal would dare take on the General in the midst of this snowstorm, to be sure. Well, you two certainly gave the press their money's worth. I must say they were thrilled at your arrival, my dear. However, I'm glad Monsieur Lavel had the lot hauled away right after your grand entrance. I simply couldn't face an entire evening with the press taking pictures at every turn."

Gary nodded his head empathetically. "Your country seems to have some of the worst paparazzi."

Adelaide rolled her eyes and took a sip of pink champagne. "Beastly, the whole lot of them!"

"Well, it is part of the package, I'm afraid," said Martha with a sigh of resignation. She looked around the room. "Where is Alan by the way? I still don't see him anywhere."

"Alan? He's back in the Apollo room with President Gallo, President Voronova, and Prime Minister Laurent."

Martha raised her eyebrows with interest. "Oh, really? Talking shop?"

Mrs. Foster shook her head and grimaced. "No, they're playing cards. Monsieur Lavel says the Sun King used to have these grand parties at night and the King, his family, and friends would play card games back in the Apollo Room. So, tonight they put up the game tables again with velvet green cloths, just like they did long ago. Well, Canada, Italy, and Russia had better watch out. Alan is dashedly fierce when it comes to playing cards and completely insufferable when he wins! Come to think of it, he's completely insufferable when he loses, too, which is why I leave him alone at the card table. Oh, look, you can see the other wives over there by the windows chatting away. No doubt they left their husbands alone for the same reason I did. My, they look lovely, don't they?"

Gary glanced over to see Michelle Laurent, Rosa Gallo, and Natasha Voronova standing around one of the great gilded tables in the Hall of Mirrors. The dress designers of their respective countries had done them proud, for each of them was splendidly attired for the Ball—Michelle in a mauve and gold gown, Rosa in a white organza gown with pink rosebuds (how fitting!), and Natasha in a bold black and white gown with an ermine collar. Adelaide Foster glanced down at her own spectacular pale blue silk dress and sighed.

"Imagine having to dress this way every day! No wonder France went bankrupt. And this corset! It's frightfully tight. I can hardly breathe!"

"Sweetheart," said Martha to Gary. "I want to go over and have a word with the Japanese Prime Minister and his wife. Do you mind?"

"Oh, no, go ahead. I'll stay here with Mrs. Foster. But hurry back. Dinner should be starting very soon."

Martha smiled and left to greet the Japanese couple. Adelaide glanced over at the blonde wife of the Japanese Prime Minister and frowned.

"You know her," questioned Gary, trying to read the British woman's face.

'Hmm, indeed, yes," said Adelaide sipping her drink. "She was Beatrice Woods when I knew her back at Oxford. She was an only child, dreadfully indulged and absolutely spoiled rotten as a result. Her father was a member of Parliament and a very successful businessman, too. I believe he was into computers and cows."

"Computers and cows?"

"Agricultural software, dear boy," smiled Adelaide. "Anyway, Beatrice's mother died when she was quite young, and her father simply doted on the poor girl. It ruined her, I'm afraid. He sent Bea across the pond to attend Harvard and then promptly brought her back to Oxford and London society. He had high hopes of marrying his daughter into the Royal Family, but unfortunately for him (and fortunately for us), all of the Windsor boys were taken at the time. So he sent Beatrice over to Japan and hoisted her upon the Japanese government and royalty. Their loss, our gain, if you ask me. Still, I confess she's made a rather good go of it. Ghastly dress, though. One should never wear that particular shade of yellow with that shade of blonde hair! It just doesn't do."

Gary laughed. "Well, maybe I can arrange for her to meet Roland Martin or a private consultation with Max. You know Max?"

Mrs. Foster leaned forward and patted Gary playfully on the cheek.

"Everybody knows Max! Isn't this party wonderful? This room is splendid. I can't wait to see what they serve us for dinner. It should be fabulous! After eating, my husband and I are going for a stroll in the gardens. Can you believe what Dumont and his staff accomplished?"

"They had lots of help," added Gary sipping his drink. "Volunteers from the town came out this afternoon to assist, and city officials sent over two bulldozers that helped clear away a lot of the snow from the main walkways."

Mrs. Foster smiled. "Well, they must have worked like demons to clear those garden paths and to put out all those candles. It looks like a fairyland out there. I don't care how cold it is. I brought my heavy winter coat, and I'm walking down to the Royal Canal. Oh look, the lady chefs have arrived. Isn't that Camille a beauty? Simply smashing! I hope she wins the competition. Girl power and all that, you know!"

Camille Aumont entered wearing a spectacular lavender silk gown. Behind her, Isabelle followed in black velvet. The two ladies picked up glasses of pink champagne and joined the reception.

Gary glanced around the room, taking note of who else was present. There was no sign of Janet and her beau, Senator Daniels, anywhere. Strange. Janet was usually front and center at any social occasion. Gary felt cheered. Maybe they decided to avoid the cold weather and stay in tonight. Gary did see Chef Gerald Matisse and Claude Breton standing near one of the glass windows, drinking red wine and laughing. They seemed to be having a great time. Then he spied Josette. She was at the other end of the hall chatting with Pierre and Antoine. She appeared to be unaccompanied this evening. She was wearing a stunning dress of pure white silk taffeta.

"Have you seen Chef Bonnet?" asked Gary.

"He was here earlier, but left to go lie down, poor man," replied Adelaide sympathetically. "I overheard him talking to Monsieur Lavel. George Bonnet was decidedly not feeling well after this afternoon, and who can blame him. I believe I heard Lavel tell him he could go lie down in a room called the Meridian Cabinet, just off the Queen's bedroom somewhere. I've seen it, lovely little place, blue silk curtains, and coverings, has a small couch where Monsieur Bonnet can rest. I do hope he comes back and joins us for dinner."

Gary agreed.

Suddenly Jack and Monsieur Lavel approached looking extremely worried.

Lavel begged their forgiveness for interrupting.

"There is a problem in the Apollo Room," he said earnestly, "at the card tables."

Adelaide huffed, promptly handed her empty glass over to Lavel, and resolutely gathered up her silk skirts. "Let me guess. My husband and the Russian President are in dispute over a hand of cards, and it's come to blows."

"Not quite," said Jack grimly. "They've stopped playing bridge and have moved on to poker, and if you don't get in there fast, we're afraid it might start another Cold War."

Gary inwardly cringed, suspecting the worse. Janet and Evan hadn't stayed away after all. She was up to her old tricks, causing havoc whenever and wherever possible "It's Janet, isn't it? She's cheating at cards with the leaders of the free world?"

Jack shook his head and looked at Gary sheepishly. "Well, she is in there, alright, but she and Evan are playing some French card game with Secretary Campbell. The problem rests with my Aunt Dee and Madeleine. Aunt Dee is dealing the cards and is taking Mr. Foster, the Russian, the Italian, and the Canadian to the cleaners. And that old trout, Madeleine, is at the table, drinking schnapps and keeping score. When I left, she was winking at the Russian."

It was a race to the Apollo Room, but Jack, Gary, and Adelaide arrived just in time to avert an international crisis. Fortunately for all, dinner was announced, and the guests were immediately led into the red Mars Drawing Room where the dinner tables were set. A magnificent feast was served featuring some classics of French gourmet cuisine that Gary loved:

Hors d' oeuvres
Foie Gras Toast
Almond Cheddar Pastries
Brie Sticks
Escargot
Fish Course
Grilled Oysters with Fennel Butter
Crab Bisque
Salmon and Tomato Quiche
Bouillabaisse
Main Course
Duck Confit
Sirloin Croquettes
Lemon Rosemary Chicken with Roasted Potatoes
Haricot Beans
Artichokes à la Lyonnaise
Stuffed Cucumbers
Salad Course
Bastille Salad

Cheese Course:
Assorted Imported Cheeses and Fresh-Cut Fruit
Dessert
Chocolate Mousse
Vanilla Soufflés
Crèpe Suzettes

After dinner, the guests proceeded to the Hall of Mirrors for an evening of dancing and good cheer. Due to the weather, the live string quartet booked for the occasion was not able to appear. But Monsieur Lavel had the music that normally played into the gardens during summer piped into the hall. As the recorded sound of strings, harpsichords, and horns filled the room, Gary proudly took his beloved Martha into his arms for a waltz. They twirled across the floor in splendor, and Gary purposefully danced close to Al several times so that he could get a good shot. If there was a photograph that Gary wanted to bring home to remind him of this trip, this was it. Martha looked and felt every bit like a queen, her dark blue gown and diamond necklace shimmering beneath the lighted cut-glass chandeliers. The room was bursting with light, as rays of January moonlight flooded into the hall through each of its seventeen floor-to-ceiling glass windows, mixing with candle glow from forty-one chandeliers

Others joined them on the dance floor. The Fosters, the Herrmans, and the Gallos took up the waltz. Jack danced with his Aunt Dee, Ambassador Porter with his daughter Marie, and Blaze with a radiant Angelique. Josette danced with Pierre; and to Gary's surprise, the three-star General McKay took his new bride and proved to be quite the sure-footed dancer! Maddie continued to cast flirtatious glances towards the Russian President, and Voronova grabbed his wife and stuck close to her for the remainder of the evening. Philippe and Abigail stood in a corner near the entrance to the War Room. Philippe had his fiddle out and was playing along with the recorded music, and Abigail twirled and tapped. Babette pulled up a chair near the children and began to draw. Max informed Gary, with glowing pride, that tonight the gorgeous Babette was wearing a Giorgio Armani gown and matching shawl in watermelon red. She even wore watermelon red gloves to match. The cat, Sebastian, sprawled out by the artist's feet, washed his paws and eyed the fringe hanging off the artist's shawl with fascination.

The dancing lasted nigh until midnight, although most of the chefs began leaving the dance floor earlier to walk down the Royal Avenue to the heated tent. The dancers exchanged partners freely. Gary danced with Aunt Sophie, Maddie, Aunt Dotty, Isabelle, Abigail, Babette, and Adelaide Foster. Jack danced with his aunt, Abigail, Camille, and all the Blue Hairs, including Maddie. Sometime during the evening, Blaze switched partners and danced with Marie Porter for the rest of the evening. Kindheartedly, Dean Dubois took notice of a solemn-faced Angelique and led her out onto the dance floor, whispering words of encouragement into her ear. As the evening wore on, Gary noticed that Chef Camille Aumont was absent. When he asked Isabelle for a dance, she informed him that Camille had a headache and left.

At midnight, the music ended. Most of the chefs were gone, and the remaining summit leaders and their wives retrieved their coats for a scenic carriage ride down to the tent and a walk around the candle-lit gardens. Several other carriages from the Coach Museum had been dusted off and fitted with horses for the evening gala. Gary and Martha gathered up a sleepy Abigail and descended the steps to their waiting carriage. They decided to forego the tent and hot drinks and return directly to the Grand Trianon. As they walked towards their carriage, Gary noticed Blaze walking hand and hand with Marie Porter down the snowy Royal Avenue. Quickly, he glanced back to see Angelique at the top of the stairs staring down at the couple. Dean Dubois and

Louis approached her, said something, and supportively took her by the arm. They walked south towards the Orangery. Josette La Claire appeared briefly at the top of the steps and then she, too, was gone.

The First Family got into their coach and slowly rode down the Royal Avenue. They passed Gerald Matisse standing alone near the Fountain of Latona. Where had Claude gone? The two chefs left the Hall of Mirrors together earlier to walk outside. Gary hoped the nervous chef had not taken ill. Then Gary saw Antoine Bernard walking alone back up to the castle, holding a steaming cup in his hand. As they approached the tent, they passed Ambassador Porter and Secretary Campbell walking down the Avenue together. Janet and her fiancé were walking behind them. The Fosters and the Herrmans trailed behind in their own coaches. At the tent, Gary could see the Japanese, Italian, and Canadian couples were already inside enjoying their hot drinks. Their coaches were parked outside waiting to carry the world leaders back to their hotels nearby. The British artist, Tom Parker, was inside taking pictures, no doubt to use for sketches later on. As they rode past the tent, Gary saw Isabelle Villeneau and Pierre Rousseau standing close together, laughing, bundled up, and perhaps too close and too full of hot liquor. Where was Chef Michel? Gary hadn't seen him for quite some time.

The ancient golden coach slowly ground its way towards the Grand Trianon. The sound of the snow crunching beneath the old carriage wheels almost put Gary to sleep. Upon arrival at their quarters, Gary tenderly lifted his sleeping daughter and silently followed his Secret Service Agents Pullman, Lewis, and Harkin into the snow-covered palace. The agents left him to assist Martha in removing and securing the Hope Diamond. Gary met up with an anxious Gabrielle, and together they put his little girl to bed and tucked her in. It was close to two in the morning when Gary made his way to the Queen of Belgium bedchamber to find his beloved wife waiting for him. She had removed her blue evening gown and was now wearing a simple white nightgown. She never looked lovelier. Gary removed his shirt, went over to his wife, and put his arms tightly around her waist. Together they gazed out into the night as storm clouds once more began to fill the winter sky. The January moon slowly vanished, and heavy snow began to fall. One by one, the luminary candles along the Royal Avenue were extinguished, the lights inside the main palace were put out, and darkness fell across Versailles once more.

* * *

Josette La Claire clutched a burning candle as she made her way carefully towards the Hall of Battles. With her free hand, she pulled her white winter cape tight against her chest and congratulated herself on her boldness, quick thinking, and ingenuity. As the ball ended, she had followed Angelique, Dean Dubois, and Louis out towards the Orangery, but then she doubled back and entered the Hall of Mirrors where a few guests remained. She chatted with them and some of the staff. Then she managed to remove a candle from one of the tables and slip into the Queen's apartments without being seen. She stayed inside the Salon des Nobles for some time, waiting till she was sure everyone had gone. She then moved steadily forward, down the darkened southern passageway. The play of soft candlelight danced across the walls within the gilded royal apartments, creating dark shadows that floated close around her.

But Josette was not afraid. Unlike Bonnet who was an idiot! Bonnet lacked the courage to take chances, the courage to take the risk, the courage to get ahead. But she did not! She was driven by her passion, by her curiosity, and most importantly, by her overwhelming desire to win. So Josette was quite prepared when she turned the dark corner of the Coronation Room to come face to face with a surprised security guard. She would greet this guard, talk to him, and seduce him if necessary in order to gain access to the cooking stations. Only no one was on guard at the Hall of

Battles when she arrived. The arched doorway stood open, black, and unprotected.

How very strange!

Josette stopped and gazed towards the darkened hall. Why wasn't there a guard here? She was so sure there would be. She held her candle up and looked around but saw no one. Ah, well, she thought as she shrugged her shoulders, perhaps no one considered bags of sugar, flour, and chocolate worth guarding. Besides, there were no finished creations yet to protect, no need to worry about sabotage. Perhaps the castle security had been pulled away to watch the guests as they walked up and down the Royal Avenue! There were more important possible dangers outside to consider. Yes, that must be it.

Satisfied, Josette tiptoed into the vast hall and made her way carefully around the chairs towards the middle station. She knew exactly what she was after, a bottle of food coloring the shade of teal apatite gemstones. She had spotted it when Louis displayed his dye creations to the guests, and she couldn't get that particular bottle out of her mind. She had to have it for her water creation. She approached the cooking station and held up the candle. Light spilled over the work area, but no bottles appeared. Where were they? Oh, but of course! Louis kept his little bottles in the refrigerator. Josette slowly walked around the front table and made her way towards the grey metal icebox. She grasped the handle and pulled it open. The refrigerator light popped on, spilling white light into the darkened work area.

Voilà. There they were. Tray after tray of tiny clear glass bottles were before her eyes, like sparkling jewels, so many beautiful colors. Instantly she found the teal one she wanted. She could see at least five of them. Surely Louis would not miss one? She eagerly reached into the refrigerator and took it. Then she spotted another dark blue one and lime green one that caught her eye, and she took those and put them in her pocket. Now, if she could get just one more of the green shade, she liked, for there would be much foliage to create in their sugar fountain scene. She looked down at the lower shelves where more bottles of many green shades were located and found it along with some of Louis's sugar figurines. These she handled and admired, selecting the best green one to keep. Her eyes grew wide with wonder at what she saw.

"How beautiful," she whispered as she reached her hand forward and touched it with her finger.

Spellbound by her discovery, Josette did not hear the rapidly approaching footsteps nor feel the presence of a stranger until it was too late, when the sharp edge of a heavy metal flashlight came crashing down on the back of her skull, killing her instantly.

Chapter Twelve

The Hall of Battles and The King's Garden

Wednesday
January 9, 2002

*H*e stood beside the Pyramid Fountain and watched the water cascade merrily over four marble bowls into a shimmering turquoise pool. The season was spring, the month was May, and all around him were row upon row of roses in outrageous bloom. Gary walked slowly through the royal gardens of the North Parterre, spellbound by the sight and intoxicated by the floral scent. Everywhere he turned, he saw historic roses in grand display. There were hedges of the graceful Cabbage Roses with their deep cups of dark pink petals. Here was a species of rose that would one day cross the channel and find itself planted in many a Victorian English garden. There was the golden yellow Sulphur Rose that came to France from the ancient Middle East. There was Old Blush China, the pink and red rose that introduced everblooming properties to the European June flowering roses. Gary walked past beds containing the red Austrian Copper rose, the crimson Apothecary rose, and White Moss Damask rose. Of course, here would be the Autumn Damask rose and the grand pink and white striped Rosa Mundi.

He was leaning over and relishing the fragrance of a deep purple Gallica rose known as the Bishop when he heard the sound of a violin playing.

The music made him pause. It called to him.

He walked back to the palace where he found the doors to the Hall of Mirrors standing wide open.

He entered and was almost blinded by the treasures before him. There stood the king's throne made entirely of solid silver. Other magnificent pieces of silver furniture surrounded it — sparkling tables and vases and chandeliers. Beside the windows were flowering orange trees planted in large silver pots. The sweet smell of orange blossoms almost overpowered him. The old Sun King sat upon his silver throne with his eyes closed, listening to the music. Gary was astonished to see Philippe standing before the king playing his old battered violin. Behind him stood a handsome young general and a tall red-headed gentleman.

It was Jefferson.

Somewhere in the dark recesses of Gary's slumbering mind, he knew this was a dream. Still, it didn't make sense. What was Thomas Jefferson doing here? Jefferson came to Versailles during Louis XVI's reign, not during the reign of Louis XIV. And who was the decorated soldier proudly watching Philippe play?

Suddenly the music stopped.

Gary then heard the sound of gunfire, the loud sound of an approaching, angry mob, and of heavy booted feet marching down marbled hallways. Jefferson quickly approached and grabbed Gary by the arm.

"You are in danger," said Jefferson urgently. "Take the boy. Run!"

"Run," yelled the General as the footsteps drew nearer.

They were close. Very close!

"Hide in the Maze!" ordered the King. He stood and pointed towards the gardens.

Gary grabbed Philippe's hand and ran.

They ran out of the palace, through the garden, and disappeared into the king's labyrinthine maze of thick green hedges. They quickly *became lost, disoriented. Gary heard the exploding sound of guns as they opened fire...*

Gary gasped and woke suddenly.

It was morning, Wednesday morning to be exact. Light softly flooded their Grand Trianon bedroom. Gary lay flat on his back, his heart pounding in his chest. What a dream! He hadn't had a dream like that since — well, not since last summer when they first faced The Seven. He didn't like these vivid dreams of his.

Sometimes they were too real.

Sometimes they came true.

He took a deep breath and turned over to check on his wife. Martha was beside him snugly curled up into a ball. She awoke at his touch.

"Morning, sweetheart," she whispered. "Sleep well?"

"Not really. I had a nightmare. Thomas Jefferson came to visit me here at Versailles. King Louis XIV and Philippe and a handsome young general were in the Hall of Mirrors. There was an angry mob approaching, and Jefferson told me to run."

"You and your dreams," said Martha yawning and rolling over on her back. "I'm beginning to think you are psychic. Why doesn't Jefferson visit me in my dreams? I'm the Jefferson scholar in the family, you know. I could use a little of his advice now and then. Did President Jefferson happen to offer any insights on the new trade agreements I'm working on with Japan? That would be helpful."

"No, he didn't say. He seemed to think we were in danger. But if I see him again, I'll ask him. In the meantime, you should check with Adelaide Foster. She went to school with Beatrice Yutaka, the wife of Japan's Prime Minister. Adelaide is a wealth of information."

Martha yawned and stretched like a contented cat. "Sounds like a good idea. I'll speak to Adelaide later. Anything else in your dream you should tell me about?"

Gary closed his eyes and remembered the fragrance of the potted fruit trees.

"There were orange blossoms," he said, savoring the scent.

Martha laughed softly. "You've been talking to Dumont again. I can tell. Didn't he say something about lime trees, too, the day we arrived?"

"Yes. Did you know that King Louis XIV loved the smell of orange blossoms so much that his greenhouses had over 12,000 seedling trees planted? They were planted so that trees were in constant bloom throughout the year, with potted trees rotated through the garden and in his palace in two-week cycles."

"Why do I have a sneaking suspicion there'll be potted orange and lime trees at the White House this summer?"

"You must be psychic, too, Madame President," said Gary.

Martha took a deep breath and sighed. "An orange blossom dream sounds rather nice. I think I'll go back to sleep and try to have one. There isn't a session until this afternoon, and I need to sleep in."

"I'm sorry if I woke you," said Gary apologetically.

"No, my head and stomach already did that. Remind me not to eat that much ever again."

Gary smiled and reached over to touch Martha's forehead. He lovingly brushed back her hair from her face.

"I will. Want some aspirin?"

Martha sighed and closed her eyes. "That would be lovely."

"Need a vase to throw up in?"

Martha smiled.

"That would be lovely, too!"

"One Ming vase coming right up."

*   *   *

Breakfast at the Grand Trianon that Wednesday morning was an all-male affair. McKay arrived late, after the snow plows cleared the walkways, and announced that Aunt

Sophie had chosen to forego breakfast. The jet lag and the late-night ball were catching up with her, and she wanted to catch up on her beauty sleep. Upon hearing this, Abigail (who did not forego breakfast) announced she, too, needed her beauty sleep and left the breakfast table to crawl into bed with her mother. Martha, with a headache and queasy stomach, remained in bed as promised. That left wife number one and her boyfriend to possibly contend with. Mercifully, Janet sent word that she and Senator Daniels would be having breakfast in bed.

That left Gary to enjoy his breakfast with his uncle-in-law McKay, Jack, Blaze, and Max. This morning they dined on blackberry crepes, raspberry tarts, freshly baked croissants, butter, orange juice, and coffee.

"Man, that was some party," declared Jack pouring himself another cup. "Madame P's entrance was *spec-tac-u-lar*! It knocked everyone's socks off, mine included. You two made my producer one very happy man. There are visions of publishing awards dancing around his head."

"Happy New Year!" said Gary sipping his OJ.

"I still can't believe you actually got the Hope Diamond over here on the q.t.," said Jack. "Where is the little sparkler, by the way? Can I hold it for a second?"

Gary shook his head. "Sorry. It's gone."

"What?" Jack stared at Gary in disbelief. "In this snow? It dumped another foot or two of white stuff last night after we turned in."

"Well, it's not here at Versailles anymore. We took care of it right after the ball. A security detail provided by the French Police took the necklace to a local bank that's a few blocks away via the golden carriage. The bank president himself was waiting for it and put the diamond in his vault and shut the door. The police have posted extra guards there until the roads and airport open, and then we'll fly the diamond right back on Air Force One."

"Speaking of airports, any word on when they will open again?" asked Max.

"No telling," said Blaze grimly. "I got a report this morning before coming over. Listen to this. They're saying this is the worst snowstorm in Paris in over a hundred years. Everything is shut down for today and tomorrow, as another round of snow is headed our way."

"Wonderful," said Max sourly. "No one told me to design parkas for the First Family."

Gary laughed heartily. "Don't worry, Max. After last night, your reputation as a designer is quite secure. Martha's and Abigail's blue ball gowns will be the talk of the town."

"Yeah, but with all the roads blocked, I can't get into town to hear what they are saying!"

Jack pushed back his plate and wiped his mouth with his napkin. "Tut, tut. All this talk of doom and gloom—all bad weather and bad press. Look on the bright side, kiddies. The adverse weather has done wonders for Blaze's love life. By the way, how's it going, Casanova? Which one of the young *femme fatales* has captured your poor innocent heart?"

Blaze stared down into his coffee cup miserably.

"I don't know!" he muttered. "I like both of them!"

Jack carefully draped his arm over the back of his chair. "Not good, Blaze, my boy. If you aren't careful, you might end up in a *ménage à trois*."

Blaze frowned. "What does that mean?"

"It's French for one-hell-of-a-mess!"

"Jack, lighten up," ordered Gary as he helped himself to seconds on the blackberry crepes. "You're scaring him."

"What do I do?" asked Blaze with acute frustration. "I mean, on the one hand, Marie is loads of fun. When we're together, we can talk just about anything for hours. The connection is incredible!"

"Sounds promising," said Jack sagely. "Connections are good."

"What about Angelique?" asked Gary.

Blaze sighed. "That's just it. Angelique is so beautiful. She's not talkative like Marie, but then I don't feel the need to talk much around her. Just being with her and looking at her is wonderful. She's so smart and kind of mysterious. There is more to her than meets the eye. And she leaves me wanting to know more!"

"I'd go for fun," recommended Jack authoritatively.

"I'd go for smart and beautiful," said Gary.

"You did go for smart and beautiful," quipped Jack.

"Exactly, "replied Gary happily. "And look where it got me!"

Max looked down at his watch and scowled. "Hate to break this up, boys, but I have a fashion show to put together. You, Blaze, have a press conference to deliver. You, Jack, have cameras to face. And you, Gary, have a cake competition to kick off. So, let's get going."

Gary downed the rest of his orange juice, slipped into his room to quickly kiss his sleeping wife and daughter goodbye, and joined the others outside in the bitter cold. When they arrived at the palace, Blaze left the group briefly to make a phone call to the White House. Ned was expecting an update. When Gary arrived at the Palace, the cake contest was ready to begin officially. Today, the chefs would be constructing the major sections of their baked and iced creations. Gary saw a flurry of activity at all the stations as they readied for the signal to begin. He also found Roland Martin standing in the Hall of Battles with a rack of clothing beside him. He was talking to the Blue Hairs. There seemed to be an acute difference of opinion.

"I'm not wearing pink or red or blue," said Maddie flatly with her arms crossed.

"But you would look lovely in this gown," insisted Roland holding out the crimson sample.

"You can't wear all the black ones," groaned Olivia.

"Be a good sport and wear one other color," begged Gertrude. "Pick one that would look lovely with your complexion."

"How about hot pink, Sugar?" asked Aunt Dotty sweetly pointing to the nightgown. "It's much more sexy."

"I like black," declared Maddie. "Besides, it matches my bag." She lifted an old black leather satchel that looked more like a small suitcase.

"You're impossible," said Eileen in a huff. "Oh, hello, Mr. Craig. Thank heavens you've come. Maybe you can talk some sense into Madeleine. She likes you."

Gary, Max, and Jack greeted the ladies and the French designer.

"What's the problem?" asked Gary.

"Madame Madeleine, she insists on wearing all the black gowns," announced Roland with acute frustration in his voice. "We are at what you call an *impasse.*"

Maddie beamed at Roland's pronouncement. She seemed to like the sound of that.

"Oh, I see. Too bad," said Max disappointedly. He shook his head and sighed. "I was so hoping she would be wearing that red silk gown. It's the best and the most *expensive* one in the collection, you know."

"That red gown?" asked Maddie eyeing it more closely.

"Oh, no, Madame. I can see that your mind is made up. I will not say another word. See. My lips are sealed!" Max made a dramatic motion of zipping shut his mouth and throwing away the key.

"Let me see that gown," demanded Maddie.

Max threw up his hands. "Oh, no. If you want to wear black—cold, traditional, unimaginative, boring black—far be it from me to change your mind. Such a shame, too. The high heel red shoes down there on the rack—Prada, I believe—are a perfect match! Don't you agree, Roland?"

Martin stared at Max open-mouthed, caught on, and quickly agreed.

"Oui, Monsieur. The red shoes, they are stunning. And just her size. As a matter of fact, she could try them on now if she wished."

"Well, Mr. Martin, if Maddie doesn't want it, then I think I'd like to wear that red set," said Aunt Dotty in her best southern drawl. She caught Gary's eye and winked.

"Who said I didn't want to wear it," exclaimed Maddie. "I'm the oldest, and I get to wear the best! Give me those shoes!"

Max smiled at Gary and Jack. "Well, Madame, if you insist. Why don't we pull over a chair so you can sit down and try them on...."

Max's invitation was interrupted by a loud wail. Gary turned and saw Philippe and Monsieur Lavel standing in front of the BBC news platform. The orphan looked like he was about to cry. Beside the boy, Gary could see the famous BBC reporter, Derrick Brown, arguing with Monsieur Lavel. Gary immediately left his group to see what was happening. Jack followed.

"Look, mate, I don't know what all the fuss is about!" said Brown looking annoyed. "It's like this see. I got here early this morning and found that dreadful cat mucking about my platform, playing with the wires. I couldn't have that animal chewing on my cables. Plus, I'm allergic to cats, so I had one of the blokes toss the bloody beast outside. End of story."

"Outside?" shrieked Philippe hysterically. The boy looked up at Gary frantically. Gary was so stunned at the thoughtlessness and cruelty of Brown's actions, he couldn't speak. But Jack could.

Jack stepped forward and took Brown by the arm. "In case you didn't notice, there's a lot of bloody snow outside, you jerk. Not a very humane thing to do to the poor boy's pet. This boy is an orphan, and that cat is all he owns in this world!"

Brown sneered at Jack and pulled his arm away. "Well, we aren't talking about people, are we, mate? It's just a stupid cat, for Christ sake."

"That cat is part of the Versailles family," bellowed Monsieur Lavel furiously stepping into the argument. The old man bravely squared his shoulders. "If anything happens to the cat Sebastian, Monsieur, I'll...I'll..."

"You'll do what?" snapped Brown hatefully. "You're just a glorified butler, old man. You can't hurt me."

"I can," said Jack hotly pushing up his sleeves. "So apologize to Monsieur Lavel and Philippe, or you'll be saying goodbye to your front teeth."

"We must go find Sebastian," cried Philippe near tears as he pulled on Gary's shirt sleeve. "We must hurry!"

Philippe's cries echoed loudly throughout the big hall. People were staring.

"Oh, shut up, you little blighter!" exclaimed Brown, and he smacked Philippe across the face with his hand.

Instantly Gary found his voice. He stepped forward, grabbed Brown, and spun him around. "You touch the boy again, and I'll break your arm," said Gary with a low, threatening growl. Two of Gary's Secret Service team, agents Lewis and Pullman, immediately stepped forward as backup.

Brown stepped back and looked at Gary defiantly. "Think I'm scared of you and your little Secret Service team? Sorry. In case you didn't notice, old chap, I have the press behind me, literally. Which means you, Mr. Madame President, can't lay a bloody finger on me or else we'll splash it across the European headlines. Sorry, mate, but I'm afraid you can't touch me!"

Suddenly, a large black handbag sailed through the air and hit Brown squarely in the groin. The Brit instantly doubled over and fell to his knees in excruciating pain.

"Pardon-moi," said Madeleine. "I must have slipped on that marble floor. Damn these red shoes."

"Oooww," moaned Brown.

Agent Pullman came forward and stood over the writhing BBC reporter. Behind him came Agent Lewis and three other Secret Service men ready to lend a helping hand.

"Perhaps it would be best, Mr. Brown, if you went back to your hotel room to... to recuperate," advised Pullman in an authoritative voice. "We'll escort you out front to the French police, and they shall see to it that you remain in your hotel room for the remainder of the day...to rest." Pullman took Brown by one arm, and another agent grabbed the other, and together they hauled him away. Agent Lewis nodded his head and gave Maddie a rare smile and a little salute.

Philippe looked up at Maddie appreciatively. "Thank you, Madame!"

Maddie protectively put her arm around Philippe's thin shoulders. "We pickpockets must stick together, kid. I don't think Mr. Brown will bother you anytime soon. If he does, you just let me know. Now, let's see what we can do about finding your kitty cat."

Philippe turned and implored Gary. "Will you help me, Monsieur?"

Gary nodded reassuringly at the boy. "Absolutely! Jack, want to help us?"

"I'm in!" said Jack.

"Me, too!" said Blaze rushing up to join them.

Gary looked down at Philippe and took stock of the poor boy's attire. He was not dressed for braving the elements.

"Maddie, why don't you go up with Philippe to his room and help him pick out some more clothes to wear, another pair of socks, a scarf, maybe another shirt. It's very cold outside. I don't want him catching cold."

"But I don't have a scarf, Monsieur," said Philippe.

The honest admission tore at Gary's insides.

This child lived inside a royal palace and literally had nothing to wear.

Max, who had just walked over, resolutely handed over his own expensive black cashmere scarf. "Here, kid, you can have mine. And I'll see what I can do today about getting you a nice new winter coat and gloves to match! My treat."

God bless Max!

Maddie and Philippe left to go upstairs. Gary thanked Max for his kindness, then turned to Monsieur Lavel who looked like he was about to have a stroke. Clearly, Lavel needed to do something to occupy his mind and calm his nerves.

"Monsieur Lavel, once we find Sebastian, I'm sure the cat will be very cold and very hungry. Perhaps you could go to the kitchen and see if something special, something hot, would be ready for him when he returns?"

Lavel's shoulders relaxed. "But of course! I will go and see that cook makes Sebastian's favorite dish — Lobster Newburg!"

"Lobster Newburg?" echoed Jack his eyes widening.

"Oui, Monsieur. Sebastian, he has the discriminating palate!"

Lavel rushed off to attend to Sebastian's lunch.

"That cat," said Jack pointing to Blaze, "eats better than you!"

Just then Ambassador Porter approached and announced there was yet another problem to deal with.

"Josette La Claire is missing," he said gravely. "George Bonnet is quite upset, quite worried. His assistant hasn't shown up, and he hasn't been able to get her on her cell phone. The first round of the competition is set to start in less than a half hour, at 10:00 AM, and is supposed to run for 6 hours. Josette should have been here an hour ago to help him prep."

"Well, isn't it possible that she's just sleeping in or maybe, to be more accurate, sleeping it off?" asked Jack judiciously. "I mean, the girl hasn't shown herself to be the world's most dependable employee, and she was having a pretty good time last night, if you catch my drift."

Ambassador Porter shook his head. "But George insists that whatever Josette's faults were regarding her attitude and her flirtations with men, she is a fierce competitor. He insists she wants to WIN, and she wouldn't show up late."

Gary thought for a moment, recalling when he last saw her. "Well, I saw Josette when we left the Hall of Mirrors. She was standing out on the terrace right after Angelique, Dubois, and Louis went out into the Orangery. I wonder if she followed them outside and got lost? The gardens are huge, and it would be easy to get turned around even during daylight hours."

Blaze added to the worry. "What if she did have too much to drink and then passed out somewhere?"

"And another foot of snow fell last night," added Gary uneasily. If that happened, she would be dead now due to hypothermia. He turned to Agent Lewis. "Did she leave the grounds last night after the ball?"

"No, sir," said Lewis. "We checked the records at the gate. Only the chefs and the members of the G-8 summit and their wives left the grounds last night in their carriages to return to their hotels." The agent cleared his throat. "We assumed... well, we assumed she was spending the night in Trianon with Mr. Phillips."

Blaze shook his head and said candidly. "I ended the evening with Marie Porter."

"Then I think we should contact the French police immediately," ordered Gary. "Get them and the rest of the agents in my detail ready to go outside. While we look for Philippe's cat, we'll also start looking for Mademoiselle Josette. Maybe we'll find something by the time the police get here.'

"Yes, sir," said Lewis. He pulled out his cell phone and stepped away to make the necessary arrangements.

"What about George Bonnet's entry? What is he going to do?" asked Gary with concern. "I'd hate for him to have to withdraw."

Ambassador Porter smiled. "My daughter, Marie, has offered to step in and help until they locate Josette. She's an accomplished pastry chef in her own right, you know. Bonnet was most appreciative."

"She did?" asked Blaze. He looked over at Bonnet's station and gazed in wonder at the little redhead working diligently behind the far right counter.

"So much," whispered Jack to Gary, "for *ménage a trios*."

* * *

Philippe told Gary that Sebastian's favorite garden spots were the Orangery, the Ballroom, the King's Garden, and the Baths of Apollo. Gary informed the French police that he had seen Josette briefly at the end of the ball and thought she must have followed Angelique and Louis south towards the Orangery. Consequently, the police sent the majority of their men in that direction. They also sent a small group north towards the Baths of Apollo. Gary, with his Secret Service detail, and Philippe headed west to check out the other two locations.

First, they walked past the Water Parterre on their way to the Ballroom, a little amphitheater grove with water fountains that cascaded down circular steps into a round pool below. The pool stood frozen, and the waterfalls silent, the steps covered with ice and freshly fallen snow. No cat was in sight. They next searched the surrounding trees in the grove, but again, Sebastian was nowhere around. Gary encouraged Philippe not to give up hope. He firmly took the boy's hand and asked him to lead them to the King's Garden.

Philippe led them out of the Ballroom section, across the avenue, and into the next section of the garden. The boy indicated there were five walkways in this area, all leading towards the Mirror Pond. The walkways were packed with snow, which made walking difficult. Gary directed his team to split up, each taking one of the paths with the plan to meet up at the center pool. Philippe and Jack remained with Gary. They slowly pushed their way up the shortest walkway on the north side. Consequently, they arrived first at the Mirror Pond. There they found Sebastian, sitting on the embankment at the edge of the frozen water. Philippe yelled out Sebastian's name, but the cat did not move. Instead, the cat bent down and licked an object sticking out of the snow.

Something instinctively made Gary grab hold of Philippe.

"Stay here with Jack," he instructed firmly, quickly thinking up an excuse. "The bank might be slippery. I don't want you to get hurt. Let me go down and get Sebastian."

"Hurry!" urged Philippe earnestly.

Gary carefully made his way down the sloping ground and cautiously approached the big gray cat. Sebastian looked up at Gary and meowed. Gary looked down at Sebastian's feet. Projecting out of the deep pile of fresh snow was the thing Sebastian was so carefully guarding.

It was a woman's hand.

Chapter Thirteen

The War Room

Wednesday
January 9, 2002
Twelve noon

They brought the body back to the palace and laid it out in the War Room on a table that had been set up for last night's ball. The War Room was located on the north end of the palace, situated between the Apollo Room and the Hall of Mirrors. Dr. Edward Goldman, White House physician who accompanied the First Family on all overseas trips, agreed to examine the body, as the local medical examiner was stranded somewhere in downtown Paris due to the inclement weather. It didn't take long for Dr. Goldman to conclude that Josette La Claire died due to a blow to the head.

"It appears the blow killed her instantly," said Dr. Goldman. He added thoughtfully, "Which is a blessing. I'd hate to think of this poor girl out there freezing to death."

There was a moment of silence in the room after Dr. Goldman's statement. A muted light fell across Josette's pale face, her white silk dress wet and frozen against her slim body. The stark, gray marble walls surrounding her in the War Room added to the feeling of lifelessness and chill. Josette's eyes were open and staring up at the ceiling. It was hard to look at her, and Gary turned his face away to gaze towards the large oval stucco bas-relief of Louis XIV riding on horseback. The majestic artwork dominated the room in its position above the fireplace.

Gathered around the table in a closed-door meeting were French President Mansart, Ambassador Porter, General McKay, Secretary Campbell, Agent Pullman, Dean Dubois, Monsieur Lavel, Captain Henri Berling of the French National Police, Martha, and Gary.

"How awful," whispered Martha, standing near the table and holding Gary's hand tightly.

"When do you estimate the time of death?" asked the French captain sharply.

The old doctor rubbed his chin thoughtfully. "Again, difficult to say. Normally we can judge time of death by the rate of change in body temperature and the setting in of rigor mortis. But because the body was found outside in this extreme cold, it is hard to tell. It would be like immediately placing a dead body into a deep freezer. We know Mr. Craig saw her at midnight. Tentatively, I would say death occurred somewhere between midnight and perhaps 3:00 A.M."

"So any of the guests out wandering in the gardens after the ball could have done it," declared General McKay grimly.

"Yes, General," said Dr. Goldman. "That would be about right. Oh, I found one other thing, most unusual." The doctor reached for Josette's right hand and raised it up. "Look here at the tip of her index finger."

Everyone stepped closer to look. Gary leaned in and saw that the tip of her finger was stained dark green.

"Frostbite, so soon?" asked Lavel, stepping back and looking horrified.

"No, no. It's a stain—given her profession, I'm guessing it's food coloring."

Gary stared down at the hand, remembering that Josette stole a bottle of green food coloring close to that color the other day from Louis Girard. Gary reminded the group of that fact.

"That is right," confirmed Dean Dubois. "She took a green one for her sugar piece. The sugar construction starts tomorrow, but perhaps, how shall I say it, she tried to get an early start?"

"And someone found out?" asked Secretary Campbell.

"Obviously," murmured Dubois shaking his head.

Agent Pullman stepped forward. "We found a couple more bottles of food coloring in her coat pocket." He held them out in his hand, little bottles sparkling blue and green in the cold sunlight.

The doctor sighed. He gently put Josette's hand down on the table and proceeded to close her eyes and then cover her body with a plain white sheet.

"Tragic," said Dr. Goldman as he removed his blue latex examination gloves. He gathered up his black leather bag and prepared to leave. "I suggest you find the means of getting this body out of the castle and to the morgue as quickly as possible. We must preserve evidence. And frankly, it's not good to have a dead body lying around. I know with the weather conditions outside this is a big order, but it must be done."

"You can use the carriages," said Monsieur Lavel softly. "Actually, we have the funeral carriage of Louis XIII still in the museum. It can carry a body, and we have the horses from last night on the property to pull it."

President Mansart looked worried. "But that means the press will see. They're gathered outside right now at the gates, even in this weather."

"It cannot be helped!" declared the captain. "But the press, you will leave them to me. A death has occurred at Versailles— that they will be told. That a murder has occurred—that they will *not* be told. Not yet. Now, if you will assist, Monsieur Lavel, I'll get our men ready to move the body at once." He turned to Agent Pullman. "I know your primary duty is to protect the president, but could one or two of your men assist our security officers in standing guard over the body until we have made the arrangements?"

"Certainly," said Agent Pullman. "No one will be allowed in this room without your authorization."

"Merci," said Captain Berling. "Now, Monsieur Lavel, if you will be so kind."

The two men left the War Room. Martha then turned to Dubois.

"Dean Dubois, did Josette have any family?"

"Oui, Madame President," said Dubois sadly as he stared down at his dead, former student. "She has a sister living in the south of France. Unfortunately, her parents, they are deceased."

"Then could I ask you to go and locate her sister's phone number. Captain Berling will need it, of course, to notify the next of kin; but once done, I would like to call her sister personally and express my condolences."

Dean Dubois smiled appreciatively at Martha.

"How kind. But of course, I will go and call my office. We have her family information in our records. *Excusez-moi.*"

"I'll go with you, Monsieur Dubois. This has become a matter of state, and I would like to help," offered Secretary Campbell.

Dubois and Campbell left. Once they were alone, Gary looked over at McKay and nodded. The National Security Advisor turned to the French President and spoke.

"President Mansart, we can speak freely. Before the summit, we communicated to you a matter of the greatest secrecy and national importance."

"The Seven," replied Mansart, staring down at the draped lifeless body.

"Yes," said McKay gruffly.

"You think this death, it was done by the ones you seek?"

"I do."

"But why kill her?" queried Mansart. "She is so young and just an assistant. She cannot be the chef you are searching for."

They stood silent for a moment around the table where Josette's body lay. Gary closed his eyes and thought back to the information they obtained from the agent, De Silva. Something suddenly clicked in Gary's brain.

"Maybe she found the jewels De Silva promised The Seven. Josette was very nosy. Remember she snuck around Louis's station and stole that food coloring. Maybe she saw something last night in one of the stations she shouldn't have seen, like the delivery of the emeralds."

"Delivery of the jewels here, in Louis's station?" asked Martha skeptically.

"No, not that," said Gary. "More likely she was in the Hall of Battles stealing more food coloring, and upon leaving, somewhere out in the Orangery or the garden, she witnessed the exchange."

"But no one entered the palace without authorization," countered Agent Pullman.

"Remember De Silva said the emeralds would be delivered to a bank in Paris," added Martha.

Gary huffed. "Okay, scratch that idea. Well, then maybe she overhead The Seven's chef making a phone call, getting the instructions for the delivery."

McKay nodded his head. "That's more like it. And she stepped in and tried a little blackmail on the side. Quite possible. She would be the blackmailing type."

The French president took a deep breath and looked at General McKay.

"Tell me again about The Seven. What do you know about them?"

"The intelligence we have about The Seven was intercepted the day of Martha's wedding," said McKay. "It came to us rather...unexpectedly. The intelligence revealed that The

Seven is a criminal organization of seven individuals — a U.S. senator, a French chef, a Vatican priest, an English lord, a world banker, a U.N. ambassador, and their leader, a man they call the Master."

"Technically, they are the Six now," added Martha, "since Senator David Miller was discovered and took his own life."

"They had another agent who infiltrated the White House and tried to kidnap our daughter, Abigail. Fortunately for us, an agent we placed inside the family residence killed their agent instead."

"I see," said Mansart frowning. "That's why you brought the children here. It was not safe to leave them there?"

"Yes," said Martha. "If they managed to get inside the White House once, they could do it again. I wasn't going to leave my children behind."

"Understood," said the French President. "So one of The Seven is a French chef. You believe it is one of the master chefs at this competition. And he or she is possibly the murderer of this poor girl?"

"Yes," said McKay darkly. "Intelligence we intercepted recently said the chef would be here at this competition."

"So, five teams are competing, ten chefs. With the death of this young woman, that leaves nine suspects, does it not?"

"Correct," said McKay. "So, Captain Berling will need to question all nine as soon as possible."

Mansart looks narrowly at Gary. "Could the Master of The Seven also be here? This Seven sound extremely powerful. Could the Master of The Seven be one of the world leaders? In fact, how do you know it's not me?"

"It's not you or any of the other G-8 leaders," replied McKay with confidence. "We've checked all the outgoing calls placed by Mr. Craig's former assistant, Ryan Adams, who worked for The Seven. None of those calls is linked to any of the G-8 summit leaders, including you. There are records of international calls he made to his wife and other calls to New

York and in the Washington, D.C. area. Unfortunately, those calls were placed to various hotels and public pay phones."

"I see," said Mansart. He paused and then looked over at Martha and McKay. "Perhaps then, in light of what has happened, we should cancel the remainder of the Summit."

"Absolutely not," contradicted McKay. "What good would that do? The airports are closed, and the roads to Paris are still not passable. The leaders and their wives can't leave here even if they wanted to. If anything, they are more at risk coming and going from the palace, especially at night. The murderer struck once and placed a body unobserved in the gardens. He or she could do it again."

"Then what do you suggest?" asked Mansart.

"Well, I have a little idea," offered Gary.

"Oh, good God, no! This is not the time for one of those," snapped McKay.

"On the contrary," said Mansart gazing steadily at the lifeless body of Josette La Claire. "Desperate times call for desperate measures. This, General, appears to be just one of those times."

"I agree," said Martha decisively. "We must act quickly."

"Then with your permission," said Gary hurriedly to the French president, "I think we can do something quite radical, something that will both ensure the safety of the world leaders and also prevent The Seven's French chef from escaping before we can capture him. It will require, however, an historic direct order from you."

Mansart squared his shoulders and lifted his chin with absolute authority.

"Then you shall have it!"

"All right," said Gary. "When Monsieur Lavel returns, we will need floor plans of the palace and a few pencils....."

Chapter Fourteen

The Chapel

Wednesday afternoon
5:00 PM

News concerning Josette's death spread rapidly throughout the palace. Inside the Hall of Battles, the chefs managed to complete their first day of competition in spite of the tragedy. Now, late in the afternoon, the G-8 summit leaders, their wives, the guest artists, and the competing chefs had been asked to gather inside the Chapel. Around the room, there were various looks of shock, uncertainty, and disbelief. George Bonnet stood apart from the crowd, his hands over his mouth, his head bent over in a confused mix of emotions. Paul Dubois stood next to him, his paternal arm stalwartly around the shaken chef. Angelique stood on Bonnet's other side, her small hand resting gently on his shoulder. Also present were the designers, Max and Roland, and the Blue Hairs. They stood huddled in a small circle, whispering quietly among themselves. Aunt Sophie and the General stood guard next to the children. Abigail didn't fully understand what was happening, but there was a look of great concern on young Philippe's face. Gary could tell Philippe was not afraid. The only face in the room showing neither signs of grief nor strain belonged to Janet. She sat dismally in a chair, looking very annoyed for having been forced out of bed and into the cold alone. General McKay and Secretary Campbell had insisted that Senator Daniels quietly move to the nearest hotel to act as their external liaison with the French Government during the crisis. Thus, Senator Daniels had left Versailles literally on foot, trudging through the deep snow, bags in hand. But no surprise to Gary, Janet resolutely remained behind. His ex-wife wasn't going anywhere.

The only press allowed in the room was Jack minus his cameraman, Al. The rest of his CNN news team and the other two groups of television reporters were anxiously waiting for word in the Hall of Battles. Jack fiddled with his cell phone. He had been firmly instructed by Gary to NOT relay any information to Washington until after this meeting. Jack looked over at Gary and reluctantly put his cell phone back into his pants pocket with a sigh. Washington would have to wait a few more minutes.

President Mansart, Captain Berling, Martha, and Gary stood at the head of the rectangular summit table. Gary's thoughts were racing, and mentally he tried to calm himself down. His proposal was a good one, and he and Martha had made the necessary contacts before bringing everyone together. After Mansart had given his approval, Gary and Martha made two important phone calls. Martha called the White House and briefed Ken Friedman on the situation. Ken would alert the folks at CIA while McKay handled communications directly with the FBI, NSA, the Secret Service, and the Department of Defense. Ken would also assist Blaze in briefing the reporters at the White House Press Room once this meeting was over. Meanwhile, Gary called Mildred in downtown Paris to fill her in on the situation and to check on the other two children. Mildred reported that Eliza and Josh were fine, albeit a bit bored to death at being cooped up in their hotel room and lonely for their parents. Gary reassured Mildred that they would be brought to Versailles as soon as it was safe. He then talked to Eliza and Joshua, instructing them to be careful and telling them he loved them. He handed the phone to Martha, and she did the same.

Thus the stage was set. Monsieur Lavel and two of his staffers appeared in the room. Lavel gave an affirmative nod of the head, and President Mansart cleared his throat to begin the briefing.

"Mesdames and Messieurs, thank you for coming at short notice. I apologize for the interruption of your leadership meeting and pastry competition. I will get straight to the point. No doubt you have heard the terrible news. Today, the body of Josette La Claire was discovered in the gardens. She was immediately brought back here, and Madame President's physician, Dr. Edward Goldman, examined the body. It is his medical opinion that Mademoiselle La Claire was murdered."

The crowd stood in shock at the news. Death was one thing. Murder was another.

"Oh, how ghastly!" exclaimed Adelaide Foster. "The poor girl! She was just a child."

"God rest her soul," whispered René Michel softly while crossing himself.

Pierre Rousseau looked visibly shaken at the news, and Claude Breton's face turned ashen. Gary looked over at the female chefs. Isabelle was crying. Camille Aumont was grimly silent, her lips pressed hard together, her eyes facing downward. She looked angry, not sad.

"Do you know who did it?" asked Dean Dubois boldly, his arm still protectively around Bonnet.

President Mansart sadly shook his head. "No, mon ami, we do not. However, we hope to take action that will quickly solve the crime. May I introduce to you Captain Berling of the French National Police, who will be conducting the investigation. Captain Berling?"

"Investigation?" It was Beatrice Woods Yutaka who loudly spoke up out of turn, much to her husband's dismay. He gave her a disapproving look which she ignored. "But surely, Captain, surely you don't believe anyone here killed that poor girl. You see, none of us really knew her." She glanced around the room at the other leaders and their wives for confirmation. "Someone from outside, an old boyfriend perhaps, must have entered the palace last night and did her in!"

Captain Berling stepped forward. "Mais non, Madame. No one was allowed onto the palace grounds last night. Of this, we are most certain. So, unfortunately, that does mean someone here at Versailles is responsible for her death, someone perhaps in this very room."

This official pronouncement drew a swift reaction from the crowd. There were gasps of disbelief and looks of suspicion and outrage. The most outraged was Janet.

"This is ridiculous," said Janet haughtily as she stood and pulled her thick fur coat tightly around her waist. "Why would anyone want to kill her? She was a mere cook, a rather pretty girl I will admit, but nothing more. This obviously has nothing to do with me. So, if you don't mind, I'm going back to bed!"

Instantly, two of Captain Berling's men came forward and promptly assisted Janet back to her seat.

"Not yet, Madame. You will stay until I say you can go. Since you have chosen to stay at the castle, you will not be permitted to leave until the investigation concludes."

"And what about us?" asked Prime Minister Foster indignantly. "Dash it all! Are you suggesting that one of the summit leaders or their wives had anything to do with this sordid affair? It's preposterous!"

"Alan, do be quiet," whispered Adelaide impatiently.

"No, Prime Minister," answered Pierre darkly. "He doesn't mean you. He means us. Isn't that right, Captain Berling? You believe, Monsieur, it was one of the chefs who killed Josette."

Captain Berling stared at Pierre narrowly and nodded his head.

"Yes, that is what we think."

Suddenly Camille burst out, "It is discrimination to suspect only us, n'est-ce pas? Those of us who disliked her will be unfairly examined."

"Dislike?" said Gerald almost laughing. "You didn't dislike her, Camille. You hated her!"

Camille cast a wicked smile at Gerald. "There are others here who hated her, too. And I know their reasons, their secrets!"

"Enough!" shouted Captain Berling. "Please, Mesdames! Messieurs! Calm down. There will be time tomorrow morning to talk, I assure you."

"Tomorrow morning? Captain, do you expect us to carry on under these circumstances? The summit must end immediately!" shouted Chancellor Herrman. "We will take our wives and leave this place before one of us is murdered, too!"

Several of the other leaders nodded their heads in swift agreement.

"And where will you go?' asked Captain Berling softly while turning his head towards the irritated Chancellor. "The airport, it is closed and will remain closed for at least two more days. The main roads have drifts of snow ten feet high. No traffic at all. The drifts are even higher on the train tracks. No trains are running between Versailles and Paris. I and my men, fortunately, were stationed in the nearby hotel for the summit or otherwise, we would not be here. Senator Daniels had trouble just walking across the street to the nearest hotel, which is full. You cannot leave, Chancellor."

Chancellor Herrman's face grew dark. "Then we will leave the palace like Senator Evans and return to our hotel rooms."

"And will you be safer there?" countered Captain Berling candidly. "How do you know this murderer acted alone? Might he or she have accomplices outside the gates, at the hotel, waiting for you to leave the security around the palace? Will any of you be safer apart? If you split up, our protection, it will be spread thin. Will murder end with Josette La Claire?"

"Captain Berling?" asked Natasha Voronova, who spoke some rudimentary English, "you have not said motive. Why did girl die?"

Captain Berling frowned. "It is too early to say. For now, you must trust us with your security as we try to solve this crime. President Mansart, Madame President, and I believe that you will be safer here inside the palace together in one group. So, we suggest that the summit, the competition, and the fashion show go forward as scheduled. For that to happen and for us to provide you with the maximum security possible, Mr. Craig has made what you might call a historical and imaginative proposal, one which President Mansart and Monsieur Lavel have both approved. I will let Mr. Craig have the honor of revealing to you the details. Mr. Craig?"

The Captain stepped back allowing Gary to come forward with his map, which he spread out on the table. Gary looked up at Jack who gazed at him wide-eyed and open-mouthed. Jack knew something BIG was about to happen, and his cell phone was out again. Gary shook his head. Reluctantly, Jack grimaced and put it back. Gary took out his pencil and made a startling announcement.

"The best way to isolate the killer and to protect the innocent at the same time is to sequester everyone inside the palace. So, with President Mansart and Monsieur Lavel's permission, all of you will be moved into the palace immediately."

There wasn't a sound in the room. No one moved, no one spoke, not even Jack. Philippe, however, looked ecstatic. He would have houseguests!

Gary smiled at the orphan and continued. "This means no one can leave the castle until the summit ends and the police catch the murderer. We hope to solve the crime in the next 48 hours, before the roads, train service, and airports reopen."

"Good Lord! You mean we will actually live inside the palace?" asked Prime Minister Foster incredulously.

"That's exactly what we mean. Monsieur Lavel with his staff, most of them local people who can walk here, with help from Captain Berling's men and our snowmobiles and carriages, have agreed to come and assist us. They shall live here, too."

Suddenly, feelings of excitement began to spread across the room. Gary was not surprised to see that Beatrice Woods Yukata and Janet looked the most enthusiastic at his proposal.

Gary provided one more detail. "Additionally, to prevent the murderer from contacting any accomplices outside the palace gates, all communication from inside the castle will be strictly forbidden. That means everyone will turn in all of their cell phones and laptop computers immediately. This includes all communication devices belonging to the summit leaders."

President Gallo exclaimed, "But you said, Mr. Craig, that none of the world leaders were suspects in this case! Why should we hand over our phones and computers?"

"Because having phones and computers would put you at risk," answered Captain Berling gravely. "If the murderer becomes desperate to make contact with the outside world and you had a cell phone, he or she might kill you to steal your phone or computer from you."

"Very well," said President Gallo reluctantly. He bent his head over and whispered something to his wife in Italian.

"But what if there were an emergency in our own country that required our immediate attention," asked Prime Minister Foster. "Are we to remain in isolation?"

"General McKay and Captain Berling will have all the cell phones and computers stored at the Queen's Hamlet. In case of emergency, any of your governments will contact them directly and, they in turn, will allow you to communicate with your governments. Remember this situation will last only two or three days at most."

"But will not this danger, this situation, draw the world's attention?" asked Canadian Prime Minister Laurant. "There could be utter chaos."

"They already know about the death. One of the palace's historical coaches already transported Josette's body from the palace. The reporters were outside the gates when the coach left. However, we will not announce that her death was murder," replied Gary. "Not now, at least. So, that means NO press." He stared at Jack directly. Jack scowled.

"But surely, won't the reporters at the gates notice us all moving inside the palace?" asked Foster.

"Yes, and the cover story for the historic move will be the historic weather, which is partly true. Now," said Gary looking down at his blueprint, "we have assigned the rooms. Except in two cases, these were randomly assigned. I'll let Monsieur Lavel make the announcements."

Lavel came forward and stood beside Gary. He had some photocopied papers which he handed over to his staffers to distribute. Gary paused and admired this great man. Lavel had not hesitated at their request but instantly had gone to work in making the mammoth arrangements. Gary wondered how Lavel must be feeling, to see Versailles opening up and becoming a functioning home once again.

"The first assignment was made purposely. Madame Foster, since you bear the name of Adelaide, we have given you and your husband Mademoiselle Adelaide's apartment on the ground floor."

"Oh, how lovely!" said Adelaide graciously.

"If you will consult the drawings that we have passed out, you will see that this apartment consists of three rooms—a bedroom, a private cabinet, and a state cabinet. We will make accommodations in the state cabinet room for your security to sleep there."

"Quite right," confirmed Prime Minister Foster. He vigorously nodded his head in approval.

Lavel continued. "The other ground floor assignments, they are as follows:

Germany will take Madame Victoire's suite.

Italy will have the Dauphine's apartments.

Russia will have the Dauphin's apartments.

On the first floor of the palace, Japan will have Louis XV's bedchamber.

Canada will have the King's bedchamber and adjoining rooms.

France will have the bedchamber in the Mercury Room plus access to the Apollo Room."

"There are additional rooms for each location in which your assistants and staff may stay. You are to give Captain Berling the names of your support staff before moving in. If possible, we would like to restrict the number of staff for each nation to five."

Lavel then turned and smiled radiantly at Martha. "And for you, Madame President, we have assigned the Queen's bedchamber, including the State Cabinet and all of the Queen's private rooms. For Mademoiselle Abigail, she will have the bed in the blue Meridian Cabinet. We will put her maid, Gabrielle, in the Duchesse de Bourgogne's Cabinet which is beside the Meridian Cabinet."

"She gets Marie Antoinette's room?" objected Janet loudly. "That's not fair. You said that room was unavailable! I wanted it first!"

"Madame," said Lavel with obvious pleasure, "These decisions are most fair and based on, how shall I put it, the seniority? Surely you cannot dispute that the Queen's bedroom should rightly go to Madame President? Is she not the most high-ranking woman in this room?"

Janet opened then closed her mouth tightly. She threw a hateful glance at Gary which he pretended not to see.

Suddenly Philippe exclaimed, "Abigail! You will come and live in the palace with me! Come! I will show you your room!"

"He lives in the palace?" echoed Adelaide Foster. "Why, how extraordinary!" She turned and smiled approvingly upon Philippe.

"Can I, Papa Gary? Please?" asked Abigail excitedly.

"Okay," said Gary. "But Agents Lewis and Harkin will go with you. Philippe, keep an eye on her."

"Oh, yes, Monsieur, I will!"

Philippe took Abigail's hand, and they headed for the back of the Chapel. The happy children stopped momentarily at Jack. Abigail suddenly gave Jack a big hug, and so did Philippe. Grinning, Jack playfully patted each child on the top of the head and shooed them away. Once the children had gone, the crowd turned to Lavel for more specifics.

"All of the chefs, including Dean Dubois and his assistant, will be staying in rooms in the South Wing near the Hall of Battles. Since the teams of chefs are suspects in the case, Captain Berling has restricted their movements to the South Wing except during meal times when they will have access to the dining rooms on the first floor. For security, the Secret Service and officers of the French National Police will be guarding the passageway between the Hall of Battles and the rest of the palace. We assigned those officers to rooms on the north side of the ground floor in the Captain of the Guard's apartment. The male artists, they will stay in Marie Antoinette's original apartments on the ground floor. And finally, we will ask the artist, Babette Moreau, to stay in the south wing in Madame de Maintenon's apartment, which is near the Queen's bedroom."

"Merci," said Babette quietly.

"Unbelievable," whispered Roland looking astounded at the invitation.

"Ambassador Porter and his daughter, Secretary Campbell, and Madame Benson-Craig will remain at the Petit Trianon."

Janet let out an audible groan.

Lavel gave her a rare smile.

"The — models — for the fashion show will be given rooms at the Grand Trianon."

"I want a room near the bathroom," demanded Maddie.

Laughter erupted in the room.

Lavel blushed. "Oui, Madame. I will arrange it. To continue, General McKay and his wife, Madame Johnson McKay, will remain at the Queen's Hamlet. That leaves Monsieur Parish and his news team. They will also be moved into the palace and share rooms with Philippe upstairs in Madame DuBarry's suite."

Jack's mouth dropped open for the second time. Gary hoped this honor would make up for the cell phone restrictions.

"But what about food and linens and well, I don't know how to put this delicately, but what about facilities?" asked Adelaide Foster.

Lavel smiled reassuringly. "Do not be troubled, Madame. Our kitchens are well stocked with supplies. There is enough food for the summit in the restaurants which normally serve our tourists. Also, as mentioned previously, our local chefs and staff have agreed to come and stay as well. Believe me, they are most excited to be part of history, also. They will have rooms in the north wing and outer surrounding buildings. For linens, towels, soaps, and other toiletries, we have put out a call to nearby shops for necessary purchases. I've spoken with several local businessmen. Shop owners know me and will assist."

"And facilities?" asked Adelaide politely.

"There are modern toilets located throughout the palace. Not all are near the rooms. However, we are providing maps with a handout with the facilities clearly marked. For bathing, however, you will have to rely on old-fashioned bowls and pitchers. Freshwater will be brought to you daily. And—," Lavel cleared his throat with modesty, "we will provide chamber pots to those who request them."

Despite that inconvenience, the thrill of being able to live inside one of the world's most famous palaces began to sink in. People started to whisper back and forth excitedly. Lavel concluded his remarks and turned the floor back to Captain Berling.

"We ask all of you," said Captain Berling, "to immediately go to your assigned rooms with your staff. The leaders may use their cell phones and laptops for the next hour to make the necessary arrangements with their respective governments. However, we ask all the chefs to immediately turn in their cell phones as they leave the Chapel. They are to turn in their laptop computers immediately as well. Captain Berling's men will follow them to their rooms and retrieve them now. My men will assist each of you in checking out of your hotels and bringing your belongings here to the palace. Monsieur Lavel's staff will assist you in settling in. Tomorrow morning, we will begin interviewing each of the chefs, and tomorrow afternoon and evening, the pastry competition will proceed as planned. This meeting is now concluded."

Gary waited for the summit leaders and the rest of the crowd to leave before going over to speak to Jack.

"Well, "said Gary, "Say something!"

"Words fail me," replied the flabbergasted reporter. "Never in my wildest dreams did I ever think I'd be camping out in Madame du Barry's boudoir. If only I had packed my silk pajamas."

"Stop it," said Gary, "or I'll send you back to the Petit Trianon to stay with Janet."

"Threats? After all I've done for you?"

Gary smiled at his friend. "Lavel must really like you, for he gave you one of the most interesting parts of the palace to stay. Have you looked at that map? Louis XV created those attic suites for his private use. None of his noblemen were ever allowed up there. It's a veritable maze of rooms, with laboratories and workshops, libraries and kitchens, bedrooms and bathrooms..."

Jack's eyebrows shot up. "Bathrooms? Oh, thank God. I'm too young for a chamber pot."

Gary continued unsympathetically. "Listen, you said you wanted to live like a king. Well now, here's your chance!"

Jack finally grinned. "My producer is going to absolutely die, you know. Can I call him now and get his reaction before you take my precious cell phone away?"

"Go ahead, but make it brief. And make it crystal clear he can't release any information until Ned back at the White House gives his briefing! This is your last call, by the way. I get your phone after you are done," said Gary laughing.

Jack reached down and put his hand in his pocket. A startled look crossed his face.

"What the heck? It's gone!"

"What's gone?"

"My cell phone. I put it right here in my pants pocket. But it's not there now!"

Suddenly Gary felt frightened.

"You don't think the murderer took it, do you?" exclaimed Gary.

"No," assured Jack. "None of the chefs came near me during the briefing or when they exited."

Another thought came to Gary, equally distressing

"You're right. It wasn't the chefs. Think, Jack."

Jack's eyes narrowed as he concentrated. Then his eyes widened in enlightenment.

"The kids? All that hugging? You mean one of the kids lifted my phone?"

"I'm afraid so," said Gary. He bent his head and rubbed his forehead. He was getting a royal headache.

"One of the children picked your pocket." Gary looked up with exasperation. "The trouble is — which one?"

Chapter Fifteen

Notre Dame and the Porcelain Dining Room

**Wednesday evening
7:00 P.M.**

*C*arlos De Silva stood inside Notre Dame Cathedral, bundled
up in his winter coat. He quietly lit a candle. His hands were
freezing as he held a burning stick over the white wax and
touched the curled blackened wick. He observed this ritual not for
the welfare of some other poor soul but for his own welfare, of which
stood in need this dark winter night.

He looked around the nearly deserted church and shivered.

It was freezing inside the enormous cathedral, so cold that his
very bones ached. The black and white tiled floor was cold. The
wooden chairs inside the Nave were cold. The air inside the church
was cold. It was almost too cold to breathe.

Why was he here, Carlos questioned himself bitterly, as he
gazed down at the table covered with votive candles in red and blue
glass containers? The candlelight barely illuminated this part of the
darkened church. Shadows danced eerily around him, and it made
him nervous. He should be back in his warm hotel room, dressed
in his black silk pajamas, enjoying a glass of red wine and a Cuban

cigar. But, no, a single phone call had sent him outside and straight here. Thankfully, his hotel was nearby, and the city had managed to clear some sidewalks in this section of the Latin Quarter. At least it was not snowing now. However, another snowstorm was forecasted to start after midnight, and Carlos prayed this meeting would not last long. He wanted to get back to his hotel before the damn snow began falling again.

Carlos left the candles and went to sit miserably in one of the many chairs set up in the Nave. He swallowed hard and focused his troubled mind on staying warm. An organ was playing softly. Carlos saw a few of the faithful, an old priest and three elderly nuns, way up front near the altar, kneeling in obedience and saying their prayers.

He marveled at their presence.

Such devotion.

Such faith.

Carlos had no faith, not anymore. True he was born and raised a Catholic. He attended Mass faithfully as a small boy, and he attended Catholic school. His mother even hoped her son would one day aspire to the priesthood. But her son's aspirations rose not to heaven but eventually descended in the opposite direction, down into the dark world of the Columbian drug cartel, who now owned him body and soul. What soul? Any light, any decency that was once in Carlos De Silva's spirit had long ago been extinguished.

Suddenly, there was a harsh rush of frigid night air inside the church, and the sound of feet swiftly approaching. Carlos turned and saw a man in a dark wool coat coming towards him. The man greeted him and sat down.

"It is a night for prayer and contemplation," said De Silva in English, the memorized line he had been instructed to say.

"May joy come in the morning," answered the man.

Carlos relaxed slightly at hearing the correct reply. Excellent! His contact was punctual and hopefully would be brief. The sooner this meeting was over, the sooner he could return to the comfort of his bed.

"Who are you?" asked Carlos nervously.

"Wait," ordered the man as he pulled something out of his pocket. It was long and silver. "We are in a house of God. I must first pay respect." The man bent his head, crossed himself, and began mouthing the ritualistic words of prayer while fingering the thing in his hand.

Praying a rosary? Now? Carlos sighed impatiently. There was not the time to pray a whole rosary! Carlos shifted in his chair and turned his gaze towards the old nuns praying by the altar. The only prayer Carlos could think of at this moment was a petition to God for this meeting to come to a quick conclusion. Finally, the man beside him crossed himself again and spoke.

"You were not followed?" asked the man quietly as put his hands into his pockets.

Carlos shook his head emphatically. "There is no one outside tonight, not even police. I was the only one on the street."

"I had to ask," said the man. He looked up at the altar and grimaced. "But we are not alone."

Carlos shrugged. "Just some old nuns. Don't worry. They are probably deaf and will not bother us. Now, what is it you want?"

The man continued to stare serenely at the altar.

"We are in a church, Mr. De Silva. Please whisper. You have heard the airport is closed?"

"Of course," snapped Carlos irritably. "What does that matter?"

"The Master of The Seven wants to know if the closing of the airport prevented the delivery of the emeralds."

Carlos smiled with satisfaction. "No, señor. The emeralds arrived early, very early in fact."

"They did?" The man's voice echoed his surprise. "We did not know this."

"The emeralds are here in Paris, safely stored inside the bank's vault. I put them there myself." Carlos nervously fingered a small package in his right coat pocket, a small envelope which contained three large emeralds he had kept for himself. Why not? There were so many stones in the delivery package from South America. No one would miss three.

"That is good news indeed," said the man. "And the information we need to access the safe deposit box? Do you still have it?"

Carlos felt himself getting angry. He hated having his abilities questioned.

"Of course not! Do you think I don't know how to do my job? I am professional! I do what I am told! I take all necessary precautions! I put the emeralds in the bank when they arrived. Then, this morning as instructed, I emailed the account number to The Seven's chef at Versailles. The chef should have the information. Then, I destroyed all the evidence. That is what I was told to do. That is what I did. The chef knows this. If you doubt me, ask the chef yourself!"

"I cannot," was the cool reply. "Something has happened inside the palace. We cannot reach the chef by phone or email, so we did not know that the emeralds arrived early. And as we on the outside cannot communicate with the chef, we cannot access the account."

"That is not my problem. I did my job."

The man turned, smiled at him, and stood up.

"Thank you, monsieur. You have indeed done your job. And now, it is time I did mine."

Before Carlos could speak, the hands came out again, and the long silver object was wrapped tightly around Carlos's neck.

It was not a rosary.

It was a chain.

Carlos was right.

The nuns were quite deaf.

They did not hear a thing.

* * *

Thursday morning
Jan 10, 2002

When Gary opened his eyes early Thursday morning, all the glare bouncing off the gilding inside the royal bedroom momentarily blinded him.

Waking up in the Grand Trianon was one thing.

Waking up in Marie Antoinette's bedchamber was quite another.

This would take some getting used to.

Everything inside the historic room seemed as if covered in gold—the balustrade at the foot of the bed (which split the room in half—the public half and the private half), the large mirror hanging over a black marble fireplace, the furniture (which included chairs, small stools, and a large jewelry cabinet), the window frames, the crown moldings, and the sculpted reliefs on the ceiling. The walls were painted pristine white, adding to the brightness of the surroundings.

Gary yawned and gazed up at the wall behind the bed and the recreated "summer furnishings"—the rich fabrics woven, painted, and embroidered with pink and white roses. Splashes of light teal leaves were also woven into the fabric's design, providing a pleasant contrast to the pink floral print. These elegant fabrics covered the bed, the chairs, the stools, and the curtains and were used in the wall tapestries.

Gary felt Martha stirring beside him.

"You awake?" he asked lazily, stretching and reaching out for her.

"Hmm," was the muffled reply. Martha's face was half hidden in the middle of an overstuffed pillow. She was curled up in a ball below a very thick down comforter that had been placed over the recreated bedspread, a gift from a kind Parisian storekeeper. Gary marveled how quickly the news of opening Versailles to the summit leaders spread throughout the neighboring streets. Shopkeepers, it appeared, also wanted to be a part of history, to be a part of *their* palace returning to life. Despite the snow-filled streets and bitterly cold temperatures, dozens of the local townspeople and merchants walked up to the palace gates. They handed over cut wood, coal, linens, pillows, blankets, toiletries, bottled water, porcelain basins, freshly baked breads, cheese, pastries, candles, flashlights, fireplace tools, and (most importantly) toilet paper. Some presented themselves with suitcases in hand and the offer to stay and work inside the castle, providing relief to Lavel's overworked support staff. All of this was caught on camera by frozen yet enthusiastic reporters ready to pounce on the unfolding, unbelievable story.

It had been a well-timed miracle, frankly, that last summer, Monsieur Lavel, in an attempt to do a thorough cleaning of the palace, had the foresight to have all the old fireplaces cleaned and restored to actual working order. Gary glanced over and gratefully saw a fire lit in the fireplace. Warmth filled the room.

"How are you feeling?" asked Gary.

"A bit overwhelmed," said Martha as her head popped up from the pillow and blankets. She stared up at the feathered canopied headpiece that hung majestically over the bed. "I really can't believe where we are."

"My ex-wife can't believe it, either," replied Gary chuckling.

"She'll have to get over it," said Martha yawning.

"You know, sweetheart, since meeting you, I've had some pretty incredible experiences, but this one is way, way over the top. This room has so much history. Do you know how many royal children of France were born in this very room?"

Awake, Martha stretched herself out on the royal bed. "Nineteen! Lavel has been telling me stories, too. And it was all done in public! Can you imagine that? Hundreds of people came and sat down over there on the other side of the balustrade and watched the *Royal Birth*. What a horrible requirement for the Queen! I had a nightmare about giving birth. It was very painful, and I was fighting hard against the contractions!"

"That would explain why you kicked me in the shins in the middle of the night," replied Gary.

"I'm sorry, dear," said Martha. She reached over and grabbed Gary's hand and pulled it close to her chest.

Gary sighed. "It's okay. As long as you don't take up kickboxing, I'll survive. You know, other Queens called this room their own. Lavel told me about the Spanish bride of Louis XIV, Marie-Theresa. Did you know she and her husband were double first cousins?"

Martha yawned again and buried her head beneath the blankets. "I know. Poor girl. She was stuck in a political marriage so France and Spain could share their wealth and form alliances during times of war. That might explain why King Louis had so many mistresses," she muttered as she settled back in.

"Exactly. Lavel listed them for me. One mistress was named Louise. She was the first mistress — young, devoted, and a bit innocent. She ended up a very rich nun. Then there was the blonde Marquise de Montespan. There was nothing innocent or religious about her at all! She reveled in her position and all its 'fringe benefits.' You know the Blue and White Porcelain Palace that Chef Michel is creating? Louis XIV built that palace for her, a secret place for them to rendezvous. She also eventually fell by the wayside. There was a brief fling with another blonde named Angelique (a popular name around here). Finally, there was Madame Maintenon, the King's secret wife in his later years. She actually began as a governess to the King's bastard children by Montespan, but Maintenon ended up his best friend, someone he truly depended upon."

"I don't think I like all this talk about mistresses," was the reply from beneath the blanket. "Don't let any wayward ideas enter that creative head of yours or I *will* take up kickboxing!"

Gary laughed. "My shins and my heart won't let me stray. What's on your schedule for today?"

"Meetings, meetings, and more meetings. And you? Are you ready for the police interviews with the chefs? I've given Captain Berling instructions for you to be present on my behalf."

Gary nodded. Given Gary's history with The Seven, Martha requested that Gary sit in on the interrogations as a U.S. representative. "We're supposed to start after breakfast. Then I'll have lunch with Abigail."

"Did the little thief tell you where Jack's cell phone is?"

"No, she's being very tight-lipped on that subject."

"She wouldn't tell me either. None of my usual bribes worked. How is Jack faring being cut off from the modern world?"

"He's not. He's a reporter. Without his phone, he's a fish out of water. I reminded him he would have had to turn his cell phone over anyway, but that didn't seem to help."

Martha sighed and rolled over on her side.

"Well, he's not the only one complaining. The leaders are, too, especially their spouses. Rose Gallo was very upset because she wants to stay in touch with her children. She has five. Natasha Voronova was upset because she wanted to stay in touch with her mother. She calls her mother every day. And Beatrice Yutaka complained the loudest, I think, simply because she likes to complain. She's a lot like your Janet."

"Janet is not my Janet anymore."

Martha ignored Gary's protest. "Adelaide Foster wasn't complaining, thank goodness. Such a wonderful woman! But her husband, Alan, was still murmuring when we took his phone away. Secretary Campbell wasn't very pleased with me, either, when we took his cellphone and laptop computer. He wants to stay in close touch with Violet, especially after all her health problems this past year. I don't blame him."

Gary frowned. "Well, I guess we could make an exception in his case. I mean he is Secretary of State."

"No," said Martha firmly. "McKay and I are sticking to the rules. And besides, if George wants to call his wife or needs to speak to his office back in D.C., he only has to ask. He'll be fine. It's only for a few days. The person who is really raising holy hell is guess who?"

"How many guesses do I get?"

"Three. And the first four don't count."

"Let's see. Janet, Janet, Janet, Janet, and Janet?"

"You must be psychic."

"Perhaps we should make your ex-wife move over to the hotel with Senator Evans."

"No. She'd just complain even more until she weaseled her way back inside the palace," predicted Martha with another yawn.

"True. Well, I'll deal with her this afternoon during the second half of the pastry competition. Speaking of food, you hungry?"

"A little. Pastry sounds good although I really shouldn't indulge. My pants and skirts are beginning to fit too tight. I'm going to ask Max to adjust the buttons on my clothes this morning, and I'm starting a major diet when we get home."

Gary laughed and patted his own burgeoning waistline. "Tell me about it. I'm packing on the pounds as well. I'll join you in that diet, but not until I've had some more of those raspberry tarts! Now, let's see if I can find us some hot coffee for starters."

Gary sat up and dangled his legs over the side of the bed. It was then he discovered they were not alone. He saw the big grey cat, Sebastian, sitting sentinel near at the foot of the bed.

"How did you get in here?" asked Gary.

The long night over, the guardian feline blinked his wide eyes at Gary and then sashayed out of the room.

It was time to eat.

* * *

After the First Family had breakfast in the blue and white Porcelain Dining Room, Martha kissed her husband and children good-bye and left for her morning round of summit meetings. The maid, Gabrielle, complained of a headache and asked to be excused. Philippe and Abigail announced their intentions of exploring the King's upstairs rooms, and the artist, Babette, announced she would go with them to sketch the children at play. The artist, Tom Parker, along with Agents Lewis and Harkin and three other Secret Service men, would be joining them. Palace staff appeared and quickly cleared the large square wooden table. Captain Berling and his assistant, Colbert, arrived for the morning interrogations. Berling bid Gary a good morning and then complained about the snow. Another foot had fallen during the night, and the wind had blown up more snow drifts. He introduced his young associate, and they quickly got down to business.

The first chef to be interviewed was Pierre Rousseau. The tall man appeared as imperturbable as ever. However, Gary thought there was something queer in his facial expression that morning, something a bit contrived. Pierre entered the room and lazily sat in one of the teal-blue velvet chairs. Captain Berling wasted no time in getting started.

"Bonjour, Monsieur. Thank you for coming. Since Monsieur Craig is here, we will conduct our interview in English."

"But of course," said Pierre, flashing a smile in Gary's direction.

"Now, your name please," said Berling. Both the Captain and his assistant had a pad of paper and pen on the table, and both were ready to take notes.

Pierre looked at the policeman a bit annoyed. Pierre was famous in his own mind and thought everyone else should be equally aware of his fame.

"Pierre Rousseau."

"And where do you live?"

"Here in Paris in the Latin Quarter. I own my own restaurant."

"How nice. Now tell me, Monsieur Rousseau, did you know the victim, Josette La Claire?"

Pierre shifted slightly in his chair.

"Josette? No, not very well. I heard of her before the competition, of course. We both have ties to Dean Dubois's school. I taught there, she was a student, but she was very young and not my type."

"Yes, of course," said Captain Berling scribbling on his notepad. "She was not your type." He picked it up and studied it carefully. "Nevertheless, I understand from my preliminary discussion with the palace staff yesterday evening that you were seen at the reception talking to Mademoiselle La Claire and dancing with her after dinner as well." Captain Berling paused and gazed at Pierre intently. "You were being very attentive to someone you claim you did not know well."

Pierre shifted again in his chair and casually shrugged his shoulders. "I pitied the girl. She looked lonely at the ball. That was her fault. She was a talented chef, yes, but she was a devil to work with. She had a reputation, Monsieur. She was not liked here by some of the chefs, nor was she well liked in town. I understand from Camille that Josette was having a hard time getting work. So I asked her to dance."

"Very kind of you," said Gary.

Pierre looked over at Gary appreciatively and continued. "I pitied George Bonnet for having to work with her. George is a good chef, very hard-working, very opinionated. So, I do not understand why he chose to bring her of all people here to the competition as his assistant."

"A mystery we hope to solve," replied Berling coolly. "Now, after the dinner, tell us about your whereabouts."

Pierre took a deep breath and gazed upwards toward the gold and crystal chandelier hanging over the table.

"Let me think. As you said, I danced with Josette at the ball. I danced with several young ladies. Then about 11:00 PM, I walked down the Royal Avenue with my assistant, Antoine, and Isabelle Velleneau. She is a beauty, that one. I like her very much. We stayed in the heated tent for almost an hour and had cocktails."

Berling turned to Gary. "Can you verify that, Monsieur Craig?"

"Yes," said Gary. "I saw Pierre and Isabelle talking together at the tent."

"Very good. Tell me, Monsieur Rousseau, did you three leave the tent together?"

"No," said Pierre quickly. "Antoine left us before midnight. He was not feeling well. About 12:30, Isabelle and I decided to walk around the north end of the gardens before going back to our hotel. It started snowing when we left. We spent a good bit of time there. Anything else?"

Captain Berling put down his pen.

"Did you see anyone on your way back to the hotel?"

"Yes. We saw Dean DuBois, Angelique, and Louis walking down towards the tents."

"Excellent. That is all—for now. Please send in your associate, Monsieur Bernard."

Rousseau left, and Bernard was promptly admitted into the Dining Room. He quickly sat down at the table with his jaw set and his arms firmly crossed. Berling again asked the usual introductory questions about name, place of residence, and current employment. Then he turned to specific questions about the murder.

"You were at the ball?" asked Berling.

Bernard frowned. "Yes, yes, of course. I was there all evening for the reception, the dinner, and the ball."

"Did you see Josette La Clare at the reception?"

"Yes, I spoke to her. So did Pierre."

Berling made a notation. "And after the ball, what did you do?"

Antoine appeared quite agitated. "I walked down to the tent with Pierre and Isabelle. We had some drinks, and then I left."

"Alone?"

"Yes, alone!" snapped Antoine.

Berling patiently made another note.

"And why did you leave alone?"

Antoine's frown grew deeper. "I was tired. I wanted to get back to my hotel. I left the Palace around 12:30."

Captain Berling smiled. "I see. Now, what can you tell us about the victim? Did you know Josette La Claire?"

"Yes!" said Antoine, and he abruptly turned his head away.

"What did you think about her?"

"The truth?"

Berling sat back in his chair and folded his hands placidly across his chest. "The truth, yes, it would be helpful."

Antoine turned his head around and spoke in a fierce whisper, almost spitting his words at the policeman.

"I hated Josette La Claire, and I'm glad she's dead!"

Berling smiled and patiently made another note.

They could get no more out of Bernard. He hung his head sullenly and refused to answer any more questions. He was dismissed with a stern warning that they would likely be interviewing him again. Once he left the room, Gary immediately spoke up and confirmed to Captain Berling that he had seen Antoine walking up the Royal Avenue by himself after the ball.

Next in the room was Josette's teammate, George Bonnet. The man looked horrible. Clearly, he had not slept well. His clothes were disheveled, his face unshaven, and his eyes puffy and red. A whiff of alcohol floated across the table, evidence that Bonnet had been drinking. Drinking heavily, it would seem. Bonnet plopped down in the chair and faced the policeman.

"I didn't kill her," declared Bonnet bluntly.

Captain Berling's eyebrows rose ever so slightly.

"No one has said that you did, mon ami."

"But that's what you think," replied Bonnet miserably. "It's what they all are thinking."

The captain responded in a voice that was both direct and kind. "I assure you, Monsieur Bonnet, I come to the table this morning with no preconceived notions. Everyone will be treated fairly and objectively. This situation, it is a shock to you, and you have much on your mind with your competition. That I understand. I simply wish to ask you some simple questions."

Bonnet nodded his head.

"Very good," replied Berling. He glanced down at his paper. "Now, let us begin with the reception last night. You were there?"

Bonnet nodded his head again. "Briefly. But I left early. I—I had a headache and needed to lie down. Monsieur Lavel graciously offered me the use of the Queen's Meridian Cabinet just down the hall. I went there to rest."

"Can anyone confirm this?"

"Yes, ask Monsieur Lavel, he will tell you!" said Bonnet emphatically. "He came and checked on me once or twice."

"I see. What about dinner?"

Bonnet shook his head.

"I missed dinner. I had some wine early, before the reception, and then I had more as the reception began. I drank too much. That happens sometimes. I fell asleep and slept through both the dinner and the ball. Lavel finally came and woke me."

"What time was that?"

Bonnet thought a moment. "I believe it was 1:30 in the morning. All the guests had gone. Lavel thought I had gone to the tents with the rest of the guests and only happened to find me when he was leaving the castle. I walked out with him and then returned to my hotel."

Berling turned and looked at his assistant, who rapidly shuffled through his papers and confirmed. "Yes, Captain, the information we have from the guards at the front gate is of Monsieur Lavel and Bonnet leaving the grounds at 1:45 AM." Bonnet visibly relaxed in his chair.

"Very well. Now, I'm afraid, Monsieur Bonnet, I must ask you about the fight that you and Mademoiselle La Claire had in the Hall of Battles. You do not need to give us the details of the disagreement. We already have that information. Tell us, several persons have reported that Josette was most difficult to work with. Is that true?"

"Oui, Monsieur. Josette La Claire, she caused me much trouble, much embarrassment."

"And she made you angry? "

Bonnet sank deeper into his chair and gazed at the floor.

"Yes. At times she could make me so angry, my blood pressure, it would shoot through the roof."

Captain Berling leaned forward. "Then why did you hire her?"

Bonnet hesitated and nervously licked his lips. "You must understand. She — she was a talented chef and worked hard when she needed to. Yes, sometimes she was lazy and flirted with men. But Josette La Claire was a fierce competitor. She wanted to win this competition, and believe me, Messieurs, that woman would do *anything* to win!"

There was bitterness in Bonnet's voice when he said that last line. Berling made note of it and quickly dismissed George. Next to be interviewed was the master chef, René Michel. He wore a placid expression as he entered the room and took his place at the table.

"I hope this will not take long," said Michel before Berling could speak. "I have many things to do today, and the interviews are interfering with my schedule."

It was an audacious if not arrogant thing to say. A girl had been killed for heaven's sake, thought Gary. Her death was far more important than a pastry competition! But, if Berling was offended, he did not show it. He too could play the cool customer.

"We will not keep you very long," assured Berling mildly. "Just a few questions. First, did you know Mademoiselle La Claire?"

"No," said Michel bluntly. "I did not know her at all."

"Did you see her at the ball?"

Michel grimaced. "Yes, but I didn't speak to her. I'm afraid I didn't speak to many people. You see, I do not like big crowds. I do not play the social scene."

"I see," said Berling scribbling. "And after the dinner, what did you do?"

René folded his arms confidently across his chest. "I left the ball about 10:30 PM and walked down the Royal Avenue by myself. It took about twenty minutes or so to get to the tent. I was, I believe, the first person to arrive. I had a hot chocolate, and then I left about 11:30, just as other people began to appear."

"Where did you go?"

"For a very long walk."

Berlling's eyes widened. "Alone?"

Michel smirked. "Yes, alone. I walked along the north end of the garden, which was illuminated up to the Neptune fountains. I smoked a cigarette, and then I left the palace grounds for my hotel."

"What time was that?"

Michel sighed sounding a bit annoyed. "I really don't know. One o'clock perhaps? It was already snowing, but I didn't care. I like the cold and the snow. I wasn't looking at my watch."

Berling checked with his assistant.

"It was 12: 48 AM when he left the front gate according to the guard's testimony," said Colbert.

"There you are," said Michel coolly. He rose to leave.

"I am not done," said Berling firmly. "One more question, *s'il vous plaît.* What about your assistant, Claude Breton?"

Finally, René flinched. "What about him?"

"Can you give us any information about his whereabouts that night?"

René pursed his lips and shook his head. "Non, Monsieur. I only know that he was talking to Matisse before the dinner, and he and Matisse arrived together at the tent. When I left, they were still there. Now, may I return to the hall? I have a tight schedule." René looked down at his watch impatiently. Berling thanked him and dismissed him.

René's assistant was next ushered into the room. Unlike his teammate, Claude Breton was a bundle of raw nerves. His face was pale, his eyes darted about the room, and his hands were fidgety. He sat in his chair and smiled weakly at the French policeman across the table. Berling greeted Claude politely, asked for his personal information, and then got right down to his questions.

"Now, Monsieur, let me first ask you about the victim, Mademoiselle La Claire. Did you know her?"

Claude licked his lips nervously. "Mais, non, Monsieur. I did not know her. I am much older than she, and I taught at Dean Dubois's school long before she was a student there."

"Did your associate, René Michel, know her?" asked Berling coolly.

Claude grimaced and shook his head adamantly. "No, he did not."

"I see," said Berling crisply. Claude watched Berling anxiously as Captain Berling wrote some notes on his pad of paper.

"Did you know anyone who wanted to harm Mademoiselle La Claire?"

Claude laughed nervously at the question. "How could I know that? I just told you I did not know her."

"You might have heard something?" suggested Berling mildly.

Claude bit his lip and shook his head again. "*C'est impossible*! I have been busy at my station. I have not time for the idle gossip."

"Very well," said Berling with a hint of skepticism in his voice. "Now, let us turn to last night. You were at the reception."

"Yes, yes," said Claude immediately. "I was there all evening."

"Did you speak to anyone?"

Another nervous laugh. "I spoke to many people, Monsieur!"

Berling looked up from his notepad and narrowly looked at Claude.

"Anyone in particular?" he asked smoothly.

Claude Breton coughed and reached for a glass of water placed near his chair. He lifted the glass and swallowed some water. Gary noticed that when Claude put the glass down, the chef's hands were slightly shaking.

"Well, yes," said Claude, clearing his throat again. "I spent some time with Gerald Matisse at the reception."

"Only at the reception?" asked Berling softly with a knowing smile.

Claude shifted nervously in his chair and took another drink of water.

"Monsieur Matisee was kind enough to walk with me to the tent. It was after 11:00 o'clock when we left the palace.

René had gone ahead. Matisse is an excellent chef, you know, and very generous. We talked a lot about the competition, and he told me much about Louis's special color dyes. I was very interested in learning about Louis's creation."

"Were you at the tent long?"

"No, Monsieur. We got to the tent about 11:30, just as René was leaving. Matisse and I had one drink, then Gerald, he said he wanted to find Louis. He left. I had another drink, and then I went to look for René. I didn't go up the Royal Avenue. René said he was going to the North Gardens, so I went up the north side, near the Obelisk Grove."

"Did you find him?"

Claude hesitated and stared at his hands now in his lap. "Eventually, yes, I found him. But," he added quickly, "René wanted to walk some more, so I took my time to enjoy the gardens and then went back to the hotel by myself."

"I see," murmured Captain Berling making note of the testimony. "That will do."

Claude nodded his head and looked up. "Thank you, Monsieur. May I go? I must get back. René is very precise, you know, about the time. He is very strict and will be most angry if I delay."

Berling nodded. "You may go."

Camille Aumont breezed into the room with an air of confidence and plopped herself down in her chair with a smile and a nod. She, not the captain, initiated the conversation.

"I will waste no time with you, Messieurs. I knew Josette La Claire, and I hated her. I, like many others, am glad she is dead."

Berling regarded the handsome woman with a smile and a look of great appreciation.

"Madame, you are a woman who knows her mind. I like that. You are not the first person to express those sentiments about Josette."

"And I won't be the last," was the cool reply.

Berling's assistant chuckled, and the French Captain also seemed amused. However, he kept a straight face and pursued the questioning.

"For the record, Madame, please tell us why you hated her."

Camille drew a deep breath and squared her shoulders. "I have my reasons."

Berling picked up his pen. "I am listening."

Camille smirked. "For one thing, I have lost several competitions to that woman."

"So you envied her talents?"

Camille glared at the Captain. "No, I resented her for winning unfairly."

The Captain arched his eyebrows. "And how did she do that, Madame?"

Camille snorted. "Hasn't anyone told you? Captain, Josette La Claire was a blackmailer and a cheat!"

The Captain's eyes now narrowed, and he cast a hard glance at the female chef. "Those are strong accusations, Madame. Do you have proof?"

Camille laughed. "The fact that she, the obvious fake, was here is proof enough. George Bonnet must have something most terrible to hide or else he would never have brought her to the competition."

"Chef Bonnet mentioned nothing like this to us," insisted Captain Berling.

Camille jutted out her chin. "*Précisément.* Someone who is being blackmailed would not report it to the police."

"What other reasons did you have for hating Josette La Claire?"

Camille Aumont frowned severely. "That one reason is enough. Now, aren't you going to ask me where I was during the time of the murder?"

Berling tilted his head. "Madame, it is my job to conduct the interview! But since you have brought it up, please tell us your whereabouts last night, *s'il vous plaît.*"

"I was at the reception, of course. Monsieur Craig can vouch for me. I was at dinner as well, but I left afterward before the dancing. I had a headache."

Berling turned and looked at Gary for confirmation.

"She is correct," said Gary plainly. "I saw her at the reception and dinner; and at the ball, I danced with her assistant, Isabelle Vinneneau, who told me Madame Aumont had a headache and had retired early."

"Very good," said Berling as he took notes. "Did you go straight back to your hotel?"

Camille paused, her eyes darting side to side as she thought. A look of acute embarrassment crossed her face. Or was it guilt?

"No, Captain. I have migraines, and I take a very powerful medicine for it. You can call my physician if you do not believe me. I took the medicine before dinner and the medicine, it suddenly made me drowsy. I had too much wine with dinner and it caused a bad reaction. I meant to go back to the hotel, but I decided to lie down so my headache would leave. I am quite embarrassed. Monsieur Lavel kindly offered the use of the rooms on the ground floor. So I went to the Dauphin's Bedchamber to rest. I must have dozed off."

"Did anyone see you there?"

"No one, Monsieur."

"When did you awake?"

"It was well after midnight, I think. The music of the ball, it had stopped. I awoke and quickly came up the steps and departed for my hotel room."

Berling glanced over at his assistant who already had the necessary timesheets in hand.

"The guard at the gate notes Madame Aumont left Versailles palace at 12:55 AM."

Captain Berling indicated that the interview was over and excused Madame Aumont from the room. Next to be questioned was Isabelle Villeneau. Gary looked forward to hearing her, as she was both forthright and delightful. The lovely young lady entered the room quickly and sat at the table with a pleasant smile, ready to talk. Captain Berling greeted her graciously and got down to business.

"You are not French, Mademoiselle. A Brit?" he began cheerfully. "A challenge, is it not, in an all-French company?"

"Indeed," agreed Isabelle honestly. "Although I must say everyone has been very kind. Camille can be outspoken, that's for sure, but she's really quite an extraordinary chef. And she's very protective of me."

Berling nodded his head and made a note of it. Gary regarded the young woman with an appreciation for her expression of loyalty.

"Now, tell me, Mademoiselle," said Berling, "about what you saw at the Ball. Did you see Josette La Claire?"

"Oh, yes. I saw her at the reception and then at dinner. After dinner, I saw her, too. But she looked rather dreadful really, a bit peevish."

"When did you see her next?"

"Well, I don't think I saw her again. I left the dance early, about elevenish, with chef Rousseau and chef Bernard. We walked down to the tents for some drinks. To be perfectly honest, I did overindulge. I'm not usually a big drinker, but it was a perfectly splendid evening, and I'm afraid I rather lost my head. It was all so exciting. Of course, we had no idea such a horrible thing would happen. That poor girl! Her murder is simply too horrible for words!"

"Oui, Mademoiselle, it is *très horrible*. Now, tell me, how long were you at the tent?"

Isabelle bit her lip and calculated. "I should say it was definitely after midnight. We saw the carriages ride by with Madame President and Mr. Craig and the other diplomats. More like 12:30 I should think. I left with Pierre, and we walked around the north gardens for such a long time. It was all lit up, you know, and quite lovely. It was like a fairyland."

"Did you see anyone else?"

"Oh, yes. We saw Dean Dubois, Angelique, and Louis walking towards the tent. They arrived just as we left. Louis went in for drinks, and Dubois stayed outside with Angelique. I think he was trying to cheer her up. She had on the loveliest green velvet cape with a hood. She had her head resting on Dubois's shoulder. I think she was crying." Isabelle turned and stared wide-eyed at Gary, the friend of the evil man who had broken Angelique's heart. Gary sympathetically nodded his head, acknowledging Blaze's transgression.

"What about Antoine?" asked Berling intently.

Isabelle hesitated. "I really shouldn't say."

"Mademoiselle," lectured Captain Berling softly, "this is a police investigation. You must say!"

"Very well then. Antoine was jealous."

Berling's pen stopped midstream. "Of Pierre?"

Isabelle giggled. "No, Monsieur. He was a little jealous of me and very jealous of Josette—any woman actually whom Pierre pays any attention to."

Berling finally put down his pen and looked at Isabelle.

"Why should he be jealous of her?"

Isabelle looked shocked. "What? You mean, you don't know? Good Lord, I was sure someone had told you by now."

Berling was getting impatient. "Told us what?" he prodded.

"Josette La Claire and Pierre Rousseau were lovers. They've secretly been together for several years now."

The revelation stunned Captain Berling. He put down his pen and stared at the young woman.

Gary had an idea and spoke up. "Does this have something to do with your teammate, Camille Aumont's, feelings towards Josette? Is that why she hates Josette so much?"

Isabelle nodded. "Yes. Mr. Craig. It happened at Dubois's school when Camille and Pierre were both teaching there. She was simply mad about Pierre. She fell for him completely.

Many women do, I suppose. Josette was the women who stole him away from Camille."

"I believe that will do, Mademoiselle," said Captain Berling, "unless you saw anything else of importance."

Isabelle frowned slightly. "There was one more thing. It's ever so small, but then I suppose it's your job to sort it all out."

"What did you see?" asked Berling with interest.

"It was rather odd, really. But after dinner, before the ball began, I saw Josette give something to Claude, which he put in his pocket. He left right after that."

Isabelle's news gave them something to ponder as they took a short break. Captain Berling declared he needed to step outside for a smoke, and Gary went in search of a bathroom of the modern-day variety. When they returned, they found Gerald Matisse waiting for them. The dark-haired young man, courteous and affable, appeared more than ready to answer their questions.

"Let us start with the victim," declared Berling, taking his seat across the table. "Tell us how you knew Josette La Claire."

"I did not know her before the competition," replied Matisse. "But I had heard of her from Louis. He knew her. She, of course, was not—what is the English expression—my cup of tea?"

Matisse grinned at Berling and Gary as they processed his meaning.

"Understood. You prefer les *jeuns hommes*, not les *jeunes dames*."

Matisse shrugged. "Many artists do."

"So, while you were here," inquired Berling delicately, "you took an interest in Claude Breton? Yet he is at least ten years older than you."

Matisse shrugged again. "Age means nothing. Claude interested me, yes. He is a great chef."

"You spent time with him at the ball?"

"Oui. We talked at the reception and at dinner. Then we left early and walked down to the tents. It was 11:30 when we got there. We had a drink and visited with some other people. I then went to find Louis. "

"Yes, I saw Matisse at the Latona fountain around midnight when we left the palace," confirmed Gary.

Berling picked up his pen and began scribbling quickly. "What did you do next? Did you find Louis?"

Matisse shook his head resolutely. "Not right away. I walked up to the Palace but did not see him there. So I went over to the Fountains of Neptune and waited for him for quite some time. He mentioned earlier that day he wanted to see those fountains, so I thought he would show up there. The fountains, they were lit up with many candles. Magnifique!"

"What did you do when he didn't show up?"

"I decided to go back to the tent, thinking he might be there. So I walked all the way down the Royal Avenue. It was about 1:15 when I got back. I had another drink and spoke with some of the Summit leaders. Madame Foster, she is quite the talker! Then Louis showed up about a quarter to two, just as the service at the tent was ending. He told me he had been with Angelique and Dubois. We had one more drink and then left the Palace. It was 2:00 AM when we got to the gate."

Captain Berling's assistant was already rifling through his papers. He told his superior Matisse's testimony was supported by the witness of the workers at the tents and the gate.

"One more question, Monsieur," said Berling respectfully. "At the dinner, did you see Claude and Josette together at any time?"

Matisse looked surprised at the question. He shook his head.

"No, Captain, I did not."

There was one more chef, one more suspect to question, and that was Louis Girard. The master chef strode into the room and sat down with an air of relaxed confidence.

"How may I be of assistance?" asked Louis smiling.

Berling chewed on the end of his pen and regarded the young man thoughtfully.

"By telling the truth," was his reply.

"But of course!" said Louis eagerly. "I want you to catch this killer for it involves me. I knew Josette La Claire very well. I cared for her. In fact, I dated her briefly a few years ago."

"Is that why you were so tolerant of her bad behavior," asked Gary quietly, "when she took the bottle of green dye?"

Louis bent his head slightly and grinned. "Josette, she was always a bit of a thief, such a child. She liked to get her way, to be indulged, to be spoiled. Yes, that is why I let her take the food coloring."

"I see," said Berling writing furiously. "Tell us more about your relationship with her."

Louis pursed his lips. "Oh, there is not much to tell. I am older than she, you know. She is twenty-six, and I am thirty-seven. I was teaching a night class at Dean Dubois's school. She was my student. It was a no-no, of course. We were not supposed to date the students. But Josette, she was not one for obeying the rules. Honestly, she is not the greatest chef, but she worked hard."

"Did she sleep with other chefs?" asked Gary bluntly.

Captain Berling stopped writing and stared.

Louis sat back in his chair and began tapping the edge of the table with his finger.

"Yes, Josette slept her way through school. She stole more than food coloring and recipes. She stole Pierre from Camille. Did Camille tell you that?"

Berling took a deep breath. "No, Monsieur, she did not."

Louis grinned. "Camille has never forgiven Josette for doing that. Camille and Pierre were also teaching at the school when Josette was a student. "

Berling consulted his notes carefully.

"Madame Aumont did, however, tell us that Josette was a blackmailer."

Louis laughed at the news. "Ah, that explains it. Josette must have discovered George's little secret."

"What do you mean?" demanded Berling impatiently.

Louis sat up straight and leaned towards the table.

"I mean, Messieurs, that George Bonnet got in trouble once when we were teaching at the school. I do not know all the details. Perhaps Dubois can tell you. But George, he was suddenly let go. If Josette found out the reason, I do not doubt she would blackmail him into getting the chance to be at this competition."

Berling wrote all this down. "This is very helpful, Monsieur Girard. Now, just one more thing. Please outline for us your whereabouts the night of the murder."

"Certainly. As Monsieur Craig can testify, I was at the reception and the dinner and the ball. About midnight, when most of the guests left to walk down the Royal Avenue to see the luminary candles, I was with Mademoiselle du Pré and Dean Dubois. Angelique, she was most upset at Monsieur Phillips's transfer of affection from herself to Mademoiselle Porter, so Dubois and I took her for a long walk around the Orangery."

"You were with them the entire time?"

"Yes. You may ask them both. They will tell you."

"Continue," ordered Berling.

"Let's see. Angelique finally said she wanted some hot chocolate, so the three of us walked down the Royal Avenue to the tent. She was embarrassed and did not want to go inside. She had been crying, and her eyes were red. Naturally, I understood, as Monsieur Phillips and Mademoiselle Porter were still inside the tent together. So she and Dubois stayed outside while I went in and got the drinks."

"What time was that?"

"About 12:30 or 12:35. Something like that. We stayed only about ten minutes, and then Angelique wanted to go for a walk around the south part of the grounds. She did not want to run into Monsieur Phillips and Mademoiselle Porter. We ended up at the Bacchus Fountain. Angelique finished her drink there, and I smoked a cigarette while Dubois told funny stories and tried to cheer Angelique."

"That is near the Ballroom garden, where Josette was found," interjected Berling with a hard stare.

"Is that where they found her?" asked Louis in surprise. "Strange. We saw no one. And we were all together, Messieurs. I never left them, if I need an alibi. Well, Angelique finally said she was tired and wanted to return to her hotel, so I walked her and Dubois both up to the palace. Then I decided to go back to the tent and find Gerald."

Berling turned to his assistant for confirmation.

"Yes, I have it here, Captain. The waiter at the tent says Monsieur Girard returned to the tent around 1:45. He and Matisse had a final drink together before the tent service closed. The guard at the gate has them leaving the palace grounds at 2:00 AM, the same time as the Fosters, the Herrmans, and the Voronovas."

Louis chuckled. "That Madame Foster, I like her very much. I hope someday she invites me to England so I may cook for her."

"I'm sure she would like that," replied Gary pleasantly, remembering the nectarine dessert the other night Louis had made for them.

Berling, however, was staring at his meticulous notes.

"I find it interesting, Monsieur, that you left the tent the first time at 12:45 and then you do not return until 1:45. That is over an hour, n'est-ce pas?"

Louis looked at the Captain with perfect assurance. "As I said before, I walked the south grounds with Dean Dubois and Angelique for a very long time. She was most upset, and

Dubois and I were attending to her. We did not rush. Then I had to walk all the way up to the palace and all the way back to the tent. That took an hour. Again, please ask Dean Dubois. He will tell you."

"I intend to do just that," answered Berling candidly. "I have no more questions at this time, Monsieur Girard. You have been most helpful."

"One more thing," offered Louis as he stood. "It might not mean much. But this morning when I checked my refrigerator, several bottles of my food coloring were missing. Is that significant?"

Berling gazed up at Louis and nodded his head gravely.

"Oui, Monsieur. I think it is most significant. You may go."

They had completed interviewing all the suspects, but Captain Berling begged Gary to stay a bit longer so they could get Dean Dubois and Angelique du Pré's testimony. The young woman was admitted to the room first. She looked quite pale, and she greeted the Captain and Gary apprehensively. She clutched a small white lace handkerchief in her hands.

"You wanted to see me?" asked Angelique timidly. Her eyes darted back and forth from Gary to Captain Berling.

"Calm yourself, Mademoiselle. There is no need to be frightened," assured Captain Berling.

"Oh, but there is cause," the young lady exclaimed tearfully. "The killer he attacked a young single woman. There are only three other female chefs here at Versailles. Camille Aumont, no one would dare harm her, and everyone likes Isabelle Villeneau. That leaves me! I could be next, Messieurs!" She fought back a sob and blew her nose.

"Mademoiselle, do not upset yourself so," advised Captain Berling. "The police are here. We will protect you. Now, please, try to concentrate. It is important that we get your account of last night, to help corroborate the testimony of the other chefs."

Angelique sniffed, wiped her nose, and sat up straight in her chair.

"Yes, Captain. I was at the reception. I—" She paused and looked hesitantly over at Gary. "I was with Monsieur Phillips at the reception and at dinner. Then...then he left with someone else!" She spat out the final words and buried her face into her handkerchief.

"Tut, tut," whispered Berling paternally. "It does no good to be so upset over a man, *mon enfant*. There will be other men. Now, compose yourself and tell us what happened next."

Angelique lifted her head and nodded obediently at the Captain.

'Well, I danced with others. Secretary Campbell, he was kind. And of course, I danced with Louis. He is like a big brother to me. At midnight," she paused and took a deep breath, "when I saw Monsieur Phillips and that other woman walk down the Royal Avenue, Dean Dubois and Louis took me for a long walk in the Orangery to calm my nerves. After that, I wanted a hot drink, so we walked down to the tent. Of course, I did not want to go inside."

"Of course," replied Captain Berling.

Angelique continued. "Louis got our drinks, and then Dubois and Louis took me for another walk around the south gardens, near the King's Garden and the statue of Bacchus. I was very tired, so Louis walked us back to the Palace, and Dean Dubois escorted me to my hotel room. I took a sedative and went to sleep."

"Very wise of you," commended Captain Berling with a nod.

"Is that all?" asked Angelique brightening slightly. Clearly, she was anxious for this interview to end.

"One more question. Did you see Josette La Claire at all when you were in the Orangery?"

Angelique shuddered just hearing the name of the victim. She shook her head resolutely. "Non, Captain. I did not see her at all after the ball."

The Captain stood and came over to help Angelique to her feet.

"Thank you for your assistance. Now go and try to calm yourself. Things have a way of working themselves out. You will see. Trust a man who has weathered many a storm in life." Angelique smiled weakly, thanked Berling for his kindness, and quickly escaped from the room.

The last man to enter was Dean Dubois. He came to the table with a most distressed look. Gary could tell that Dubois felt the loss of Josette La Claire deeply.

"Thank you, Monsieur, for speaking with us," Captain Berling began graciously as he acknowledged Dubois's feelings. "I know this is hard for you, mon ami. Your reputation, it precedes you. These chefs are like your children, are they not? You are their surrogate father."

Dubois kept his emotions in check, but he bent his head as he whispered, "Yes, they are that to me."

Berling nodded in understanding. "All the more reason I need your testimony, your perspective. Also, I need for you to confirm the testimony of your assistant, Angelique."

The mention of her name made Dubois smile. "I trust she was forthcoming. She is so dedicated to the school and to me. She is so modest, so kind and honest."

Berling agreed. "Yes, she is most charming."

Dubois sighed. "But she is not wise with the men, which brings me to last night. No doubt others have told you about her feelings for Monsieur Craig's friend."

"Yes," responded Berling promptly.

"Well, Angelique was most upset when Monsieur Phillips left with Mademoiselle Porter for the walk down the Royal Avenue. Chef Louis and I took Angelique to the Orangery for her to regain her composure. Then we walked down to the tent for some hot chocolate. After that, we walked the gardens, to the south I think, to look at the lights and the statues. Amazing how Monsieur Dumont's men were able to clear the main pathways of much of the snow! It was very beautiful to see by candlelight. Where was I? Oh yes, we came to the Bacchus Fountain and stayed there a long while. I told old stories from the school's past to cheer her up. Angelique announced she was tired and wanted to retire. Louis walked us up to the palace and then went to look for Matisse, who we understood was spending his evening with Claude. They are, you must be aware by now, how do you say, 'an item.'"

Berling smiled as he wrote. "Yes, Matisse told us that. Thank you, Dean Dubois. Your story confirms that of Angelique and Louis. Tell me, did you see Josette after the ball?"

Dubois stared directly at the Captain and said he did not.

"Very good," said Berling. "Now, just a few things more. First, could you tell us more about George Bonnet? Did something happen at your school that was not proper?"

Immediately Dubois appeared anxious, and his eyes darted about the room as he wrestled with his private thoughts.

Berling quickly added, "Do not fret. You are the good papa and do not wish to speak ill of any of your protégés. But it is important, Monsieur, that I get all the facts."

"Yes, I understand," said Dubois resignedly. "George Bonnet, he is a good chef, but at times he lacks the confidence. Years ago, in a little competition we held at the school, I discovered he had copied a recipe from another source and used it as if it was his own."

"Plagiarism?" asked Gary.

"Yes, Monsieur. I, of course, did not want the public scandal and kept the matter most quiet. But Bonnet was let go immediately. There is no record of it, however, in his file."

"Is there any chance that Josette La Claire discovered this?"

Dubois's eyes popped open in surprise. "You think George killed her?"

"It is one possibility," replied Captain Berling frankly. "It has been suggested that Mademoiselle La Claire, she was trying to get ahead. Perhaps she used the information on his cheating to force George to bring her to the competition. This murder could be a simple case of blackmail."

Dubois sat thoughtfully and considered the Captain's theory. "It is possible, yes. Josette, she was like a child, headstrong and selfish. She would do almost anything to get her way."

"Would she cheat?" asked Gary sharply.

"Oui," said Dubois quietly. "She wanted to win this competition and would stop at nothing to do so."

"Chef Bonnet was very angry when she took Louis's food coloring?" queried Berling as he consulted his notes carefully.

Dubois nodded. "George has the hot temper. You saw it, Monsieur Craig. But commit murder, that I do not know."

Captain Berling picked up on the hesitation in Dubois's voice and put his pen down. He leaned towards the gentleman and softly questioned him directly.

"Who do you think killed Josette La Claire?"

Dubois stared down at his hands folded in his lap for a moment. Gary studied the man's distinguished features and felt the agony he must be going through. He cared for all his chefs. How could he pick one for such a terrible crime?

Finally, Dubois looked up and reluctantly answered the Captain's question. "George Bonnet, he is the obvious choice. And Camille Aumont is a woman scorned. I would not want to be someone who crossed her path, one who has angered her so. She could easily do it. But if I were you, Captain, I would watch René Michel very closely."

René? The answer stunned Gary. René was the chef he least suspected.

"I don't understand," said Gary adamantly. "René Michel seems to be a very confident man, a man very much in control."

Dubois pursed his lips tightly then grimaced. "Yes, he is that on the outside. But do not be deceived, Messieurs. René Michel is a fierce competitor, also. Winning for him, it is everything. And this historic competition, with the whole world watching and with Louis as his competitor, this he wants to win most of all. He drives himself and poor Claude to the point of collapse. You have observed Claude and his nerves. I fear he will soon have a breakdown if he doesn't stand up to René and take better care of himself. Michel has, I'm afraid, a terrible temper, one he does not display in public like George. If René Michel ever found out that Josette La Claire was cheating, if he believed she would win this contest dishonestly and deprive him of this most coveted victory, I have no doubt whatsoever, Messieurs, that he would kill her."

Chapter Sixteen

Salon Des Nobles

Thursday Afternoon
January 10, 2002

D ubois's pronouncement rang in Gary's ears as he rushed to join the children for lunch. The ever-wise Lavel, perhaps sensing Gary would be in need of quiet as well as refreshment after the long, difficult interviews, set up a private luncheon in the green colored Salon Des Nobles. This room stood adjacent to the Queen's bedroom and had once served as the Queen's throne room where she held her official audiences. A painting of King Louis XV still hung on the wall next to the table; and this afternoon, the former Lord of Versailles seemed to extend his watchful royal eye upon them as they ate their lunch.

Jack and Blaze joined Gary, the nanny Gabrielle, Abigail, Philippe, and the cat, Sebastian, for the midday meal. The children enjoyed brie-cheese sandwiches and hot tomato-basil soup. The adults dined on a superb spinach soufflé and crisp green salad. Underfoot, Sebastian devoured his specially prepared plate of Beef Burgundy. For dessert, there was Crème

Brulee. No one ate till Sebastian had his food properly blessed, and Abigail surprised Gary by standing up and reciting the child's prayer in perfect French. Jack gave Gary a narrow look after the prayer. The little girl with perfect auditory memory was absorbing a few French phrases. However, Gary seriously doubted Abigail had any real comprehension of French — yet. At least that was his hope. Time would tell.

Gary did not bring up the subject of the police interviews in front of the children and Gabrielle. Instead, the topics of conversation focused on the weather and Janet. On the bright side (literally), the weather had finally taken a turn for the better. After last night's record snowfall, the afternoon Parisian sun finally broke through the morning's purple clouds, and glorious sunlight filled the salon with welcome warmth and cheerfulness. On the downside, there was nothing cheerful to report on Janet's continuing nasty attitude and behavior. Between mouthfuls, Blaze detailed how the former Mrs. Craig was driving the staff and guests in both Trianons mad with her endless demands. Gary well-remembered life with his former wife and nodded his head sympathetically.

After lunch, Gabrielle promptly gathered up the children and the grey cat and took them off to play upstairs in Philippe's rooms until the cake competition resumed. Once they left, the conversation quickly turned to the topic of murder.

"So, okay, tell us already," demanded Jack as he leaned back and sipped his red wine. "And don't you dare hold anything back. My professional ears will pick up all signs of prevarication. Rest assured my mouth will remain shut — at least until you find my cell phone."

"Go through each suspect and their testimony," insisted Blaze, finishing off a second helping of dessert.

Gary toyed with his dessert while giving his two friends a detailed replay of the morning's interviews.

"What do you think?" he asked as he finished his dessert.

"Sounds like your Captain Berling is one cool customer," pronounced Jack authoritatively. "Did he give you any indication as to his take on the testimony, any suspicions he might have?"

Gary shook his head. "No, he took careful notes, asked his questions, and left."

"Too bad," observed Blaze as he wiped his mouth.

"What do you think?" asked Jack thoughtfully. "Do you agree with Dubois, that René is the chief suspect?"

Gary bit his lip and thought for a moment. "Hard to say. Our experience in September with Ryan Adams and Senator Miller taught us it could be anyone, including the least likely person. No one suspected them. Honestly, I would have to disagree with Dubois and say René was at the bottom of my list. So, maybe he should be moved to the top."

"Don't forget that Jim Myers was the obvious suspect last time," reminded Jack, "and he did turn out to be the guilty party. So I say go with obvious, go with the woman. My bet is on Camille."

"I agree with Dubois," contradicted Blaze. "René is the most reserved of the chefs. He was the first man at the tent, and he has no alibi. He says he was in the north section of the gardens, but he could be lying. He could have gone to the north end at first, and then he could have crossed over at the Water Parterre when most of the guests had gone down to the tent."

"True," said Jack as he put his wine glass down on the table. "But the best motive for murder, I think, is still the woman scorned. Camille did it. She hated Josette, and her alibi is flimsy. She says she went downstairs, but she could have gone to the Hall of Battles and waited in the dark. If she knew that Josette was a cheat, she could have predicted Josette would go back into the Hall to steal more food coloring. Camille sneaks up on her old enemy Josette, knocks her on the head, and it's a done deal."

"So how did Camille get Josette's body outside?" asked Gary. "I can't see Camille dragging Josette halfway across the gardens in all this snow."

Jack huffed. He hadn't considered that and did not like having his pet theories shot down.

"Well, maybe she had an accomplice. The best murderers do! Our intelligence said a chef and assistant would be here working for The Seven. Maybe the sweet and innocent Isabelle isn't so sweet and isn't so innocent."

"No way," argued Blaze indignant. "If anyone is innocent, it's Isabelle."

"Can you be sure?" asked Jack cynically. "Ryan Adams appeared rather innocent, too."

"What about Isabelle's alibi?" retorted Blaze hotly. "She was with Pierre."

"So she says. But Pierre could be lying as well," countered Jack smoothly. "Pierre lied about knowing Josette. Isabelle told us Pierre and Josette were lovers. What if Camille and Isabelle laid the trap, with Camille waiting in the Hall and Isabelle directing Pierre away from Josette by keeping him company and walking him down to the tent. Then once they are walking in the north gardens, Isabelle could have suggested to Pierre that they split up and look for Josette. He looks in the north gardens while she looks in the south."

"And she goes to the Hall, finds Camille, and helps her move Josette's body out to the garden," added Blaze skeptically. "I don't know, Jack. Your theory is a stretch."

"Never underestimate a woman, Sam," warned Jack. "I keep telling you that. And you best start listening before you get yourself knee-deep in trouble with Angelique and Marie."

Blaze ignored Jack's last comment. "What about Pierre? He confirmed Isabelle's alibi. He says he was with Isabelle the whole time!"

"Of course he does," replied Jack. "He's worried the police will learn that he and Josette were lovers, thus making him *the* prime suspect. Police always suspect husbands or boyfriends first. The last thing he needs is to be without an alibi. So, before the interviews today, Isabelle finds him and convinces him to lie, to tell the same story as she does, to protect them both. And he instantly agrees, wanting to save his own backside. It's quite a masterful plan, I think, worthy of a powerful and conniving female."

"I don't know. It's just so hard for me to believe Isabelle would do such a thing," said Gary considering Jack's theory.

"Gary, who do you think killed Josette?" asked Blaze.

"Well, they all had an opportunity," Gary reflected. "If I had to pick, I guess I'd go with the obvious, with George Bonnet. He has a bad temper, he was being blackmailed by Josette, and he disappears after dinner with no real alibi for the rest of the evening. Knowing how unethical Josette was, he could have gone down to the Hall to wait and see if she showed up to steal or cheat again. She did, they fought, and he killed her by accident. I think perhaps it was an accident. Panicked, he takes her outside and then rushes back to the Palace for Lavel to discover him later sleeping it off. It is a solution as that is simple and straightforward solution."

Jack frowned with disgust. "Totally boring! I prefer my theory, complicated and exciting, as any adventure with a woman should be."

Gary looked at his watch. "One thing is for certain," he announced as he stood. "We all must be on our guard. Blaze, you keep your eyes open for anything strange, and Jack, you film anything that looks suspicious."

Lunch concluded, Gary headed off for the Hall of Battles for the final judging while Blaze and Jack went to observe the afternoon session of the G-8 summit in the Chapel. When Gary entered the hall, he saw the children had already arrived and were sitting on the floor next to Babette. She was seated in a chair busy sketching. General McKay was standing directly behind her, observing over her shoulder with a critical eye of her artwork and today's high fashion outfit: a tight-fitting Cerruti blouse and miniskirt, accessorized by a full-length, cream-colored coat lined in luscious fur. He whispered his commentary into the artist's ear, but Babette blithely ignored all of the General's critiques. Abigail was at Babette's feet, mimicking the female artist by "sketching" with her crayons. Philippe sat next to Abigail with his fiddle in hand, playing a light tune. Pullman and Lewis and three other Secret Service agents stood nearby, closely watching the children. Sebastian sat at Agent Lewis's feet grooming his front paws.

Gary quickly joined Aunt Sophie, Ambassador Porter, and Dean Dubois. Now that Ambassador Porter's daughter was working as Bonnet's assistant, Porter asked to be released from his official judging duty. However, Porter joined them for the walk-through. The judges picked up their clipboards and began their inspection of today's work, the completion of cake construction and the creation of additional spun sugar pieces that would adorn their cakes.

They began at Pierre and Antoine's station. The Royal Palace of Marly, with its twelve petite palaces surrounding it, was constructed with yellow cake and a light, cream-colored icing. Antoine was still icing one of the cake palaces, constructing the fine detail of the windows, doors, and roof tiles. Pierre was busy coloring a batch of bright blue spun sugar, which he was ready to put into molds that would become the surrounding pools and fountains. Gary noted that Pierre was silent and wholly absorbed in his work, not making any eye contact whatsoever with Gary or the other judges. Antoine seemed even more attentive to Pierre, but unlike the other day, he appeared relaxed and confident. Was this because his chief competition for Pierre's affection was now permanently removed?

They next walked to the ladies' station. Camille and Isabelle moved with precision within their workspace. There was a white board propped up on the countertop with a detailed list of "things to do," most of which had been crossed off. Isabelle was in charge of crossing items off once completed. She was working on the decoration of the Octagon-shaped palace and its fences and gardens, while Camille displayed her masterwork with spun sugar as she brought forth the small, wild animals for placement around the spice-cake Menagerie. She was busy constructing a sugar lion as the judges passed by. Gary noticed that on Camille's face, there was a look of great satisfaction, perhaps even a smug smile. The look gave Gary a sudden chill. Was Camille pleased with her sugar work, or was she pleased with murder?

Louis and Gerald's station was a blur of activity. Gerald was standing at a hot stove, melting sugar into large pans. There were bottles of various shades of blue food colorings on a nearby cart, along with the mold for use in constructing the Grand Canal. On the counter, small statues of white spun sugar represented the statues that lined the Royal Avenue. Louis was bent over a tin sheet filled with pieces he was cutting for the construction of Louis XIV's flotilla. An intricate colored drawing of the Italian ship was also on the counter. Gary was stunned at Louis and Gerald's miniature Versailles palace, made from pale, golden gingerbread. It was a gingerbread "house" that rivaled the White House Gingerbread Houses created each year at Christmastime. Gary was quite certain Abigail would be absolutely enchanted with this creation. He noted Louis and Gerald's demeanor. Neither of them seemed nervous or guilty or unduly upset. Louis even glanced up once and cast a pleasant smile in Gary's direction.

Suddenly, there was a loud thundering crash.

"Idiot!" screeched René.

The reprimand echoed powerfully through the hall.

Gary jumped at the sound and turned to see Chef Michel standing over his assistant, Claude, with his fists clenched. A metal tray was lying at his feet, and a group of small sugared, blue and white square tiles was scattered and broken on the floor. Michel's eyes narrowed, and he raised his hand, ready to strike. Gary thought Michel would hit Claude. But Michel brought his arms down to his side and yelled at his assistant.

"A whole tray of pieces lost! It is good that I made extras, or we would be ruined! RUINED! DO YOU UNDERSTAND???"

"I am sorry," whimpered Claude pitifully, kneeling on the ground, rushing to gather the ruined pieces. "It was an accident. I didn't see you behind me."

"Watch what you are doing and where you are going! NOW CLEAN THIS MESS UP!"

Michel took in a deep breath, exhaled angrily, pulled out a pack of cigarettes from his pants pocket, and marched out of the Hall of Battles for a smoke.

"Please continue the review," said Dean Dubois in a soft voice. "I must go and see to René. I will judge Bonnet's work later." With that, Dubois hurried off after his former student.

"Let me help you."

Startled, Gary heard the comforting sound of Aunt Sophie's voice. He smiled as he saw that she had put down her judge's clipboard and had gone around the cooking station. She was kneeling beside a humiliated Claude Breton.

"It's alright," she assured him kindly as she gently began picking up blue and white sugars pieces off the floor. "We all make mistakes in the kitchen. This could have happened to anyone. Heavens, I once dropped a whole pan of gravy on the floor right before a Thanksgiving dinner for twenty guests."

Claude looked up and managed a grateful smile, amazed at Sophie's kindness.

Sophie continued chatting away, the maternal sound of her voice soothing the nerves of the embarrassed chef. "My family likes their turkey well done, on the dry side actually, so gravy is an absolute necessity. And there I was, with gravy spattered all over my new dress and all over the kitchen floor. Fortunately, I was able to find a little packet of gravy mix in the cupboard — it was not anywhere near as good as my own made from scratch, mind you—but it turned out fine. So, no worries. Things always work themselves out. We'll clean this mess up in a jiffy," she said cheerfully. "Then you can get back to work. By the way, I think your cake is coming along very nicely."

"Merci," muttered Claude. His hands were still shaking as he worked alongside her, picking up the sugar pieces, but there was now some reassurance in his eyes.

"She's wonderful," whispered Ambassador Porter coming up next to Gary.

"She is that," agreed Gary heartily as he watched the First Lady help Claude regain his composure. "General McKay is one lucky man. Well, let's finish up with Bonnet and leave Aunt Sophie with Claude. She has things under control here."

Gary and Porter went to the final station. Bonnet was standing over his cake creation of the Baths of Apollo. Marie Porter was standing beside him, handing him sparkling pieces of mint and sage green sugar leaves and greenery, individually made, which Bonnet was arranging and attaching to the scene. Already, the white sugar versions of the Baths of Apollo's famous statuary were in place. Those statues were extraordinary, and Gary gave them very high marks on his judge's sheet. Marie glanced up at her father briefly and grinned. Then she refocused her attention on Bonnet and his assembly. An intricate drawing of the creation was on the countertop in front of her showing the detailed plans for the construction, a clear map of Bonnet's design. Porter beamed proudly at his daughter as he watched her work.

Gary's attention shifted as he noticed Captain Berling's arrival. The French captain's face was dark as he strode quickly across the hall and whispered something to McKay. The artist, Babette, paused with her drawing, glancing up at Berling with a sudden look of alarm. She had overheard some bad news. McKay caught Gary's eye and motioned for him to come over.

Gary excused himself and hastened to McKay, fearing perhaps something might have happened to Eliza or Joshua. Being separated from his other children in the midst of this crisis put his nerves on edge.

"What is it?" asked Gary anxiously. "News from the city?"

McKay grimaced and swore under his breath.

"Yes, bad news I'm afraid. I'll let Berling tell you."

"Eliza? Joshua? Are they safe?"

"Do not be anxious about them," assured the Captain quickly. "Your other children, they are quite well. But I come with grave news. You and your Secret Service must take every precaution to increase the security for you and your family."

"What's wrong?" demanded Gary gazing at the policeman's grim face.

"There has been another murder. The body of Carlos De Silva was discovered this morning. They found him shoved behind a table of candles at Notre Dame Cathedral. He was strangled to death. It looks as if The Seven has struck again!"

McKay stared over at the cooking station where his dear wife was still assisting the berated assistant chef. "And after what we just witnessed," said the General somberly, "I would venture to say René Michel now is officially our chief suspect."

Chapter Seventeen

The Grand Canal

Thursday. late afternoon

A feeling of utter vulnerability came over Gary when he learned of De Silva's death. Suddenly, he felt completely overwhelmed and terrified. He and his young family were stranded here, partly by his design and partly by the unexpected weather. The reality that The Seven had the means to murder at will both inside and outside the palace walls hit him hard. Fear shot through his veins like ice water.

It was time for him to take action, a decision not well received by those standing around him. Agent Pullman protested, Captain Berling frowned, and General McKay swore. But Gary didn't care. He was acting now as a husband and father driven to protect his family. And to do that, he needed help, and he knew just the person to enlist. Despite everyone's objections, Gary immediately left the Hall of Battles and went in search of Monsieur Lavel. He found the noble gentleman in the Hall of Mirrors. Gary pulled Lavel aside, and in a hushed whisper, told him everything.

Lavel stood there stunned.

"But the murder of Mademoiselle La Claire? Was it not the crime of passion?" he asked in a daze.

"Passion had nothing to do with it, "said Gary flatly. "It was a cold and calculated murder, one based on greed and power. So I've come to you for your help, Monsieur Lavel. I fear the lives of my wife and my children — "

Children.

Gary stopped, aware that mentally and emotionally, he also included Philippe as if he were his child, his own son. The revelation startled him. He glanced at Lavel in amazement.

Monsieur Lavel smiled knowingly and raised his hand. He needed no further explanation.

"Say no more, mon ami. I understand, and I, too, can be discreet. This situation, it calls for delicacy, does it not? Of The Seven, I will say nothing, but you can rest assured, Monsieur Craig, that I and my staff, we will keep a very close eye on your wife and Abigail and Philippe. We will guard them with our lives!" Lavel threw back his shoulders and stood, chin held high, with all the pride and power of France behind him.

Gary exhaled a sigh of relief.

"Thank you, Monsieur Lavel. I knew I could count on you."

Lavel looked immensely pleased with the compliment. Then he glanced around at the group of Secret Service agents standing apart from Gary, only a few feet away. Agent Pullman's face was unreadable, but Agent Lewis gave Lavel a brief nod. Lavel then spoke with some hesitation.

"If you do not mind, may I offer a petite observation and suggestion, in front of your men?"

"Please do," said Gary sincerely.

Lavel put his hands together and placed them under his chin thoughtfully.

"First, a suggestion for the children. We should get them out of the palace, away from the chefs, as much as possible. Philippe, he will not like it. He considers the palace his own.

Fortunately, the snow has ended, and the temperature outside will begin to rise. So, if you will, I will make arrangements for the children to play at the Grand Trianon and outside — starting today!"

"That sounds very good," agreed Gary.

Lavel smiled with satisfaction and glanced again at Gary's Secret Service detail. Agent Pullman was already taking notes.

"Next, I will need shoe sizes of Mademoiselle Abigail and — all of your men."

Agent Lewis cleared his throat.

"Shoe sizes?" asked Gary.

"Yes, right away. Please write them down. Now, as for the chefs, I admit I do not like Monsieur Michel. He is too quiet, that one. I do not like the way he treats his young assistant — most unkind. You can tell a lot about a man in the way he treats others."

Gary nodded his head in agreement. "Your thoughts match those of General McKay and Captain Berling. Chef Michel is their chief suspect."

"That is right," replied Lavel. He turned and gazed out the window. The vast expanse of the snow-covered gardens sparkled beneath the clearing sky and the January sun.

"Another one to watch," cautioned Lavel solemnly, "is Madame Aumont. She is one who holds the grudges, no?"

"Yes," answered Gary as he, too, turned to gaze out the window, basking in the warm sunlight. The frozen ice-blue waters of the Water Parterre were glistening in the afternoon rays. "I hear that she can be resentful."

Lavel squared his shoulders again and sniffed. "Ah, then, we too will watch her closely, mon ami. It is not wise to underestimate a woman, particularly an angry woman. You should not ignore Camille Aumont."

"I appreciate your counsel," said Gary sincerely, "and your willingness to help. It gives me great comfort. The situation is more dangerous than I anticipated."

Lavel placed his strong hand on Gary's shoulder. It gave him great comfort.

"Do not fear. There is great evil in the world, it is true, but there is also great good. And the good will always triumph. Behold! The storm unleashed its worst nightmare upon us. We felt its terrors and survived the long night. But now, the light returns, and soon it will burn every bit of the darkness away. Trust Papa Lavel. You will see."

*   *   *

Gary felt tremendous relief after speaking with Lavel. Upon consulting with General McKay, they rewarded the Frenchman by giving him back his cell phone. Lavel immediately put it to good use and placed a call to a local merchant willing put on his heavy boots and plow through the snow-covered sidewalks to be of service. Miraculously, within the hour, Lavel managed to have a large box delivered to the palace gate containing *ice-skates!* There were skates for Abigail and Philippe, Gary, Blaze, Jack, Al the cameraman, and most of Gary's security detail. In addition, one of the carriages from the night of the ball was hitched up to a team of black horses. The carriage was waiting for them in back of the Palace. Dumont, the gardener, and one of his men drove the team themselves. Happily, Gary and the children boarded the carriage and rode down the Royal Avenue for a late afternoon of skating on the frozen Grand Canal. When they arrived at the Baths of Apollo fountain, Abigail jumped out of the carriage and squealed to see a golden sleigh waiting for her at the edge of the embankment. Monsieur Lavel himself was standing at the fountain beaming. He pointed to the sleigh with pride.

"This sleigh, it was made in 1730 and was used by the King's children to play on the Grand Canal in wintertime," said Lavel proudly. "I thought the children would like to ride in it."

"This just gets better and better," quipped Jack as he slowly got out of the carriage. "No telling what Lavel does for an encore."

"Stop complaining and get to work," warned Gary as he knelt to help lace up Abigail's skates. "You're getting exclusive rights to film everything."

Jack's cameraman, Al, was already in his skates and out on the ice with his camera.

Jack scowled. "A figure-skater I am not, unlike my Joe Friday over there who went to Yale and played in an amateur hockey league."

Gary looked up to see Al gliding effortlessly across the ice. Already Philippe was in his skates and chasing after the large cameraman. Al managed to skate backward and film at the same time.

"Show off!" muttered Jack as he struggled to get his skates on.

"Don't worry. I can't skate either," assured Blaze. He confirmed this fact by promptly falling flat on his face in the snow.

"Come on, Papa Gary! Hurry!" urged a wiggling Abigail anxious to get out on the ice. Gary managed to get his own skates on, carefully took her hand, and helped her walk around the Apollo fountain and onto the ice. Half of his Secret Service detail (the half with any skating abilities) were already out on the canal waiting for them. Those without skating skills stood sentinel around the edge of the frozen water with their pride and weapons intact. Two of the guest artists, Mr. Parker and Mr. Ito, also stood nearby with cameras, ready to capture scenes that they would later put on canvas. Lavel and Dumont stood on the embankment and cheered.

"Here goes nothing," said Jack wobbling as he tentatively put his right foot on the ice. "If I fall and break something important, Sam, you'll be hearing from my lawyer and my producer."

It turned out to be an enjoyable outing. Gary, who had spent some Christmases up in New England early in life, could skate reasonably well and was able to teach Abigail some of the basics. Abigail fell a lot, but she didn't mind. She just laughed and promptly got back on her feet with her stepfather's help. Once she was able to stand alone and skate forward slowly all by herself, Gary and Al each took one of her hands and skated around the canal in a big circle. Philippe, true to form, was a natural in skating just as he was in music, and the imp raced around the pond, showing off for the cameras. After a while, Gary put Abigail and Philippe in the golden sleigh and had two of the Secret Servicemen push them around on the ice while Al skated ahead and filmed. Gary followed behind offering a strong arm of support to Jack, who was slipping and sliding his way over the ice.

Somewhere in the middle of the sleigh ride, Jack managed to remember he was a reporter and started quizzing Philippe about his beloved ancestor who once frequented Versailles.

"He was a rich nobleman," explained Philippe proudly. "He was my great, great, great, great, great granduncle. He owned a castle and fought in many battles."

"Was he here during the Revolution?"

"Oh, yes!" exclaimed Philippe happily. "He was here and almost died defending the King and Queen against the new Republic. My ancestor's wife, she was thrown in prison, and her mother and grandmother all died most tragically!"

Gary cast Jack warning glance. He did not want vivid descriptions of the Reign of Terror aired around Abigail.

Jack ignored it. He liked terror. Terror was his business.

"Did your ancestor die, too?"

"No," said Philippe sadly, shaking his head, "But he was put in prison and suffered all the same."

Gary decided it was time to change the subject.

"Abigail, why don't you let Jack go for a ride in the sleigh? Philippe, you get out and skate with me."

Jack was thrilled at the idea of NOT skating and eagerly climbed inside the sleigh with Abigail. Philippe got out and skated alongside the sleigh as it was pushed around on the ice. Gary held Philippe's hand, and they skated together behind Abigail and Jack for another trip around the canal. Al then offered Philippe the chance to hold his camera and film Abigail, so Gary took the opportunity to skate over to the bank where Lavel and Dumont were standing and take a rest.

"Thank you for the sleigh, Monsieur Lavel," said Gary heartily. "Abigail is having the time of her life! She'll never forget it!"

"Nor will I," said the old gentleman wistfully.

Gary turned to Dumont and expressed his appreciation to the old gardener. "And thank you for the carriage ride. The horses are fantastic creatures. Tell me about the king's horses. I read his stables were once as fabulous as his palace."

Dumont nodded. "Oui, Monsieur! They were that! Two stables flanked the front courtyard in the old days, the Great Stables on the left and the Little Stables on the right. In the Little Stables, the King had 25 teams of ten horses each for his carriages. There were the black horses from Spain, the Brandenbourg Bays, the French dappled grays, and the spotted stallions from Poland. Oh, it must have been glorious, Monsieur! The King's horses wore white bridles trimmed with red ribbons."

"Most regal," observed Lavel with an approving sniff.

Dumont continued excitedly. "It was recorded that the King had over 600 horses in the Little Stables. There were rooms for the saddles and glass cases which held the royal saddles and harnesses. The King had one favorite saddle covered in violet velvet and gold trim. In the Great Stables, there were over 200 more saddle horses from Spain and Italy, and there were over one hundred English hunters that the King used in the chase.'

"The King loved the hunt," added Lavel with an authoritative nod.

"It must have taken hundreds of people to man the stables and care for all those horses," said Gary in awe.

"Oui, Monsieur," said Dumont enthusiastically. "Many worked there—quartermasters, footmen, pages, grooms, coachmen, sword-bearers, saddlers, couriers, and eight fife players!"

Gary grinned. "Maybe that's what I need to get me going in the morning—a cheery fife player to hasten my steps!"

Dumont laughed gaily, and Lavel allowed himself a rare chuckle. They suddenly turned their attention to some commotion on the ice.

'Teach me how to skate backward!" demanded Abigail to Al, the cameraman.

'Sure, kid!" he said. He retrieved his camera from Philippe and handed it to an agent for safekeeping.

"Teach me, too!" demanded Blaze, who by this time had pretty much mastered the art of going forward.

"It's easy," said Philippe demonstrating the art.

"I'm out of here!" announced Jack. He was having none of it.

While the children skated off with Al and several Secret Service agents in tow, Jack gingerly slid over to the edge of the embankment for a well-deserved rest and a private talk with Gary about the case. Lavel and Dumont assisted the tired, wet reporter into the waiting carriage, and Gary followed him inside and shut the door.

"The things I do for you," said Jack as he rubbed his sore ankles.

"They are most appreciated," said Gary sincerely. "And stop bellyaching. That little bit of filming should earn you and your network a prime-time special when we get back home."

"Then why wait? How about giving me my cell phone so I can call in the story now?" asked Jack holding out his hand.

Gary shook his head. "Sorry. Rules are rules. Besides, I haven't been able to get Philippe or Abigail to confess which one took your phone or where they hid it."

"Terrific. Foiled again by a six-year-old. Well, at least we are all safe and accounted for today. I got to tell you, Sam, this setup is starting to get to me. First Josette bites the dust, and now De Silva kicks the can. Did they find the jewels, by the way?"

"Yes and no," said Gary sourly. "Captain Berling reports that three emeralds were found on De Silva's body, in his coat pocket, which confirms the stones were successfully smuggled into the country. It also confirms De Silva was a consummate crook holding back a few jewels for himself. But the rest of the emeralds were not found in his hotel room."

"Which puts us back at square one."

"Not necessarily. Since not all the emeralds were not with De Silva, we can assume that they were deposited in the bank before the airport closed. And, thanks to the snowstorm, neither our chef nor even the Master of The Seven, for that matter, have gained access to them. We just have to solve the mystery before the snow melts."

"Do you still think it's Chef Michel?" asked Jack as he leaned back in his seat.

"It's certainly looking that way to the police," replied Gary.

Jack looked at Gary unconvinced.

"But you don't think so."

Gary stared out the window as he spoke. "This afternoon, I told Monsieur Lavel that this was not a crime of passion. But suppose it was? I keep thinking about the fact that Pierre and Josette were lovers. Pierre lied to us about that. Suppose we are wrong in assuming Josette's murder has something to do with The Seven. It might have nothing to do with The Seven at all! Suppose it was simply due to a heated argument between two lovers."

"You're not serious!" replied Jack.

"Weren't you the one to suggest Isabelle and Pierre were lying to cover up for each other?"

"Yes, but that was so I could incriminate Camille."

"But what if Pierre was the mastermind and, though I hate to implicate her, what if Isabelle is his *new lover*? Maybe they weren't walking in the north gardens at all as new acquaintances, but in the south gardens as true loves. Suppose Josette, who was last seen in the area of the Orangery, was out walking alone in the south part of the park enjoying the night air when she stumbles onto Pierre and Isabelle locked in a passionate embrace. A fight ensues, and Josette is killed."

"An accident?"

"Yes. *Le crime de passion*, not a premeditated murder."

"Interesting theory. You could be right," said Jack coolly. "And if you are right, just remember it was I who said it was a woman. Go for beauty, that's my policy."

Gary chuckled. "Yes, I know!"

Jack sighed. "Except this time my record has been abysmal. I've been in Paris almost a week now, and the only woman chasing after me is older than my grandmother and wears red Prada shoes." He shivered at the thought and continued.

"Well, I'll keep my eye on Camille, and I bet you a candy bar you'll find a strand of sparkling emeralds around her neck before the week is out."

There was a noise. Gary looked out the window and saw two motor carts fast approaching. Between Dumont's work crews and the returning afternoon sunlight, the Royal Avenue must be clear enough now for the carts to transport again. Things were looking up.

"Speaking of women," said Gary. "Here comes my wife."

"Which one?" asked Jack.

"That's not funny."

"I think it's hilarious," said Jack as he opened the carriage door and made his exit as the motor cart carrying Martha arrived. "I'll leave you two lovebirds alone. I think I'll try the backward skating deal. If the boy wonder Blaze Phillips can do it, then certainly I must give it a try. After all, I have my reputation to consider."

Gary laughed. "It's not your reputation that's in danger."

Jack slapped his backside with a twinkle in his eye. "With this ridiculously thick parka that Max purchased, my hinder regions are quite safe. Afternoon, Madame President! Your carriage awaits! Now, Messieurs, if you would be so kind to assist?"

With Dumont and Lavel each offering an arm for support, the reporter wobbled away. Martha took his place inside the carriage. She sat down beside Gary, took his arm, and snuggled close to him.

"How are you?" asked Gary as gave Martha a little kiss on the cheek.

"Tired," said Martha truthfully. "I thought the afternoon session would never end. The Italian President talked our ears off, and then Japan had even more to say."

"Did the Russian President behave himself?"

"Well, he was a bit cranky when the meeting started," said Martha yawning. "But during our first break, Secretary Campbell took him aside and had a word of prayer with him."

Gary smiled to himself, well remembering his former college professor's frightening powers of elocution and private persuasion. Against Campbell, President Voronova didn't stand a chance!

"And did Voronova have a spiritual experience?"

Martha grinned. "Let's just say we gained a reluctant convert. We certainly had a lot to cover on our agenda this afternoon—global health initiatives, the enhanced HIPC initiative, and the global digital divide initiative."

"Sounds very initiating."

"It was. And you?" asked Martha.

"I did some initiating of my own," said Gary.

The President's eyes widened.

"I'm listening," she said.

Gary took her gloved hand in his and told her about the startling news of De Silva's death and his decision to bring Lavel into his confidence. Martha turned her head and gazed out the carriage window to watch her youngest daughter skate.

"Is that why our daughter is outside this afternoon skating around King Louis XIV's Grand Canal in a sleigh made of gold?"

"Correct. Lavel suggested it, and I concurred. We must keep the children away from the main palace and the chefs as much as possible without appearing we are doing exactly that."

"I see. So De Silva is dead?"

"Yes."

"Damn."

"Those were Charles's exact sentiments," said Gary smiling.

"I can well imagine. So, now we don't have a lead on the outside to track. It comes down to us, doesn't it? Well, at least there is some good news to tell. The airport is open again, and the main roads should be open by tomorrow morning. What do you think? Given what's happened, should we have Mildred and the children stay put or come here tomorrow?"

Gary took a moment to ponder the question. Until this morning, his answer would have automatically been yes. He missed the kids. But after the news of De Silva's death, he wasn't sure bringing Joshua and Eliza here was the right thing to do. It was enough of a worry to keep track of Abigail. With Joshua and Eliza here, there would be three possible targets for The Seven to attack instead of just one.

Gary shook his head. "No, let's stick to the original plan, even if things get rough. The children will come when the meeting is over. In the meantime, Mildred can handle the situation just fine."

"True," agreed Martha, trusting her husband's judgment. She knew that Mildred was one of the original founders of the CIA's top secret organization known as the Blue Hairs. Many years ago, she and McKay's first wife, Isabelle Michaels McKay, created the covert organization of retired military wives with their husbands' support, oversight, and direction. Gary and Martha both knew Mildred could keep her wits about her in the midst of any crisis. "I'll call Mildred when we get back to the palace and update her on the situation." She paused. "Gary, why is Jack lying face down on the ice? Is he alright?"

Gary looked out the carriage window and managed to keep a straight face.

"Oh, he's fine. He's just learning how to skate backward."

"Shouldn't he be standing up then?"

"He's building up to it gradually," said Gary.

"I see," said Martha smiling. She relaxed in her seat and leaned her head against Gary's shoulder. "Well I, for one, am in dire need of a nap before dinner. This summit is exhausting. I swear I haven't been this tired in years. Care to join me?"

"Absolutely," said Gary happily. "Should we get Abigail?"

"No," said Martha firmly. "She's having too much fun, and she's surrounded by at least a dozen men, most with weapons. That should be sufficient, especially with Lavel supervising. I really like him, by the way. They all can bring Abigail back when she's finished playing. Would you mind telling Agent Pullman that I want to go back to the palace for a rest?"

Gary opened the door and called for Pullman to come over so that he could tell him their plans. Pullman and his team were never far away. He called Dumont back to the carriage. The old man climbed into the driver's seat, and soon the carriage slowly moved forward. As it pulled away, Gary glanced out the window towards the ice-blue canal. Jack was back on his feet and holding on to Al's arm for dear life. Abigail was in the golden sleigh being pushed by one of the agents. The sound of her bright laughter rang through the cold winter air and made Gary smile.

Where was Philippe?

Gary looked around in alarm. Then he spotted the waif standing off to the side of the canal by himself. Philippe was staring after the carriage, watching them depart. The look on his face was poignant, and it wrenched Gary's heart, for in those wide, honest eyes was the stark expression of a boy very much alone.

Chapter Eighteen

The Contest

Thursday night

After a refreshing nap with his beloved wife and an early dinner in the Porcelain Dining Room with his family, the Fosters, and the Mansarts, Gary walked towards the Hall of Battles, ready for an evening of entertainment. The chefs had completed their cake and sugar designs, and all the G-8 summit leaders and their spouses were present for the conclusion of the competition.

Night had fallen, but the expansive historic hall was all lit up with bright lights erected on three television podiums. Tall candelabras added a touch of elegance beside each cooking station, each lit with dozens of honey-colored beeswax candles. Monsieur Lavel and local merchants had added this touch of old to mix with the new. As Gary stared at the dancing candlelight, he realized this is exactly what they needed. They needed new light to shine on the mystery.

Jack ambled up to Gary and greeted him brightly.

"Why the serious face, Sam? This is a party! Cheer up!"

"Sorry. Just thinking about the case."

"That's your trouble. You think too much."

"I know. But we're running out of time, Jack, and we need something to happen."

Jack shrugged his shoulders nonchalantly. "Well, who knows? Perhaps fate will lend a hand."

A shrill voice spoke up from behind them.

"Hello, boys!"

It was Janet.

"Speaking of fate," said Jack, "here comes an ill-fated one."

Janet threw back her head as she passed by and gave them a wide fake smile.

"Having fun?" she asked.

"We *were*," said Jack sarcastically, returning her toothy smile with his famous flashy white teeth bared.

"Ha ha," said Janet spitefully. "Be nice, Jack, or I'll sic my politically powerful boyfriend on you. Remember. He's just a stone's throw away." She gathered her thick fur coat about her person and sashayed pretentiously into the hall.

"If only I had a stone to throw at her," replied Jack grimacing in Janet's wake. He sighed. "Well, I better get to work. Don't forget. I get first dibs on an interview with you and Aunt Sophie when the judging is over."

"You got it," said Gary.

Jack hurried off to his television crew, and Adelaide Foster immediately came up to Gary and handed him a chilled glass of Coke.

"Here. Drink this. It's the real stuff, loaded with sugar and caffeine. You look like you need it. Too bad you don't drink alcohol. Otherwise, I would have brought you a double scotch. No ice." Mrs. Foster held up her glass filled with amber liquid and toasted Gary.

Gary chuckled and took a sip of the soda.

"Thanks," said Gary appreciatively.

Adelaide took a few sips of her beverage, looked in Janet's direction, and declared, "Good Lord! How did you ever put up with that woman?"

"I'm not sure. It wasn't easy."

Adelaide Foster sighed sympathetically. "I actually feel sorry for her, you know. I suspect underneath that bash exterior she is quite insecure. Pathetic, really."

Gary smiled. "You are too kind."

Adelaide sipped her drink again and then changed the subject. "I heard the airport is open finally, thank the Lord. With the meeting winding down tomorrow, we'll be leaving the palace soon."

"Probably. Are you enjoying your stay in Versailles?"

"It's been perfectly splendid. I know I'll never have such an opportunity again. We have a whole suite of lovely rooms downstairs. Honestly, the rooms are a bit cold at night, and one does have quite a hike to the loo. But I'm not complaining. Nor is my husband—well, not too much. He is rather thrilled to have this experience. The townspeople are as giddy as we are, I daresay. They think of this palace as their palace, you know." Mrs. Foster's eyes suddenly popped open. "Good Lord, don't tell me those two are teaming up!"

She pointed towards Janet, and there indeed was Gary's ex-wife merrily chatting away with Beatrice, the Japanese Prime Minister's wife.

Mrs. Foster groaned. "Look at them! Name dropping, comparing diamond rings, and seeing which one can brag the loudest, no doubt."

"My money's on Janet," said Gary with the voice of authority.

"Don't be so sure," said Mrs. Foster. "Beatrice is the most selfish, most shallow woman I've ever known. She'll give your Janet a real run for her money."

Adelaide finished her drink. "Well, if those two start behaving badly, we can always send in Madeline to give them a quick kick in the shins. The old gal is standing back there with Mr. Parish, and I see she's got those bright red shoes on again. Bully for her!"

Maddie and Aunt Dotty were indeed standing back with Jack beside the CNN platform. They were admiring the fat cat, Sebastian, whom Philippe was holding tightly in his arms. Jack patted the kitty, leaned over, and whispered something into Philippe's ear. The imp grinned. Maddie sipped her wine, listening and keeping a very close eye on Derrick Brown. The British reporter had returned to the Hall, but he was keeping a healthy distance away from Philippe and his Prada-shod protectress.

Gary turned his attention to the chefs. The teams were standing at their stations, ready for the final requirement of the competition, the all-important move of their sugar and cake creations from the sturdy steel countertops to a square table set up in front of each station. This was a nerve-racking task, for the slightest wrong move could result in disaster. Once each chef positioned their pastry creations, the judges would make their final pass for scoring, and Dean Dubois would announce the winner. Gary was ready, and it appeared that all the guests had arrived. Dean Dubois took the microphone and asked everyone to take their seats. Gary decided to sit beside an overexcited Philippe and share the happy moment with the boy. Gary wouldn't have to stand and judge till all the works were successfully moved.

Dean Dubois welcomed the leaders and their companions to the conclusion of the pastry competition and formally reintroduced the teams to the media who were filming. Then Dubois began with Pierre and Antoine's team and asked them to move their work. The room fell silent as the two men came around, picked up the heavy cake and sugar work, and carefully moved it to the table. Gary was so nervous he could hardly breathe. But everything went smoothly, and Pierre's masterpiece was there for all the room to see. It was breathtaking. The king's palace was masterfully recreated with exquisite icing detailing around the windows and doors. The most beautiful part was the sugar recreation of the large fountain in the center of Marly with large sprays of aqua-colored spun sugar up into the air. The pale blue ribbons of sugar were so thin and delicate that they looked like frozen water. The crowd clapped and cheered, and Pierre took a majestic bow. Antoine stood close by his mentor looking radiant and proud.

Next, the female chefs took center stage. They lifted and carried their work slowly from countertop to tabletop, and for a slight second, it seemed Isabelle stumbled. Camille said something quickly in French, and the girl recovered. The crowd watched closely as the creation was gently placed on the table, and then the crowd began its applause. Isabelle let out a big sigh of relief and turned to grin at the cameras. Camille maintained her calm exterior and merely nodded in the direction of the press. Their creation was equally beautiful. The Menagerie had come to life; the recreation of sugar animals—the elephant, the lion, the ostrich, and the camel—captured Gary's eye. Such fine details!

"The animals look real!" whispered Philippe excitedly into Gary's ear. The poor child was literally standing in his chair while holding his cat and straining to get the best view. Gary had a hold of Philippe's legs for security, and he agreed with the boy that the animals did look life-like.

Next, it was Louis and Gerald's turn. They had been standing right in front of their station, blocking the view of their creation. When Dubois called their names, the two men looked at each other, smiled, and moved apart, allowing the crowd to get their first view of the Girard and Matisse creation. The crowd gasped and began cheering immediately. Even Gary was taken aback.

"Oh, Monsieur! Look!" exclaimed Philippe wildly. The boy almost slipped from Gary's gasp.

The pastry creation of the wedding of Marie Antoinette was extraordinary. Louis and Gerald had managed to recreate the main palace, a shortened version of the park, and the Grand Canal. The flotilla was unbelievably detailed. But the most magnificent part was Louis's recreation of the fireworks that exploded over the Canal. There were slivers of thin, sparkling spun sugar, each one dyed in delicate hues of blue, red, white, and gold, shooting upwards. Amazing! The two men carefully lifted their creation and moved it to their assigned table.

Now it was René and Claude's turn. All eyes turned to the fourth team as they lifted a spectacular masterpiece into the air. Gary was too far away to make a final judgment, but the shining blue and white palace was superb and just might win René the competition. The team was half the distance to the table when a series of horrific sounds exploded through the Hall of Mirrors. Everything happened so quickly that it wasn't until later that evening when Jack replayed the event in slow motion on his camera, did Gary fully comprehend what took place.

Philippe was straining to see the Porcelain Palace when he suddenly slipped, fell crossways into Gary's lap, and the cat Sebastian was hurdled straight into the lap of the buxom Mrs. Voronova sitting directly behind them. Philippe's flying legs and feet upset the metal chair and caused it to bang hard against the floor. Terrified, Sebastian's claws sunk deep into the Italian woman's thighs, and she stood and shrieked. The cat hissed angrily and darted from the room. The over-anxious Claude, startled by all the loud commotion, lost his grasp, and the entire sugar and pastry creation went tumbling to the floor in a thunderous crash, the delicate sugar tiles of blue and white shattering everywhere as they fell.

There was a stunned moment of silence in the room as the crowd stared at Mrs. Voronova, at Philippe, at the ruined cake and disqualified chefs. Cameras rolled. Even Dean Dubois, who held the microphone, was speechless. René exploded.

"IDIOT!" he screamed in a cruel voice. The master chef's face was darkening red as he drew deep, angry breaths. "Look what you have done! YOU have ruined me!"

"René, forgive me!" Claude cried pitifully. "I was startled by the noise! It was an accident!"

Michel lost all control and flew into a rage.

"I'm tired of your excuses! I HATE YOU!!!"

René lunged towards Claude and grabbed him by the throat, choking him. It took only seconds for Captain Berling's men, positioned at the back of the room, to rush forward and reach the two chefs. However, the artist, Tom Parker, dropped his work, jumped towards the two chefs, and got there first, for he was sitting on the side near the front row. The amazingly strong artist grabbed Michel by the shoulders and threw him deftly to the ground. Despite being on the floor, René continued to hurl angry threats towards his shaking assistant. He tried desperately to get off the floor, and it took Parker and two of Berling's largest men to keep him pinned to the ground, preventing him from attacking Claude again. Then the artist, Mr. Ito calmly came forward, reached down, and applied force to an area around Michel's neck. The chef let out a final scream and immediately collapsed into unconsciousness.

Gary instinctively pulled Abigail and Philippe close to him, turning their young faces into his chest, blocking their view of the violent scene unfolding before his eyes. During the attack, Claude's face turned red and purple by the time Parker pried René's fingers off his swollen neck. A stone-faced Captain Berling stepped forward and motioned for René to be taken from the Hall immediately. Still unconscious, the other chef's wrists were, nevertheless, cuffed behind his back; and then Mr. Parker and one of the large French policemen carried the broken man out of the room. Mr. Ito followed closely behind, ready to step in again if needed. Meanwhile, Aunt Sophie reached the shaken Russian President's wife and was assisting her out of the room.

The sound of shocked voices began to echo inside the hall as the crowd whispered and watched. A clearly mortified Dean Dubois finally took the microphone and resumed what was left of the pastry competition.

"Mesdames et Messieurs! Your attention, *s'il vous plaît.* Our apologies for what has taken place. But we have one more team to present, and it is best for us to continue, *n'est pas?* Let us conclude with Monsieur Bonnet's presentation, then we will break for some wine and refreshment while the judges make their final decision—and we clean up the mess. Please give Monsieur Bonnet your attention!"

"I must find Sebastian," urged Philippe impatiently into Gary's ear.

Gary refused and held on tightly to the boy. He wasn't about to let Philippe out of his sight. "No, Philippe," said Gary firmly. "I want you to stay with me, especially when there is a dangerous man about. I don't want you to get hurt. When the competition ends, I'll go with you and help find your cat."

Philippe looked at Gary steadily, and for a brief moment, Gary saw a fleeting expression cross the poor orphan's face. It was a relieved look of a child secure in a stern adult's authority, safe in a father's trust. Philippe meekly sat down and didn't argue. As Gary turned his attention back to the chef's station, he felt the warm, thin hand of the poor boy grab hold of his arm. Gary covered the child's hand with his own and held onto it tightly.

Bonnet and Marie were carefully lifting their recreation of the Baths of Apollo from their workspace, and Gary couldn't believe his eyes. Yesterday, there had been a very simple plan in place, but clearly, the addition of Marie Porter had sparked a fire beneath Bonnet's ingenuity. What was placed on the judging table was truly magnificent. The sugar statues of the horses rising out of the water were exquisite in their own right, but now, in addition, there was a miniature sugar golden carriage parked in front of the fountains, sculpted and executed in the greatest detail. Surrounding the carriage were freestanding forms of the Sun King himself, with several of his royal household. There were even tiny sugar pink and yellow roses surrounding the fountains. The crowd, overwhelmed by the drama of René's arrest and full of empathy for George Bonnet's situation, broke out in loud applause for the masterpiece. A rare look of pleasure and relief crossed the master chef's face, and modestly, he took a bow. Marie stood behind him, eyeing her proud father in the audience. Blaze stood up and clapped the loudest.

Dubois thanked the chefs, announced there would be a half-hour break for refreshments, and invited the panel of judges to make their final reviews. As Gary stood, Philippe let out a sound of joy and let go of his grasp. Mr. Parker was standing in the doorway of the Hall of Battles with a fluffy gray ball of fur wiggling in his arms. Philippe started towards the artist, stopped, and turned to ask permission to leave.

"May I go get Sebastian?" asked the child dutifully?

Gary nodded. "But stay inside the Hall and stay in sight. No hiding."

"I want to go, too," insisted Abigail getting out of her seat beside her mother.

"Ask your mother," instructed Gary.

Martha gave her permission. "The same rules apply to you, sweetheart," she added firmly. "No hiding for you either. And once you get the kitty cat, go help yourself to some refreshments. Look! Monsieur Lavel is waiting for you beside the table near Uncle Jack's cameras. He will get you something to eat. And there is Auntie Madeline. She'll want to see Sebastian. I'll be along in a minute. I need to talk to President Mansart while Papa Gary judges the cakes."

"I'll be good," promised Abigail. She took Philippe's hand, and together they darted off in the direction of the British artist who handed over the large cat to a happy waif.

"She promises to be good, but for how long?" mused Martha skeptically. She didn't wait for Gary's time estimate but left to find the French President. Gary caught the British artist's eye, gave him an appreciative nod, then took up his clipboard and got to work. Dean Dubois and Aunt Sophie quietly joined him in the final pass by the tables. There was muted discussion after witnessing such a violent scene. Gary breathed deeply and tried to focus on the task at hand. The trio walked past each entry, discussed the merits, critiqued the flaws, and weighed the artistry of each creation. Each one was glorious and worthy of the grand prize, but only one could be the winner. After examining the four remaining pieces, the three judges huddled in a corner and quickly made their final unanimous decision.

There was just enough time for Gary to grab some refreshment before Dubois took the microphone again to announce the winner. He glanced at the food table where Philippe and Abigail were standing with Jack, Maddie, and Babette. Philippe was holding Sebastian up for Babette to pet. Then Jack pulled out his wallet, pulled out some money, and handed it over to Philippe, which the boy pocketed immediately. It took only a moment for Gary to understand.

The brazen little con-artist!

And here Gary had been worried sick over the boy's safety! Safety?

For that child?

Gary inwardly fumed. How could he even think that Philippe, the street-smart Parisian pickpocket, the boy who nimbly dances atop castle ledges, would slip and fall off his chair?

Exasperated, Gary marched right over in time to hear Jack say, "Nice, work, kid."

"Jack!"

"Yes?" replied the savvy television reporter smoothly.

"I want a truthful answer from you," demanded Gary. "You set that whole thing up, didn't you—Philippe falling all over himself, the cat thrown high in the air, the accident that set René off? You planned the whole thing, didn't you?"

"Well, I did suggest that fate would lend a hand. And it did, although, in this instance, fate needed a pretty good shove. And you must admit it paid off. You wanted evidence that René can turn violent. Now you have it. McKay and Captain Berling should be able to take it from there. Case closed. Why all the fuss? I thought you would be pleased."

"Well, first of all, it was unfair. This is a competition. René and Claude should have been able to compete with the others and have their work judged fairly. Second, you put Philippe at risk! AND third, you paid him to do it! That is totally unethical. It's contributing to the delinquency of a minor!"

"Yes, wasn't Philippe wonderful?" said Maddie proudly, patting the attentive child on the head. "When this is all over, I just might take him home with me and teach him some of my best tricks." She looked at Philippe and winked.

Philippe looked thrilled at the prospect.

"Philippe, don't look so happy!" chastised Gary firmly. "I'm very disappointed in you. It was a dangerous thing to do, and you could have gotten hurt!"

"But I wanted to help Uncle Jack protect Abigail," explained Philippe sincerely.

"Uncle Jack?"

"Yes, Papa Gary. I told Philippe to call him that. That's what we call him," said Abigail helpfully.

"Aren't they sweet?" said reporter.

"Jack, be quiet. Abigail, you stay out of this. Philippe, don't you ever do anything that dangerous again. Understand?"

Philippe nodded, unscathed by Gary's rebuke.

"I think I will take Philippe and Abigail to see the cakes," said Babette judiciously. She quickly took the two children by the hand and dragged them off to safety.

There was a moment of uneasy silence.

"Well, just don't stand there," said Gary testily to Jack while pointing at the exit. "You're a reporter. Investigate! Find out what's happening with Captain Berling's interrogation of Chef Michel. And no more funny stuff!"

"You're so cute when you're angry."

"OUT!"

Jack laughed and skedaddled away.

"Here. Drink up," said Maddie handing Gary another glass of Coke.

"Where did you get this?" asked Gary gratefully accepting the offer. He gulped down several swallows.

"Adelaide Foster sent it over."

Gary took another long swallow and sighed. "Kids! I just don't get it. Philippe looked thrilled when I scolded him."

"Of course he did," observed Maddie mildly while sipping her wine. "Children crave attention, even if it is negative."

"You sound like the voice of authority."

"I should," replied Maddie sagely. "I have six children."

"SIX!" Gary stared at the small woman with his mouth agape.

Maddie took another sip of champagne. "Hmmm. Yes, Johnny and I had six children—three boys and three girls, and we have nineteen grandchildren, with our first great-grandchild on the way in late April, a baby girl. She'll be a Taurus like me, an extremely bull-headed child I hope." Madeleine blinked blissfully at the thought. "Shame Johnny is gone now and won't be here to welcome her into the world."

Gary took a sip of his soda and stared at the petite woman with new appreciation. "Well, since you have so much experience raising kids, tell me then, why should Philippe crave such attention. I mean, the boy lives in the most exquisite castle in all Europe and he has the entire staff of Versailles at his beck and call. Philippe is surrounded in luxury!"

"True," replied Maddie finishing her drink. "But there is one treasure Philippe desperately needs that's not found inside even this palace."

"And what is that?" asked Gary cynically.

She resolutely handed Gary her empty glass.

"A mother and a father," said Madeleine.

Chapter Nineteen

The Cabinet Room

Thursday Night and Friday Morning

Maddie's words echoed inside Gary's head as he returned to his seat. Babette brought the children back, leaving the cat with Lavel and Gary feeling a bit guilty. Gary pulled Philippe close as Dubois took the microphone to announce the winners.

Despite the drama of René's arrest, the pastry competition ended without further incident. Pierre and Antoine came in fourth, but by the look on Pierre's aristocratic face, one would think they finished first instead of dead last. Camille and Isabelle came in third. Isabelle was thrilled. Camille wore a detached smile as she received her medal, coolly thanked the judges, and took her place at her station. That left two teams vying for first place. It had been a close call, but in the end, it was an upset victory, with first place going to the worn out George Bonnet and his stand-in chef, Marie Porter. Louis and Gerald handled second place with professional grace and were the first to congratulate a stunned George Bonnet on his achievement. The diplomats and their wives cheered when

Bonnet received his medal and check for ten thousand Euros. Bonnet clutched his medal gratefully and thanked the judges and audience profusely. Ambassador Porter and Blaze rushed forward to congratulate Marie, who hugged her father with joy and then gazed with anticipation into the adoring eyes of Blaze Phillips. Gary smiled as he watched the pair walk over to the refreshment table side by side, lost in a private new world only they shared.

The competition over, Gary and Martha stood and prepared to retire for the evening. The Fosters came over to say good-night.

"Well, I'm rather glad that's finally over," said Adelaide. "Perhaps now I can get some sleep knowing the murderer has been caught. I do hope the Captain gets a full confession out of that ghastly man."

"No worries there," observed Prime Minister Foster with certainty. "Captain Berling is a clever chap. All in all, I'd say it's been a rather exciting evening, what? Lots of excitement, outbursts, egos, and surprises. Reminds me of Parliament during one of our 'Ask the Prime Minister' sessions."

"Oh, Alan, do be quiet," ordered Adelaide emphatically. "Wonderful job, Gary. I'm so pleased with the outcome. Bonnet most deservedly should have gotten the prize. And he definitely had the sympathy vote. We were all pulling for him after what happened."

"Well, he deserved it," said Gary sincerely. "The detailing on the carriage and the water fountain was stunning. Dubois said it was the best sugar work he's ever seen. It was a good conclusion to a difficult week for everyone. And honestly, I have to say, the judging was fun."

"It was wonderful to watch you in your element, sweetheart," said Martha smiling proudly.

Adelaide yawned. "All this fun has worn me out. Alan, say good-night, dear."

"Good night, dear," said Prime Minister Foster.

Martha laughed and said goodbye to her friends. The Hall of Battles was quickly emptying, with chefs, summit leaders, and television crews making for the exit. Gary had to pull Martha aside as Janet and Beatrice walked by, Janet on one arm of Louis Girard and Bea on the other.

"I'm *so sorry* you lost, dear boy," complained Janet loud enough for Gary and the rest of the Hall to hear. "I don't know *what* the judges were thinking! They must be blind! Yours was clearly the winner."

"It was the best, I assure you," agreed Bea haughtily.

"You are very kind," said Louis.

"Don't despair, Sugar," purred Janet as she turned and eyed Gary coldly for just a fleeting moment. "I have the perfect consolation prize. I've decided you can make the cake for my wedding! You've met Evan. He's the most popular man in the Senate, and anyone who is anyone in Washington will be at our wedding!"

For once, Louis appeared to be at a loss for words, and the women hurriedly pushed him forward before he could reply. Gary grinned. Poor Louis! He knew just how the chef must be feeling. Gary then noticed the shy Angelique followed Louis, Janet, and Bea quietly out of the Hall looking quite unhappy. Gary felt her pain. Rejection is not easy to bear.

"I'm exhausted, too," Martha admitted to Gary as Monsieur Lavel approached. "I'm ready for bed.

"I'm not sleepy," declared Abigail.

"Do not argue with votre mère, petite!" instructed Lavel solemnly as he handed Sebastian over to Philippe. "The sleep you must get, for tomorrow there will be much sunshine outside to enjoy."

Nice try, thought Gary. But Abigail wasn't buying it. She pulled intently on her mother's sleeve. "Mommy, don't make us go to bed! You promised to play the harp for us. Play something for us now!"

"Oui, Madame President," urged Philippe enthusiastically. "Play your harp, and I will play my violin with you!"

At the prospect of hearing Martha play, Lavel instantly changed course.

"We moved the new Antoinette harp into the Hall of Mirrors this morning, Madame President, and the instrument, it is in tune. The candles from the ball are there ready to be burned again. I would be most happy to light them for you."

Gary decided to join in.

"It would be nice to hear you play, darling," he said.

"Oh, alright," said Martha giving in. "But only on my terms. I insist on changing into something more comfortable. I refuse to play the harp in this dress and these heels!"

"Deal!" said Gary happily.

"I will ready the Hall of Mirrors," said Monsieur Lavel. He dashed off.

"Can Philippe sleep in my room tonight?" asked Abigail as Gary took her hand and led her out of the Hall of Battles. "The bad man might get me!"

Gary turned and looked at Philippe, who was walking behind him at Martha's side.

"Are you scared, Philippe?"

"Mais, non," said Philippe wide-eyed. "I am not scared."

Philippe, of course, was lying. Gary saw the fear in the boy's eyes.

"Well, perhaps it would be alright this one night. We can always use another man on the case to help protect Abigail. And we will ask Jack to join you. He likes camping out." Gary turned and instructed one of his Secret Service detail to go upstairs to Philippe's room to get the boy's violin and the necessary blankets, pillows, and pajamas.

Thirty minutes later, Gary was standing in the Hall of Mirrors watching a magical scene unfold. The news that Madame President would be giving a concert with the poor orphan French boy rapidly spread through the palace corridors like a cool winter wind and a crowd gathered silently in the deepening blue shadows of the Hall of Mirrors. Presidents and prime ministers alike waited and listened, some still dressed in their formal evening wear, others attired in their warm pajamas and dressing gowns.

Monsieur Lavel set up the harp at the south end of the hall, placing three large candelabra stands around the golden instrument. The white candles were lit, and their flickering light danced across the mirrored walls. Martha sat behind the harp, dressed in a cornflower blue silk dressing gown edged in white lace. Her hair, which had been pulled up during the pastry competition, was down and lay like a golden veil across her shoulders. Gary stared at his lovely wife, thinking that she looked every bit like a French royal queen.

Martha instructed Philippe to stand to her left. She struck an A-string, and Philippe deftly tuned his old instrument to her majestic harp. The tuning done, Martha turned and asked Lavel, "Does he know the Pachelbel *Canon in D*?"

"Oui, Madame President," assured Lavel. "The song, it is played outside on the grounds. He knows it well."

Martha nodded, then turned and instructed Philippe. "I'll start the piece, Philippe. I'll play the first few measures. Then you join me."

"Oui, Madame," said Philippe dutifully. He placed his treasured violin to his neck and waited for his cue.

Martha struck the Canon's well-known notes softly and slowly, and the rich sound of the harp music filled the historical, mirrored hall. Then the pure sound of Philippe's violin joined in, first meekly matching the harp in unison, then boldly breaking into its sweet melody against the harmony. The haunting music encircled him and carried Gary's mind across the centuries to the days of the old Sun King, when noblemen and women gathered and danced inside this palace, inside this very room. Gary listened contentedly. He could almost hear the rustle of royal silk gowns, could almost smell the aroma of potted orange trees in full blossom, could almost see the glitter of gleaming tables made of solid silver.

The touch of Abigail's hand brought Gary back to the present as his daughter grasped his hand tightly in her own. She looked up and smiled at him, comforted and cheered by the music. The cat, Sebastian, brushed up against his ankle. Gary leaned over and picked up the purring, gray beast. All watched and peacefully listened to the sound of the harp and violin. The melody rose to a bright crescendo that swelled and spilled out into the hall and the night, music and light arising against the dark, against the brutal cold. Gary watched the dancing candlelight, warmed by the miracle of music and the overwhelming love he had for his magnificent wife.

*   *   *

The next morning after breakfast, Gary met with McKay, Jack, Blaze, and Agent Pullman in the King's Private Cabinet, a small room located on the north side of the first floor of the palace. Per Gary's request, Monsieur Lavel was also invited to the briefing. The men stood huddled around the massive roll-top writing desk trimmed in gold and situated in the middle of the room beneath a gold and crystal chandelier. Gary stared down at the desk as General McKay broke the bad news.

"He let Michel go?" exclaimed Jack.

General McKay frowned and nodded, his arms crossed gravely against his towering broad frame. He was not pleased.

"Captain Berling interrogated the chef for several hours, but they didn't have enough to formally charge him with murder. Berling has nothing concrete to arrest Michel on, other than assaulting his assistant."

"Assault is good," quipped Jack.

"I agree," said Blaze looking unnerved. "We don't want Michel running free in the castle. He might turn and assault one of us!"

McKay pursed his lips. "Unfortunately, Claude refused to press charges, either out of loyalty for Michel or out of fear. Anyway, Michel was let go—for now—and Berling assures me he will keep Michel inside the Palace until the weekend. Berling will watch him closely, as will I. Trust me, gentlemen, my men will be on guard."

"That's right," added Agent Pullman. "Our agents will be monitoring Michel's every move."

"I vote we lock him up in the Bastille," suggested Jack.

"The Bastille, it was torn down years ago, Monsieur," observed Lavel.

Gary heard a sound, something like a giggle. He moved over to the window and stood by the thick crimson red drapes. He pretended to be interested in gazing down on the Marble courtyard. The red curtains fluttered ever so slightly in greeting.

There was a knock at the doorway.

One of Pullman's agents entered and announced that Chef Gerald Matisse wished to speak to them. Surprised, General McKay told the agent to bring the chef right in.

Matisse was ushered into the room immediately, clutching his chef's hat and looking anxious.

"You wanted to speak with us?" asked General McKay sharply.

Matisse bit his lip. "Oui, Messieurs. I—it is most awkward."

"Your conversation will be kept confidential," assured McKay.

Matisse nodded. "I mentioned in our interview the other day that I had spent some time with Claude." He paused and looked down at his hands gripping his hat. "What I did not tell you, Messieurs, is that Claude recently told me he thought his life was in danger. After what happened at the competition, I fear it is so."

McKay gazed at the chef narrowly. "Chef Breton did not tell us that."

Matisse looked up sharply. "He would not! He knows too much! He fears René too much!"

Gary pulled one edge of the curtain close to him protectively. The obedient curtain remained ever so still.

"Go on," demanded General McKay.

Matisse licked his lips nervously. "René and Claude spoke briefly when we arrived at the tents the night of the Ball. I think I told you that. René left just after we got there. Claude told me later that René actually told him that he was going to check on his station before retiring to the hotel."

"He was going back inside the Hall of Battles?" queried Jack, ever the good reporter.

Matisse nodded his head guiltily. "Oui, Messieurs. That is what he said."

"But he told us Michel was walking alone in the North Gardens," replied McKay.

"No, Messieurs," said Matisse emphatically shaking his head. "He is lying. That is why Claude is so upset. He knows the truth, and he is afraid if he decided to tell you, René would kill him too."

"Why didn't you tell us this before?" asked McKay in a low voice.

"I feared for my life also," answered Matisse with a sigh. "You have seen what Michel can do. But I could no longer hide the truth. I care too much for Claude!" He spoke this last sentence with great earnest.

"Very well," said McKay after a long pause. "We will report the information immediately to Captain Berling. I don't have to tell you how foolish you were in keeping the information from us. If you hear or see anything else, you must report it to us immediately. Understood?"

Matisse swallowed hard and nodded affirmatively.

McKay waited to speak until Matisse was ushered out of the room. "Well, I guess that confirms our suspicions. I better find the Captain and relay this information immediately. Mr.

Phillips, would you care to join me? We should be working on today's press release with the Captain as well. I want anything you tell the press to be approved by the Captain."

"Absolutely!" said Blaze.

McKay and Blaze left the Cabinet. Gary let go of the curtain and stepped towards the King's desk.

"Well, well, well," said Jack, the seasoned reporter. "This case just gets better by the minute. Too bad I can't call it in."

At that moment, they suddenly heard a phone start ringing. Agent Pullman stiffened. Jack looked around the room. Gary looked down. It was coming from inside the desk.

"Can you open this thing?" asked Gary.

Monsieur Lavel quickly stepped forward, turned a key that was resting in the lock, and opened the desk.

There was a cell phone hidden inside.

Gary picked it up and answered it.

"It's for you," he said and handed it to Jack.

Jack warily took his missing cell phone from Gary and began speaking with his worried producer.

As Jack talked, there was another soft knock at the door. One of Pullman's agents entered looking perplexed. He immediately glanced over at Gary with an apologetic, wide-eyed stare.

"Sir, we were wondering if you had recently seen the children? I—we, that is—are having some difficulty in locating them inside the Palace. The girl, Gabrielle, is most upset. They were playing Abigail's favorite game of hide and seek, and now she—we can't find them. We found Abigail's tracking sensor on the tip of the gray cat's tail."

Agent Pullman lowered his head and placed his palm to his forehead.

"Oh, God, not again, not here."

Lavel was very worried. "Mon Dieu! And Philippe, he knows all the secret passages."

"She'll turn up soon," said Gary confidently, turning slightly towards the window. The curtains remained very still. "Perhaps, Monsieur Lavel, you could assist Agent Pullman in searching Philippe's rooms upstairs? You must know of places where he likes to hide?"

"Of course. Please, Monsieur Pullman, follow me."

Lavel and the agents exited the room. Jack finished his phone call and announced he needed to find his crew.

"You can keep your phone for now," said Gary. "I'll clear it with McKay. Go on. I'll join you in a moment."

Jack left, leaving Gary alone in the Cabinet.

Gary paused and admired the white paneled walls of the King's private, ornately gilded chamber. He looked at the historic desk once more, then slowly pulled the roll top down and locked it again. Before he left, he turned and addressed the curtains sternly.

"You can stay here for a few minutes longer, then go find Gabrielle. I don't want you to go off hiding again. It's not safe. And shame on you both for stealing Jack's phone! We'll discuss that later. The weather is beginning to warm up. We can have an early lunch, and then we can go for a nice walk outside in the Orangery. You can invite Babette to join us. Would you like that?"

"Oui," chorused the chastised curtains in unison.

Gary smiled and bid the naughty curtains *adieu*.

Chapter Twenty

Opera

Friday afternoon

"I can't look!"

Jack Parish covered his eyes with his right hand and resolutely clutched the banister bordering one of the Versailles Opera's ornate "spectacles" with his left. He and Gary were standing in a second-story theater box situated between two wooden columns that were painted to look like marble. The men were looking down on the stage of the palace's grand theater. A magnificent eighteenth-century space designed by Gabriel, the Versailles Opera was once the site of the celebration of Louis XVI and Marie Antoinette's marriage. The theater was an oval shape with an orchestra floor that could be raised to the level of the stage, allowing it to also serve as either a banquet hall or ballroom for special occasions. Tonight, on this historic stage framed by plush, cornflower-blue curtains, Roland Martin's haute couture fashion show was a hit. Leading off the event, Madeleine strutted her stuff across the wooden floor, dressed in a crimson-red silk nightgown. She turned and struck a winning pose in her matching red Prada shoes. Leaders of the free world and their wives enthusiastically clapped and cheered.

"You're not missing anything," quipped Janet haughtily. She and her new best-friend-forever, Beatrice, stood beside Jack, not passing up an opportunity to needle the CNN reporter. "She is old enough to be my grandmother!"

"Ghastly," said Beatrice with a curt nod.

"Well, I think she's great!" exclaimed Al while filming Maddie's slinky return walk across the stage.

"That's because you have no taste," replied Janet.

"Too true," concurred Beatrice.

"Janet, leave Jack and Al alone," ordered Gary. "You promised to be a good girl, remember?"

Janet cast Gary a pained look. "But it's *so hard* to keep such silly promises, my sweet, when faced with that!" She pointed to the stage where Gertrude was now modeling a gown of hot pink satin.

Lack of vision did not impair Jack's verbal observation. "Janet Marie Benson-Craig being good? Mac, that ain't possible."

Janet ignored them both. "That only goes to show that Roland Martin has no taste. I certainly won't allow someone who uses *geriatric models* to design my wedding dress. Come along, Bea. Let's go see if Monsieur Lavel has set out something decent on the refreshment table."

"Too right," agreed Bea with a sniff as they left in search of food and drink.

Gary gave Jack an encouraging pat on the back. "You're safe. They've gone. Now look, there is your Aunt Dorothy. She's wearing a fabulous bright leopard print!"

There were more cheers and some catcalls from the floor below where the chefs and summit leaders were sitting.

"It's low-cut with fur trim," added Al.

"Oh, no, not animal prints!" whined Jack. He lowered his hand and took a brief look. Then he announced, "That's all I can handle for one evening. I think I'll take my chances and follow the Furies down to Lavel's refreshment stand. Catch you later. *Au revoir.*"

"I better go, too," said Al quickly putting away his camera. "Knowing those two, Jack will need either a chaperone or a bodyguard."

The shaken reporter and his sidekick left the box just as Martha arrived.

"What's wrong with Jack?" she asked as she entered the box.

"He's just feeling a bit modest."

Martha looked incredulous. "Jack?"

"He's very sensitive, my dear," said Gary.

Martha eyed her husband skeptically. "Since when?"

Gary laughed. "Since about five seconds ago. Don't worry, darling. He'll be his old conceited self by morning."

Gary paused to gaze down at the chefs seated on the floor of the Opera. He noticed that Isabelle and Camille were sitting with a cheerful Pierre Rousseau, Claude Breton was seated by an attentive Antoine Bernard, Gerald Matisse was sitting with a subdued George Bonnet, and Louis Girard was bravely sitting beside a brooding René Michel. Dean Paul Dubois and his assistant, Angelique, sat directly behind Girard and Michel, closely supervising their protégés.

Gary turned his attention back to his wife.

"So, where've you been?"

Martha stared at the shining chandeliers hanging from the theater's painted oval ceiling and sighed. "Working, of course. It never ends. McKay cornered and updated me on pressing matters over at DOD. His assistant in charge of International Security Policy is ready to announce our 'Nuclear Posture Review,' and they wanted to finalize details before they do a press release and chat with oversight committees in Congress. Secretary Campbell went back to his rooms at the Trianon to review the documents and prepare his communications with other countries on our new defense position."

"Everything going okay?" asked Gary.

Martha nodded. "Oh, yes. Everything's fine. We're reducing our stockpile of nuclear warheads from 6,000 to 3,000, officially changing our focus from enemy threat to enemy capacity."

"I love it when you talk strategy," said Gary. "Let's just hope our strategy with the chefs will prove just as successful."

There was a loud roar from the audience below. Gary glanced down to see Madeleine on the catwalk again, this time wearing a sexy little black dress.

Gary put his arm around his wife and grinned.

"Look at it this way, sweetheart. Who needs nuclear warheads when we have her?"

*   *   *

The fashion show proceeded without incident. Each of the Blue Hairs modeled three Roland Martin high-end creations. For the finale, all of the ladies walked the stage with the world-famous designer. The crowd gave them a standing ovation. All the guests were then invited to partake of Monsieur Lavel's refreshments set up outside in the hallway leading up to the Opera. It was a long room with black and white tiled floors and creamy arched walls and high ceilings. Running the length of the hallway on one side was a series of life-sized, white marble statues standing on square stone pillars. The glass windows and doorways located on the other wall let in the January afternoon sunlight.

Gabrielle was in charge that evening of watching Philippe and Abigail, who had magically re-appeared from their afternoon's absence. Neither of the children expressed any interest in watching a fashion show, so Gabrielle took the children upstairs into Philippe's realm, the King's private apartments, to play board games. This arrangement suited

Gary nicely since he sensed the investigation was concluding very soon. And that conclusion could prove to be dangerous.

Gary grabbed a diet Coke from the bar and went to congratulate the Blue Hairs on their catwalk performance. He found the ladies talking with Captain Berling, Blaze, Jack, Babette, and General McKay. Gary arrived in time to hear the conversation was indeed on fashion, but not on any of Martin's creations. General McKay was in the middle of a caustic review of Babette's latest outfit. Tonight, she was wearing a knee-length black skirt, a steel-gray top, and a mid-calf, black fur-lined coat that buttoned at her neck. Her knee-high black boots completed the look. It was the most subdued outfit the artist had worn during the week.

"I see you've toned it down, young lady," observed McKay critically. "About time, too. No more pink fur, if you please."

The artist grinned, not taking offense at the General's bluntness. "I thought a traditional look would be appropriate for tonight," she said looking down at her skirt. "I'm wearing Yves Saint Laurent."

"I liked the pink fur," said Gary stirring the pot. He enjoyed getting the General's goat.

McKay cast him a threatening glare.

Captain Berling offered a rare smile. "Come, General, you are in Paris! You must expand your fashion horizons."

The General looked horrified. "My horizons are fine just where they are, Captain! And Gary, don't encourage her! Sophie might get wild ideas for her wardrobe, and I can't cope!"

Gary laughed. He was about to say something more when suddenly Louis Gerard approached them.

"Pardonnez-moi," he said urgently while glancing back towards the tables. "I do not wish to disturb, but I must speak with you."

One of the General's eyebrows arched sharply at Louis's request.

"Concerning what?" Berling asked. "You may speak freely."

Louis nodded, looking quickly over at Gary.

"It may mean nothing, but as we were leaving the theater, I saw something very strange. Perhaps it is important for your investigation."

"Continue," ordered Berling curtly. "What did you see?"

Louis swallowed hard. "I was sitting near René in the theatre. When the show ended, his assistant, Claude, came towards us and walked out with René. Claude looked very anxious. Then I saw René give Claude something as they exited, and Claude put it in his coat pocket."

"Did you see what it was, Monsieur?" questioned Captain Berling.

Louis shook his head no.

McKay glanced at Gary with alarm. Gary knew what the General was thinking. They had to act fast. The General looked at the Captain and Aunt Dotty and nodded his head. Gary wasn't sure, but it appeared to be a prearranged signal of some sort.

Aunt Dotty suddenly walked over to Louis and patted him maternally on the shoulder. "Thank you, son. We'll take it from here."

Louis looked a bit confused. Nevertheless, he nodded his head obediently towards the Captain and General and walked away.

"You'll take what from where?" asked Jack once Louis was out of earshot.

Aunt Dotty looked at her nephew reassuringly. "You ask too many questions, Sugar," she drawled in her thickest Texan accent. "But seeing how you are family and a reporter, I guess you just can't help it. Say nothing, Jack Parish. Turn your camera off and turn your professional gaze aside. Captain, may we?"

The Captain stared at Aunt Dotty with a look of both apprehension and appreciation. He turned to the General for guidance.

McKay silently nodded.

Aunt Dotty smiled calmly and said, "Madeleine, Sugar, time for you to do your thing."

Maddie's eyes instantly lit up. She was apparently ready to do her thing. She took a big sip of champagne, handed her glass over to a mystified Jack with a wicked wink, and casually walked over to the refreshment tables where Claude, Campbell, and Dubois were idly chatting. Gary watched breathlessly as the little lady greeted each man with a charming smile and a flirtatious hug.

"What the hell is going on?" whispered Jack.

"Be quiet," ordered Babette sternly. "Trust Madeleine and your aunt. They are smart women. You will see."

Jack let out an exasperated huff and polished off the rest of Madeleine's drink.

After a few minutes of lively conversation, Maddie returned to the group anxiously waiting on pins and needles.

"Well?" said Dotty.

"Where's my drink?" asked Maddie.

"To hell with your drink!" said Jack impatiently. "What in blue blazes was that all about?"

Captain Berling politely cleared his throat.

"Did you get them?" he asked.

Maddie nodded, reached into her jacket pocket, and pulled out a small bundle tied up in a man's white handkerchief. She promptly handed it over to the French policeman.

"I believe this is what you're looking for, Captain," she said sweetly. "It was in Claude's coat pocket, just as Louis said it would be."

Jack's eyes practically popped out of his head.

"Why, you're...you're...you're a pickpocket, too! You're as bad as Philippe!"

"Oh, no," said Madeleine blithely. "I'm much better!"

"And it's a good thing she's on our side," added Gary. "Nice work, Maddie! Alright, Captain. Let's hope it is evidence we are looking for!"

Captain Berling carefully untied the bundle and stared at the contents.

"What is it?" asked Jack restlessly.

"Hold out your hand, Monsieur Craig," ordered Berling.

Gary extended his right hand. The Captain carefully poured out the bundle's contents, a shower of shining green stones, into Gary's palm.

"Oh, my God!" gasped Jack.

Gary stared at the glittering green gemstones in his hand. Here were the South American emeralds promised to The Seven. And here was the proof that René Michel was indeed a murderer and the member of The Seven they were looking for. Their search was over!

"The case, it appears to be closed," announced Captain Berling with certitude. "This should be all our government needs for an arrest and a conviction. This proves that René and Claude killed Josette. She must have discovered they had the emeralds."

"We have them!" said the General with satisfaction in his deep voice. "Both of them!"

"No, Messieurs, you do not," said Babette stepping forward. She picked up a single stone from Gary's outstretched hand and examined it carefully. Then, to their amazement, she placed it in her mouth. Then she spit it out.

"Gentlemen, these emeralds, they are not real gems. These stones are made of sugar," said Babette. "They are fake!"

There was a moment of silence as everyone stared at the sugar stones glittering in the palm of Gary's hand. Gary could hardly believe it! They looked so real! The wonderful feeling of success and relief suddenly plummeted into utter defeat and confusion. He didn't understand. Then he realized something important, a fact that made his blood run cold.

"We've seen that color green before. It is the same color as the one on Josette's finger. Is this why she was killed? Josette went back to the Hall of Battles to steal more of Louis's green dye. Remember what Louis said to us? He gave some of this dye to René for his sugar garden! He warned Josette not to steal from him again. So the night of the ball, she sneaked back and went looking for more bottles of this dye in René's station. She discovered these. Then someone found her and killed her."

"But where did she find them?" asked Jack. "That would tell us who was guilty! If she found them in Louis's refrigerator, then it's him! He always says he is the best in sugar!"

"Not necessarily," said Babette studying the stone. "Louis gave this color dye to René. Perhaps René used it to make the emeralds and hid them, in either his refrigerator or perhaps even in Louis' refrigerator, just in case he was caught. What is important now is that Claude had them after the murder."

Aunt Dotty looked at Gary narrowly. "So, René and Claude used Louis's dye to make fake emeralds? But why?"

"For the simplest and oldest of all reasons," said McKay gravely.

Captain Berling picked up another green crystal and examined it with a resigned sigh. "Could it be that simple? Mon Dieu! I was a fool not to see it before!"

"Oui," said Babette looking at the Captain with complete understanding. "It is all so obvious now."

"What's so obvious? What reason are you three talking about!" demanded Jack. It was not obvious to either him or to Gary.

Babette picked up another sugar stone from Gary's hand and held it up to the light.

"Double-cross!" she said.

Chapter Twenty-one

The Clock Room, the King's Staircase, and the Ballroom

Late Friday afternoon

Gary stood frozen to the spot as he held the green sugar stones tightly in his hand and gazed out the window, grasping the full truth and implications of Babette's statement. Lavel's promise had indeed come true. All the darkness and uncertainty that surrounded them during the week had vanished, bringing with it new light and understanding. Outside, the snow and ice began to melt, and inside, the mystery began to unravel.

"I can't believe it!" was Jack's professional reaction to the news. He looked plaintively at Gary, with an imploring look for permission to use his newly acquired cell phone. Gary shook his head. Not yet.

Captain Berling spoke in an urgent whisper to Gary.

"Mon ami, we must hurry. It is time."

Gary exhaled and handed the fake emeralds to the Frenchman.

"I agree," said Gary. "But first, we must tell Martha and get her out of the palace. Our agents must take her over to the Grand Trianon immediately. I don't want her inside the palace when it happens. If anyone questions her about her departure, she can claim her stomach is upset again, which it will be when she hears the news."

Agent Pullman, not three steps behind Gary, silently left to alert the rest of Martha's Secret Service detail of the situation and to make the necessary arrangements with Lavel.

McKay began issuing orders.

"Ladies," said McKay to the Blue Hairs, "you are to stay here in the hall. Act normal and stay close to the heads of state. If there is any danger, take immediate action. Mr. Parish, against my better judgment you will join us. You may watch, and you may report *later*. But keep your mouth and your camera lens shut! And Mademoiselle Moreau, I want you to go upstairs, find the children, and stay with them. Keep them upstairs till you hear from me. Should they come in harm's way, take any action you deem necessary."

"Yes, General," murmured Babette. "The children, they will be safe."

The General paused and gazed affectionately at the young artist.

"I know they will," he said. "But just in case, please take the Japanese artist with you."

Babette gave the General a knowing grin and quickly exited the hallway.

Jack opened his mouth to say something, thought better of it, and shut it again quickly, deciding to quietly obey the General's orders.

"Gary," said McKay, "get Monsieur Lavel. We'll need his help in selecting a good location, one that is private and away from the other guests. We have their security to think of as well. And everyone, try to appear calm! We don't want to alert anyone to the situation."

Despite Mckay's warning, Gary involuntarily glanced across the room. Evidently, their side gathering had already drawn attention from some in the hall. Pierre and Isabelle were staring in their direction, as was George Bonnet. Louis was staring, too, looking most curious. Gratefully, René had his back to them, talking to Dean Dubois and the Canadian couple. But where was Claude Breton? He wasn't in the crowd. Nor was Dubois's assistant, Angelique. Where had she gone? Was she safe? Would she be the next victim?

Captain Berling was right.

They must act now!

* * *

The trap was set in the Clock Cabinet, a small room just east of the bedchamber of Louis XV. The elaborate little white and gold room was named after a gilded astronomical clock permanently on display there, an ingenious device created for the king that could indicate the time, day, month, year, and even the phase of the moon. On top the clock was a crystal globe around which the tiny planets of our solar system circled the sun. How fitting, thought Gary to himself in a brief moment of mental diversion as he watched the ancient clock spin around and around. He was restlessly waiting for their trap to be sprung. The little-jeweled planets circled the tiny crystal orb, just as the kingdom of France once circled faithfully around this very room and its noble king. Now the elements of their modern play were tightening and spinning around this one moment, here inside this inner sanctum of the former Sun King.

Would things spin out of control?

Gary fought to contain his breathing against the tension rising inside his chest.

The Clock Cabinet had large windows looking over the Marble Courtyard. As the main players took their positions, the pale light of the afternoon sun shone eerily through the thick window panes. Gary stood erect beside the marble fireplace, his hand on the mantle to steady himself, feeling chilled in anticipation. The marble was ice cold to the touch, for there was no fire burning in this fireplace. The cold did nothing to help Gary calm his nerves as two of Berling's men led René Michel into the cabinet.

To his credit, René remained outwardly calm. The chef took a languid stance, his arms crossed coldly across his chest, as he quickly took stock of the situation. René's facial expression was positively indifferent, almost aloof, as he glanced about the room, eying one by one Captain Berling, Gary, General McKay, and President Mansart. He took the lead, wasting no time in demanding an explanation.

"What is the meaning of this?" he queried haughtily, the disdain clear and chilled in his deep voice. "What do you want with me? I have answered all your questions!"

Captain Berling took his time in responding. He did not react to René's scorn with emotion of his own but resolutely stared straight at the chef.

"We have one more question for you, Monsieur. Something has come to light that is most interesting," replied Berling smoothly. He took a small package out of his coat pocket and unwrapped it slowly in the palm of his left hand. The green sugar emeralds sparkled beneath René's gaze. Gary waited anxiously for the chef's response.

"What, monsieur, can you tell us about these?" asked the Captain.

If Michel knew anything about the emeralds, he hid it well. His own pale- green eyes narrowed as he looked at the sugar stones. Yet his face remained impassive. Gary glanced over at Jack, who was watching the chef closely for any signs of guilt. From the look on Jack's face, the seasoned reporter wasn't able to discern anything definitive.

"Emeralds?" said René finally with a disbelieving laugh. His lips curled into an ugly smile. "Is that why you brought me here? I know nothing about jewels, Captain Berling. I am not a jewel thief. I am a pastry chef."

"Look closely," replied Berling, ignoring René's insolence. The Captain picked up one of the sugar emeralds with his free hand and showed it to René. "These stones, are they not familiar? These stones, they were made of sugar and with the special dyes created by Chef Louis Girard."

"Then," said René with a sneer as he looked at the Captain, "you should be questioning Louis, not me."

"But I have, Monsieur, and Chef Girard assures us that you gave these sugar emeralds this evening to your assistant, Claude Breton."

René's eyebrow shot up with indignation at the accusation.

"Then Louis lies!" he replied hotly. René's voice was defiant, but Gary thought he saw a glint of fear in the chef's eyes. Michel was more than angry and annoyed. Now he was afraid.

"And why, Monsieur, would Louis Girard do that?" asked Berling.

"I do not know, Captain," said Michel. "You'll have to ask him. Perhaps he wants me arrested and out of the competition. Besides, what does it matter? What concern is it to you if I made some imitation stones out of sugar or not?"

"Because," said McKay stepping into the conversation, "the dye used to make those stones was the same color as that taken from Louis Girard's refrigerator by Josette La Claire the night she died. We found traces of it on her hand at the time of her death. We believe she came back to the Hall of Battles, Monsieur Michel, the night of the Ball, to steal more of that green dye from Louis and *from your station*. Louis had given some of it to you. You discovered her there, didn't you when you went back to check your station before leaving? And you killed her!"

René glared at McKay, the rage building in his face.

"And now you want to pin her murder on me? I already told you. I didn't know her! Why would I want her dead?"

Now Gary spoke up. He had to. After all the deaths that had happened last year — President Taylor, Eric Peters, and Donald Hooper — all who had died at the hands of one of The Seven — it was Gary who needed to confront and unmask this killer.

"Because," said Gary, "you are a member of an international organization, known as 'The Seven.' The competition was moved here on purpose, Monsieur Michel, because we knew one of the members of The Seven was a chef working in this competition. We had intelligence that a group of emeralds was to be a gift to The Seven. We believe you are that chef and that you created those fake sugar emeralds in order to steal some of the real ones for yourself once you left the Palace. And tonight, the fake emeralds were found in your assistant's coat pocket. You gave them to him."

René said nothing against the accusation, but his hands flexed open and shut. He breathed heavily through his nose, like a bull ready to charge.

Captain Berling folded up the handkerchief that held the fake gemstones.

"René Michel, I charge you with the murder of Mademoiselle Josette La Claire. You will come with us immediately to police headquarters. You may contact your solicitor there."

René Michel again did not speak.

Words mattered very little now.

He was surrounded, caught in their net.

Frantic and enraged, René took action instead.

In a quick move, he turned and pushed over a free-standing carved pedestal located in the middle of the room. The pedestal and a small, priceless bronze statue that stood on top of it came crashing to the floor. In the pandemonium that ensued, René made a mad dash for the door and for the King's stairway that lay beyond it.

Instantly, there was yelling, panic, and disarray.

U.S. Secret Service agents immediately rushed over to Gary to form a human wall of protection around him and prevent him from moving. Berling's men, the Captain himself, and even Jack rushed after the fleeing Frenchman. Gary had trouble seeing what happened next, but he heard the loud shouts of the policemen reverberating within the marbled corridor, the commands for René to stop, the pounding of heavy steps racing down the marble staircase, and the explosion of gunfire that followed.

Then there was a terrible silence.

Jack was the first to return with the news.

He looked at Gary and shook his head.

"Dead?" asked Gary.

Jack nodded.

"He's lying at the bottom of the stairs, shot in the chest and neck broken, a goner," said Jack.

"Sir, we need to get you out of here," insisted Agent Pullman with a firm grip on Gary's forearm. The agent practically lifted Gary's feet off the ground. "We must follow protocol, sir."

"Go," said Jack. "The General and I will stay here. It's over, Mack. I was never good at math, but with Senator Miller and Chef Michel gone, The Seven is now officially reduced to The Five, by my reckoning."

Guarded and led by his Secret Service detail, Gary bundled up in his winter coat and hurried outside. He wanted to return as quickly as possible to the Grand Trianon to be reunited with his wife, to hold her in his arms, and privately release all the feelings that were churning inside. With the outdoor temperature rising, the garden walkways were starting to clear, and Gary elected to walk, not ride, back to the Trianon. He wanted the time to settle down, to clear his head, to calm his nerves; and the gardens were beckoning to him, offering him their particular solace.

He and his security detail were all the way down to the Apollo Fountain when they ran into the gardener, Monsieur Dumont. The old man was walking up towards the palace carrying an old shovel and a large tin bucketful of salt. He must have been clearing the walkways and placing salt out by the fountains by hand.

"Bonjour, Monsieur Craig!" called out the humble man as he approached. Dumont was all smiles and happiness, placidly watching over his vast domain like a merry old king. He was innocent, unaware of all that had just transpired inside the castle.

"Hello, Monsieur Dumont," replied Gary rushing by, not wanting to stop and chat.

The old gardener chuckled. "It is the beautiful day, Monsieur, full of the sunshine! Perhaps you will soon see the fountains turned on. Enjoy the gardens…with the others."

Gary stopped dead in his tracks.

"What others," he asked turning his head around. Captain Berling's orders were to ensure all remained safe *inside* the palace.

Dumont put down his heavy bucket, took out a handkerchief, and rubbed his brow.

"The young French girl, the shy pretty one who works with Monsieur Dubois. She is here."

Gary felt a dreadful chill race down his spine, a cold that had absolutely nothing to do with the weather.

"Angelique? You saw her?" demanded Gary.

Dumont's head bobbed up and down affirmatively, pointing west.

"Oui, monsieur. I saw her not long ago. She was headed towards the south grounds, just over there."

"Do you know where she was going?" asked Gary urgently.

Dumont's face lit up with a kind expression.

"Oui, monsieur. I overheard her saying they were going to the Ballroom."

"They?" quizzed Gary, feeling his throat tighten with cold and dread. He could hardly swallow.

Dumont shook his head, put away his handkerchief, and bent over to pick up his bucketful of salt.

"Oui, Monsieur. She was out for a walk with that man, the nervous one, Chef Claude Breton."

Gary began to run.

Behind him his detail and even Monsieur Dumont followed in pursuit, calling after him.

Gary ignored them and protocol. He doubled his pace feeling the sharp panic rushing through his veins, filling his head with a pounding terror. What if René was partially telling the truth up there? What if they got it wrong? Certainly, René possessed the dye from Louis and the skill to make the sugar emeralds. But what if it was Claude who discovered Josette in the Hall of Battles, if it was Claude who actually killed the girl sneaking around the stations? Angelique could be out there right now, walking with a murderer.

Gary called out Angelique's name as he neared the grove.

He called out again as he entered.

And he was the first to see her.

Angelique stood terribly close to the edge of the circular steps, her face buried in her gloved hands, weeping.

Gary raced towards her and arrived just in time as she looked up at him with a look of pathetic desperation. Then she fainted dead away into his arms. Gary clasped the overwrought girl tightly to his chest and gazed over the edge, below the steps of the outdoor stone amphitheater. Parts of the stone steps were still covered with rigid sheets of shining white ice that were slowly beginning to melt, glistening brightly in the January sun. The light almost blinded him, but Gary could see lying at the bottom of the grove, on the edge of the frozen pond of water, the broken body of Claude Breton. Claude's eyes were wide open, unseeing. There was blood pooling around his skull, violent red mixing with the pure white snow and ice.

Claude had fallen down the steps, broken his neck, and cracked his skull.

Claude Breton was dead.

*   *   *

"Claude, he tried to take me hostage, said he needed a way to escape," said a trembling Angelique. They were gathered back inside the warm palace in the blue Porcelain Dining Room. The distraught young woman was seated at the table, and Monsieur Lavel and his staff were plying her with hot tea, lemon, and sympathy. Captain Berling had returned to the palace and sat next to her. McKay and Dean Dubois hovered close behind. Gary, Jack, and Berling's assistant sat across the table, waiting for the girl to continue her story. The policeman was taking detailed notes as usual.

"Must she do this now?" complained Dean Dubois furiously. "My assistant, she was almost killed by Breton. Look at her, Monsieur! She is in shock. Please, I beg you, let her come with me and rest!"

"Mais non," said Berling regretfully. "We must question Mademoiselle du Pré now while the facts, they are still fresh in her mind. But we will be gentle. We will be brief. Now, Mademoiselle, tell us what happened. Take your time."

Angelique nodded, took a sip of hot tea, and placed the steaming cup slowly down on the table. Her elegant hands were shaking.

"Claude asked me to go for a walk with him. He was upset, so I said yes. I wanted to help him. The sun, it was warm and the walkways were clearing, so it would be a pleasant walk. He was very nervous and—what is the word—preoccupied? But it did not bother me. Monsieur Breton, he was always nervous. Claude said very little, and we walked all the way down to the Apollo fountain. That's where we saw Monsieur

Dumont working. Claude didn't want to talk to him, so we turned around and began walking back towards the castle. When we got near the Ballroom, he suddenly grabbed me and pushed me inside the grove and began talking like a crazy man."

She paused to pick up her cup and drink again. Dubois looked like he couldn't take much more. His facial muscles flinched with every word she spoke. Finally, he bent his head and covered his face with his hands. Angelique continued.

"He said…he said he could not stand it. He said he needed me to help him escape, that he could not stay here any longer."

"Did he say why?" prompted Captain Berling gently.

Tears filled her eyes as she shook her head no.

"No, he did not," she said in a small quivering voice. "He looked so desperate, so pathetic. He grabbed my arm and began to pull me. I fought him off. Then…it was an accident, believe me! Claude slipped on the ice and fell down those steps. I almost fell over the edge, too. Then I saw him lying there like that…"

Her voice broke. She put her elbow down on the table, rested her head against her arm, and began to sob.

"That is enough," insisted Dubois tersely, stepping forward and placing his hands protectively on Angelique's thin shaking shoulders. "Please, Captain, spare her."

"Very well," said Captain Berling. "You may go, Mademoiselle."

Angelique stood up unsteadily. Dubois immediately put his arm around her and assisted her out of the room. At the doorway, Angelique paused and cast a fragile look of thanks towards Gary. Then she left.

"Monsieur Lavel, go and see if you can do anything else for her," requested Gary.

Lavel nodded with compassion and followed them out of the room. Gary felt assured Lavel would see to the girl's needs. She would lack nothing, poor thing. Gary made a mental note to have the White House physician also have a look at her. She might need something to help her sleep tonight. Her nerves must be shattered. He turned his eyes to the Captain.

"Well, what do you think?"

"I believe," said the Captain sagely, "that the case, it is finally closed. This is what I think happened. Claude and René, they must have gone back into the Hall of Battles the night of the ball. They were going to double-cross The Seven and take some of the real emeralds for themselves. Josette La Claire, she also returned to the Hall of Battles to steal the same food coloring. She must have discovered René and Claude in Louis's station. Or perhaps she was there first, and René found Josette looking inside his station or even Louis's station. René might have hidden the emeralds there. The order of who arrived first, it does not matter. One of the men, probably René, he hit her on the head with something, some heavy object from his cooking station. Then René carried her out to the garden while Claude cleaned up the workspace."

"It fits with the testimony and alibis we have," said McKay authoritatively. "Both Claude and René were in the North Gardens alone, according to their testimony. They said they didn't spend time together, but in truth, they were together committing and covering up their crimes."

"I still find it hard to believe," said Gary.

"Nevertheless," said Captain Berling with a satisfied smile, "our business here, it is concluded. Sadly, we may never know which of them actually killed Josette. Both men had the opportunity. I believe it was René. His temper, it was very bad. I have seen such cases before! Fortunately for us, both men are dead, and we have the fake emeralds, proof positive they were allied with The Seven." The Captain stood up. "Now, I leave it to you, gentlemen, to find the real emeralds. I wish you well in your search for the real jewels and in hunting down the remaining members of The Seven.

If you have further need of my services, you only have to call. Messieurs, adieu."

With that, the Captain and his assistant, Colbert, bid everyone goodbye and left the room.

"Well, it's over, thank God," said McKay. He looked at Agent Pullman, part of Gary's Secret Service detail. "Agent Pullman, inform the rest of your men. The murderer, or perhaps I should say 'murderers,' are dead, and this particular danger is finally over. They can stand down."

"Yes, General," Pullman responded. He stepped over to the window to radio the news to his fellow agents.

"Does this mean I get my laptop back?" asked Jack. "And, can I finally call in the full story to my producers?"

Gary chuckled. "Yes, you will and you can...tomorrow."

"Tomorrow?" exclaimed Jack.

"Tomorrow. All your communication devices are stored all the way out at the Queen's Hamlet. It's late, the sun is setting, and I'm hungry. And if I know Monsieur Lavel well (and I think I do), there will be a great feast at the palace dinner table tonight, celebrating the end of the summit meeting and the capture of the killers. We will return all the phones and computers tomorrow morning. Don't worry. You'll get your scoop. Besides," said Gary with a pleased expression, "we don't want it to look like you are getting any special treatment."

"But I like getting special treatment!" said Jack.

"Sometimes, my friend," said Gary smiling, "I think you were born three hundred years too late! You should have been a prince or perhaps even an English Lord!"

"Well, there's no chance in hell that will never happen," replied Jack with a covetous sigh as he looked around the over-gilded room.

"Come along, your highness," said Gary. "At least you can eat like a king tonight."

Chapter Twenty-two

The Queen's Bedroom

Friday night

It was their final night in the castle, and Gary's prediction of a royal feast did indeed take place.

Monsieur Lavel, with the assistance of the remaining competition chefs, put on a banquet splendid enough for the old Sun King himself. Long tables again lined the historic Hall of Mirrors; ornate silverware, crystal goblets, and colorful porcelain plates were set upon gold-colored tablecloths; yellow beeswax candles burned brightly in a long row of crystal chandeliers, and course after course of exquisite food was served on shining silver platters. Isabelle made a delicious ratatouille for the children. Camille created a simple yet stunning roasted chicken with vegetables that was Martha's hands-down favorite. George Bonnet made a Duck a L'Orange that had everyone talking. Antoine made a smashing Beef Burgundy that Aunt Dotty demanded the recipe for, promising to share it with her lady friends back home in Texas. Pierre made a Hollandaise sauce for his fish platter that made Gary want to stand up and cheer! Gerald Matisse made sizzling sirloin croquettes that were the favorites of Alan and Adelaide Foster; and even Paul Dubois graced them with a dessert, rolling up his sleeves and delivering a chocolate soufflé that put Blaze into sheer ecstasy. But the grand finale was produced by Louis Girard, who dusted off his worn copy of Antonin Carême's historic recipes and produced two grand desserts from the old master — the Château Rothschild *Gelée D'Orangees En Rubans* (*oranges* stuffed with orange and almond jelly) and the Brighton Pavilion *Fromage Bavarois Aux Noix Verts* (Bavarian cream with walnuts). The Bavarian cream was simply the most delicious thing Gary had ever put into his mouth.

The evening was a fitting counterpoint to the day's drama.

The food was comforting.

The conversation was cheering.

The mood was restful. Even Janet managed to be on her best behavior. Her beau, Senator Daniels, per Secretary Campbell's request, had managed to get to the airport and was flying back to the U.S. that night on joint business for the Congress and the Department of State. Janet elected to stay behind to enjoy one last day of the French royal treatment.

The friendships formed with leaders from around the world were uplifting, with a hopeful promise of further collaboration in days to come.

The only drama at the dinner table proved to be Madeleine, who kept winking flirtatiously at the Russian President, much to his horror and much to Jack's delight.

The dinner ended with the January moon shining peacefully upon the golden palace, sending presidents and prime ministers yawning to their beds.

Gary carried a sleepy Abigail to her plush blue bed inside Marie Antoinette's Meridian Cabinet. He tucked his little girl snugly into the silken sheets and covered her with a modern-day down comforter. Gary leaned over and gave her a goodnight kiss. He was just about to leave when Abigail piped up.

"Papa Gary?"

'Yes, sweetheart?"

"Philippe is very sad."

"Sad?"

"He doesn't want us to leave. He says he will be lonely when we go home. He doesn't have a mommy or daddy. Papa Gary, I didn't have a daddy once, before you married mommy. I was sad, too."

Her words made Gary feel terrible inside.

He took a deep breath and tried to be encouraging.

"I know it will be hard to say goodbye, sweetheart," assured Gary, perhaps trying to convince himself as much as Abigail. "But Philippe has Monsieur Lavel and Monsieur Dumont. He won't really be alone. They will take good care of him."

"Could Philippe come home with us?" asked Abigail hopefully.

Gary wondered for a moment.

Could he?

"I tell you what. I'll speak to Monsieur Lavel and see if Philippe could come visit us this spring, at Easter time. He could be your guest at the White House Easter Egg Hunt."

"Can he bring Sebastian?"

"Of course!" said Gary happily. "Philippe can come visit you and Sebastian can come visit your kitty, Sheba. Now go to sleep."

Pacified, Abigail rolled over and drifted off to sleep.

Gary quietly entered the Marie Antoinette bedchamber to find his wife already in her pajamas and in bed. She was wearing her reading glasses and had a big red notebook marked "PDB" in her lap.

"Bit of light reading?" quipped Gary as he sat down on the edge of the bed. The "PDB" or President's Daily Brief was a top-secret document compiled every day by the CIA summarizing new international intelligence warnings and detailed analysis of situations worldwide that warranted concern to American security. Jack referred to it as the ultimate big scary book.

"A woman's work is never done," replied Martha flipping a page. "Just a few things I needed to review this evening. Thank goodness for fax machines! Charles had these new memos brought up from the Hamlet this evening."

"You never get a break," observed Gary thoughtfully. He reached for her hand and squeezed it tightly. "This trip has taken a lot out of you. I've been worried about your health. How's your stomach? Better?"

Martha peered over her glasses. "Honestly, it's still a bit queasy, but after everything that happened today, I'm not surprised."

"Need a vase?" teased Gary.

Martha pushed her reading glasses up. "No, thanks. I don't think I need any rare Chinese pottery this evening. As long as I have you, darling, I'll be just fine."

"You do wonders for my ego," said Gary grinning.

"Another part of my job description," said Martha resolutely closing her briefing book. "Enough of national security for one night! I want to hear the latest palace gossip!"

"What makes you think I know anything about that?"

Martha crossed her arms and cast Gary a wifely skeptical look.

Gary sighed. "Okay, okay! Well, I did hear after my interview with Captain Berling that Pierre Rousseau offered George Bonnet a job in his restaurant in the Latin Quarter. And Bonnet accepted."

"Must have been the duck dish," said Martha thoughtfully. "You know, I kind of like Pierre, despite his very, very big ego."

"Me, too," agreed Gary. "And I heard after dinner that the Fosters had invited Camille and Isabelle to England this spring to cook a banquet for Parliament and the Queen! I was there when they issued the invitation. Isabelle was blown away!"

"And Camille?" asked Martha raising her eyebrows.

"Camille accepted the offer with almost a yawn. You would think she got to cook for the Queen of England every other day."

Martha laughed. "Adelaide liked Camille's cooking. Her chicken dish was very tasty. I like Camille, too. She is one very cool customer, unlike your former wife. By the way, how is Janet? She was awfully quiet at dinner tonight. That usually isn't a good sign with her."

"That's because she is saving up her energy to pester some poor designer in Paris to make her wedding dress once she gets out of here. Max, of course, is thrilled *he* doesn't have to deal with Janet any longer."

"I thought Max looked somewhat triumphant when he said goodnight. I don't blame him for that. What about the Blue Hairs?"

"I'm not sure what all of them are doing once the summit is over. You and General know more about that than I do… But Maddie, Eileen, and Aunt Dotty plan to go with us to the Queen's Hamlet tomorrow to officially have lunch with McKay and Sophie."

"Which means they will get a briefing with our National Security Advisor and get their next assignment," interpreted Martha.

"Exactly," said Gary. "I can't wait to see what new adventure you and the General dream up for them next!"

Martha smiled. "It will be quite something. By the way, how is Abigail?"

Gary shrugged. "A bit tired and a bit overly concerned about Philippe." Gary got up off the bed and went searching for his own pajamas. He found them laid out on a chair at the foot of the bed, pressed to perfection. Monsieur Lavel again? Gary marveled for a moment at this amazing man and then continued. "She just asked if we could take Philippe home with us."

Martha laughed softly and removed her reading glasses with a maternal sigh.

"Why am I not surprised? And is Abigail the only one who wants to take Philippe home?"

"Okay. You got me. I wouldn't mind a visit either. I suggested we invite Philippe over for the annual Easter Egg Hunt," said Gary pulling off his shirt. "And Abigail insisted that Sebastian, the cat, come, too."

"Abigail is a good negotiator!"

"Just like her mother," replied Gary.

Martha tilted her head contemplatively. "Why don't we invite Monsieur Lavel and Monsieur Dumont as well? Dumont can spend some time tinkering around the Rose Garden with you, and Lavel can spend some time with Usher Morgan down in the kitchens. Somehow I think those two would be great friends!"

Gary got into his pajamas and joined his wife in bed.

"Madame President, that's a splendid idea! I must admit I'm getting rather accustomed to Monsieur Lavel's extraordinary attention to details. We'll invite him, Dumont, and Philippe for an Easter visit in the morning, just in time for Joshua and Eliza's arrival tomorrow afternoon. Joshua and Philippe will hit it off with them, I'm sure. Now, my dearest girl, have I told you lately how much I love you?"

Martha tossed her briefing book onto the floor.

"No, my darling, you haven't! Tell me now!"

Gary took Martha into his arms and was just about to kiss her goodnight when a human cough interrupted them. Gary fumed. It was Agent Pullman standing at the doorway clearing his throat.

"Yes, Agent Pullman, what is it?" asked Martha testily, sitting up in bed and pulling the overstuffed comforter around her shoulders.

Pullman remained straight-faced. "Sorry to disturb you, Madame President, but someone has requested permission to come say goodnight."

Martha looked at Agent Pullman narrowly.

"Is it that important, Agent Pullman?" asked the President.

"It's *important*," stressed Pullman.

"Oh, alright! Bring them in," directed Martha sitting up straight in bed.

Agent Pullman nodded, his lips slightly curling into a pleased smile. He stepped back and motioned for the guest to enter.

Philippe came into the room carrying with him his old brown fiddle.

"Philippe!" exclaimed Martha in surprise. "We were just talking about you! What are you doing up so late?"

The poor boy nodded his head shyly, his brown curls framing his handsome young face beautifully in the candlelight. Philippe's expression was poignant.

"What do you want, my boy?" asked Gary kindly.

My boy.

How easily the words came. Gary suddenly he realized just how deeply he cared for this Parisian waif, this lonesome child of Versailles. Abigail's sentiment was also his own. Leaving Philippe behind was going to be very hard.

Philippe meekly stepped forward.

"Madame President, Monsieur Craig. Soon you will leave the palace. I wanted to give you a gift, but I have little money. But I have the music. So I come to play for you... something I wrote for you, Madame President."

Martha gasped with delight.

"You wrote something... for me?"

Agent Pullman, still standing sentinel in the doorway, folded his arms in satisfaction and smiled down at the child approvingly.

"Oui, Madame President. May I play it for you?"

Gary saw Martha's green eyes glistening. A maternal tear slipped down her beautiful face. She wiped the tear away, pressed her lips together and nodded.

"I would like nothing better than to hear you play," said the President.

Philippe stood in front of one of the massive floor-to-ceiling windows in the Queen's bedchamber, his small figure framed by the former Queen of France's rose-patterned silk draperies of majestic pink and blue. Martha nestled into Gary's strong arms as Philippe brought his violin up to his chin and rested it on his shoulder.

The music began, sweet and simple, filling the royal bedchamber with an angelic melody. Martha reached for Gary's hand underneath the covers and held onto it tightly. Gary fought back his own tears as he listened to the song, his heart flooded with love for his beautiful wife and this wonderful abandoned son of France.

Chapter Twenty-three

The Queen's Hamlet

Saturday late morning
January 12, 2002

G ary did not sleep well that night.
    He lay in bed wide awake for quite some time after Philippe played his farewell song and bade them goodnight. He was awake long after Martha drifted off to sleep in his arms. He was awake when the fat cat, Sebastian, jumped onto the end of the bed and curled up in a fluffy ball at his feet.

When sleep did come, it came with fitful dreams.

He had nightmares of Josette — breathless and frightened — the poor girl clutching her long white skirts in her pale, trembling hands as she ran down a snow-covered Royal Avenue. She was pursued by a terrifying shadow, in form like a hideous dark fallen angel flying low to the ground. The shadow's black wings spread out menacingly and wide across the gardens ready to engulf her. A demon's skeletal hands reached for the girl, grabbing her bare shoulder with a deathly grip. Josette faltered and fell, screaming as she collapsed in the snow.

Gary then dreamed of a royal banquet taking place inside the Hall of Mirrors, a dinner set on rows and rows of solid silver tables, all laden with exquisite food. Prominent people of the past packed The Hall: princes and princesses in their finest laced attire, dukes and duchesses bewigged and bejeweled, and royal attendants and milk-white maidens serving their guests with propriety and precision as required by the earnestly observed laws of etiquette. Gary saw Blaze sitting beside Louis XIV at the head table, toasting the old king with a silver goblet in hand. Chef Louis Girard was approaching the royal table with a covered dish.

Finally, Gary dreamed of the Versailles gardens at the height of springtime, full of flowers, full of light. He saw Philippe in the outdoor Colonnade, dancing the waltz with a pretty young girl dressed in a light blue gown. A young General looked on, enthusiastically clapping his hands in time with the music. He wore a sword at his side. And there was Jefferson again, this time playing his fiddle, all the time watching Philippe closely with a fixed paternal eye.

Then Jefferson stopped playing and looked at Gary with an imploring stare.

What did he want?

What was Jefferson trying to tell him?

Gary woke sharply to bright sunlight flooding into the palace bedchamber. He yawned and lazily shrugged off his myriad dreams, reaching towards his wife for comfort. But Martha was not there. Sebastian was in her place, however, curled up in a ball at her pillow. Gary petted the gray cat a cheerful good morning and then leaned over and glanced at the floor on Martha's side of the bed. The big red briefing book was gone, too. Obviously, his beloved had arisen long before to attend to her civic duties.

Gary yawned again as he pondered his wife's job. Oddly, it reminded him of football. Gary loved football. Most men do. In the moment, it struck him as odd that he was married to a woman who daily handled "the nuclear football," carrying around the secret codes of America's nuclear arsenal. Martha was like a quarterback, and Gary was her cheerleader. An amusing image of Martha dressed in heavy shoulder pads and throwing a big football to the Russian President entered Gary's thoughts, with himself, Aunt Dotty, and Madeleine on the sideline with pom-poms!

He rubbed his forehead hard. It was too early in the morning to contemplate such paradoxes and fanciful analogies and fitful dreams. So he got out of bed and went in search of his terrycloth bathrobe. Sebastian arose, stretched, and jumped off the bed to follow him. The marble floors were ice cold, despite the presence of a roaring fire in the fireplace. Gary hurriedly found his slippers and put them on. He looked out the window to see the sky clear and brilliant blue. The weather was rapidly warming, and that made him smile, for it meant Eliza, Joshua, and Mildred would be coming to Versailles today!

After finding his old bathrobe (a hideously striped garment that he refused to part with, despite Martha's insistence), Gary went to the nearest modern bathroom in the building. While he enjoyed being part of history, he drew the line at chamber pots! After he finished his toilet, he wandered into the Porcelain Dining Room with Sebastian close at his heels. The cat was ready for breakfast as well. Given Monsieur Lavel's pampering of the palace pet, Gary was anxious to see what extravagant breakfast would be waiting for him. Gary found Jack Parish alone at the table, barely awake and looking worse for wear. The reporter's white hair was a tangled mess, his face unshaven, his eyes bloodshot.

"You look awful," said Gary in greeting.

"I've looked worse," was the caustic reply.

Gary sat down at the table and poured himself a steaming hot cup of coffee. A java jolt was just what he needed.

"Rough night?" he asked taking a sip. The brew tasted perfect.

"Rough week," amended Jack miserably. "I've eaten too much, drank too much, worried too much, and seen too much, not necessarily in that order. And please pass me some of that coffee before I collapse."

Gary promptly pushed the steaming coffee pot in Jack's direction. He then helped himself to some hot Belgium waffles, butter, and syrup. Sebastian jumped up on the table and pranced over to a small plate full of Eggs Benedict. There was a small bowl of cream beside the eggs with Sebastian's name written on it.

Eggs Benedict and fresh cream — not bad.

"I've overeaten, too," said Gary guiltily staring at his piled-high plate. "Martha and I are both feeling our clothes tighten around the waistline."

"Yeah, but you went to bed at a decent hour. I went to the after party upstairs. Did you know Aunty Madeleine can Rumba?"

Gary almost choked on his waffle.

"Who exactly did she Rumba with?" sputtered Gary reaching for his napkin.

Jack crossed his heart with his fork. "I'm sworn to secrecy, but if diplomatic relations with the former Soviet Union suddenly improve, you'll know why."

"But I thought," said Gary between bites, "that the Russian President was terrified of Madeleine and her advances."

"He was, but that was before the Moscow Mules were passed around."

"Pardon?" asked Gary uncomprehendingly.

"Lime juice, vodka, ice, and ginger ale. They're rather tasty late at night, but trust me, son, they are hell come morning."

Jack paused to rub his forehead and nurse his cup of coffee. "The Russian Mules were the Russian President's wife's idea of a nightcap. She, her husband, and Madeleine polished off quite a few. You know, Sam, this trip has been a thrill a minute. Thank heavens we caught the murderer because, at this rate, I don't think my nerves could stand much more."

Gary frowned unsympathetically. "Well, the case is closed, so you've got nothing to worry about except your hangover and your headache."

The case was closed, thought Gary pensively as he set his fork back on the table for a moment. Then why didn't he feel any better? Why did he still feel so apprehensive? Then Gary thought about his strange dreams. He pictured Josette frantically running from the Shadow of Death and Jefferson staring at him with that plaintive, paternal look. Jefferson almost looked afraid.

What did it all mean?

Probably nothing, except the fact he was tired and hungry. So, Gary shook off his feelings once more, deciding it was simply a bad case of nerves. He must think positive. He must think about this day and the happy reunion with his other stepchildren. And he must have more of those waffles!

He looked over at Jack with a forced smile. "Drink some more coffee, Jack, and cheer up! Today you get your computer back and permission to phone in your first-hand account of all this week's events. It will be the story of a lifetime."

Jack immediately poured himself another cup.

"I know. Why do you think I'm up so early?" he said testily.

Gary glanced at his watch. It was 10:30.

"Right," he said. He didn't want to argue and left Jack to deal with his hangover. Gary determinedly focused his attention on consuming a second helping of waffles and on watching Sebastian lick his paws.

An hour later, a fairly large group left the palace for the long ride to the Queen's Hamlet. Piling into several tourist carts were Gary, Philippe, Abigail, Eileen, Madeleine, Aunt Dorothy, Louis, Gerald, the Fosters, the Voronovas, Angelique, Jack, his cameraman Al, and Max. Martha elected to stay behind due to a last-minute private meeting with Canada's Prime Minister. Gary suspected that Martha would also manage to sneak in a late-morning nap once her conference finished. She looked very tired to Gary. She needed rest.

The midday sun had burned away most of the snow and ice from the walkways, so the carts were able to make the journey along the garden paths to the secluded hideaway that once belonged to Marie Antoinette. Abigail was full of wiggles after being cooped up in the Palace for so long. She bounced and squirmed on Gary's lap as the motor carts headed down the Royal Avenue. Gary had invited Lavel, Dumont, and Philippe after breakfast to visit the White House this coming spring, and Philippe was ecstatic, chattering away excitedly with Abigail about the upcoming trip. The children were comparing their famous homes, and Jack, now somewhat sober, was making a forlorn face at Gary, wanting to film this little conversation. Gary shook his head no. Jack stuck his tongue out at him.

They made one brief stop along the way at the Petit Trianon to pick up Janet, who loudly insisted she be the first to get her cell phone back! She, after all, had a wedding to plan. After leaving the Petit Trianon, about halfway down to the Queen's Hamlet, they passed Marie Antoinette's Temple of Love, a twelve-column, round, outdoor pavilion that housed Bouchardon's famous statue of Cupid carving his bow. Inside the pavilion this morning were all four of the guest artists. They were taking pictures of the statue as the carts rolled by. Abigail called out and waved at the pretty Babette, who enthusiastically waved back at the child. The Japanese artist made a solemn bow towards the children as they went past them.

They rode on in relative silence except for the sound of cartwheels crunching the remaining snow beneath them and of Jack's occasional moaning with his leftover headache. Soon enough, they rode into Marie Antoinette's fairytale hamlet, a collection of ten buildings built around a small artificial lake for the former queen's pleasure and escape. They passed a stone cottage mill standing beside the water and another building called the Boudoir on the right before approaching the Queen's Cottage where the General and Sophie were staying. The newlyweds and their own Secret Service detail were waiting outside to greet them as the carts arrived.

Abigail and Philippe jumped out first and dashed towards Aunt Sophie, who greeted the children with open arms.

"Philippe is coming to visit us at Easter!" announced Abigail loudly.

Jack and his hangover flinched at the sound of the child's squeaky voice.

Aunt Sophie smiled at the children. "That's wonderful news! We'll have to plan lots of special outings for Philippe when he arrives."

"Can we take him to the zoo?" asked Abigail.

"Of course," agreed Aunt Sophie, "and to the Smithsonian, too."

"I've never been to a zoo, Madame," said Philippe full of excitement. "Will there be lions? I wish to see lions and elephants!"

"We could take him on safari to Africa," offered Maddie getting out of her cart. "Lots of big lions there."

"I hope you are joking," muttered Jack. He didn't trust Aunt Maddie as far as he could throw her.

Maddie winked at the reporter and then turned to walk with the Russian and English couples up the walkway towards the cottage. Angelique walked quietly behind them. Her face was still a bit pale. Gary hoped the poor girl would be able to retrieve her things and go home soon. Her nerves were shot.

"Can we hurry this up?" complained Janet as she stood up. She pulled her fur coat tightly around her chest. "I need to speak with my publicist. God only knows what this disaster of a trip has done to my image back in the states!"

"Don't worry," replied Jack. "Your image was already a disaster before you came."

Janet threw Jack a hateful glance and stomped away towards the cottage.

"You must be feeling better," observed Gary as he took the reporter by the arm. "Your sarcasm is back."

"With a bang," added Jack. "Who knew your ex-wife would be a natural cure for a nasty hangover? It must be the effect of two negatives cancelling each other out."

Gary laughed and led his friend out from the cold and into the historic cottage. The General and Max walked ahead of them with Louis, Gerald, and the rest of the Blue Hairs following behind. The group marched upstairs to the room holding all the computers and cell phones. The General and two of the Secret Service agents stood by a wooden table on which the laptop computers and a box with the cell phones sat. The General had Gary assist him with the disbursement. Gary would pick up one device at a time, and the General would supervise as agents checked each item off the master list.

Against his wishes, Gary decided to let Janet have her cell phone back first. There would be hell to pay if he didn't.

Janet snatched her phone from Gary's hand and immediately dialed her fiancée:

"Evan? Darling, it's me. How was the trip back? ... Wonderful, Darling. Oh, you heard from Violet Campbell? She was worried about me? How kind she is! At least she cares about what happened...."

Gary sighed. Before this conversation was through, Janet would be blaming him for all the murders and the snowstorm. It was classic Janet.

He turned his back on his former wife and and took pleasure in telling Jack he could use his cellphone now. The reporter pulled his cellphone out and kissed it.

"I've missed you," murmured Jack.

"You're pathetic," said Gary.

Louis and Gerald surged forward ahead of Max, the Fosters, the Russians, and Aunt Dotty and requested their phones and laptop with some urgency.

"We are in a hurry," explained Louis impatiently. "We must get back to our restaurant in town immediately."

"Naughty, naughty," said Max wagging his finger at Louis. "You can't break in line, boys. I was ahead of you."

"But we must go," demanded Gerald with great uneasiness. "There is much to do in town. You can send us our cell phones later if you wish, but there is one computer, that one over there, we must have." The chef pointed to his laptop computer on the table.

"Of course," said General McKay. The General himself reached down to retrieve the laptop and showed it to his agent to get the serial number.

Gary nodded his head in agreement. The chefs had been extremely friendly this morning and were apparently anxious to leave.

A bit too anxious to leave, perhaps.

Gary suddenly had that bad feeling again.

At that moment, something startling occurred to him, an idea that shuffled all the pieces of the week's puzzle into a new arrangement neatly inside his mind. Now it formed a vastly different picture, one more horrifying than any they had theorized before.

McKay was about to hand Louis his laptop when Gary suddenly stepped forward and intercepted it.

"Not yet," said Gary taking the computer away from his uncle.

McKay looked at him narrowly, his face darkening.

"What is it?" demanded McKay gruffly.

Louis instantly protested. "What are you doing? That is my property!"

Gary didn't answer either of them but sat down at a small wooden table, opened the computer, and turned it on. The computer started humming, and quickly a prompt appeared on the screen asking for a password.

Could it be so simple?

Gary carefully typed in the French word for SEVEN.

The password was accepted.

Gary heard McKay gasp.

"I don't believe it!" uttered Jack, gazing over Gary's shoulder.

There was an icon on the computer for email. One message was marked urgent.

Gary hit it quickly with the cursor. Louis's email appeared on the screen; and near the top, there was it was, an email from Carlos De Silva.

"Get them!" barked McKay to the Secret Service Agents in the room.

But Louis was too quick for them.

He grabbed Angelique and quickly dragged her over to his side, pulled out a knife from his coat pocket, and brought it up to the flesh of her exposed throat.

"OH MY GOD!" exclaimed Janet in horror. "He has a knife! He's a madman! HE COULD KILL US ALL! SOMEBODY DO SOMETHING!"

Philippe did something. Instantly the boy ran forward and threw his arms around the chef's waist and wailed.

"Do not hurt the beautiful girl, Monsieur!" cried Philippe in tears, hugging Louis tightly.

With Matisse's help, Louis managed to extricate himself from Philippe and forcefully push the boy away while keeping the blade at Angelique's pulsing jugular vein.

"QUIET!" spit out Louis angrily. "Do not take another step closer, Messieurs, or Angelique, she will die!"

Angelique's eyes filled with terror as Louis edged the point of the knife deeper into her neck.

"Please. Do as he says," whimpered Angelique in a quivering voice.

Agent Pullman lowered his gun, and Philippe stepped back towards the window where Abigail was standing.

Louis began issuing orders. "Gerald, take the weapons and the communication devices from the agents. Get their earpieces, too. No one else move."

Gerald Matisse went over to Pullman and took his gun away. He did the same to the three other agents in the room.

"Bring me the communication devices and a gun," said Louis.

Gerald brought them over.

Louis now took a gun and put away his knife. He held Angelique's arm tightly as he picked up one of the communication devices and began speaking into it.

"I have Monsieur Craig, General McKay, the Russians, and the British Prime Minister. We are armed with guns. Do not attempt to come inside or I will shoot them all."

Something was said in reply, but Gary couldn't make it out. Obviously, they got the message.

He glanced over at Abigail, who was frightened and clinging to Aunt Dotty. The old woman's arm was protectively around his daughter's shoulder. Dotty looked at him with a silent look of assurance. Gary noticed that Madeleine had inched her way toward Philippe and was shielding him from Louis's direct line of gunfire with her body and her big black handbag. Gary nodded a brief expression of gratitude to the daring secret agent. Jack and Al were watching wide-eyed, Al holding his camera, his knuckles white. Max had collapsed to the floor and was hiding behind the General. Aunt Sophie gripped Charles's hand tightly, and Charles McKay looked like he was about to explode. He was breathing hard like a pent-up bull. The Fosters and the Russians clung to each other in fear. Janet looked like she was about to faint.

Louis spoke again harshly.

"Now, Monsieur Craig, please continue what you started. Please open for me the email from Monsieur De Silva."

Gary's mouth was dry, and his hands were shaking as he slowly moved the laptop's cursor over towards De Silva's email. He hit enter, and the email popped up on the screen.

"What does it say?" demanded Louis.

Gary cleared his throat. He glanced over again at Abigail. She was listening.

"My French isn't very good," said Gary honestly, "but I believe it says the emeralds are here. I recognize the *Banque Nationale de Paris*. And there is a series of numbers."

Gary paused, and then he read the numbers out loud and very slowly.

"1-8-2-0-1-3-7-8-5-1-2."

"Merci, Monsieur," said Louis. "Now, turn the computer off and hand it over to Gerald."

Gerald took the computer away from Gary with a sinister smile.

Gary remembered the artists were nearby taking pictures at the Temple of Love. They were supposed to walk down to the Hamlet and join them for the afternoon. He had to buy them some time. Gary started talking.

"So it was you all along, wasn't it? You made the fake sugar emeralds."

Louis cast Gary an ugly grin.

"I told you before. I am the best in the world at sugar creations."

Gary nodded. "You made the emeralds but why?"

Louis clutched his gun and laughed. "Because I wanted some of the real emeralds for myself! No need for the Master of The Seven to get them all. Gerald and I, we make the fake emeralds for the double cross."

"But Josette discovered them in your refrigerator, didn't she?" continued Gary. "She went back for more dye and discovered the fake gems. You lied to us about that. René didn't plant them in your refrigerator. You hid them there!!"

Louis's mouth turned into a frightening grin. He glanced down at Angelique and pressed the gun deeper into her back. The lady chef was hyperventilating.

"Young women these days, they must be more careful!" Louis repeatedly drove his gun into Angelique's back, punctuating every word.

Adelaide Foster let out a small gasp. Her husband pulled her close and held her more tightly.

"What about René and Claude?" asked Gary, trying to continue the conversation as long as possible.

"René and Claude, they were idiots," continued Louis turning his head to face Gary.

"You planted the emeralds on Claude during the fashion show and then lied to us about it. You set him up!"

Louis shrugged. "It was easy. You and the Captain were looking for a suspect. We gave you one. And you believed everything we told you."

"And you took Josette's dead body out to the gardens," finished Gary swallowing hard.

"Yes," said Louis turning again and smiling devilishly at a petrified Angelique. "I took the dead girl and dumped her outside in the snow. I did not believe you would find her so soon. Too bad. And fortunately for us, Claude had a nervous breakdown. He tried to kidnap this poor girl to escape the palace and accidentally ended up killing himself instead. Now, Messieurs, enough talk! It is time for me to get the real emeralds. I will do what Claude Breton tried to do and take this hostage with me. Gerald, see if you can find some rope. We should tie up the agents before we go."

Unfortunately, given the setup of the Hamlet as the former farmhouse of Marie Antoinette, Gerald found some rope with very little trouble. Louis ordered Mr. Foster and the Russian President at gunpoint to assist Gerald in binding the hands and feet of the Secret Servicemen. They did so quickly.

"Now," said Louis menacingly into the agent's microphone, "Gerald and I will go outside. Gerald will take your guns before we leave. I and my hostage will leave the Palace. I will go to the bank and retrieve the emeralds while Gerald stays inside with his hostages. The Master of The Seven will want us to finish our mission here before we escape the country. We will use your communication devices. If anything happens to me or to him, we will shoot to kill."

The demand was acknowledged.

Louis took hold of Angelique's arm and pulled her close to him. He then gave a slight bow to Gary in departure.

"Bonjour, Monsieur Craig. Please give my regards to your lovely wife."

Louis, Angelique, and Gerald exited the room, heading for the long gallery that connected this part of the building with the Billiard room. There was an outside stairwell on that side of the building where they could escape to the carts. Gary quickly stood and grabbed Philippe by the shoulders.

"Philippe! We don't have much time! Is there a secret passageway out of THIS ROOM?"

Philippe's eyes widened.

"Oui, monsieur. It is over there." Philippe pointed toward a curtain.

Gary let out a huge sigh of relief. He then grabbed his little girl and pushed her towards the orphan boy.

"Philippe, take Abigail and sneak out of the Hamlet. YOU MUST NOT BE SEEN! Wait till you see Chef Girard and Angelique drive away in their cart Then I want you to run through the woods to the Pavilion. Find the artist, Babette

Moreau. *Tell her everything. Get Abigail to tell her the numbers.* Babette will know what to do."

Gary quickly hugged Abigail goodbye and then reached out and hugged Philippe, too.

"You can do this!" urged Gary with more faith in the children than he felt. He stared into the eyes of the boy with reassurance. "Go quickly! And make sure no one sees you!"

Philippe took Abigail by the hand, smiled bravely at Gary, and disappeared behind a curtain at the window.

The children were gone.

Now Jack suddenly went into action. He turned and grabbed his aunt.

"Aunt Dee, there is no time to waste! Which of your girlfriends is the expert with computers?"

Dotty hesitated.

"This is no time to be shy, Aunt Dee," said Jack sharply. "I need to know now!"

Eileen quietly stepped forward.

"It's me," she said. "I'm the computer expert on the team."

Jack grabbed her arm, pulled her over, and sat her down hard at the table where Gary was sitting. Then he motioned for his cameraman to come over. Al lumbered over with his laptop and small video camera in hand.

"Fantastic! Eileen, this is my cameraman, Al, who works for CNN. Al, this is Eileen, who works for the CIA!"

"Jack!" cried Dotty in disbelief. "You knew?"

"My dear aunt, of course, I knew. I've known for quite some time. Give me a break. I'm a news reporter, remember?"

Dotty gazed at her nephew in proud amazement. "I don't understand. When did you figure it out?"

Jack smiled. "I suspected something was up when you appeared with that ghastly shade of blue hair. Only something really important, like working undercover for Uncle Sam, would convince you to make such a fashion *faux pas*." Jack turned and started speaking in an urgent whisper.

"Now, kiddies, you two need to put your heads together fast and find a way to download what's in Al's camera into our computer and send it over the airways to Langley and Atlanta *toute de suite* before our not-so-sympathetic guard returns. Al has some technological magic built into our digital computer that can connect us to the internet even at this remote location. Once it's sent, our two companies can fight over who gets the rights to what bits of information."

"What are you talking about?" asked Gary. "What's in your camera?"

"Everything. We filmed it."

"Filmed what?" demanded McKay.

"Louis's confession," replied Jack. "I got it. I got it all."

McKay drew in a breath sharply. "All of it?"

Jack nodded confidently. "Yes, sir. That's what I'm good at. Reporting. We recorded every single rotten word he said."

McKay stared at Jack with a look of rare approval. "Son, I've severely misjudged you. You're not so bad."

'Thanks," said Jack beaming. It wasn't every day Jack got a compliment from the National Security Advisor.

Eileen handed her laptop to Al, and Al worked frantically to connect his camera. He quickly handed it back, and Eileen's fingers flew across the keyboard. McKay hovered behind them, whispering additional information and access codes they would need. They were almost finished when they heard the metallic click of a gun.

Gary's head turned.

Gerald was standing at the door with his gun pointed straight at his chest.

"What are you doing?" snarled Gerald suspiciously.

"Nothing," Gary lied, frantically trying to think of an excuse. He couldn't think of one.

Gerald wasn't buying it.

"Stand up and move away from the table," ordered Gerald. "NOW!"

Gary and Eileen stood up.

"Now, back away," said Gerald motioning them away with his gun.

"Please don't shoot us!" cried Janet suddenly. "I don't want to die! I'm supposed to get married soon!"

The edges of Gerald's lips curled into an evil smirk. "Mademoiselle, if and when I start shooting, it will give me the greatest of all pleasures to start with YOU! You are *the loudest, the most self-centered, bossy, aggravating, annoying woman* I have ever met! Now, be quiet!"

Janet closed her mouth, her face contorted with anger and fear.

Finally, McKay spoke up. His voice was level, soft, and convincing.

"You don't have to do this, son. Give us the gun, and we'll go lightly on you."

Gerald's eyes widened in surprise.

"You think I'm a coward?" he asked.

McKay stepped cautiously forward.

"No, I think you are smart. Think, man. You've been left behind. Louis is a smart man, too. What makes you think Louis will come back for you? How do you know he hasn't just left you here to take the heat while he escapes with all the jewels for himself?"

A serious look of doubt crossed Gerald's face.

"Louis would not do that," cried Gerald forcefully. Yet there was a hint of panic in his voice now. He then pointed his gun at the Fosters and the Russian couple. "But if he doesn't, I have my hostages. I will escape. Now, step away from the table all of you! I want to see what is on that computer."

Gary and the others edged away from the computer as Gerald moved in their direction. The chef bent his head over the screen when suddenly there was a commotion. Three people burst forth from behind the curtain. One large male headed in Gary's direction, one short man in the direction of the British and Russian couples, and a female form in the direction of the chef.

"Freeze!" yelled Babette, pointing her gun at Gerald.

Startled, Gerald snarled and deliberately turned the gun towards Gary's head.

Suddenly a big black handbag went sailing through the air, hitting Gerald's arm. It was another direct hit by Madeleine. There was an explosion, the sound of shattering glass, the sound of Janet screaming, and then another explosion.

When it was over, Gerald Matisse was dead, lying flat on the floor, deftly shot through the head by MI6 agent "Babette Moreau." She calmly walked over to inspect the body. Satisfied, she lowered her gun and smiled at the General.

"Hello, Father," said Jane Michaels McKay, dropping the fake French accent and resuming her British one. "Are you quite alright? I ran as fast as I could."

The General let out a blustery sigh of relief and heartily welcomed his beloved daughter with a warm embrace.

"Thank God you came in time, sweetheart," said McKay with open arms. "Perfect timing, as usual, nice bit of shooting, just like your mother, and what in hell's name are you wearing now?"

"Michael Kors," replied Max, getting up off the floor. "Marvelous choice, Darling. Just the thing to wear when shooting criminals. It was *the* hit of Fall Fashion Week this year in Paris!"

"No one asked you," snapped the General in warning. Max sank back on the floor under McKay's withering look.

Jane grinned at her Dad. "Well, you said to come to Versailles dressed to kill, so I did!"

"And did so quite nicely," observed Prime Minister Foster. "Well done, my dear. Well done!"

"Good heavens," exclaimed Adelaide Foster awestruck. "Is this really your daughter, General?"

"Yes," replied the General proudly. "My daughter and your country's agent. Please offer my sincerest apologies to the MI6 budget officer for the excessive clothing expense."

Adelaide laughed merrily and reached out to shake Jane's hand. "It was money well spent."

Her husband also extended his hand. "I daresay the Queen's Government can foot the bill. If there is any difficulty, any extraordinary clothing expenses will be our treat!"

"Thank you, Prime Minister Foster," said Jane. "I would like to keep the clothes."

Alan Foster puffed up his chest and nodded. "Absolutely, my dear girl! Good to see England had a role in the capture. National pride and all that, you know!"

"Who are the others?" asked the Russian President pointing to the Japanese and Canadian "artists."

"Special agents from Japan and Canada, here on my orders," replied McKay. He looked at Gary and said with the rarest of smiles, "It was one of my little ideas!"

Mr. Bardou smiled, and Mr. Ito bowed in recognition.

McKay continued. "And your other British agent, Mr. Foster, I will assume is outside, assisting our men?"

"He is," confirmed Agent Bardou. "Mr. Parker is untying your Secret Service agents. He will be here shortly. Fortunately, we were on our way here, not far away actually, when we spotted the children sneaking out of the Hamlet and into the woods.

It took us a moment to intercept them and learn what was happening. We ran as fast as we could." Now it was Gary's ex-wife's turn to make a statement.

"This is all *your fault*," said Janet hotly recovering her composure. She looked at Gary and then at Max.

"My fault?" exclaimed Max.

"Yes," said Janet coolly. "If you hadn't been so nasty about making my wedding dress in the first place, I wouldn't have been here and this," she paused and tilted her head in the direction of the dead chef, "would never have happened."

Max stared at Janet in disbelief.

Funny, but Janet's overriding self-centeredness was oddly comforting to Gary in this moment. Things were finally getting back to normal.

Janet put on her gloves haughtily. "Well, I'm through with Paris. Beatrice knows a lovely designer in Japan. I'll hire him. Now, can someone escort me out of here? I want to go home to North Carolina immediately!"

By this time, Secret Servicemen had been found, untied, and were flooding into the room. Agent Pullman himself took Janet by the arm and led her away from the situation. Perhaps one of the nicest things he's ever done for me, thought Gary gratefully.

Suddenly, the Russian President and his wife approached Madeleine. The Russian President shook her hand resolutely, and the wife gave her a kiss on the cheek.

"You are the brave woman, the good secret agent!" observed President Voronova with appreciation. "You help save us! You come to Russia soon and be our welcome guest."

"I'd be honored," said Madeleine batting her eyelashes shamelessly.

"I think lots more Moscow Mules are in her future," whispered Jack in Gary's ear.

McKay's cell phone rang, interrupting the conversation. The room abruptly fell silent as McKay snapped it open and took the bad news with his usual grace. He swore.

"Hellfire and damnation!" yelled the General into his phone after hearing the report. "How in hell did he get away?"

The phone meekly informed the General of the details.

McKay swore again.

"Well, what about the girl? Is she alright or did you manage to lose her too?

The phone gladly reported the whereabouts and condition of Mademoiselle du Pré .

"Well, thank God for that! Take her to the hospital immediately... I don't care if she protests. The poor girl seems to attract danger like a magnet. She should be suffering from shock and hypothermia by now. Call Captain Berling, tell him what's happened, and get him to close the airport, the train stations, the borders, and anything else he can think of. Now go and don't screw it up!"

McKay ended the call and folded his cell phone with a harsh snap.

"Louis got away?" ventured Gary.

McKay scowled. "Yes. He managed to use Angelique as a human shield, got ahead of all our men at the gates, and dumped our lady chef somewhere in town after he left the premises. Police found his car abandoned not far away. He must have had another agent waiting for him, most likely the person who killed De Silva. No telling where he is. Probably miles away by now."

"Monsieur Girard, he will not get far," contradicted Philippe politely.

All eyes turned towards the orphan boy. In the midst of all the commotion, no one noticed that Philippe had returned.

McKay sighed wearily. "What makes you say that, son?"

Philippe slowly reached into the pocket of his worn woolen coat and produced a man's black leather wallet. He meekly handed it over to the General.

"I took his wallet," confessed Philippe.

The General's eyes practically popped out of his head.

"You...did...what?" sputtered McKay.

"Chef Louis, he was a bad man. He tried to hurt that lady. He must not get away. So I took his wallet. *I took all his money.*"

For one of the few times in Gary's memory, General Charles McKay was rendered utterly speechless. Jack was not.

"I *love* this kid," exclaimed Jack pumping his fist in the air.

"Do you mean to tell me," asked Adelaide Foster incredulously, "that you stole his wallet? Good heavens, I didn't see a thing!"

"I picked his pocket," explained Philippe to an amazed group of adults.

Jane, still holding her gun, threw her head back and burst out laughing.

General McKay looked up and communed with the ceiling. "How in hell am I going to explain this to Captain Berling and President Mansart?"

Madeleine walked over and gave the boy a congratulatory hug.

"Okay, kid, you win. You really are the best pickpocket in all France."

Chapter Twenty-four

Eiffel Tower

Saturday Afternoon

C aptain Berling knelt beside the body and shook his head wearily in disbelief. He carefully lifted the edge of a white handkerchief draped across Gerald's face and stared at the dead chef.

"This case, it never ends," murmured Berling with a heavy sigh.

"I'm sorry," said Gary apologetically, feeling a bit guilty for dragging the Captain out yet again to another crime scene.

Gary was standing alone with Berling and his men. The rest of the party—the Fosters, the Russians, the Blue Hairs, Max, Janet, and the children—had been taken back to the Palace after giving their statements to the French Police. Only McKay and Jane remained inside the cottage. McKay was standing by a window talking briskly on his cell phone to Langley CIA headquarters. The crusty old General was frowning as he relayed the latest news to the CIA chiefs. Jane was sitting at the table giving Berling's assistant a detailed account of what happened from her perspective. The assistant was writing furiously.

Berling stood up.

"The apology is not needed, Monsieur. If not for you, the real murderers, they would have remained unidentified. But tell me, how did you know something was wrong?"

Gary shrugged. "I don't know. It was a feeling. Something just felt wrong."

The Captain smiled. "You have the good intuition, n'est-ce pas? Or perhaps you are a bit of the visionary, the psychic!"

"Oh, I don't know about that!" replied Gary modestly. "I've never been good at predicting the future. I do what I can just to live in the present!"

"Come, mon ami," directed the Captain as medics arrived to remove the body. "Let us go outside. Both of us could use the fresh air."

Gary followed the Captain out to a long, second-story gallery that connected the main house with the adjoining billiard room. From this vantage point, they could see the entrance where Jack and his entire press team were assembled. Jack was standing in front of the camera delivering his live report via satellite to the states. He was getting his promised scoop. Blaze had also arrived and was being briefed by Agent Pullman on the events that had just transpired. Blaze would be giving a press conference to other reporters outside Versailles's gates once Jack's report aired.

Captain Berling pulled out a pack of cigarettes and lit up. He offered one to Gary, who refused. Gary had given up smoking years ago and did not want to go back. He pulled out a roll of lifesavers and popped a peppermint into his mouth instead. Peppermint was his flavor of choice during times of stress.

The Captain took a long drag and blew the smoke out slowly.

"I must confess," said the Captain candidly, "I am sorry it was Matisse. I liked him."

"Yes, me, too," said Gary. "Any word about his boss, Louis Girard? Has he been captured?"

The Captain shook his head and puffed away on his cigarette. "Non. Chef Louis has—how do you say—vanished into the thin air."

"What about Angelique? Did she know anything, hear anything about where Louis was heading when she was being held captive?"

Captain Berling paused and stared down at his burning cigarette. "Ah, that poor girl! Always she finds herself in the middle of danger. She was most upset when we picked her up. She is in the hospital now. She protested, of course. But seeing that it was our fault for not arresting the right men and thus putting her in danger once again, we—that is to say, France—feel responsible for her additional suffering. We will do what we can for her and will pay for all her medical expenses. And I personally have assigned two men to stand at her door and a policewoman to sit by her bed for the next twenty-four hours to make sure danger does not threaten that poor girl again. And yes, she was most helpful. Louis mentioned something during his escape. Angelique told us he spoke of Switzerland."

Gary looked at the Captain in shock.

"Switzerland? That's weird. None of The Seven are located there!"

Captain Berling inhaled the smoke and smiled knowingly at Gary. "It is a good place to hide. Perhaps he goes to the mountains for his retreat."

Gary let out a deep breath. This wasn't good news.

"Have you told the General this?" asked Gary.

Berling nodded. "Oui. The General, he knows. I have issued orders for the Swiss border to be watched carefully. And we've contacted our allies in Geneva. They are watching for Chef Louis from their end. Do not worry, Monsieur Craig. He will not get far."

Captain Berling's cell phone rang, and the policeman excused himself for a moment to take the call. Gary put another lifesaver in his mouth and watched Jack finish up his reporting. The Captain soon returned, this time smiling.

"That was from my man stationed at the main Palace. The roads have all opened, and all of the Summit leaders and their parties are about to depart. The Fosters wished to extend their goodbyes and good wishes to you. Your ex-wife has also left. She did not extend such sentiments."

"I completely understand," said Gary ruefully.

The Captain put his strong arm around Gary. "But there is good news, mon ami. Your wife, she instructs me to tell you your other children have arrived! They are waiting for you at the Palace. Go, mon ami. I will attend to matters here. Let your mind rest. It is finished. Go to your wife and children with my blessing."

It didn't take much persuasion to get Gary back into his cart. Accompanied by his Secret Service detail and Canadian agent, Jean Bardou, Gary left Blaze and Jack behind and rode quickly through the massive gardens back to the palace. As his cart approached the Latona Fountain, he saw his wife and eldest stepdaughter, Eliza, anxiously waiting for him on the steps of the Water Parterre. Gary jumped out of the cart and dashed up the steps straight into Martha's outstretched arms. She broke out in tears as he held her tight.

"Thank God you are alright," she cried softly, her head pressed hard against his shoulder. "When the word came that they were holding you hostage, I was afraid I would lose you forever."

"Shhh," comforted Gary softly, as he stroked the back of her hair. "It's over now. We are safe."

Martha pulled back and looked up at him with glistening eyes.

"I've been a total wreck waiting for news. I threw up at least three times!"

Gary smiled and leaned over to kiss her cheek.

"Did you run out of vases?" he murmured into her ear.

Martha pulled back again and sniffed with a glorious smile.

"No, Uncle Gervaise kept me well supplied."

"Uncle Gervaise?"

Gary felt another set of arms grab him tightly from behind as Eliza joined the happy reunion.

"Monsieur Lavel!," said Eliza laughing. "But Abigail is calling him Uncle Gervaise now."

Gary let go of his wife briefly to turn and hug his eldest stepdaughter. She looked stunning. Unlike Abigail, who had her mother's blonde hair and big green eyes, Eliza took after her biological father with his black Irish coloring. Eliza had ivory-colored skin, coal-black hair down to her shoulders, and luminous blue eyes the color of a clear October sky. Staring at his teenage child, Gary took in the effects of staying a week in Paris.

"You look lovely, my dear," said Gary. "You've cut your hair."

Eliza blushed. "Just a trim and some layers put in."

"It's beautiful," declared Gary with fatherly approval. "And I like the new lipstick. Better hide it from Abigail though. You know how she likes to pilfer shiny cosmetics! Where is she, by the way?"

Eliza grinned, knowing her little sister's proclivity for stealing lipsticks and using them as crayons.

"She and 'Uncle Gervaise' are giving Nanny Mildred an official tour of the Palace. Mildred bought Abby a new doll in Paris, and Abigail is absolutely thrilled. When I last saw them, Abigail was clutching the doll in one hand and tightly holding onto Nanny Mildred's hand with the other."

"That ought to keep Abigail busy and secure for a while!" said Gary, knowing that "Nanny Mildred" was the co-founder of the Blue Hairs and an excellent CIA agent herself. Abigail couldn't be in better hands!

Gary suddenly looked around the Water Parterre.

"Where is Joshua?"

Eliza shrugged.

"He and Philippe are in the palace, too. Philippe is showing Joshua all the rooms upstairs! They took one look at each other, and they were instantly B.F.F."

"B.F.F.?" asked Gary clueless.

"Best Friends Forever," offered Agent Bardou stepping forward. The handsome agent turned and stared graciously at Eliza with his warm brown eyes. Eliza looked up enthralled. Well, thought Gary happily, maybe he was a bit psychic after all. At least he predicted this scenario accurately. Gary performed the necessary introductions.

"Agent Bardou, may I present my oldest daughter, Eliza Johnson Craig. Eliza, this is Agent Jean Bardou from Canada."

Eliza offered the young man her hand and a winning smile.

The agent looked instantly smitten

Now it was Martha's turn to play cupid.

"Agent Bardou, my daughter hasn't seen the gardens yet, and I'm sure my husband would like to walk around now that warmer weather has returned. Would you care to join us in what I believe the old Sun King called a 'promenade?'"

"I would be honored," replied the agent.

Agent Bardou and Eliza walked ahead while he and Martha followed, arm in arm, behind them. Gary and Martha walked slowly, allowing Eliza and Agent Bardou some space and privacy.

"So Mildred bought Abigail a doll?" asked Gary. "That's nice."

"Yes, she brought everyone presents. She brought me some lovely perfume, *Ce Soir Ou Jamais* by Annick Goutal. You'll like it. It smells like roses."

Gary smiled. Before meeting and marrying Martha, he used to live in a backyard cottage in Greensboro, North Carolina owned by Mildred's sister-in-law, Harriet. Mildred and Harriet had nursed him through his messy divorce from Janet, and Mildred had encouraged Gary to plant a rose garden in Harriett's backyard. She knew how much roses meant to Gary.

"She bought you a present, too," continued Martha as they meandered around the Latona Fountain. The fountain stood quite still, but the waters had melted and were sparkling beneath the afternoon sun.

"Let me guess! A cookbook?"

"She did, and Jane has sent you a review copy of her husband Trevor Allyn's latest thriller, *Waiting in the White House*, based on everything that happened to us last year."

"Well, being married to Jane Michaels McKay certainly gives Trevor a lot of exciting material to write about. I guess his next novel will be *Vigil at Versailles.'*"

"Great title! I'll let Jane know. Oh, I almost forgot to tell you," she said as they ambled down onto the Royal Avenue. "We've been invited to stay one more night in the castle."

Gary's heart leaped with the news. "You're kidding!"

Martha smiled happily. "Well, you see, everyone else has left—all the members of the summit, their wives, their associates, and most of the press, thank heavens! The only people left are us, the Blue Hairs, Max, Blaze, and Jack and his crew. Secretary Campbell has also left. He was in a hurry to get back to the states. He looked very upset. I know he's been awfully worried about Violet. We must see her when we get back. Anyway, Monsieur Lavel (or perhaps I should say Uncle Gervaise) was positively insistent that we stay another night. Do you mind? I think I can rearrange my calendar."

"Of course, I don't mind," said Gary. "But why do you think Lavel asked us?" Martha gazed at the Grand Canal wistfully. "He says it's because Eliza and Joshua haven't had the chance to stay inside the castle, which is true. And believe me, they are THRILLED to be staying. Lavel is putting Eliza in the Duphine's apartments, and Joshua is bunking upstairs in Philippe's lair. But I think it's more than that."

"You do?"

"Hmmm. Yes, I do. Honestly, sweetheart, like Philippe, I think Monsieur Lavel doesn't want us to leave."

Gary nodded, acutely aware that he didn't want to leave, either.

"So you really don't mind staying one more day?" asked Martha.

Gary stopped walking and turned towards his wife.

"We can stay on one condition."

Martha laughed playfully. "You and your conditions! Okay, what condition would that be?"

Gary stepped towards his wife and pulled her close, tenderly placing his hand under her chin and lifting her face up towards his own. He leaned slowly towards her, his lips almost touching hers, and murmured, "I get to cook."

*   *   *

"Are you sure you won't stay?"

An hour later, Gary stood at the front of the Marble Courtyard where a black stretch limo was parked, trying to convince Jack not to jump ship.

"Sorry, but I've had all the fun one man can possibly take," said Jack handing his suitcase over to an agent ready to put it in the trunk.

"But you like the high life," argued Gary pointing to the magnificent palace behind him. "You can stay another night, Jack! NOBODY ever gets to do that! Plus Lavel promises to give you any room you want!"

"Sorry, Charlie, but this poor boy has had enough!"

"What do you mean you've had enough?" asked Gary.

Jack folded his arms. "Mmmm. Let's see. In this latest case, we started with a little suicide, and it has been going downhill ever since. We've had death by poison, death by blunt force trauma, death by falling from great heights, and death by gunfire. There's been an 18th-century ball, a fashion show featuring retirees, and a cooking contest that kills. There's been petty theft upon my person, grand theft auto, and international smuggling of precious gemstones. We top it all off with secret passageways, secret computer codes, and secret agents who paint like Monet and who shoot like hell at 50 paces. Oh, no, Fred, I'm done! I'm fried! I'm cooked! I'm toast! I'm going home where the buffalo roam and only deer and antelope play!"

Gary laughed and patted Jack playfully on the back.

"Sure you don't want to wait and ride home on Air Force One? I know how you hate flying commercial."

"Who says I'm flying coach? Not me, Mack. Janet told me that 'Evan Darling' has sent his private jet to fetch his princess home, so I'm hitching a ride with your ex-wife!"

Gary's mouth dropped open.

"You're flying home with *Janet*?"

"Uh-huh. We've downed arms and declared a ceasefire — at least until we get across the Atlantic."

Gary's eyes narrowed.

"Jack, if I know Janet — and trust me, I do know Janet — she doesn't do anything for free. So, what did she demand in return?"

Jack shrugged his shoulders. "So okay, I did make her one itsy-bitsy, little promise to cover her wedding on the news — in primetime."

"That's some promise," observed Gary.

Jack grinned. "Yeah, but I didn't say *who* would be doing the coverage. Tell me, how does Janet feel about Joan Rivers?"

Gary shook his head smiling. "You do like living on the edge. But you really shouldn't fly alone with Janet. She might get mad and toss you into the ocean. Want me to loan you an agent or two for protection?"

Jack grinned. "I already got my own agent, thanks. Aunt Dotty will be riding to the airport and on the airplane with me. If Janet says something nasty, Aunt Dee can set her straight!"

Gary sighed. "Okay, you win. But if you don't mind, I think I'll ride to the airport with you. I've been cooped up inside that castle for so long, it will be nice to get out and about and see some of Paris along the way."

Jack wagged his finger at Gary. "Naughty, naughty! You just want to ride in the stretch limo. And you know that's not protocol."

"You forget. I have a posse. Agent Pullman, call the posse. I'm going to town."

Agent Pullman grimaced. This excursion wasn't planned. And Agent Pullman liked making and sticking to plans. However, orders were radioed out, and two more black cars soon rolled up to follow the limo. Aunt Dotty arrived and got her suitcases and coat stowed away. The party was getting into the car when Dean Dubois suddenly appeared, carrying his briefcase and overnight bag.

"Messieurs! Wait!" he called out urgently, running towards them.

Gary gave orders for everyone to stop.

Dubois raced across the Marble Courtyard and arrived completely out of breath.

"Is everything alright?" asked Gary with concern, fearing more bad news. "Did something bad happen to Angelique?"

"Mais, non," said Dubois out of breath. "Angelique, she is recovering. I just heard you were going to the airport. May I join you? I just received an urgent call to go to Rome. A former student of mine, he is having a great problem with his restaurant and asks me to come immediately to help him."

"Of course!" said Gary magnanimously. "There is plenty of room. You can ride with me, Jack, and his Aunt Dotty."

"Merci, Monsieur Craig. You are ever the good friend."

Dubois handed his suitcase over to the agents but clung to his briefcase.

"This stays with me at all times. It has my cooking tools. They are most expensive, and I trust them to no one!"

Agent Pullman did not look happy. This definitely was NOT protocol.

"I completely understand," said Gary to the gourmet chef. "It's okay, Agent Pullman. Come, Dean Dubois. Let's get going. Perhaps you can recommend a place where I can do some shopping in town today. I'd like to buy Martha and the kids some gifts, and maybe I'll just buy a few cooking utensils for me!"

Dubois smiled radiantly at him. "I know just the place to go!"

"I knew you would," said Gary.

They crammed into the Limo. Agent Lewis was driving, and an agent named Hawkins rode in front on the passenger side. The passenger seats formed a luxurious circle. Jack and Gary sat in the seats that ran behind the driver, another agent named Wood sat in back, and Dean Dubois sat next to Aunt Dotty on the passenger side.

They rode along for about five minutes with Jack and Gary admiring the sights, pointing here and there at the windows. Aunt Dotty was immersed in a review copy of *Waiting in the White House* that Jane had sent. The agents up front and in back were quiet. Dubois sat quietly too, staring at his watch, until suddenly he opened his briefcase, apparently searching for something.

He found it.

Dubois took out a knife and rammed it into the chest of Agent Wood, killing him instantly. Then, before either Agents Lewis or Hawkins could react, Dubois grabbed Wood's gun from its holster and fired one shot at the back of Hawkin's skull. The agent slumped over in the front seat, bloody and dead. Dubois then placed the gun at Aunt Dotty's temple.

"Now, Agent Lewis," said Dubois calmly. "You will use your communication device and tell your friends behind to stop following us or I will kill the woman and Mr. Craig."

Dotty's eyes were wide with fear, and Jack's face went ashen white.

Agent Lewis spoke into a wrist microphone, and the two cars following them peeled away.

"Very good," said Dubois coldly. "Now radio your men and tell them to down any overhead helicopters. Also, I better not see ANY French police cars or motorcycles or hear any sirens. If I do, I will start shooting. Go ahead. Tell them."

Agent Lewis again spoke thickly into his microphone. There was an instant reply and then silence.

"Where do you want to go?" asked Lewis.

"Downtown. Head towards the Eiffel Tower. We aren't far. I suddenly feel like sightseeing."

Gary's heart was pounding as the events of the past week shifted once more inside his mind to paint another horrible picture.

"It was you all along," said Gary bluntly. "Louis wasn't the master chef of The Seven and Matisse his assistant. YOU are The Seven's chef, and Louis is your assistant!"

Dubois's face said it all. His lips curled into a terrifying grin. He then took the bloody knife out of Wood's chest, held it close to Aunt Dotty's exposed throat, and pointed the barrel of the gun directly at Gary's chest.

"You are the smart man, Monsieur Craig. You have finally figured it out. Yes, I am one of The Seven."

Keep him talking, thought Gary. Keep him talking, and we stay alive.

Gary continued. "You were in control of everything. As head of the school and director of the competition, you were in a perfect position to select the chefs who would participate.

And you selected Louis, since he was your assistant, and Matisse assisted you both! You had Louis make the fake emeralds. You were the one who planned the double-cross!"

"But of course," said Dubois staring at Gary with hate-filled eyes. "Do not think I wanted to betray The Seven fully. I am loyal to the Master, but really, what would a few emeralds less matter to our cause? Once they were discovered, we would blame De Silva, of course. And once De Silva told one of my agents that the emeralds were in Paris, we killed him so he could not refute our story."

"Matisse must have found Josette in the kitchens the night of the ball when he went back to get them. He killed her while you and Angelique and Louis were at the tent drinking hot chocolate."

Dubois said nothing and continued to stare at Gary, his eyes narrowed. Gary proceeded with his theory of what happened next.

"Then he met up with you and Louis in the gardens, told you what happened, probably in a moment when Angelique could not overhear. Then you took Angelique away while Louis carried the body out to the park. Matisse went back and waited inside the tents. And you managed to keep poor Angelique away both of from them and then use her as your alibi!"

Dubois laughed wickedly.

"Angelique! She is the very useful girl. She makes the good hostage, no? Too bad she is not here. She would be very useful again!"

Suddenly the Eiffel Tower came into view. Gary silently prayed for a miracle but feared he might not live long enough for one to appear. They approached the road which ran alongside the river. Dubois called out new orders.

"Pull up and stop at the Promenade, in front of the bridge. Again, if I see any police, I will kill the woman and the reporter."

Agent Lewis did as he was told and brought the car up to the front of the Tower. Several tourists were milling around.

"Now get out," demanded Dubois in a sinister voice, "and come around and open the door. Then step back and keep your hands in the air!"

Lewis got out and walked around the front of the black limo. He opened the door and backed away.

"Now, Mr. Parish, you first."

Jack nodded weakly and crawled out of the limo.

"You next, Mr. Craig. And keep your hands up."

Gary slid out of his seat and stepped outside the car with his hands held high. Some of the tourists passing by stopped and stared. Gary tried to warn them with his eyes. But he knew if he spoke, he would be dead.

Dubois and Aunt Dotty emerged from the car. Almost immediately, some tourists saw the gun and began screaming and running in all directions. There was instant chaos! Gary saw two guards stationed at one of the towers. He prayed they would stay still and somehow radio for help. But foolishly they did not. They began walking towards them. But Dubois was too fast for them. Two more shots rang out, and both guards fell to the ground dead.

There were more screams and more panic.

Suddenly they were all alone, except for a few cars and taxis passing by on the highway.

Dubois held tightly to Dotty's right arm. Jack's aunt looked both terrified and angry, and she clutched her book to her chest. Gary hoped it was thick enough. Maybe it would be a shield for her if Dubois shot towards her heart.

"Now, Agent Lewis, it's time you were out of the equation," announced Dubois, who fired the gun at Lewis's right thigh. The agent fell to the ground in a shriek of pain.

"But I like you, Agent Lewis, and I want you to live to witness what I do next. So, be grateful I didn't aim for your head. Now pay attention."

Dubois let go of Aunt Dotty's arm and turned his gaze and his gun squarely on Gary.

"I happen to know, Monsieur Craig, that it was largely due to your interference that The Seven's attempt to gain control of the White House failed miserably last summer. It is thanks to you that our agents outside and inside the White House, they are all dead. The Master of The Seven will be very pleased to know I've finally taken revenge for our losses. Goodbye, Monsieur Craig."

Dubois leveled the gun at Gary and began to pull the trigger.

Gary braced himself for impact, for the explosion of metal hitting his head or chest, of leaving this life without being able to say goodbye to Martha or the children.

WHACK!

Aunt's Dotty's right fist, armed with her mystery novel, landed a punch and knocked the gun out of Dubois's hand.

Stunned Dubois stared frozen for a moment.

"Get the gun!" yelled Dotty reaching for Dubois's hair, which she yanked with all her might.

The chef screamed but managed to pull away and push Dotty to the ground. Jack ran towards his aunt and threw himself between her and Dubois. Gary lunged for the gun, but Dubois, seeing his opportunity lost, quickly got up off the ground and scrambled around the limo. He opened the door and jumped inside.

Gary got to the gun and picked it up. But he didn't know how to use it. He'd never fired a gun in his life!

Dubois slammed the door and started the engine.

Jack pulled Dotty up off the concrete and shoved her in Gary's direction.

"Give her the gun!" he yelled.

Gary obeyed. He handed the gun over to Dotty.

Dubois engaged the engine, quickly put the car in reverse, and started backing away. Then he turned the car towards the bridge.

Dotty ran forward closing the distance between her and the limo.

"The limo is bulletproof," cried Agent Lewis, "and there are only two shots left."

"I only need one," said Aunt Dotty confidently taking aim.

Dubois's car began to pull away fast, but there was a large garbage truck crossing the bridge, not far off, approaching them at a pretty good speed in the opposite lane. Dotty aimed and fired. The truck's front tire exploded, and the truck suddenly veered straight into the opposite lane, blocking Dubois's path and slamming straight into the limo. Dubois's car was pushed and smashed into the side of the bridge. The truck and it's driver were unharmed, but the impact proved too great for the limo and the bridge's rails. The rails gave way, and the limo fell through, out, and over into the muddy waters of the Seine below.

Suddenly there were sirens. Gary turned. Lewis was yelling into his wrist transmitter. Help was on its way.

Jack went over to his Aunt and retrieved the gun.

"I better give this back to Agent Lewis, Aunt Dee. You don't want your cover completely blown when the cops arrive."

Aunt Dee smiled fondly at her nephew. Jack walked back to Agent Lewis and handed over the firearm.

Lewis was sitting up, his hand clasped over his bleeding leg. He looked pale, but he would live. He took his weapon and used it to salute Aunt Dotty.

"Nice shot," said Lewis, as the sirens pulled closer.

"Ah, that was nothing," said Jack proudly as he knelt down to give Lewis some assistance. "She was born on a ranch in Texas, Agent Lewis. You should see what she can do with a rifle!"

The two Secret Service cars that had been following them before suddenly appeared along with five French police cars. An ambulance also appeared, its red lights blinking like a beacon of hope to Gary. Agent Pullman was first out of the car and by Gary's side.

"SIR, ARE YOU INJURED?"

Pullman's face was twisted with an expression of extreme anger and extreme panic.

"I'm fine, Agent Pullman, I'm fine," assured Gary. "And the next time I decide to do something outside of protocol, you have my permission to stop me."

Gary expected Pullman to smile or appear relieved. But a grave look of concern remained. Sudden Gary felt the terror return.

"What is it?" demanded Gary. "What's wrong?"

"It's your wife, sir. We've just heard. They've taken her to the hospital. She's very ill."

Chapter Twenty-five

Paris

Saturday late afternoon

The next ten minutes were the most agonizing of Gary's life.

Pullman picked Gary up off the sidewalk and shoved him and Jack Parish into a black vehicle. By the time the car started moving, a French police escort had appeared to lead them through the traffic-filled streets of Paris to the hospital. Gary held onto the door tightly, white-knuckling the handle as pure panic consumed him. He thought of last summer when one of The Seven's agents nearly succeeded in killing Martha by slipping poison into her lipstick.

Had Dubois succeeded this time?

Was it possible?

Yes.

Dubois was a famous chef in France's most prestigious culinary school. He had trained many chefs, perhaps several who worked inside the palace. It was very possible for Dubois to have more than one assistant, a mole cleverly placed inside Versailles's kitchens, ready to strike when his master so ordered.

Gary closed his eyes as he mentally played back the week inside his head. How could he have been so blind? The signs were all there—Martha's nausea, episodes of vomiting, and worsening fatigue. He should have recognized it, should have sensed the danger she was in! And now, if she died, what would he do? How could he live without her?

Gratefully Jack said nothing and didn't pull out his cell phone during the car ride. However, as the car pulled up to the hospital, it was evident the news of Martha's illness had already been leaked to the international press. A sea of reporters was waiting outside in the cold as Gary and Jack got out of the car. Flashing cameras blinded them as they rushed through the sliding-glass hospital doors. Inside, Gary was immediately greeted by a hospital administrator who led him and his associates down a long hallway, into an elevator, and up several floors.

Gary's nerves were raw as he exited the elevator. He was led towards a private room.

The door opened, and he saw her.

She was lying on a bed, covered with a white sheet.

IV bottles were hanging on tall metal poles beside her bed.

Her blonde hair was loose, falling gracefully across the pillow.

She was pale, almost as white as the bed linens.

But she was not dead!

Martha turned her head towards Gary and smiled as he rushed towards her. He grabbed her slender hand.

"Martha! Are you alright?"

"I'm fine," she said softly. She lifted her other hand to touch his cheek. Her touch calmed his shattered nerves.

"Oh, thank God," he said with a sigh. "I was so worried! I thought I had lost you!"

"You won't get rid of me that easily," said Martha.

"That is good news," said Jack stepping over to the other side of the bed. He leaned over and patted Madame President gently on the shoulder. "We don't want you going anywhere. Without you in the White House, my life would be so very boring."

"I promise to keep you entertained, Jack," said Martha smiling. "And thanks for taking care of my husband. I hear you two had another close call at the Eiffel Tower."

"You could say that," said Jack blithely. "But next time we go on a little driving excursion into town, I'm having Aunt Dotty bring her own weapons from home, starting with her big old shotgun."

"Martha, Dean Dubois was The Seven's real chef, and Louis was his assistant," said Gary. "Dubois is dead, so the case is truly closed. Now I want to hear what happened to you," he said tenderly.

"I passed out," said Martha simply. She paused and looked at him with a strange expression on her face. It was apparent there was more to be said. Again, Gary's nerves were on edge, and a million horrible scenarios ran through his mind.

She opened her mouth to continue, but into the room strode the White House physician, Dr. Edward Goldman, followed by a French doctor, a young man with dark hair and tortoiseshell glasses carrying a medical chart. Dr. Goldman greeted Gary and introduced the other physician.

"Mr. Craig, this is Dr. Fournier. He is a specialist, and I wanted his assistance in this matter."

Gary extended a grateful handshake.

"Thank you so much, Dr. Fournier," said Gary fervently.

"It is my pleasure to assist you," Dr. Fournier replied. "I was just going over the chart with your doctor, Monsieur Goldman. We have thoroughly examined your wife, have run blood tests, and did some imaging tests. We have the results here."

"Well, what can you tell us?" asked Gary anxiously. "I mean, clearly Martha made it through alright. She's alive, but will there be any lasting effects from the poison?"

"Poison?" The French doctor clutched the chart tightly and tilted his head with a bewildered look on his face.

"Yes," said Gary. "Do you know what kind of poison they used? Dean Dubois managed to have some poison administered to Martha at the castle! Is she out of danger?"

"Gary," Martha began hesitantly. "There is something I need to tell you..."

The French doctor beat her to it.

With a little smile he said with amusement, "Your wife, Monsieur, she is not poisoned. You wife is pregnant."

Gary felt all the air instantly leave his lungs. His mouth dropped open in shock. So did Jack's.

Dr. Goldman politely coughed. "Gary, Dr. Fournier is a doctor of obstetrics. His specialty is handling multiple births."

"Oui, Monsieur," Dr. Fournier hastened to explain. "As I was saying, we ran all the tests. It is my estimation that your wife is about three months pregnant. And after looking at the sonogram images, I can tell you the babies, they look healthy and strong."

"Babies?" said Gary.

"Babies," said Martha, glowing.

"Babies!" exclaimed Jack.

Out came Jack's cell phone.

Dr. Fournier cast Jack a narrow look and continued counseling Gary. "We will keep your wife here a little longer for observation. She merely fainted back at the palace—very understandable, I think, in light of her responsibilities at the Summit, her condition, the jet lag, and from all the *other activities* happening at Versailles. From what little I have seen on the television and in the newspaper, she has been under much stress. Let her rest here while I consult with Dr. Goldman, and we will release her *toute de suite.*"

"I'm going to be a father?" murmured Gary in a daze.

"A proud papa of twins!" confirmed Dr. Fournier looking down at the chart.

"Twins," said Martha happily, as she gazed up at Gary.

"Dr. Goldman," said Jack, "could I make an appointment with you right away? I think I'm going to need a steady supply of valium during the next six months. Can I get it in an IV drip?"

In that moment, the full weight of everything settled down upon poor Gary's frazzled nerves. And he did what any self-respecting man in his position would do.

He fainted.

Chapter Twenty-six

Peace Room and Latona Fountain

Saturday afternoon

When Gary awoke, he was lying in the hospital bed, and Martha was standing beside him holding his hand.

"What happened?" asked Gary.

"You keeled over, champ," replied Jack who was standing behind Martha.

"Keep your editorial comments to yourself," ordered Charles McKay, who was standing at the foot of the bed. "After what he's been through this week, he's earned a nervous collapse. How are you, son?"

Gary took in a deep breath and rubbed his forehead.

"Okay, I guess. Just a bit overwhelmed at the moment." He paused and looked at Martha reassuringly. "Overwhelmed in a happy way, of course!"

"I'm so glad," said Martha a bit sheepishly. "I wasn't sure how you would take the news. I must confess it shocked me, too. I should have known the signs. But I am 45 years old, and well, it just didn't occur to me. I've been irregular in my cycles this past year, so when it happened again, I thought that was due to menopause coming on. I blamed the upset on my nerves. And the weight gain, well, I blamed that on the French pastries."

"Amen," said Jack patting his own bulging waistline.

"Young man, you can't write any of this," cautioned McKay spying the cell phone still in Jack's hand.

"General, I could fill volumes with what you people won't let me publish," said Jack with a sigh.

"Any good news to report?" asked Gary as he propped himself up in the bed. "Something Jack can phone in. Don't forget, Charles, he did help capture Dubois!"

McKay frowned and relented. "Well, alright. Although technically, his aunt did most of the work. Nice bit of shooting on her part. Fine woman. I'm thinking we should send all our agents down to her Texas ranch for some specialty training. Anyway, the latest news is that Captain Berling and his men went to the bank. They were successful in retrieving the emeralds. The stones are in their custody now. So we can rest assured The Seven will NOT have those jewels to help finance any future operations."

"That works for me!" said Jack happily. "Pardon me while I step outside and have a word of prayer with my producers."

"Parish!"

"Yes, General?"

McKay's voice softened. "Don't mention The Seven in your report. Not yet. Just mention that the emeralds were part of the murder plot. And do me a favor. After you call in your story, go downstairs and visit Mademoiselle Du Pré. She's in a private room one floor below us. You can't miss it. It's surrounded by policemen, evidence of Captain Berling's guilty conscience. I broke the news of Dubois's near escape and death to her myself a few minutes ago. She was very shaken. Poor girl. She could use a friend about now."

Jack nodded. "No problem, General. I'll be happy to check on her."

"And be sure to invite her to dinner tonight," added Martha generously. "And if she can't make that, tell her I'd like to meet with her before we leave."

"Will do," said Jack.

Jack stepped outside into the hallway and closed the door behind him.

"Well, it is good news the emeralds were recovered," said Martha. "At least we know our mission to France was successful."

Gary agreed. "So, *'the case that would not close'* is finally closed. That should please Captain Berling."

McKay offered a rare smile. "Not really. Captain Berling begged to ask you, Martha, in all humility and respect, to please go home as soon as possible. He and his men are exhausted and in much need of a holiday."

Martha grinned. "We will go home tomorrow, Charles. But we have one more night at Versailles. And Gary, this should get you back on your feet fast. Monsieur Lavel also called. He was very upset about the car chase and was most concerned about you. He said to come 'home' as soon as possible — imagine calling Versailles home! — and that he would open up the kitchens for you as requested! Darling, you will get to cook! And Camille, Isabelle, and George Bonnet have offered to be your line chefs!"

That did the trick.

Gary was up and at 'em in no time flat. He relinquished the hospital bed to Martha. Within an hour, they were both in their limo heading for the palace with a whole host of reporters in tow. He and Martha arrived at Versailles and were greeted enthusiastically by their children, Philippe, Aunt Sophie, Blaze, Marie, Ambassador Porter, the Blue Hairs, and a very emotional Monsieur Lavel. As promised, Gary and the remaining chefs cooked up a sublime dinner, served again in the Hall of Battles. After supper, there was a round of toasts and a series of announcements. Martha and Gary shared their good news, and Martha announced her plan to use some of her former husband's trust funds to recreate the historic Marly back in America. (Martha's first husband was a relation of the wealthy DuPont family and had left Martha a sizable amount of money at his death.) The recreation of the former Sun King's palace retreat would become a modern center for residential artists and eco-friendly gardeners. It would be located on property owned by the President just outside of Charlottesville, Virginia; and (the biggest surprise of all) the Versailles master gardener, Monsieur Dumont, had agreed to assist in the planning and the recreation of the Sun King's gardens at Marly.

After dinner, by popular demand, there was another impromptu concert by Martha and Philippe. Martha sat at Marie Antoinette's harp and played several duets with the young boy and his violin. Gary sat contentedly with the fat cat, Sebastian, on his lap, enjoying the beauty and peace of the moment. Their time in Paris was coming to an end. And listening to Philippe play, he knew he most definitely did not want it to.

Sunday Morning

The First Family slept in late and breakfasted together in the Blue Porcelain Room for the very last time. Almost as an apology for the harsh storms cast upon them during the week, the sky this morning was absolutely clear and blue. The sun bore down happily upon them as they gathered outside on the steps facing the Water Parterre. Joining the First Family in their farewell were Jack, Blaze, Max, the Blue Hairs, and the French President. In addition, Angelique du Pré had been released from the hospital and had just arrived. Martha had insisted that the young woman come so that she could speak with her privately before they left the country. With breakfast concluded and their suitcases packed, it was finally time to go.

The first to say goodbye was Monsieur Lavel. He gave Martha a traditional Frenchman's kiss on both of sides of her face and wished her well. He then approached Gary and did the same.

Monsieur Lavel then knelt in front of Abigail.

"Ma petite Mademoiselle," he said seriously. "I have two gifts for you!"

Abigail's eyes grew wide in anticipation. She was holding her new doll in her arms.

"First, all week long you have asked for the French ice cream. Today we have prepared for you my favorite peach ice cream, made by one of the best restaurants in all Paris!"

Abigail jumped up and down as young Gabrielle appeared carrying the promised cup of fruited ice. She took her ice cream and tasted it immediately.

"It's good!" she declared.

"And secondly," continued Lavel standing up, "I cannot let you go home without seeing this!"

And suddenly, the gardens of Versailles sprang to life as all the fountains were turned on as if by magic. Gary gasped as he watched sprays of sparkling water burst forth, dancing high above the fountain as the outdoor music began to play. It was magnificent.

"Thank you," said Gary sincerely.

"Promise to come back in the spring," requested Lavel in all sincerity. "Our roses, they will anxiously wait for your return."

"We will," promised Gary.

Then Philippe came forward and requested permission to play for them one last time. He stood on the steps, pulled out his old brown instrument, and began to play along with the outdoor music. The sound carried out into the gardens, and the fountains seemed to rejoice. When it was over, Martha stepped over and thanked Philippe for his performance. She reached for the battered violin to admire it. Her face suddenly whitened.

"What's wrong," Gary asked with concern. "Are you feeling sick again?"

Martha slowly shook her head, a dazed expression on her face. She looked at her husband in amazement as she handed over the violin.

"Look at this," she said.

Gary looked down at Philippe's old brown violin. He saw nothing special.

"Look at the back," said Martha.

Gary turned the violin over. There he saw a name etched into the darkened wood. It was a mark he had seen many times over in his wife's private study, at the University of Virginia and at Monticello....

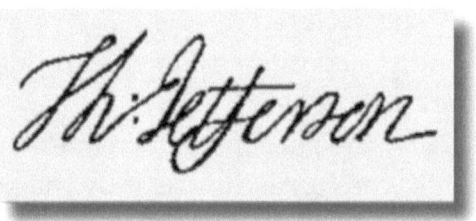

Gary looked at Martha in utter amazement.

"This was Jefferson's violin? Could it be?"

"Oh, yes, it could," said Martha, being one of the world's leading experts on Jefferson and the former Dean of the University of Virginia Law School before becoming the U.S. President. "Jefferson was a great musician, but his violin is one of the rare artifacts belonging to him that has gone missing for centuries." She looked at Philippe in wonder. "And to think we've been serenaded by Jefferson's violin all this week. I actually played duets with it and never knew."

"But how did Philippe get it?" asked Jack, his reporter's instinct turning immediately to finding out the bare facts.

"It belonged to my ancestor," answered Philippe proudly. "He was my great, great, great..."

Jack interrupted. "Yeah, kid, we know he was great, but who the hell was he and how did he get this violin?"

"Don't swear in front of Philippe," warned Gary. "He's impressionable."

Jack looked aghast and pointed at the child. "IMPRESSIONABLE? HIM? Like hell he is!"

"You did it again."

Jack glared at Gary.

Philippe piped up. "President Jefferson and my ancestor were the best of friends. Before Monsieur Jefferson died, he sent the violin to my great, great, great, great, great, great..."

"Oh, my Goodness!" whispered Martha, a sudden light of understanding shining in her eyes. Suddenly, she knew.

"Well, I don't understand," said Gary still in the dark.

Lavel stepped forward. "You do not know? But I thought we told you, the day you arrived, and Philippe played the violin for you from the rooftops."

Gary shook his head impatiently. "No, you didn't say."

"But isn't it obvious, Monsieur Craig. Philippe's ancestor was like your General Washington. He was, in fact, like a son to Washington. Philippe's ancestor is the Father of France, the author of our democracy. That fact alone was one of the reasons I, and all the staff at Versailles, allowed Philippe to secretly live here. Philippe's last name is Lafayette. Philippe is a direct descendant of the General Marquis de Lafayette!"

"That's it," cried Maddie stepping forward and putting her hand resolutely on the boy's shoulder. "You're coming home with me, kid. I'll adopt you and love you and fatten you up. You're a bit on the thin side, you know, but with some of my home cooking, that will soon change. I'll teach you everything I know, too."

"You will?" said Philippe happily.

Gary smiled and resolutely shook his head.

The choice was clear now.

He had known it for some time now.

And Gary would follow his own heart.

"That is very kind of you, Madeleine, but I don't think so. If Philippe chooses to come to America, he will come home with me as my son!"

Gary looked at Martha and implored, "One more?"

There was a hushed silence for a few moments with only the sound of the Latona fountain gratefully dancing behind them, its clear happy sprays joyfully cast into the air. Tears filled Martha's eyes, and a broad smile crossed her face. She nodded her head in radiant agreement.

Philippe looked at Gary with an expression of wondrous, hopeful disbelief. Gary knelt in front of the orphan and took hold of his slender hands.

"Philippe, I know it's been hard for you, losing both your parents and your beloved grandpapa. You've been alone in the world for a very long time, too long. But those days are over now. You don't have to hide or steal or be alone anymore. If it's okay with Monsieur Lavel and Monsieur Dumont, we want you to come home with us and be a part of our family now. We want—I want to be your father, Philippe. I want to love and take care of you. I love you, my boy."

With a look of sheer joy, Philippe threw his arms around Gary's neck and began to cry. His slender body shook with sobs of happiness, his private grief flowing out through healing tears just as freely as the waters of the Latona fountain splashing behind him. Martha knelt to place her arms tightly around her husband and her new son and kissed them both. Lavel and Dumont broke down and wept in each other's arms.

"I going to have a brother!" exclaimed Joshua in absolute delight. "This is AWESOME! I won't be the only BOY in this family anymore!"

"Can we take Sebastian, too?" asked Abigail, fearing for the cat's future.

"Sebastian, too," said Martha with a smile as she stood and wiped the tears from her radiant face.

"And it's a boy cat!" cried Joshua happily. The odds for the men in this family were getting better and better!"

"I'll send along all of Sebastian's favorite recipes," said Lavel with a sniff. He took out a large white handkerchief and blew his nose.

Gary stood and faced the old gentlemen.

"Are you sure it's okay with you? Philippe been under your care for so long."

"Of course," said Lavel smiling. "But I must insist that I am invited often to visit him."

"You may come as often as you like," reassured Gary.

"Philippe MUST have a new wardrobe," said Max interrupting, ever observant to fashion details. He gazed at Philippe fretfully. "He can't appear in front of the news media wearing *that!*"

"We'll go shopping," exclaimed Eliza clapping her hands. "Mildred and I will help. We found lots of fun places to shop while we were stuck in Paris!"

Max pulled out his cell phone and flipped it open. "I know the best designers in Paris. They'll open their shops early for me. And I better call my assistants and find Nick, too. Where are they when I need them most? We have work to do!"

"Sounds lovely," said Martha with a maternal sigh. She gazed at her new son with affection, then turned to President Mansart. "President, would you be so kind as to assist us in starting the formal adoption process? I don't know exactly what the laws of your country will require, and I would assume it will take several months at least. But the sooner we can get started, the better!'

Mansart beamed at the American President. "Madame President! I will attend to the matter personally. Philippe LaFayette will also need a passport *tout suite*! And perhaps, I can help speed up the process."

Martha smiled appreciatively. "We would be most grateful. Blaze, please work with President Mansart to begin the official adoption paperwork?"

"You bet!" said Blaze grinning. "Wait till Marie hears about this!"

Jack finally reached his breaking point.

"CAN I HAVE AN INTERVIEW NOW????????" he exclaimed.

Gary stood up and laughed. "Oh, alright! Go find your cameraman, Al, and call your producer, too. You can have an exclusive interview with the First Family's new son!"

"It's about TIME!" exclaimed Jack, ripping open his cell phone and hitting the speed dial. "This is way, way, way over-the-top!!! America is going to go HOG WILD over this story, as if the Hall of Mirrors Ball, the epic snowstorm, the Hope Diamond, and a whole host of Versailles murders weren't enough!"

Lavel blew his nose again and spoke. "If I may be so bold, Messieurs, since this is such a happy occasion, why not do the interview in the Peace Room, with the bright Hall of Mirrors in the background? I think I speak for all, perhaps even for the old Sun King himself. Let us go to the Room of Peace and celebrate."

"Perfect, as always," replied Martha with a grateful nod. "Uncle Gervaise, lead the way."

Joshua grabbed Philippe's arm. "Come on! You can share my room, and I'll show you tons of cool video games to play when you get to America. Ever play football?"

"Football?" inquired Philippe bewildered.

"You're gonna love it!" assured Joshua. "Baseball, too! We'll take you to Redskins and Nationals games!"

"I'm going to America!" exclaimed Philippe to his new brother.

The two boys ran off towards the palace.

"Let's go shopping," said Eliza to Max as they followed the fleeing children.

"Let's have a drink and a toast!" declared Maddie. "To Philippe, the best pickpocket in all France!"

"Pickpocket?" said the President of all France.

Aunt Dotty quickly took President Mansart's arm. "She's just kidding. Dementia, poor thing! Doesn't know what she's saying half the time. Shall we go?"

Everyone was ready to leave.

Everyone except for Abigail.

"I want to watch the pretty fountains with my new dolly, Mama. Monsieur Lavel turned the fountains on special just for me!"

Gary groaned and immediately looked over at Mildred for help. They both knew *that* tone of voice in the President's youngest daughter. Abigail's little bullheaded mind was made up, and not even the President of all France and the announcement of a new brother on CNN cable news would pull her away from her promised water fountain display.

Angelique shyly stepped forward.

"I will stay with her," she said softly looking at Mildred, the official nanny to the children. "Madame Harrison, you go along with Mademoiselle Eliza and Monsieur Jones to assist in the news conference and in gathering Philippe's things. It is such a beautiful day, and the gardens they are so lovely. I do not mind staying here with the little girl."

Mildred looked uncertain, never comfortable leaving her post. She glanced over at Gary and Martha for their opinion.

"It's okay," said Martha.

With the President's blessing, Mildred, Martha, and the President of France went inside the Palace to join in the celebrations. Gary paused a moment before walking into the Hall of Mirrors to gaze across the vast gardens of Versailles, alive with light and joy. He watched as Abigail and Angelique walked down the Water Parterre towards the glorious Latona Fountain. The danger was past, the journey was over. Gary smiled and went inside the palace to find his new son.

* * *

Angelique du Pré took Abigail by the hand and led her towards the water fountain. The January sun shone so warm and friendly, making the water sprays sparkling bright.

"Look! There are turtles and frogs!" said Angelique pointing to the many little animal statues in the pool of water.

Abigail giggled and watched the glistening blue water shoot out of the animals' mouths high into the air.

It was time.

Angelique pulled her cell phone out of her coat pocket. She cast a worried glance towards Agent Pullman and two of his men who were standing behind the little girl. In English, she asked for a moment to call her mother and explain what had happened to her.

Then she smiled sweetly and said something extremely rude to Agent Pullman in French.

Pullman smiled back.

Pullman didn't know French.

Stupid American.

Assured that none of Abigail's security spoke French, she took a breath, looked down at the child affectionately, and then carefully pushed the numbers into her phone. She called the man to whom she had been secretly married to for the past year.

She called her true love, her passion, her soul mate.

She called her husband, Chef Louis Girard.

The following conversation was spoken in French. None of Abigail's Secret Service detail understood a word that was said.

"Where are you, my love?... in the mountains of Pau? Thank God! I have worried so. That stupid French Captain put me in the hospital and surrounded my room with policemen. I could not call till now...No, the police they are complete imbeciles. They believe everything I tell them. They are searching for you in Switzerland. You are safe, mon cher. Now listen carefully. I have spoken with the Master's new assistant in America. He knows all that has happened.

I gave him your cell phone number. He will call tomorrow with instructions. They will have money, fake passport, and identification papers waiting for you. You will retrieve them and then travel immediately to Italy… Do not worry. The Master of The Seven's assistant will tell you how to cross the border and who to contact once you are in Italy. You should remain out of sight for a while in Naples. Stay there until you get instructions to go to Rome and report to the Vatican. You are to look for Palmer's Priest and the Book of John. I will follow as soon as I can. You know where to meet me… Do they suspect me? Of course not, my love. These men, they are blind!"

Angelique paused and smiled prettily at Agent Pullman. Agent Pullman blushed.

"These agents do not know that before I became a chef, I was once an actress on the Paris stage, a very good actress."

Louis added something to her declaration, and Angelique smiled.

"True, my love. You are the helpful husband. You and Dubois did a good job in keeping up the illusion that I was shy, that I was scared, that I was the poor victim! The authorities will never know the truth, that it was I who killed Josette La Claire. I was also Dubois's loyal assistant, his right hand! Gratefully, he did not reveal what really happened that night — how we all met in the gardens and how Gerald, who is my height, took my velvet cloak and hood and put it on! When you, Dubois, and Gerald went to the tents, it was Gerald wearing my cloak. Everyone in the tent thought it was me they saw outside the tents drinking the hot chocolate. But I was in the Hall of Battles, sent to get the sugar emeralds from Louis's refrigerator and to place some of them in René's refrigerator — to cast the suspicion on him. It was I who discovered Josette sneaking around your station, and I did not hesitate to act! She was a bothersome fool and deserved to die. Then you and I and Gerald and Dubois met again in the gardens at the Bacchus Fountain. I took my cloak and left with Dubois while you went back to get Josette's body to place it outside in the gardens. Dubois gave us the perfect alibi we needed, and the truth went with him to the grave. Now, no one will ever know what really happened."

She paused again to look at Abigail. The little girl, with the photographic auditory memory, continued to enjoy her ice cream and the fountains while listening carefully to every single word Angelique said. Abigail did not understand the complex French words, for the nice lady was talking so very fast, but she would remember them all and would ask her new brother to translate them for her and her mother later when they got home.

Angelique sighed with satisfaction.

"You worry too much, my love. The police do not know about Josette, and they will never know about Claude Breton. It was I who asked him to walk with me in the garden, to comfort poor, poor Angelique! He walked with me to the Ballroom, and I then pushed him down the steps and killed him…You know why I had to do it! The Master of The Seven does not like loose ends. They say three is a charm. Too bad I did not get the chance to kill Madame President. How the Master would have liked that!"

Louis said something else in warning, afraid for his wife.

Angelique disregarded it. She continued to look at the child.

"What if I killed the little girl? She is right here standing beside me, Madame President's youngest daughter. I could break her neck and cast her into the fountain before her guards could stop me."

Angelique patted Abigail on the head and stroked the little girl's blonde hair. She placed her hand gently on the child's neck.

The phone vehemently objected.

Angelique laughed.

"Be quiet. I am teasing you! I will not harm her. No, I like her. I like this little Abigail. She is charming, she is strong, she is brave like me! And she has given me this chance to talk to you! For that, I am most grateful. It reminds me of the words Maurice Chevalier sang long ago. Today I could not agree more —

Thank Heaven for little girls."

A Reflective Bibliography

Versailles Palace Chapter Settings

Each novel in the House Mystery Series features a famous house, villa, or castle located in different places around the world. The first few chapters of each book set-up the story in Washington, D.C. Once the main story moves its famous location, each scene is set inside a different room. Thus, by the time the reader finishes reading the novel, they have had a "virtual tour" of the house. In this book, once the plot moves inside Versailles, each chapter gives the reader a royal tour of the Sun King's famous palace. As a reader, your virtual tour includes the Marble Courtyard, the rooms of the Grand Trianon (Family Drawing Room and Garden Drawing Room), the Hall of Battles, the Venus Room, the Diana Room, The Hall of Mirrors, the Mars Room, the Chapel, The Salon Des Nobles, The Cabinet Room, the Opera, The Clock Room, The King's Staircase, The Queen's Bedroom, the War Room, the Peace Room, and the "rooms" of the Gardens (the Colonnade, the Grand Canal, the Queen's Hamlet, the Ballroom, and the Latona Fountain).

Author's Notes on Prelude Quotes and History

Every House Mystery novel opens with a Thomas Jefferson chapter set in Jefferson's time. For On The House, I chose to feature Jefferson and his daughter visiting Versailles during the time when he was the U.S. Ambassador to France. Jefferson was stationed in France until the outbreak of the French Revolution. He did indeed take John Adams's place as Ambassador, and he did know General Lafayette. I incorporated several direct quotations from Jefferson into his dialogue with his friend, the Marquis de Lafayette.

* This part of Mr. Jefferson's speech is adapted from Jefferson's own words, taken from Eric S. Peterson's Light and Liberty. Reflections on the Pursuit of Happiness." Thomas Jefferson, The Modern Library, New York, 2004.

** The royal chateau of Marly is shown in a magnificent oil painting by J.B Martin. The layout of Marly looks very similar to the layout of Mr. Jefferson's "Academic Village" at the University of Virginia (UVA). The chateau of Marly sat in the center of the U-shaped design. Six pavilions lined either side of the estate grounds with formal gardens located behind each. In like manner, Mr. Jefferson designed his academic village with a large rotunda building at the center and ten pavilions surrounding it, five on each side. Gardens of different plant varieties and landscaping design are behind each one. However, the center of Mr. Jefferson's village is a grassy lawn, whereas the center court of Marly had a series of three large pools with magnificent fountains.

The author has taken literary license in having Jefferson and his daughter attend a royal fete at the grand estate of Marly. Some of these royal parties were known to last for as many as four days. But one has only to look at Martin's painting and a picture of the UVA Lawn to imagine Mr. Jefferson walking the grand estate of Marly and using it as inspiration for his academic village at UVA. For more details about Marly and the porcelain palace, the author recommends Ian Dunlop's Versailles, published in 1970. The Porcelain Palace was taken down in 1687. Marly was lost after the reign of Napoleon.

Notes on the Palace of Versailles

In roaming through the stacks at the University of North Carolina at Greensboro (UNCG) library, I discovered several wonderful books describing the palace of Versailles. Dunlop's book, mentioned above, was where I first read about the king's fascination (obsession really) with orange trees and the wonders of his glorious greenhouses. The King's greenhouses had over one million pots for planting, and they kept the gardens of Versailles in full flower twelve months of the year. They literally defied nature. Dunlop also describes Marly, the Menagerie, and the Porcelain Palace in the greatest of detail, to the point where I could almost smell the jasmine blooming at the Porcelain Palace and envision the fountains at Marly shooting sprays of crystal water one hundred feet into the air!

Another literary jewel I found was James Eugene Farmer's Versailles and the Court of Louis XIV, published in 1905. This gem of a book is packed with much detail on the makeup and daily activities of the castle during the reign of the Sun King. Farmer describes the business and workings of Versailles office by office—food, stables, kennels, chapel, apartments—outlining the daily life inside the royal home. I came to understand that Versailles wasn't just a palace. It was a city, full of every kind of tradesmen, businessmen, craftsmen, and servants. Farmer's book has chapters describing the main characters of the Sun King's court including his second secret wife, Madame de Maintenon, his brother Monseigneur, his children and grandchildren (the legitimate ones and the illegitimate ones), and other nobles at court. Farmer also writes detailed accounts of the famous fêtes, the theater, and "the seamy side" of court life! This book was a real page-turner!

The recent work of Antonia Fraser, Marie Antoinette, gives the reader a masterful peek inside the daily life of Versailles a hundred years later, in the mid to late 1700s. I found this book entertaining and informative. The new movie, Marie Antoinette, based on this book is very true to history and gives one a good view of the palace inside and out. Speaking of movies, I highly recommend the video, Versailles, a Treasure of France, by Kronos France Films. This video gives you a photographic tour of the palace and the gardens with aerial views of both.

Finally, a word of warning: If you travel to France and visit Versailles, be sure to take the tour which lets you visit both the exterior rooms (the staterooms including the Hall of Mirrors) and the interior rooms (which will include the King's bedroom, clock room, and council room). I made the mistake of getting just the exterior tour. If possible, you'll want to tour the rooms on the lower level as well which include the bedrooms of the Dauphin and Dauphine of France. Also, if possible, give yourself at least TWO DAYS to sightsee. You will need a whole day for just touring the gardens. Trust me! And be sure to rent the cart!!!! Unless you are a marathon runner, you'll need it!

Notes on Lafayette

Perhaps the most fabulous discovery in my research for this book was Andreas Lakzko's work, Lafayette, A Life. You can still get this out-of-print book from Amazon.com. I did after reading the UNCG library's copy! It is masterfully written, reminiscent of the style and prose of Victor Hugo's great work, Les Miserables. Lakzko's book is beautifully written, and it held me spellbound. Lafayette was very much a part of our American heritage and Mr. Jefferson's times, so Lafayette had to be woven into Gary and Martha's life and this story. General Lafayette is a dear part of my life as well. When I defended my doctoral dissertation inside Jefferson's Rotunda at the University of Virginia, I did so in the oval room on the second floor. At one end of that room sits a marble bust of General Lafayette! He was looking on when I become a doctor of philosophy!

Notes on King Louis XIV

In reading Antonia Fraser's work on Marie Antoinette, I was delighted to discover another of her works, <u>Love and Louis XIV: The Women in the Life of the</u> Sun King. While this book chronicles the lives of Queen Marie Theresa and Louis's *many* mistresses, it also describes beautifully the King himself and his life at court. One gets a real feel for the palace and her famous king. I was fascinated by his great devotion to his Catholic faith; his almost perfect daily church attendance to mass on the one hand and his daily acts of adultery on the other. This book gives great insight into the emotional complexity of this famous French monarch.

Notes on the Gardens of Versailles

One little book I found very helpful was the tour book by Simone Hoog and Béatrix Saule, <u>Your Visit to Versailles</u>, which I picked up at the Versailles Palace gift shop. Along with pictures of the palace state rooms, it has a grand map of the gardens and many wonderful photographs of the royal park. You'll need this one in hand while you explore the expansive gardens of the Sun King's home.

Notes on Cooking

When Gary and the First Family arrive at Versailles, they are treated to Chef Louis Girard's preparation of a dish created by the first celebrity chef, Antoine Carême. I learned about this famous chef and his legendary recipes from a biography by Ian Kelly, <u>Cooking for Kings. The Life of Antonine Carême the First Celebrity Chef</u>. Carême emerged from the French Revolution to become the master chef for George IV of England, Napoleon, the Romanovs, the Rothschilds, and the Viennese court. This culinary master did, in fact, keep detailed journals, full of recipes and drawings of his sugar creations. Kelly's book contains the actual recipes and drawings of Carême's legendary work. Get it and check out the menu on pages

134-137 that was served at Brighton Pavilion—a dinner that consisted of eight soups, forty entrees, and sixteen desserts. This was a meal I know Blaze Phillips would definitely love!

Bon Appétit!

Notes on Fashion

Babette's high fashion wardrobe was indeed hot off the Paris Fashion Week runway. For her attire, I went on the Internet and selected outfits for her to wear. The following fashion designers are featured in this story:

- Yes St. Laurent by Tom Ford (long black coat lined in black fur)
- Louis Vuitton (love the oversized gray fur hat)
- Cerruti (cream mini skirt, cream boots, and long cream fur-lined duster coat)
- Issey Miyake (white jacket coat and deconstructed white dress)
- Nina Ricci: (I love the long pink fur)
- Michael Kors (every girl needs a little black dress by MK!)
- Salvatore Ferragamo (why stop at pink fur? Let's go lavender!)
- Christian Dior (Love that white and red floral patchworked skirt!)
- Giorgio Armani (watermelon red ball gown with matching red gloves)

I will take one of each!

THE END